Fleabag and the F

Gemma had to face the fact that she was no good.
She knew a real Fire Wielder should be able to
stand with Fire blazing in the face of any danger.
And *she* didn't know how to do that! Whatever
was happening felt stronger than the Fire.

Gemma's job is to look into the flame of the
Ring Fire and understand the ways of the Fire
Giver, to protect the Kingdom from evil and give
wisdom to the King. A former kitchen maid, she
has always felt unequal to this task, and a terrifying
event now confirms her doubts. Numbed by shock
she is deceived by an evil enemy whose actions
threaten the whole country.

From a distance, Fleabag has been watching
this disaster unfold. He is unsure how to set about
it, but the mangy streetwise cat is determined to
save his friend. And once again he is not alone...

Beth Webb lives in Somerset with her four
children and an entourage of pets. Her other
books for children include *The Magic in the Pool
of Making*, *Fleabag and the Ring Fire*, *The Witch of
Wookey Hole* and *Foxdown Wood*.

To Lucy and Catkin Patterson.
Remember: Every time a cat
walks into the kitchen
—feed it!

Fleabag and the Fire Cat

Beth Webb

A LION BOOK

Copyright © 1998 Beth Webb

The author asserts the moral right
to be identified as the author of this work

Published by
Lion Publishing plc
Sandy Lane West, Oxford, England
ISBN 0 7459 3846 9

First edition 1998
10 9 8 7 6 5 4 3 2 1

All rights reserved

Acknowledgments
My thanks to Gabriel Ralls, Cathy Patterson
and Jon Stewart for helping me to think up
this story. Thanks also to Linda Nash who
keeps me sane in so many ways!

A catalogue record for this book is available
from the British Library

Typeset in 11/12.5 Aldine
Printed and bound in Great Britain by
Caledonian International Book Manufacturing, Glasgow

Contents

1

Blue Lightning

Blue lightning flashed in terrifying sheets across the darkened sky. Everywhere the oppressive air was uncannily still. The rain had not yet closed in behind the storm. The world seemed to hold its breath between flashes. Everything was waiting for the thunder… which never came.

Fleabag stretched as he climbed out from his nest under the lavender bushes. He turned his black furry face this way and that, swivelling his ears to catch sounds of his grand-kittens playing somewhere in the undergrowth at the back of the palace gardens. He yawned and began to call their names. He would have to get them in. Their mother would have his fur if the kittens got wet or frightened.

He *was* supposed to be kitten-sitting, after all— although his idea of supervising the little ones consisted mostly of finding a warm, dry patch of earth and having a cat-nap for an hour or two with just half an eye open until lunch, or tea or elevenses or whatever excuse for eating he could think of next.

He had spent the morning dreaming about his heroic adventures on the quest to find the Queen's

Ring, two years before. Sometimes his thoughts were full of how bravely and nobly he had carried out the quest. But at other times, like today, he felt more afraid, remembering how real the danger had been. Tales were all very well, but they were scary when they were actually happening. They really made a cat's fur stand on end.

Rather like this eerie, thunderless storm.

He balanced on his three legs and stretched as he called the kittens again. As he waited for their answering calls, he looked up at the sky. The strange lightning was becoming more frequent. The rain would pour down any second now. The heavy blue-black clouds were stacked up into gigantic, ominous-looking towers, ready to pour torrential waters onto the earth below. It did not need a great deal of imagination to see fearsome faces leering down from above.

Suddenly the rain *did* come, as fiercely and totally as Fleabag had feared. The huge raindrops caught in the black cat's golden eyes and made them sting. In the walls of the palace behind him a window clattered open at the mercy of the frantic wind. A hand reached out to pull it shut.

Fleabag was about to call the kittens again but what he saw made his voice stick in his throat...

Not far away, Gemma the Royal Fire Wielder was sitting with her desk pulled up to the window so she could look out over the garden. She liked to daydream between reading official documents. From here she would watch her old friend Fleabag the talking cat, playing with his grand-kittens. Their games made her laugh.

Gemma was scarcely more than a child herself, and had once been a street urchin. Now she held the highest office in the land, higher even than her friend King Phelan. She was the Fire Wielder. It was her job to look into the flame of the Ring Fire and understand the ways of the Fire Giver, to protect the Kingdom from all evil and give wisdom to the King. But she never felt comfortable in her job. Although she loved the Ring Fire she served, she never felt she understood it properly. She never seemed to really grasp how to be the carrier of the great eternal flame. Surely it was too great and awesome for someone ordinary like her. She always seemed to get everything wrong. The Ring Fire never flared when she called upon it, but always roared to life spectacularly at the most embarrassing moments. All her ceremonies went wrong, and she was sure everyone was laughing at her behind her back. She was miserable.

She longed to be a street child or even a kitchen maid again. Then at least no one would expect her to be something she wasn't...

Official duties hemmed her in. It was bad enough having to sit inside most of the day reading difficult books or signing papers, instead of being amongst the familiar bustle of the stall holders in the market, or laughing at Fleabag as he performed his ludicrous antics. Life had been hard when she was younger, but at least she had been free.

Gemma sighed. She could not escape her duties but at least she could watch the world and laugh at the kittens, even if she couldn't join in.

But today, she was sitting with her thin face in her

hands, staring out of the window for a different reason. The lightning bothered her. It flashed again and she shivered. It was too similar to something she had known, something from not so long ago. Something she had hoped never to meet again.

Absently she scratched the itching in her palms, then jumped as the Ring Fire flared between her fingers. It did not burn her—it wasn't that sort of a fire—but the shock of its golden, exuberant flames leaping against the eerie blue lightning outside made her gasp and go cold. Its presence meant she was right: this was no ordinary storm, and *something* was about to happen!... But what?

Gemma swallowed hard as she turned her gaze back to the ominous skies. She watched the brilliant blue flashes skimming across the slate-black clouds. They seemed to be illuminating the world while an evil mind was searching for something down below.

'I thought the Chancellor and his son were dead,' she muttered to herself. 'This is the sort of magic they used. I could never forget it...' For a few moments her mind drifted back to the day when Phelan, Fleabag and herself challenged the terrible power of the Chancellor of All Wizards in the imitation Hall of Light at Porthwain. At the time she thought she was merely acting a part to scare the Chancellor. She had not realized the true power of the gift in her hands. If she had, she would never have dared to do what she did that day.

She shook her head and sighed. Perhaps part of her problem now was knowing that she really *did* carry the Ring Fire. The thought daunted her.

There was another flash of eerie blue light. She closed her eyes tightly, but she knew it would not make it go away. Normally Gemma loved storms, and had been known to climb up into the attic and out onto the roofs of the sleeping apartments so she could get a really good view.

But today she merely sat very still and watched. Her breathing was shallow and fast. She did not like what was happening. She did not like her memories. What was worse, the Ring Fire was burning in her palms. It would not go away. It was a warning. Maybe there would be another battle like the one they had fought at Porthwain, or the time she had beaten the wolves back…?

Gingerly she shook her sleeves back as she raised her hands, and let the Ring Fire blaze out properly. If there was to be a battle, she knew better than to get in the way of what the Ring Fire chose to do. She felt very small and alone and wished that Fleabag or Phelan were with her. They always knew what to do, but there was no time to go and get help. Whatever had to be done, had to be done now. As she raised her hands, a tremendous gust of wind caught the palace buildings. Doors rattled everywhere. Her window tugged on its catch and swung wide.

As she did so the heavy blue-black clouds seemed to swoop down and engulf the palace in sudden rain.

Gemma leaned out to pull the window closed. At that very second the thunder came at last—crashing with an unbelievable noise that shook the ground. Blinding lightning flashed, but this time, instead of the harmless eerie sheets of searching light, a five-fingered fork of lightning darted towards her. Then another. Then another, each groping closer and closer to where she stood.

She jumped back, but not because of the lightning. Something much worse had frightened her. Something inconceivably terrible...

For as she had reached out to catch the window, the rain had caught the Ring Fire that still burned in her palm. As the water touched the flame, it went out! The unquenchable Ring Fire that gave life and meaning to everything, had failed while *she* had been holding it!

Gemma forgot the clattering window and fled her room, running blindly down the darksome corridor. She did not stop until she reached the familiar safety of the broom cupboard. She fumbled with the wooden latch and slipped inside. Years ago, when Gemma had been a kitchen maid she used to shelter here from the wrath of the drunken cook.

It was a tiny, circular room at the top of a small, spiral staircase. There was one window in the place, a small, vertical slit which admitted enough air and light to make the hiding place tolerable for several hours.

The violent wind that had come so suddenly was now buffeting the palace like a petulant giant. A blustering draught slammed the cupboard door behind Gemma. It was difficult to open from the inside, but she did not care. Instead she curled up very small under a pile of rags and dusters, closing her eyes to the all-pervading blue lightning.

She was too dazed to cry. The last time she had seen anything that eerie blue colour it had been in the hands of the evil Chancellor at Porthwain. She had not been so frightened then. But the magical blue fire had not felt this powerful, and she had not been alone, for Fleabag and Phelan had been there too. More importantly, then the Ring Fire had flared high and wide from between her fingers. It had been glorious, defeating and swallowing the threatening evil with a burst of golden flame. It had been exhilarating and exciting! It had worked!

But now, what she had always dreaded more than anything had happened. In *her* hands, the Ring Fire had failed. It had died. She had seen the strange wind and rain quench it. There was nothing more she could do. She must have weakened it by her ineptitude. It was *she* who had brought it to this pass!

At last Gemma managed to let her feelings out. She buried her face in her hands and sobbed silently. Outside the cupboard she could hear Fleabag pacing up and down the corridor calling her. She stopped crying and held her breath. How she wished she could rub her face into the cat's knotted flea-ridden black fur and feel his thunderous purring against her cheek. She wanted to hear his impossibly awful jokes and just laugh with him. He would comfort her and say something kind and warming.

But her friend could not help her this time. Alone she had to face the fact that she was no good as Fire Wielder. Fleabag must never know that the rain from the strange, evil clouds had quenched the Ring Fire. Everyone in the land would be in deadly terror if they knew this evil menace was stronger than the Ring Fire.

The whole land was at the mercy of the blue magic

until she could find another Fire Wielder, one who was worthy of the office. Someone who would know what to do.

Tentatively she lifted her head a little to listen. Had Fleabag gone? Was it safe to cry again?

Gemma could hear nothing. There was always a hope that she hadn't allowed the blue magic to kill the Ring Fire completely. But she knew a real Fire Wielder should be able to stand with Fire blazing before whatever danger threatened the land. And *she* didn't know how to do that!

Whatever was happening outside felt stronger than the Fire.

'Please let me go,' she whispered. 'Let me be plain Gemma Streetchild again!'

Below in the kitchen, a sodden Fleabag lined up six bedraggled kittens in front of the fire to dry their fur. He was very worried. He had only glimpsed Gemma's outstretched hand reaching for the window. The Ring Fire had been dancing on her fingers as she reached out, then it had faded as the blue power gathered to strike.

But suddenly Gemma had pulled her hand back, leaving the loose window clattering in the wind. Fleabag had run upstairs as soon as he had brought the kittens inside, but he couldn't find her. Instinctively he knew something was very wrong, but Gemma had been so withdrawn of late… She didn't seem to want to know him any more. He couldn't *make* her talk to him. He would talk to Phelan. He might know what to do.

But there was nothing more Fleabag could do for now except make the kittens presentable again, so he turned his attention to washing a struggling little black miniature of himself. 'I wonder what will happen next?' he thought.

2

Fleabag is Uneasy

Fleabag twitched his whiskers. Something had brushed past his face, disturbing his dreams. Lazily he stretched out a claw and took a sleepy swipe. He missed, but who cared? Let the mice get bold. The more careless they were, the easier they would be to catch. He turned over and put a loving paw around his wife Tabitha, then went back to sleep. He was tired. Yesterday's strange storm had left everyone feeling exhausted.

Suddenly he sat bolt upright. There *was* something in the room, and it wasn't a mouse!

He got up stiffly and balanced himself on his three legs, smelling the air and turning his huge tattered ears this way and that, scooping at the night, trying to catch the slightest sound. What *was* it? He felt the fur on his back begin to rise. But why? He could not smell or hear anything strange, but ever since the storm a peculiar feeling had stayed hanging in the air...

The royal palace was silent except for the usual pacing of the guards outside and the sniffings and scratchings of the guard dogs. In the next room

King Phelan was snoring loudly. He was only a young man, scarcely in his twenties, but his snoring could shake the window panes if he had curry for supper. But the 'something' was not Phelan.

Tabitha turned over sleepily. 'What's the matter, dear?' she purred (unlike Fleabag, she could not use human speech).

'Nothing, dear. I'm just going to stretch my legs for a while. Go back to sleep.'

'I can't,' she replied sleepily. 'Something keeps brushing past my whiskers and disturbing me.'

Fleabag did not want his wife to be worried. She was pregnant with what looked like an enormous litter of kittens. She needed her sleep.

'I felt it too,' he said. 'I think there's a mouse that needs teaching some manners. I'll catch it,' he promised.

Tabitha rolled over and stretched the length of the velvet-lined cat basket, glad to have the extra space to herself, and went back to sleep.

Fleabag did not like the feeling that was running up and down his spine. It was not good. He drank some water and slipped out into the corridor. He sniffed all along the bottom of Phelan's door. No one except the butler had come in or out since the King had gone to bed. Yet something... something... was... *behind him*!

He jumped and twisted 180 degrees in the air, landing with a thump! Nothing. Only the midnight shadows on the walls. Shadows he had known since he was a kitten. Nothing strange... Yet there it was again! He jumped high this time, clawing halfway up the wall as... *something* went past.

'This is ridiculous!' he told himself. Once again he felt compelled to leap and pounce, attacking somewhere above his head, then behind him, then all around, just beyond the end of his own tail. He found himself jumping and thudding along the corridor—yet there was absolutely nothing there! He had no idea what he was after, he just had to do it. He was acting like a demented kitten. This was ridiculous—it was so undignified!

Tabitha called out sleepily, asking him either to go out and play in the garden or to come back to bed—he was keeping her awake.

Fleabag turned and growled warningly at the something-that-was-nothing. 'I'll be back!' he warned, as he slipped back into the bedroom and curled up next to his beloved. But sleep eluded him.

At breakfast a grumpy Fleabag asked Phelan if he had slept well. The young king shook his head and pushed his dark curly hair out of his eyes with marmalady fingers. 'No, you woke me up with your mousing in the middle of the night. Couldn't you let the poor little things live until morning? Honestly, it sounded as if coal was being delivered, the way you were jumping around.'

Fleabag did not think this was the right time to discuss the matter of the strange 'something' with the King. He wanted to have his thoughts clear first, so he selected a fat herring from the tray the butler was holding and took it out into the garden. There he could crunch the bones without Phelan throwing a slipper at him for being disgusting. There was only one way for a cat to think, and that was to eat a very substantial breakfast and follow it with a mid-morning nap.

He had a funny feeling about what was happening these days. Last night had not been the first time he had been woken by this strange 'something' that he just *had* to chase. He sometimes woke and found his fur on end. Some of his children had been acting rather strangely of late too, jumping and chasing at shadows in a frenzied way, just as he had.

But since yesterday's storm, the feeling that hung in the air was definitely worse, and he did *not* like it. He was suspicious, but he wanted to be certain of what he was suspicious *of* before he spoke to Phelan. Then there was Gemma. She had been so withdrawn and unhappy lately. She was no longer her old fun self, and she certainly didn't have time to see to really important matters of State such as rubbing his tummy and picking his fleas out. He felt in his whiskers that something was very wrong. In fact he felt uneasy all the way to the tip of his scraggy tail.

He finished the herring in the shade of a purple lilac tree, donating some of the chewier bits to a passing kitchen cat. Then he had a leisurely wash in the morning sun. There was something very familiar about what was happening. That was more worrying than anything, for he could not remember *why* it was familiar. He longed to get up and *do* something, to find an answer, to solve the mystery, but he knew that if he acted without the proper preparation and enough cat naps, he would miss a vital clue.

He curled up where he was, with the sun dappling through the trees, and fell asleep. But he did not get much rest, for the sound of voices woke him.

It was Gemma. She was striding along the gravel walk, dressed in her full robes of State (she was rarely out of them these days), giving orders to a group of tired-looking acolytes and acting like one of the arrogant nobles she had always despised.

But the effect was sad, rather than awe-inspiring. Gemma's heavy white robes, thickly embroidered with gold and red flames, made her look swamped rather than dignified. Her straight mousy hair had been dyed flame red and piled high, and she wore thick make-up. Her tired face was beginning to show small, irritable-looking lines. She was nothing like the timid scullery maid who had been befriended by a mangy old kitchen-cat called Fleabag. Only three years had passed, but power and authority had changed Gemma—and not for the better.

Now was his chance. With the speed and agility of an acrobat, the fat, lazy Fleabag managed to dash to a plum tree a little further down the path, and scramble up it. He flattened himself on a branch that hung out over the walkway. He lay panting, gripping the bark with his claws. 'Where did I find the energy to do *that?*' he wondered.

Just then Gemma came almost level with him. He tightened his hold on the branch with his three paws and allowed his bottle-brush tail to tickle Gemma's nose.

She looked up crossly and pushed the offending tail to one side. 'Don't *do* that!' she snapped. 'It makes me want to sneeze, and you're *filthy!*'

Fleabag grinned and landed deftly on Gemma's shoulder so he could whisper in her ear. 'It never used to bother you, Miss High-and-Mighty. Come and sit down with me for a minute. I'll share my fleas with you and I'll even pounce on bits of grass if you twiddle them for me!'

'No!' she said, removing him from her shoulder and putting him firmly back on the ground. 'Not now. I'm busy. I'm off to an important meeting.' She stood up and brushed dust and loose petals from her robes. 'Look at me, I've got muddy paw prints all over me!'

'Sit down and I'll lick them off, I'm good at that,' the cat volunteered as he trotted alongside her. 'It's time we had a talk anyway.'

Gemma stopped for a second and looked down at her friend's huge golden eyes. Despite his teasing he looked worried. 'What about?' she asked suspiciously.

'About lots of things, but first of all there's yesterday's storm.'

'What about it?' she snapped. She could feel herself going pale.

'I was in the garden when the rain started, and I heard your window blow open. When I looked up, I saw something you ought to know about…'

Gemma was almost sick. *He knows! He saw!* she thought. Swiftly she gathered her skirts and put her nose in the air. 'This is ridiculous. I told you I'm in a hurry—I've no time to discuss the weather!' She had to protect him from the truth. She had to pretend she didn't know what he was talking about. When she had found a new Fire Wielder she would sit under the trees and scratch Fleabag's tummy and apologize. But not now. She dare not say anything *now…*

21

Fleabag could do nothing to make her listen, so he darted off after a butterfly, pretending he didn't care. But from the corner of his eye, he watched her over-dressed figure disappear between the trees. His heart sank. Why was she treating him like this? They had been through so much together; they had been such good friends. She really understood how to get the fleas out of the awkward places in his fur that even Tabitha could not manage with her excellent rough tongue. But most importantly of all, whether she liked it or not, he *had* to find a way to talk with her soon. She was in deep trouble. They needed to discuss the strange things that were happening, and most of all what he had seen...

Something evil and frightening was coming close. And it was Gemma's job to know what to do about it. He wanted to talk to her, but he knew she would not listen. Fleabag was not sure what the matter was, but her message was plain: he was only a cat and she was the Fire Wielder. In other words, he had to mind his own business.

He lay on his back and rubbed the warm earth into his matted fur, making it even messier. Something was very wrong, and things wouldn't get any better with Gemma acting all high and mighty. Rolling in the deliciously scratchy warm earth was much more helpful to a worried brain than attending meetings. He waved his three legs in the air in a most ridiculous manner, although not even the boldest shrew would have dared laugh at the sight. For he was Fleabag the Magnificent, sire of over twenty kittens, and grand-sire of at least ten more (and five or six more on the way!), defeater of the evil Chancellor of All Wizards...

22

Suddenly he righted himself and sat alert, every whisker stretched in anticipation of hearing or feeling something close by. But no, it was gone again. Troubled, he resumed his rolling in the lovely, prickly earth. Where was he? Oh yes. He was the defeater of the Chancellor who had intended to claim the throne for himself, saying he was both Fire Wielder *and* Monarch...

Fleabag's fur rose again at the thought of the great Battle of Porthwain when he and Gemma had fulfilled the ancient prophecy that the Chancellor would be defeated by a black cat and a Fire Maiden. The Chancellor had raised terrible blue flames to try to destroy the Ring Fire. But he and his son Sethan had been burned to death by their own terrible magic. Indeed, Fleabag had brought about a great victory for the Ring Fire—Phelan and Gemma had helped a little too, of course!

Suddenly Fleabag rolled over and sat bolt upright. He was amazed at his own stupidity. That was it! Somehow the Chancellor's blue magic was awake again! He began to wash vigorously as cats always do when they are embarrassed. How could he have been so *stupid*? Perhaps Gemma had made the connection too, perhaps she was frightened, but why? The Ring Fire had defeated the blue magic before; it would do it again.

Things were dire. There were no two ways about it; with or without Gemma, he would have to find out what was happening.

3

Gemma Makes Plans

Her Eminence, the Lady Gemma of the Sacred Fire, Fire Wielder to the King, longed to take off her heavy robes and sit on the ground next to Fleabag. She would have loved to spend the morning scratching his ridiculous furry tummy, listening to that great deep rolling purr of his. It would be so good to tell him all her worries and fears.

But she didn't dare. No one must know.

She felt ill and weary. Knowing the terrible truth, that the blue magic could put the Ring Fire out, was a weight she found intolerable. On top of that, her shoes hurt and she was late for a reception to meet the new Chancellor of the University at Porthwain. A young man, she had been told, very anxious to meet her as he wished to be instructed in the ways of the Ring Fire. That was certainly a change from his predecessor, who had also held the office of Chancellor of All Wizards—an evil, destructive man, who had been intent on destroying the Ring Fire and claiming power for himself.

But Gemma did not feel like instructing anyone, even a keen student. After all, what could she, who had failed so badly, say to anyone? But there was always the very slim chance that he might prove to be the man to succeed her. Who knew? More than anything in all the world she wished that she had never heard of the office of Fire Wielder, so that she could be plain, ordinary Gemma Streetchild again.

'Bother the Ring Fire,' Gemma muttered, scratching the palms of her hands under the long sleeves of her formal robe. Her hands had been itching badly since the strange rain had put the Ring Fire out. She had put soothing cream on the reddened itchy places and her wardrobe mistress had tactfully chosen a gown with very long sleeves. Gemma was certain the Ring Fire wasn't dead; she had spotted a glimmer of a flame while she was dressing. But at least it was unlikely to flare up in her hands this morning, if it ever did again.

She was glad that the rain had put the flames out while she was holding them. She hated it when the Fire appeared. She never knew what to do. The responsibility was too great. She was no Fire Wielder, she was just a street urchin-cum-kitchen maid.

Gemma was angry with her life. She had never had a childhood. She had never had *fun*! When she was little she had to fight in the streets to survive. Then in the palace kitchens she had to work until she dropped. Then the Queen had ordered her to go on the quest for the royal ring. Now she was the most important person in the land—even above the King. People expected her to be something she wasn't, and it wasn't fair!

But now she had failed the Ring Fire she felt better. With a clear conscience, she would find a successor and run off to the little cottage in the rocks where she and her friends had stayed one winter when on the Ring quest. Life had been good then. She could find that cottage again, and live there with some hens and a milking goat. That was all she needed. She hated having to be the Fire Wielder. She got things wrong all the time and the Ring Fire never did what she thought it was supposed to. She dressed in these silly robes and tried to look dignified. But it didn't help. If anything it made her feel more hot and cross and stupid than ever!

She wiped away a tear surreptitiously. Her palm was burning hot! Quickly she let her sleeve drop over the reddened skin. Danger was near, she knew it; but she dare not try and do anything in case it went wrong. The best thing she could do was to have this audience with the new Chancellor, then set her mind to the task of appointing another Fire Wielder. Once that was done, the land would be safe and she could go away and never come back!

Just the thought of living in the cottage in the rocks again made her feel easier. She'd want a cat with her of course—it needn't be Fleabag, although she would love to have him. He probably wouldn't want to come now he was married and had a huge family. She'd ask for one of the kittens—one of the talking ones. The ordinary cats weren't nearly so interesting...

As Gemma day-dreamed, she began to cheer up. She forgot the burning in her hands which should have put her on guard. In her head she was far away, in the foothills of the great mountains beyond Porthwain... In fact she was so deep in her thoughts she did not look where she was going. She tripped on a step and hit her head on the banister. The pain brought her back to reality. But now she had a headache as well as too-tight shoes and sore hands.

She sighed as she climbed up the rest of the steps into the palace from the gardens. She promised herself that before she went, she would sit out in the sun with Fleabag under the lilac tree and tell him the truth.

But today she had to pull herself together. She gathered up her skirts, entered the hall and walked up the main staircase. Suddenly she smelled burning. She looked down. One of her sleeves was scorched! In her right hand was a tiny, steady golden flame of fire! Why did it choose to burn like that? The flame rarely caught things alight. It was usually more of a glow... She brushed at the scorched cloth and the flame went out.

Oh, why did it all not go away? She did not want this. She had failed the Ring Fire yesterday and now it was back to mock her! Why did it not understand that it was not right that a mere street child should become the bearer of the living flame of the Ring Fire—the heart of the Fire Giver, watching over the people of the land? She clenched her hand tightly and bit her lip to stop herself crying out. But it did no good. She longed to run all the way back to Fleabag and cry into his fur. But it was too late. She had reached the top of the stairs and the heavy carved doors of the Hall of Light were already swinging open.

The white stone walls of the circular chamber were bright with the morning sun which streamed in from the octagonal lantern set high in the middle of the ceiling. Here eight great lancet windows rose out from the roof, curved over and met in the centre, letting the sunlight stream across the great silk carpets that lay end to end across the floor in a glorious celebration of colour and design.

Gemma blinked. The light in the Hall always seemed to be intensely bright, but it was probably because the corridor outside was so gloomy.

When she was able to see clearly once more, her heart missed a beat, for across the room was a figure she had thought she would never see again.

4

The Chancellor's Offer

The young man standing in the centre of the Hall was tall, slim and fair, with a wide-boned face, typical of people from the West. He was suave, elegant and immaculately turned out in a grey silk tunic and trousers.

But what made her blood run cold was the realization that he was the image of a nightmare from her past—Sethan, the son of the evil Chancellor of All Wizards, whom she had seen die with his father in terrible blue flames in the imitation Hall of Light at Porthwain.

Gemma felt herself go pale. The burning in her right hand increased until it seared her in a way she had never felt before. So today at least, she *was* still the Fire Wielder! She was determined to keep calm.

She did not offer her hand to be kissed as the young man stepped forward and bowed to her.

The Chancellor's equerry bowed too as he said, 'My lady, may I present the Lord Domnall of Porthwain, Chancellor of the University. He presents his respects and humbly requests to be instructed in the great and sacred truths of the Ring Fire.' The equerry stepped back. Once again the young man offered to take Gemma's hand.

Keeping her arms stiffly by her sides she silently thanked her wardrobe mistress for her long sleeves. Lamely she nodded towards a chair. 'Welcome, Lord Domnall. Would you care to sit?'

As she calmed her mind and looked hard at the Chancellor, Gemma sighed with relief. The man who had died was quite a bit younger than her visitor, even allowing for two and a half years since that day. The two young men were similar, that was all, and the grey silk suit was commonly worn by university officials on formal occasions. She was just feeling twitchy. She promised herself that this would all be over very soon.

'He seems very young to be Chancellor,' she thought. 'But then I suppose I am young to be Fire Wielder.' She settled herself in an ornately carved chair opposite her visitor. Mechanically she began the formal recitation of the Holy Writings.

After about ten minutes of polite listening, the Chancellor raised a finely boned hand. 'Forgive me for interrupting, my Lady, but these writings have been familiar to me since my youth.' He leaned forward with intense enthusiasm written across his face. 'It is real knowledge and the wisdom of the Ring Fire I seek.'

Gemma stared blankly at her visitor. How was she going to answer him? Somehow she knew, just by looking at him, that he was not the longed-for replacement. She might be exhausted and miserable, but she would not betray the Ring Fire by telling its secrets to everyone who asked. After a few moments she shrugged and rose to her feet. The young man looked up anxiously then stood as well.

'I'm sorry,' she said, 'what you ask is secret. The ancient wisdom belongs only to the Fire Wielders.'

Domnall kept his composure. He had expected as much. He had not imagined Gemma would simply tell him how the Ring Fire was passed from Fire Wielder to Fire Wielder, and how he might take it from her to become the next and greatest of all—both Monarch and Fire Wielder in one. Once he had the Ring Fire, disposing of the King would be easy. He was the sixth son of a sixth son of a sixth son after all! It was his birthright to claim the crown *and* the Ring Fire. All he needed was just a little more knowledge…

His father had planned this glory for himself, and he had died for his presumption, along with his younger brother Sethan. They had perished as they deserved. Usurpers!

And this Fire Wielder was weak and a mere child. What was more he could sense that she did not *want* the power she had. This was going to be easy. The secret goal of the Ancient Order of Wizards was within his grasp. But he knew he must be careful.

The girl was watching him intently, waiting for a reply. He had been silent too long and was in danger of being ushered out of her presence. He smiled and bowed his head. 'Of course, My Lady. My enthusiasm for sacred knowledge is greater than my wisdom. Forgive me.'

Gemma smiled. 'Of course.' She had to keep her composure. She was scheduled to be with this young man for three whole hours. How was she going to cope? It was so airless inside as well. Then she had an inspiration. 'I do find the palace stuffy on a sunny day like today, Lord Chancellor. Would you care to walk in the grounds?'

Domnall bowed in response. 'Madam, I would be delighted.' And he stood back to let her pass.

Although Domnall was fairly sure the ceremony of Giving the Fire had to take place in the Hall of Light, he had only met this slip of a girl a few moments ago. There would be plenty of time...

The formal gardens were a blaze of spring colour, laid out in intricate designs between covered walkways, supported by beautifully carved and painted pillars and arches. Each area of the palace was in a separate building. The Great Hall, the Hall of Light and the library were in the main building, but dotted around the gardens were guest quarters, children's nurseries, sleeping halls, smaller dining halls and kitchens, and a wonderful ballroom. Here and there tall, elegant trees shaded patches of green lawn and children played or did their lessons in the shade.

As Gemma took her visitor along a gravelled path between the bathhouse and the guest quarters, a kindle of kittens darted out, chasing each other wildly.

Domnall stopped dead and blanched, making his already pale skin paper-white.

Gemma turned and smiled. 'I know the people of your city have a natural dislike of cats, but these are quite harmless.' The memory of how she, Phelan and Fleabag had stood against the terrible Chancellor of All Wizards, and met his evil blue flames with the Ring Fire was forever fresh in

Gemma's mind. She was grateful that this young man was only the Chancellor of the University. The Order of Wizards had been disbanded by royal proclamation after the Battle of Porthwain. She did not know what she would have said if this Lord Domnall had been one of them—probably she would have refused the audience.

As they watched the kittens, Fleabag appeared from a large clump of blackcurrant bushes and ushered his grandkittens away. Domnall stared hard at the venerable grandsire and made a slight gesture with his left hand. Fleabag and his kittens suddenly darted off amongst the shrubs chasing, or being chased, by *something*.

Gemma was so wrapped up in her misery that she did not notice.

Fleabag found himself in a breathless heap amongst the wild strawberries and began to wash himself hard, to cover his loss of dignity. 'This,' he muttered to himself, 'has got to stop!'

Gemma and her guest sat to drink tea at a little table in the rose garden. Fleabag soon caught up with them, but kept well out of sight, pricking up his wide, black ears as he began to listen intently. Almost immediately Domnall jumped, then sat stiffly with his head on one side as if he was listening. But in his intense blue eyes was a far-away look that betrayed a flicker of hate, or was it fear?

Gemma raised an eyebrow. 'Are you well, my Lord? Is something the matter?'

Domnall shook his head and relaxed again. 'I am sorry, Madam; I am just not used to the presence of cats.'

Fleabag smirked at this as he silently promised himself that this young man would have to get very used to the presence of cats. 'I'm afraid from now on, a cat will follow you wherever you go,' he promised silently. He would have a chat with his eldest daughter, Cleo. She was highly intelligent and an excellent sleuth. What's more, she had kept her ability to talk a secret. He would ask her to follow him. She would enjoy the game and was less obvious than himself. Any visitor from Porthwain would be nervous of being followed by a three-legged, black scrag-bundle with a reputation as a slayer of wizards.

'Let's face it,' Fleabag muttered smugly to himself, '*I'd* be scared of me if I saw me coming.'

After discussing the garden and sipping mint tea for a while, Domnall skilfully turned the conversation back to the Ring Fire. Gemma let her head drop a little and sighed.

Domnall did not press the point, but, feigning sympathy, gently inquired whether carrying the Ring Fire was burdensome, for her Ladyship seemed very weary whenever the subject was mentioned.

'Yes, indeed I am weary,' she confided. 'In fact, I am planning a holiday. Things will be different after that.'

Better and better! Domnall laughed to himself. This girl was like a ripe plum about to drop into his lap!

'My lady, I own an excellent lodge in the north of Beulothin, not far from the city of Beriot. It overlooks the sea and is not troubled by neighbours. The city itself is only half a day's ride away, yet in my lodge, you would think yourself alone in the whole world! It is very beautiful, set between two great hills and with a small sandy beach below. Please, allow me, as your humble servant, to give you the use of it this summer.'

The young man smiled so warmly and genuinely that, although Gemma felt worried by the pain in her hands and a burning tingling down her spine, she found herself quite taken by the idea. It would give her time to think about what to do next, and most importantly of all, the journey would mean passing her beloved little cottage in the rocks.

'That sounds wonderful!' she enthused. 'But I fear I will not make a good guest. I have little conversation these days.'

Domnall brushed her fears aside. 'I will not be there, my Lady. I would not dream of imposing myself when you obviously need space and peace for a while to recover from the strains of your work.'

Gemma looked into the young man's eyes. Their intense blue reminded her of the blue flames raised by the evil Chancellor she had helped destroy. But now she was being silly! He looked so honest and kind, she found herself smiling warmly in response. 'Thank you,' she replied quietly. 'I should like that.'

Domnall could hardly contain his glee. He stood up and made an over-elaborate bow to hide the fact he was grinning widely. He had won the first stage in his victory!

'Then, my Lady, it is agreed. No more talk of the Ring Fire, as it wearies you so greatly. Simply a month by the sea with whatever friends you care to bring. You will be my guest but left completely alone. I will provide food, servants and everything you could possibly require.

'Meanwhile, I will take my leave of you, as I fear I am trespassing on your time.'

Then, before she could answer, he swept another bow and strode smartly away towards the gatehouse, closely followed by his equerry.

Gemma leaned her head on her hands, trying to ignore the burning throbbing that would once have warned her of great danger.

Fleabag took his cue. With one bound he landed on the table in front of her, knocking the delicate china cups flying and smashing them on the gravel below.

Gemma turned to glower at the impossible cat, and stretched out a hand to shove him away. But he just sat there, head on one side, great golden eyes wide. 'You're not going to Beulothin, are you?'

Staring in the direction her visitor had gone, Gemma shrugged. 'What's the harm? I've got to have a rest!' and with that she sobbed and sobbed into his fur.

The black cat looked wistfully after the disappearing figure of Lord Domnall. There was something seriously wrong with Gemma if she had not sensed the blue shimmering danger that the Chancellor seemed to wear like a cloak. What was worse, Fleabag was angry with himself for not managing to set Cleo on that evil man's tail. Bother!

5

Sir Fleabag

To Gemma's surprise, Phelan thought the idea of a
few weeks by the sea an excellent one.

He had been worried about Gemma for some
time. The king had listened while Fleabag had tried
to describe what he had seen the day of the strange
blue storm. It troubled him deeply. He did not want
her to go so far away without being near her, just in
case something was seriously amiss. Phelan decided
he would accompany them as far as Beriot in the
hope that Gemma might confide her worries to him
while they were riding.

It was no lie that Phelan wanted a holiday too, but
he did not want Gemma to feel crowded when they
got to the Chancellor's lodge. He decided to leave
her there and visit his friend Prince Tomas, the
Regent of Beulothin. Phelan would only be a few
hour's ride away if he was needed.

So messages were dispatched. The company would
make their first official stay with Rowanne de
Montiland, the Lady Knight who had accompanied
them on their quest to find the royal ring. She had
challenged her spiteful, greedy cousin Rupert to the

Princedom, and had won. As Princess she had changed the city's name back from Rupertsberg to its ancient title of Erbwenneth. It was over a year since they had seen Rowanne, and a night or two in her palace was sure to cheer them all up. She had excellent cooks and usually followed her feasts with plenty of storytelling and music.

After seeing Rowanne, they planned to ride north by north-west as they had done on the Ring quest. The snows were thawed and the spring rains were over, leaving the roads open and dry. It should be an easy ride, taking three weeks at the most.

During the next few days, Gemma dismissed her maid and packed her own things. She did not want anyone to guess she was not planning to stay long at the lodge by the sea, but to escape as soon as possible. Her luggage was mostly filled with seeds and basic farming tools, oilskins and blankets—things she would need for living alone in a rough place. She did not pack a single robe of state.

She felt sorry for her acolytes. They would have to bear the burden of official duties until someone came to take her place. She told them simply that they must oversee all the Fire ceremonies until further notice. She gave no explanations and made no excuses.

She felt better for doing what *she* wanted for a change. The day they were to leave she pulled on her leather jerkin and riding breeches and smiled properly for the first time in many long months. First, she would have a short holiday by the sea; then, when she had thought of how to find her replacement, she would simply disappear. It would be easy to hide in the mountains. She would be the Fire Wielder no longer.

Fleabag did not wait to be invited. As the horses and pack-ponies drew up outside the stables for loading, he simply hopped onto a spare saddle-bag (making sure first of all that his daughter Cleo was safely hidden *inside* the same bag), then they were off.

The journey to Erbwenneth was pleasant, but Phelan winced at the top of the last hill where he and his gang of thieves had once hidden and ambushed Fleabag, Rowanne and Gemma.

The Fire Wielder rode past the spot, head down, as if the memory meant nothing to her.

Fleabag jumped onto the King's saddle and made as formal a bow as a cat can manage. 'Sire,' he chuckled, 'I think you ought to dub me knight for my famous deeds in the late Queen's name on this field of battle.'

Phelan laughed out loud. 'Nonsense, I ought to cut your stringy tail off for daring to bite the flesh of your future liege-lord and King.'

'Well, it was your fault for pouncing out like that. Anyone would have thought you were a thief!' the cat pouted.

'I *was* a thief!' the King replied, reddening. 'And you are quite right, you should be dubbed knight on this field of battle.'

And with that, the King dismounted and drawing his sword, pointed to the grass at his feet. 'Kneel, noble cat!' he commanded. But then he regretted it, for three-legged cats cannot kneel very well and it was hard for Fleabag to remain dignified because he kept losing his balance and falling over. In the end Phelan said, 'Just stand still, Fleabag!' and he touched the cat lightly on both shoulders with the gleaming blade. Then he pronounced very solemnly, 'In the name of Queen Sophia of beloved memory, I command you to arise Sir... er... what would you like to be called?'

Fleabag stretched up and said something very quietly, so only Phelan could hear.

The King bowed his head and replied equally quietly, but with great dignity, tapping the cat on both shoulders again.

Then he stood up straight and said, so everyone could hear, 'Arise, Sir Fleabag Scrag-Belly.'

Everyone clapped and cheered, and the King gave the cat a golden earring as a token of his new status.

Gemma turned in her saddle as Phelan remounted. 'He's not really Sir Fleabag Scrag-Belly, is he?' she asked, quite horrified.

'No,' the King replied in a voice full of awe. 'He told me his real name.'

Princess Rowanne was delighted to see them. They were feasted and fussed over, but in the middle of the party, Fleabag sat right under Rowanne's chair, and prodded a not-too-sharp claw into her leg. Before Rowanne and Fleabag had made friends, this had been his way of making her listen to him. Since then she had always worn knee-high boots when he was around.

This time Fleabag was careful not to hurt, but Rowanne knew exactly who was under the table and that he required an audience with her. She dropped her napkin and bent down, glowering at the cat hidden in the gloom below.

'Listen, *mog!*' she hissed, 'why don't you come up and talk to me like a human being?'

'Because I'm *not* a human being!' Fleabag grinned.

'Well, why don't you come and talk to me properly, then? I could have you arrested for scratching my leg, you know.'

'But you won't, because you like me too much,' Fleabag retorted smugly. 'Now, this is secret,' he said, serious for once. 'I need to talk to you urgently and in private.'

'Talking like this isn't very secret or private.' Rowanne made a face. 'And I've eaten too much dinner, so if I don't sit up straight in a minute, I'll be sick all over you.'

'And spoil my luxurious black fur you've always coveted as a collar? Never! I'll meet you at midnight in the bell tower. Don't be late!' he demanded, and stalked away under the table, nibbling at a few fallen scraps as he went.

Rowanne righted herself, smoothed her hair and continued her conversation with Phelan.

The bell tower was a tall, thin, circular building, with a spiral staircase inside, ascending for three hundred steps before reaching the bell platform at the very top. From there all of Erbwenneth was in view, as well as a wide sweep of the countryside beyond.

Rowanne had once been very fit, for she had been

a Lady Knight in the late Queen's Guard. But she had not been in action since fighting off some of her cousin's supporters after she became princess. Now she was quite out of breath when she reached the top. Fleabag, of course, was calm and composed, staring out of a small window towards the north west, his bottle-brush tail neatly curved over his three paws.

'I'm a grandfather, and I'm much fitter than you!' he mocked. 'You ought to be ashamed of yourself, puffing like a pensioned-off mole!'

'And you're an alley-cat who doesn't know how to address a princess!' Rowanne retorted.

'I would if I met one!' Fleabag would never let Rowanne best him, even though they were friends these days.

Rowanne decided against dropping him out of the window for his cheek. She knew from experience that he would scratch her hands badly, and besides, it would make a mess in the courtyard below. For now, she was more interested in hearing what he had to say than in vengeance.

'Why have you dragged me all the way up here?' she complained. 'Why couldn't we have had a nice chat in my room over a flagon of ale?'

Fleabag looked out across the rolling countryside again. 'Because I want to be sure that no one in the whole world knows what I am going to say. I wanted to be sure we would be quite, quite alone...' The cat hesitated as he looked down at a row of dead bats and mice lined up across the floor. He patted one of them that he thought he saw twitch a little. 'I don't trust anyone except you to know this...'

'Know what?' Rowanne was getting exasperated.

'I think Gemma has either lost, or forgotten, the Ring Fire. Normally there is always a little flame hovering about her wherever she goes. I suspect that humans can't always see it, but I can. For at least two weeks it hasn't been there. The flame has gone, whether by her own choice or some other reason, I don't know. She will not talk about it.'

There was silence for a few moments. Rowanne tightened her grip on the handrail, and felt her fingers become cold and sore as she squeezed the iron. This was unbelievable. It was more than dreadful, it was...

Suddenly, above their heads came cawing and clattering sounds. Rowanne and Fleabag leaned out of the little turret window to see a crow flapping its great heavy wings laboriously as it flew off into the midnight skies. 'I forgot there might be birds listening,' he said. 'Still, with any luck, it's an ordinary stupid bird, or one who is loyal to us.'

Rowanne sniffed. 'Don't be daft, Fleabag. Would a bird care about the Ring Fire?'

'It has been known,' Fleabag answered nervously, remembering the ravens who had given a clue as to the whereabouts of the Royal Ring three years before. Then he went on to tell her what had happened to Gemma, how she had changed and how she had accepted this strange invitation for a month by the sea in Beulothin from this new Chancellor who smelled and looked and moved like the long-dead Sethan of Porthwain.

Fleabag did not tell Rowanne about the strange disturbances, the 'somethings' that drove all the cats silly with distraction. Neither did he try to explain what he had seen on the night of the storm. She would just have laughed and said it was normal for cats to jump around like half-witted lunatics.

'The long and the short of it is,' Fleabag looked up at the Princess with urgent gravity, 'you have got to come with us. I think Gemma will need help.'

Rowanne leaned on the window sill next to the cat and looked out across the landscape they had travelled before. 'When do we leave?' she asked.

6

The Voice

Gemma was delighted when Rowanne asked if she could come for a few days by the sea as well. The princess never tried to discuss the Ring Fire. She was more interested in telling tales of battles whilst downing a pot of ale. She made Gemma laugh, and never once alluded to the storm or the blue magic.

Phelan was relieved Rowanne had come. He realized that Gemma either would not, or could not talk, and he found riding next to her very wearisome.

As the company neared the mountain pass, and the little cottage in the rocks came closer and closer, Gemma became more silent than ever. Fleabag sat on the pommel of Gemma's saddle and tried to joke with her, but she did not even smile. In fact she scarcely spoke to anyone. Fleabag took to annoying a small dog that Rowanne had bought with her as a gift for Prince Tomas. But the animal was so stupid, he found it meagre and unsatisfying sport.

When they came to the bottom of the grassy slope below the stony outcrop where the tiny cottage was wedged in a cleft, Rowanne and Phelan jumped from their mounts to go and look at the place. Gemma pretended she wasn't interested, and called it a 'smelly dump'. Every part of her longed to go and sit in that tiny back room and to re-kindle a fir-cone fire, as they had so long ago. The bright flames had transformed the damp little hovel to a warm home filled with golden light and soft brown shadows. Once the Ring Fire had glowed there as well, making the whole place feel joyful...

Gemma found she was aching to know whether the cottage was still standing after two bad mountain winters. Had Phelan's repairs held good? She so wanted to go and stand quietly on the earth floor and remember how good it had all been. Most of all, she wanted to remember how it had felt to hold the Ring Fire in her hands, and not feel frightened or inadequate, just loved.

As the others came back from the hidden place, slipping and stumbling down the slope towards her, she knew by their laughter and chatter that all was well. She had to feign disinterest. They must never think of looking for her there.

They camped just below the mountain pass before nightfall. Within a couple of days, Gemma's spirits lifted as they saw the wide fertile plains of Beulothin spreading out before them. Phelan ordered all royal insignia to be hidden. Three years before they had saved the land from a terrible flesh-eating monster. If their presence had been known, they would have been thronged by cheering crowds.

It was not until the travellers had reached the Chancellor's comfortable little lodge near the sea that Phelan turned back. He felt he could do nothing to help until Gemma felt like talking. Meanwhile he would make sure she had peace and quiet for as long as she needed it. With the cats and Rowanne to guard her, she would be safe enough.

'You keep an eye on her, Fleabag,' Phelan had told him. 'I'll come to see you all as often as I can, without seeming rude to Tomas. Probably quiet and sea air will do Gemma good. Then we can all sit down and talk. Meanwhile, try and relax a little and have a holiday yourself. Worrying won't help, and I suspect the Ring Fire will do something to help Gemma fairly soon.'

Fleabag wasn't so optimistic. 'Come back as soon as you can, Phelan. I've had an uncomfortable feeling about this holiday since the Chancellor suggested it. Something is badly wrong. I don't know what it is, but I can sense it in my whiskers and I know I saw what I saw! In my heart of hearts, I don't trust anything that comes out of Porthwain.'

Phelan looked at the lodge. It was a whitewashed thatched chalet, perched at the head of a pleasantly wooded valley that ran down to the sea. Everything seemed perfect for a peaceful holiday.

'It seems safe enough, but I do trust your instincts, you old ratter. I'll post sentries secretly in the woods all around. Send Cleo to them if you are worried. I know she can't talk, but tell her to carry a feather in her mouth if I am needed.'

Fleabag grinned. The King did not know that his daughter could out-talk any cat—or human—he had ever met. And what was worse, she had a great partiality for fresh game. That dear, innocent golden cat usually had *several* feathers in her mouth... along with the feathers' owner, half eaten. She rarely missed her prey.

'Don't worry Phelan, we'll get a message to you,' the cat assured him. 'Take care. May the Ring Fire light your path.'

The King picked up Fleabag and scratched him behind a tattered ear. 'Thank you, my furry friend. We can't know what the Chancellor's real intentions are, but I know the Ring Fire will be burning, with or without Gemma being there to watch and listen.'

'True!' the cat jumped down. 'And we must learn to listen to it for ourselves. But I'm still frightened for her. I am sure she is in danger!'

Phelan left after giving Gemma a warm hug. As he disappeared between the trees, an elderly manservant stepped out of the lodge to help the travellers carry in their luggage. Gemma refused the housekeeper's offer of help with her unpacking. What she carried had to remain a secret.

Soon everyone had washed and eaten. The servants bade the guests goodnight and left Gemma, Rowanne and the cats alone.

Fleabag was still nervous. The 'somethings' seemed to have gone when they left the King's palace at Harflorum. Neither he nor Cleo had been troubled by them since. But his feeling of doom and the troublesome memory of the storm had not lessened. He chewed at his claws while he sat by the fire in the cool of the evening. How he wished Cleo had had a chance to follow the Chancellor that day he had come to the palace.

Cleo was at that moment following Gemma around the house. The sleek golden cat had not remained hidden for the whole journey—just long enough to make it too far for her to go back alone. After that she had ingratiated herself with all the travellers with her deep, tuneful purr and willingness to be stroked.

Gemma's room overlooked a river that tumbled down towards the ocean. The sounds of water sang pleasantly all night, and she smiled as she fell asleep with Cleo purring gently at the foot of her bed. As soon as Cleo was certain all was well, she slipped back to sit by the fire with her father.

'Gemma is sound asleep, Dad,' she whispered as she stretched out to toast her tummy fur. 'She's as peaceful as an overfed kitten. We can relax until morning.'

But Gemma's dreams were far from peaceful. Something, someone was behind her, talking hypnotically in a low voice, suggesting the very thing she wanted with all her heart, to lay aside the Ring Fire. All night she tried to turn around and see who was talking to her, but she could never quite see who it was. It was only a voice, not a person. But what a wonderful voice—so kind, so gentle, so understanding of how very, very tired she was.

In fact she was so tired, she dreamed she fell asleep. Then she dreamed, within the dream, that the same voice was speaking to her again, and again she fell asleep within her dream. Soon she was under so many thick layers of suggestion that if anyone had seen her, they would have thought her dead. Only no one did see her, for Rowanne was just as deeply asleep herself, and the cats were not there...

7

Swept Away!

Fleabag and his daughter Cleo were walking by the shore. Once the humans were asleep, they had spent most of the night enjoying catching small fish in the pools and caterwauling at the moon as loudly as they liked without having boots thrown at them.

At first light, they were both still in fine voice, when they spotted a figure walking slowly down towards the sea. Although the sun was not yet fully up, there was enough light to know it was Gemma, by the way she stood with her hair blowing in the wind. She looked very small and lonely on the thin stretch of sand between the rocks, her long, loose night-robe tugging against her legs in the chilly morning breeze.

Gemma did not seem to notice the cold. She just stood staring out to sea, without turning to greet the cats as they ran towards her, calling happily.

Suddenly Fleabag hissed to Cleo to stop, and tugged at her tail with his teeth, pulling her back behind a rock. 'I don't like this,' he whispered. 'Something strange is happening. I'm sure Gemma is sleep-walking. My fur is all on end.'

Cleo nodded her agreement. 'So's mine... What's that, Dad?'

She pointed a paw out to sea where the grey rocks and even greyer water were tinged with dawn light. The sky was streaked with gold and rose, promising a glorious sunrise. Out at sea, a small boat was heading towards the shore. In it stood a tall, thin figure. He used no oar or sail, yet the boat seemed to move with perfect control. As sand and shingle scraped the keel, the figure stepped into the shallows and ordered the little craft to stay close. There it bobbed as surely as if a strong hand were holding it.

The figure reached Gemma's side, although she seemed quite unaware of his presence. He moved behind her and seemed to speak in her ear.

Gemma shook her head, and the cats could hear her replying faintly, although she seemed to remain asleep. Neither cat could hear what was said, but whatever it was, it had not satisfied the man. He pointed to the boat and, unprotesting, Gemma got in. Then, with a blast of blue flame that made Fleabag shudder, the little craft skidded right over the waves towards the open water.

The man stood on the shore, tall and dark in the very early morning light. For several minutes he watched the boat spinning and bobbing as the blast of blue magic faded, and the current took over, tugging the little vessel further and further away from land.

Then he laughed softly, turned, and vanished into thin air. High above, a black crow flapped slowly away...

The cats stared wide-eyed. 'Cleo,' Fleabag whispered,

'run back to the house as fast as you can and get help. It doesn't matter what you have to do to waken Rowanne, but do it. Gemma's life and my fur depend on it!'

'Shall I summon the King's soldiers as well?' Cleo asked.

'No, they could be anywhere in those woods. I need help *now!*'

Cleo was gone—a streak of rusty gold in the early light.

Fleabag gingerly took a few steps towards the sea. The icy water made his fur hang in heavily sanded points. He jumped back. He did not *like* water, but the sight of the ever-retreating little boat made him take another step, then another, deeper and deeper into the swirling sea, until the next little wave caught him under the belly, and lifted his paws off the bottom.

Cats can swim, but they do not like it. On a hot summer's day, even Fleabag might almost have enjoyed a splash (although he wouldn't have admitted it to anyone). But in this freezing cold sea, with a stiff breeze blowing from the east, Fleabag was not a happy cat.

It was only the thought of Gemma, alone in a small boat heading for the ocean, that kept him going. He was frightened for her. She had seemed so strange and unaware of everything. That man must have been Lord Domnall. He was the only person who knew exactly where Gemma was, and he wielded the blue flames as the other Chancellor had done. It was obvious to Fleabag that Domnall was a member of the Order of Wizards. He shuddered.

Simply banning them had done nothing to stop their evil work. It had only made them more secretive. Now they had some sort of hold over Gemma, and the danger he had seen threatening her in the strange blue storm was becoming a reality.

Fleabag's neck was aching as he lifted his head to keep his black nose above the water. The salt was in his eyes and he admitted to himself that he was very scared. He longed to turn back to shore. But he had to keep swimming, for Gemma's sake. He *had* to reach her and waken her.

He could sense they were all at war now, and it wasn't going to be the sort of battle that could be fought with swords and armour. Rowanne was going to find this hard to understand.

Fleabag spluttered as a wave caught him full in the face. He must stop worrying and concentrate on swimming. The lack of one back leg made his steering difficult, but Gemma's boat was still in sight, so he kept on trying. Suddenly a much bigger swell caught him, lifting him onto the glassy green curve of its back, so for a second or two he could take a good look in every direction. The shore was a long way off, and the boat seemed no closer. The size of the waves told him he was now in the open sea, and he was very frightened.

But, catfully, he kept swimming. The sun was now gleaming above the horizon, and the waves were rising higher and higher all the time. He was swallowing more and more water. His fur was completely sodden; even the tiny soft under-hairs next to his skin were drenched, making him heavy and ungainly.

He managed to breathe, but he had to close his

eyes, for the salt stung them terribly. He had water swilling around his wide ears, making glugging and whistling sounds deep inside his head. For no sensible reason, he opened his mouth and mewed 'Help!' As the waves grew bigger he could feel himself being dragged under. Desperately he struggled to keep afloat, expending precious energy as he fought the sea. He was now so stiff and cold he could hardly move.

Then another wave lifted him high again. He could no longer see the boat, but there was something that gave him a glimmer of hope. It was a piece of driftwood, a branch from an old tree. With the last dregs of his strength he steered himself towards it, hoping it was not some sort of a mirage. To his relief his claws sank into something very solid indeed.

Cleo, meanwhile, was struggling to waken Rowanne. The servants had disappeared. She was alone with the sleeping Princess. She did not dare try to run for Phelan's soldiers; it would take too much time to find them. But nothing, not even a specially sharpened claw, honed to perfection as Fleabag had taught her, could rouse the sleeper. Once or twice Rowanne reached for her sword, waved it and shouted 'To battle!' but then sank down into the pillows again, still fast asleep.

The golden marmalade cat sat firmly on her victim's chest, licking the Princess' face long and hard with a rough, warm tongue. By noon Cleo managed to get Rowanne to open her eyes.

Rowanne turned over and tried to shoo the cat away, threatening her with battlefield oaths.

But Cleo did not budge. Now, she decided, was the time to reveal that she could talk. She had kept her secret from humans, because it was the best way to gather information. She always followed her father's advice of eavesdropping whenever possible. She had noticed how people fell silent when Fleabag or one of her talking brothers came into sight. By remaining mute, she had discovered a great many useful palace secrets.

But this was an emergency of unbelievable magnitude! Gemma would be far out at sea by now, and her father was in real trouble. So Cleo dug her claws a little more deeply into Rowanne's chest, then stood, raised her tail and stretched her back into a glorious, marmalade arch and said, very politely: 'My Lady Rowanne de Montiland, I beg your forgiveness for disturbing your sleep, but Her Eminence the Fire Wielder has been kidnapped. My father may at this moment be drowning, and the servants have fled!'

Then Cleo lowered herself to glare, golden-eyed into the princess's bleary face. She was no longer polite, simply determined. '*Get up!*' she ordered, displaying her special claw. 'Get up immediately, your Highness, or I will be forced to use this, my ultimate weapon, on the fancy leather saddlebag you prize so highly!' Fleabag had done this before to make Rowanne listen, and the anecdote had been a favourite tale amongst his kittens.

At last Rowanne raised her head and managed to say, 'If you get off my chest, you walking dog-food, I will get up. While I am dressing, I would like a sensible explanation of what you have just said, and why you are waking me at such an unearthly hour.'

Cleo sprang lightly down and sat on the window-sill where the thin shaft of sunlight caught the glossy golden hues of her coat to best effect. She looked up at the chink of bright blue summer sky. 'It is now past noon. I do not know what time it is your habit to rise, but I do not call *this* unearthly. Furthermore, I have been trying to rouse you since dawn.'

Rowanne struggled over to the window, almost tripping as she tried to pull her breeches on at the same time. She tugged the curtain back and gasped. 'No! I have never slept this late in my life... except when I was under a spell, but that was different.'

Cleo turned her golden face to look at Rowanne. She was an honest-looking cat, with a neat white triangle around her pink nose. Her expression was serious. 'Your Highness, I don't think that *was* different. My father told me the story of your enchantment by the Chancellor of All Wizards, and I think this may be more of the same.'

Rowanne did not reply. She pulled on her shirt and buckled her sword by her side. Then as the two ran out of the house down the track towards the beach, Cleo told Rowanne what had happened in the early hours.

It was then that they saw the branch of driftwood bobbing near the shore, with the black, unmoving shape still clinging to the sodden bark. The cold, stiff little bundle of fur that was washed into the bay on the afternoon tide would not have been recognizable as Fleabag, it if hadn't been for a golden earring.

8

Flotsam and Jetsam

Rowanne gently lifted the cat's cold body and wrapped it in her overshirt.

Before she became a Princess, the brave Lady Knight had seen many heroes die, and had never been known to cry, but now she did not stint her tears for her old enemy and friend, the redoubtable Fleabag.

Cleo followed Rowanne up the path back to the house. She was too stunned and confused by what had happened to know how to cry.

Rowanne went inside to collect her saddle-bags and a cloak. She called Cleo to jump into one of the bags, but she tied Fleabag, still rolled in the woollen shirt, across the back of her saddle, like a great warrior slain on the field of battle. Then Rowanne sprang up onto her horse.

She looked down at the frightened little ginger cat cowering in the leather bag behind her left knee. 'We must go and find Phelan. He may think of something he can do to help Gemma, and Fleabag will be buried with full honours as a knight and a hero.'

The journey was not long, for Rowanne rode like the wind. But to Cleo, hiding in the saddle-bag, it seemed to go on for ever. Sometimes she stayed low, feeling very sick, curled up in a ball and at other times she looked out of the flap and watched her father's untidy black head bobbing up and down in time to the horse's pace. Sunlight glinted on his golden earring as water trickled from his nose and mouth, and his fur dried in untidy sandy tufts under Rowanne's loosely tied shirt.

By the time they reached Beriot it was scarcely four hours past midday. Phelan met them outside the gates as he returned from a ride across the country-side. He waved cheerfully and called out to Rowanne as soon as he saw her, but she did not reply. She simply rode, cold and stony-faced, until she was so close to him that no one else could hear.

'Gemma has been kidnapped and is drifting out at sea in a small boat, and I have brought the brave Fleabag to you for burial.' Rowanne spoke hurriedly and softly. She could not risk her grief over-whelming her, and she dare not let anyone else know that the Fire Wielder was in danger.

Phelan went pale and turned his horse so he could call his equerry to his side. 'I want my most senior sea captain in my study in one hour.'

Then with a heavy heart he beckoned to Rowanne to follow him through the streets until he came to the royal residence of Beriot. This was a fine, stately building, but more like a large country house than a palace. It was built of warm-coloured red bricks and its roof had a hundred different little gables and slopes to it. Set high on a hill at the northern edge of Beriot, it overlooked the city on one side, and the sea on the other.

The private study Tomas had set aside for the King's use had a wonderful view over the sea. Phelan leaned on the windowsill, peering out, as if trying to catch a glimpse of Gemma's forlorn little boat. Cleo had told him everything she could. Now everyone had fallen silent.

At last Phelan sighed. 'Thank goodness you can talk, young lady. We'll bury Fleabag in the royal cemetery at Harflorum. As soon as we have found Gemma we will take him home in a gold coffin.' The king spoke quietly, without turning away from the window.

Stretched out on the settee next to him, Fleabag lay in the warm afternoon sun, looking for all the world as if he were asleep.

Cleo put a paw up to the king's knee. 'If you please, Your Majesty,' she said, 'he would far rather be buried in the strawberry patch or under some brambles. He was never a cat for being formal about things. He would much rather be somewhere a little wild and untidy...'

Phelan nodded. 'I know what you mean, but he was a knight of the realm and a national hero. He was of a noble family. He told me his real name when he was knighted. My predecessor, Queen Sophia told Gemma that he had a pedigree many times longer than his venerable tail. The people will expect a proper funeral in a proper place.'

Cleo wanted to cry. 'I wish my Mum was here. She would agree, I know. He needs to be buried somewhere open and free...'

Just then a deep voice not far away murmured, 'How about you don't bury me at all? I'd much prefer it!'

'Fleabag!' everyone shouted at once. The black cat stretched a little and opened one golden eye. He smiled under his black whiskers. 'Hello,' he purred. 'Did I give you all a scare?'

'You did indeed, you incorrigible rogue!' Phelan leaned over and stroked the cat's doormat of a head. 'What happened?'

Fleabag grinned and rolled over, as Cleo jumped up next to him and began to lick his ears with delight. But the effort of moving made him cough badly. 'I felt like a little attention and I had nothing better to do at the time. Did you find Gemma?' He coughed again.

'No, I'm afraid not,' Phelan sighed. 'It appears she was swept out to sea.'

Rowanne took a few seconds to realize that Fleabag was really alive. Then without further hesitation, she flung the study door open and bellowed, 'Fetch the royal vet!' into the face of an amazed-looking chambermaid who happened to be passing at that very moment. '*NOW!*' the Princess screamed as the girl stood there with her mouth hanging open.

The chambermaid dropped the pile of sheets she was carrying and ran as fast as she could. Within minutes, she returned, leading a fat little man puffing and panting up the stairs behind her, straw and hay dropping in a trail behind him as he ran. Wiping his bald, shiny head, he bowed as he tried to dust down his clothes. 'My apologies, Your Majesty... In the middle of delivering a foal... no time to change...'

'Please do not worry yourself,' Phelan assured him, 'This is too urgent to stand on ceremony.' He

60

ushered the vet over to the settee where Fleabag lay, dazed and bleary-eyed. 'Our friend nearly drowned in the sea this morning; in fact we thought he was dead. But it appears he is very much alive!'

After a short examination, and a few drops of medicine, Fleabag fell into a healthy sleep. There were no more plans for his funeral. His chest was rising and falling steadily, and his fur was warm.

'He will be all right in a few days,' the vet announced. 'He must have taken a deal of water into his lungs, as well as getting hypothermia. Any longer in the sea and he would not have survived. Probably the ride on the horse saved him—the jolting must have revived his circulation and warmed him up. Putting him across the saddle with his head down must have helped to drain the fluid from his lungs. He is a very lucky cat indeed. Tell me,' the vet went on, 'how many lives has he had? Seven, eight?'

Phelan smiled. 'Many more than that. I have seen him use all nine at once before now, and he still comes out with his whiskers gleaming.'

The vet laughed and promised to look in again that evening. 'Just keep him quiet and warm. Plenty of rest and a little good food at regular intervals. Above all keep him well away from the sea and he'll be fine.'

The next visitor was Captain Marcus, of the King's flagship, the *Flora*. He was a lean, dark-skinned man, probably from the south like Phelan himself. His long black hair was scraped back into a tight pigtail, and his black eyes seemed to take in everything at once. He seemed to be perpetually scanning a distant horizon rather than letting his

gaze rest anywhere. He said nothing when he
entered but dipped his head in a short bow, and
tugged off his faded blue cotton cap. A fine woollen
captain's cloak trimmed in gold braid had been
hastily draped around his shoulders, but Marcus
looked uncomfortable under it, as if he were unused
to such clothing. The man stood quietly, legs apart,
as if he expected the floor to heave like a deck at any
moment.

Phelan liked him immediately. This man was
watchful and aware. He would be glad to trust his
precious mission to a man like this.

Cleo explained things as best she could, and
Captain Marcus listened quietly, asking a few questions here and there. Then Fleabag, disturbed by the
voices, awoke and told his story before eating a little
lightly steamed fish and going back to sleep.

The Captain unrolled a chart he had been carrying
under his arm. Rowanne showed him the bay and
the lodge where they had been staying. Then he
pointed out the way the tides ran, and where
Gemma's little boat had probably drifted.

'Why did Fleabag not get swept out to sea too?'
Rowanne asked.

Captain Marcus stretched a strong brown hand
across the map, pointing to the two rocky arms of the
bay. 'As long as he remained within this area, he
would be carried back to shore with the flotsam and
jetsam of the tide. But the Fire Wielder's boat may
have been swept further out and caught in the ocean
currents. I have a rough idea where she may be
floating. The currents follow a fairly regular pattern
around these waters.'

Phelan stood and looked at Captain Marcus. 'I must warn you, Captain, there are dark powers involved in this. There may be no regular patterns for you to follow and you may be sailing into a trap. This is a dangerous voyage. You may never return to your loved ones.'

The Captain rolled the map carefully, keeping his eyes down as he did so. 'Sire, five years ago I lost my wife to the monster you killed before you became High Prince over our Lord Tomas, and King over the land. What you did was too late for her, but a great service to all of us. I am prepared to do what I can for you in return. I am not frightened by evil magic, and I have no more family to leave behind. She was all I had.' And with that he bowed stiffly and left the room.

Phelan turned his gaze to the sea again, and Fleabag muttered under his blanket, 'I resent being called "flotsam and jetsam"!'

9

Adrift!

Gemma did not wake until night had almost fallen.
The layers of unnatural sleep Lord Domnall had
woven around her gradually slipped away over the
hours.

During that time she dreamed many dreams of
carrying something very, very heavy. Too heavy.
Then someone came to her from behind, always from
behind, and offered to take the burden from her. It
was a man, she knew that. He was so understanding,
so helpful. She wanted to give him whatever it was
that weighed on her so badly, but she could not...
ought not.

He told her she was being silly and obstinate, but
she wasn't. She did not know why. She was so tired,
she did not know anything, only that she still carried
whatever it was that was too heavy.

Then there were flames, and a feeling of flying, or
was it sailing? The flames were not warm and golden;
they were bright, vivid cerulean blue, and ice cold. As
they licked her skin, they burned by freezing. They
were unkind flames. They brought fear, and that
voice again.

Only this time it was no longer asking gently. Now it was telling, insisting… *ordering* her to surrender whatever it was she was carrying. She was crying. Gemma would have given up her burden if she could, but it seemed to be a part of her. She could not let it go. She tried to pluck it from her hands, but it was so tiny, she could not find it. Odd, she thought, how something so heavy could be so small.

Her dreams went on. The voice from behind begged and pleaded, cajoled, wheedled, commanded, threatened. All day long it went on, until Gemma was so exhausted, she simply decided to wake up.

And when she opened her eyes at last, she found herself in a small boat, surrounded by sea, with the rain pouring down her face and neck. An oilskin had been roughly pulled over her. She was thirsty, so she scooped a little rainwater from between the folds of the cloth, and drank.

Some instinct told her that she might need the water that was left, so she carefully arranged part of the oilskin so rain could collect and form a good-sized pool at the end of the boat. This left her feeling cold and wet around the shoulders, but she huddled down as far as she could and shivered.

Hiding under the heavy cloth, Gemma tried to collect her thoughts. She was frightened, but she could not run away from the situation. She would have to face it. She had never been at sea before, and she rather liked the gentle rising swell of the waves. It was soothing and comforted her fear, but she was still lost and alone. More importantly though, she was hungry and would have given anything for a hunk of bread. Her head span and she felt terribly tired. At long last she managed to sleep again, rocked by the gentle waves.

This time her sleep was natural and she woke in the middle of the night feeling refreshed. It had stopped raining, and she pushed back the stiff folds of her covering so she could see the stars, intensely bright in the inky blackness above. At last she found she could think.

She remembered the last few days, the way the strange storm had put out the Ring Fire, and her longing to give up being Fire Wielder, her tiredness, and her strange visitor with his seemingly kind offers of help. Suddenly she sat bolt upright, making the boat rock violently. 'That's it!' she gasped. How could she have been so stupid! That blue fire, those unnaturally blue eyes, she had seen them all in the Great Hall at Porthwain. 'Domnall *is* a wizard! He has the same knowledge that the old Chancellor had. Only this time he wants the Ring Fire itself, not just the royal Ring.

'He must have sent the storm to test my strength as Fire Wielder. He must have been delighted to see how bad I was at my job. I wonder if he succeeded in taking the Ring Fire from me?' She opened her palms and stared at them. It was too dark to see much by the faint starlight, but they felt very sore where she had scratched at the skin in her dreams, trying to pluck the Ring Fire out. But there was no sign as to whether the Fire had gone or not. But, it did not always burn when she thought she needed it most.

Gemma knew it had still been with her after the strange storm: it had scorched the sleeves of her robe. The rain and the blue lightning had simply doused the flame, it hadn't killed it... But why had the blue magic defeated the Ring Fire so easily?

For the first time it occurred to her that maybe things hadn't been as they had seemed. Maybe the rain had damped the flames as any rain would do, but she had seen that the Fire still burned. So perhaps it was only a battle that had been lost, not the war. She had been too tired and worn down to see how things were. Lord Domnall could have been plant-ing suggestions into her mind for a very long time. The Ring Fire wasn't defeated, and it mustn't be. And above all, it must not end up in the hands of a man like Domnall! It made her search for a new Fire Wielder even more urgent.

She lay back in the boat and sighed with relief. She could not have given up the Ring Fire in her dream, even though for a short time she had wanted to. She knew now that the man was Domnall, or at least his shade. He was very angry with her and had left her with threats before she had woken.

'The Ring Fire would never let itself be given,' she reminded herself. 'It is not like a necklace or a sword which can just be handed over. It is alive, after all. If the Fire Giver does not will itself to be given then it cannot go.' Gemma pulled the oilskin over herself and smiled. *She* might or might not be the Fire Wielder any more, but the Ring Fire would be safe, wherever it was. It was in the hands of the Fire Giver to give or take back. It was not hers to give.

But what would Domnall do next?

At the Battle of Porthwain, the Chancellor of All Wizards had thrown more and more magic at her and Fleabag, culminating in the blue flames that had consumed himself instead of her. If Domnall wielded blue flames, he must be the new Chancellor of All Wizards. Would he be as cunning as the old one? She lay still, watching the myriad stars above her. They were so cool and bright, with such a gentle light. Vaguely she remembered that Rowanne had tried to teach her how to find her way by the stars, using certain constellations as points of the compass. But it had meant nothing to her. And what if she *had* understood? This boat had no oars.

She was adrift, all alone on a vast ocean.

Back in his tiny room at the very top of a lonely tower, Domnall resumed his human form. He stared angrily out across the plains towards Beulothin and the sea. It had taken him almost three years to discover the secret of the blue flames that his father had used against Fleabag and the Fire Maiden. Because Domnall did not believe there *was* a Fire Giver, he saw the Ring Fire simply as a particularly potent magic to be taken and used like any other.

Now Domnall realized he had made a mistake. The girl did not have the power to surrender the Fire. He could not use his most powerful spells on her, as he did not know her real name. Moreover, she seemed protected from direct magic by the accursed Ring Fire. But he should have had her thoughts almost completely under his control. His skilled cook had prepared her food with many potent herbs, opening her mind to his hypnotic suggestion—and she had *still* disobeyed him.

Could it be that she did not know *how* to hand over

the vital flame that burned in her? She was very young and inexperienced to be a sorceress in such an eminent position. Her naïvety was partly her protection. She knew nothing, so she could divulge nothing. Perhaps she had not been taught the right ceremony before the last Fire Wielder had passed the flame on and died... Domnall caressed his leather-bound book of spells. There must be something in here to do the job. It was just a matter of time before he discovered it.

Meanwhile he must look after the Fire Wielder. He did not want her dead yet. As long as she lived, there was a hope that the right words could be found to make her give up the Ring Fire. If she died, the Fire might die with her. He could not risk that.

There was always the King's Ring, which would be relatively easy to steal. But legend had it that if the wrong person held the ring, the Fire would simply withdraw. That had been his father's mistake, to go for the Ring, not the heart of the flame itself. If the worst came to the worst, he would kill her and that so-called King, and take the land by force. If both Phelan and Gemma were dead, however, there was always the risk that the Ring Fire would be extinguished and he would have to rule by the power of the blue flames alone. They were powerful enough, to be sure: pure, distilled evil wrapped in an ice-cold all-consuming hate. But that would also eventually destroy everything in the land, including the riches and slaves he wished to control and enjoy.

Domnall gave an involuntary shudder. That would be the ultimate desolation, for above all things he feared being alone.

If he could be seen to hold the Ring and the Ring Fire, his reign would be more easily assumed, leaving him rich and famous, with every living thing trembling at the sight of him. That was what he really wanted.

He had been rash. Now he must keep the girl alive a while longer. Domnall poured water into his silver scrying bowl and said the words that would enable him to watch over Gemma while he prepared deeper spells to fulfil his aim. Peering into the silver sheen on the surface, the Chancellor could could see his captive had drinking water. She was miserable but safe.

Like a spider keeping a fly alive in a cocoon of silk for a later meal, Domnall wound her little boat in spells to keep her secure until he could see his way more clearly.

Gemma felt hot and sick. The water pooled in the oilskin tasted foul. The fabric had been sealed by boiling it in animal fat, and that left rancid rainbow oil slicks floating on the surface. There had been no fresh rain for several days, and her feeble attempts to catch fish had all failed. She had almost caught one or two small fry by tickling, as Rowanne had taught her to do with trout, but they did not seem to like that game and would not play.

She lay still and dazed in the bottom of the boat, staring up at the sky. Day after day the sky promised rain, but always lied. Her head ached.

She began to think of the Ring Fire again. She did not understand it. She had never understood it. But she wished it would help her now. If only it would either rescue her or let her die, not let her live on and on in this torment. She was so miserable. She knew she had let the Ring Fire down. Phelan and the people of the land had trusted her to be their Fire Wielder... But she was only a child who had never been allowed to be a child. She did not even have a real name. What did everyone expect?

Gemma looked over the side of the boat into the jade-green depths of the sea. It looked so cool and inviting. She longed to go for a swim, but was scared that she would be too weak to keep alongside the boat. Would being in all that water just make her thirstier? Perhaps she should just slide into the depths and go to sleep. Then it would all be over. She wanted to cry, but did not dare waste water in tears.

Just then a glistening shoal of pretty silver fish swam past. If only she could reach one... She hated the thought of eating raw fish, but she knew it would give her food and some fresh juices at the same time. It might save her life.

She leaned over the side. The fish slid below her fingers, this way, then that, darting and zigzagging, always just out of reach. How pretty they were! Gemma did not want to kill them. But she had to live. She was frightened of dying alone out there. She leaned over the gunwales of the boat and stretched out her arm. Her fingertips brushed the smooth side of a silvery fish. She opened her fingers to try to catch the next one as the shoal slipped past again, so beautifully, so silently.

Now, *now*, NOW! But as she clenched her fist around a fish's tail, the boat tipped, and Gemma fell in. She was so shocked with the sudden coldness of the water, she let go her prize and swallowed brine, which was so salty she retched. Splashing in panic she realized the boat was on a swift current and slipping away from her. Collecting her wits she began to swim, but her long white night-gown clung heavily around her legs. She tugged it up above her knees and knotted it. Now her legs were freer she kicked strongly, and soon came alongside the boat. With a weary hand she caught the gunwales and her fingers grabbed a rowlock. Lifting her head above the water she took a deep breath as she put up her other hand and tried to drag herself up out of the water.

But the boat was small and light, and the weight of her and her water-sodden robe were too much for it. Instead of heaving herself over the side, she managed only to flip the little craft over and bring it crashing down on top of herself.

The boat's plank-seat hit her very hard on the head. She gulped and swallowed more water in the darkness. She felt very cold and frightened and dizzy. She could not remember what had just happened to her. All she knew was that she must survive, at all costs.

Groping in the darkness she found the seat. She slid her arms over it so her head was held out of the water. There she clung, staring blankly at the little tiny light that flickered between her fingers.

Then she passed out.

10

Aidan

Domnall had not seen Gemma's boat capsize. At that very moment he had been searching through his scrolls and manuscripts for the solution to his problem. He had to discover the words that would release the Ring Fire to his domination. His name meant 'World Ruler', and he intended to live up to it. At any cost.

Meanwhile, there must be spells and potions strong enough to control this slip of a girl and the flame she was supposed to be carrying.

Then, suddenly, something made his heart miss a beat. He turned to his scrying bowl and peered in. There was the boat, yes, but something was wrong! He stilled the water with a gesture of his forefinger to make the vision clearer. The boat had capsized! Where was the girl? He passed his hand over the water again and commanded to be given sight of her, but there was just the naked wooden hull bobbing on the sea. Then the vision faded into nothing. Only darkness.

Was she dead? What had happened? How could his spells protecting her boat have failed? He cursed his manuscripts and kicked the table over, scattering parchments this way and that. His cup of wine tumbled too, spreading a pool of blood-red liquor across the mystic pages.

In his fury, the wizard took the scrying bowl and flung it across the room. The clear water spilled haphazardly across the floor as the silver bowl landed with a clatter, dented and misshapen.

Far out at sea, the waves stirred and rose in answer to Domnall's rage. Great clouds gathered and piled high, and the winds began to blow.

Less than two hours later Gemma's little boat came within sight of a small island, one of an archipelago scattered across the Eastern seas. A skinny lad of Gemma's own age stood on the pebbly shore and watched the storm rising, hoping that amongst the driftwood there would be something useful: something saleable, or even burnable. The sight of a small boat cheered him immensely. To own a boat was a great thing indeed! He would not have to work for his tyrannical father any more. He could be his own master and sell his own fish. If he worked hard he might even be able to rent a room and leave home entirely. No more scoldings from his mother for having eaten too much when his belly was scarcely half full.

'Indeed,' he thought as he swam strongly towards the upturned vessel, 'one day I might be able to buy a wife to mend my nets and cook for me.' Yes, a small boat was *just* what he wanted!

The boy grabbed the boat's trailing rope. Then clenching it between his teeth, he turned his face inland and soon had his prize in the shallows. But something was caught underneath, preventing him from dragging it ashore. He stood and grasped the rim of the boat then, with a great effort, he managed to flip it over.

There, under the seat, was a girl's body.

He pulled the limp form out and left her lying at the water's edge. He beached the boat first, as that was by far the more valuable find. Then he returned for the girl. She might be wearing jewellery. She looked very oddly dressed in what seemed to be a night-gown, although it was a good one with no patches or tears in it.

He grabbed her under her arms and dragged her roughly up the shingle. The stones hurt Gemma's feet and she coughed and cried out.

The boy dropped her just above the high-tide line and turned her over with his foot. So, she was still alive! He must search her quickly. She didn't look as if she could put up much of a fight, but he wanted to take no chances of being seen at his work. Quickly he unclasped a fine gold chain from her neck and slipped a heavy gold ring from her finger. It was an expensive one with a device engraved on it that might be a small flame in a circle. He would have to be careful how he sold that. It could be the arms of a noble family on the mainland. He did not want to be accused of murder or theft.

She did not seem to have anything else of value. He looked down at her. He thought she might be strong if fed a little. He did not have much to share, but now he had a boat he was his own master. He also had a gold chain to sell. For a little while at least he could afford black bread for two. He would shelter her for a day or so, and if she recovered well and seemed adept at mending nets, he would keep her. If she behaved herself and minded her tongue, he might marry her. She would be useful, and he would not have to find a bride price either.

If she was useless he would make enquiries as to what family carried the arms of a small flame, and he would collect a reward. Either way his luck was in.

But where to hide her? He scanned the shoreline. He did not want to take her home. It was too crowded there already, and he did not want his parents to think of putting her to work for them or collecting a reward for themselves. She was his prize. His alone!

He left Gemma face down on the pebbles so the water could drain from her lungs, as he stood in thought a while.

Aidan was short and scrawny. Lank, straw-coloured hair whipped into his sharp-featured face as the wild wind blew off the sea. His shirt was sail-cloth, hacked rather than cut, and his breeches were of the same material, several sizes too big and caught round his waist with rough twine. The bones in his face were square, and his eyes were pale and narrowed from squinting into the wind every day.

At last he nodded to himself and dragged the boat further up the beach. He had no paint to mark it as his own, so he found a sharp stone and into the sticky tar of the boat he scored the device from the ring, a small flame set in a circle. Then he scratched a large A. He could not write his name, but he knew it began with an A. Now the boat was marked as his, he could afford to think about his other prize. He lifted the craft onto his shoulders and, looking for all the world like a tortoise, began to carry it up the beach. Once it was secured above the high-tide line, he turned and called to the wet, shivering figure on the shingle, 'Come on then. Don't just sit there!'

Gemma looked up, a little surprised. It was only beginning to register in her waterlogged brain that she was safe on land. She could not remember who she was, or even what she was doing there. But she knew she was glad, and grateful to something, or someone. She supposed it must be the boy, although she did not know who he was, or why she should be grateful.

Aching and feeling sick, she clambered shakily to her feet. Then, slipping and struggling on the loose stones, she followed her rescuer.

They scrambled up a steep cliff path, then walked for about ten minutes across dunes and marram grass. Gemma's legs were weak and her head ached and span. She could feel a lump on the back of her head where the boat had hit her. Suddenly her legs gave way beneath her and she collapsed onto the soft, dry sand.

When she woke she was lying on old sacking in a dark, smelly place. What looked like planks arched overhead, with blueish curves of light in between each one. She blinked and rubbed her eyes. She was cold and thirsty, but her headache had lessened. Next to her was a plain earthenware pot. She peered into it. Water! Greedily she drank most of it and fell asleep again.

In the late evening, a stiff breeze blew up, whistling through the planks of her sparse shelter.

She roused herself, drank from the pot again and ate from a slab of dry black bread next to it. Then she got up. The only way out of the shelter was by crawling low under a curved opening to one side. When she was out, she stood up and looked around. Her new home appeared to be a half-rotted old boat, about the length of three men, but not quite high enough to stand up in. She shivered and hugged herself. Then she spotted a figure hurrying towards her.

Striding along the path between the dunes was the scrawny boy she had seen before. He was struggling with a cumbersome-looking bundle. He shouted. 'Oi you! Inside! You don't want them to find you, do you?'

Gemma did not know who 'they' were, but she obeyed. Crouched inside the boat, she helped to pull the bundles inside. It was mostly sacking, some of which was sparsely stuffed with straw. As she unrolled it a few bits of ragged clothing fell out. There was a sailcloth cape, a coarse apron, a skirt and a loose shirt. They stank, but Gemma pulled everything on, glad to be not so cold for once. The boy helped her arrange the rest of the sacking into some sort of bedding.

'I'll be back for you in the morning. Don't try and run away.' He shrugged. 'Not that there's anywhere to run to. This is a very small island, and you're mine now, anyway.'

'What do you mean, *yours*?' Gemma was very confused. She did not have the foggiest idea what was happening.

The boy looked at her. His face was almost moon-like in the pale half-light of the hulk. 'I found you,

you're mine. I'll be back in the morning. Don't move from here or you'll be sorry. Goodnight.'

And with that he started to slither away under the lip of the hulk.

'Just a minute—please,' Gemma called, 'Where am I? Who are you?' Then she hesitated. 'Who am *I*, come to that?'

The boy stuck his head back inside. The wind was blowing so hard he had to keep pulling his hair out of his mouth so he could talk. 'This is called Spider Island. I don't know who you are, but as you're my servant now, I'll call you Ahanet. That means 'hard work', in the old dialect of our island. My name is Aidan.' And with that he stepped back and stood up.

For a few moments Gemma could hear his bare feet walking swiftly away through the rough grass. Soon the wind covered every other sound, and she fell asleep.

11

Cleo the Smuggler

Fleabag had been most put out when Phelan forbade him to set sail with Rowanne and Captain Marcus. 'You need rest, old friend. The vet said you had to lie quietly for several days yet, and the voyage is so urgent we dare not wait an hour longer than necessary.'

Fleabag sat with his back to the King, staring out of the window towards the sea, twitching the very tip of his tail in tightly controlled fury. But he said nothing.

Phelan stood next to his friend and tried to scratch him behind the head, but Fleabag simply put his ears very flat against his skull and turned to glower at the King. Phelan tried again. 'Look, it won't be so bad. I am staying home as well. Even with Gemma gone, I still have to fulfil all my duties and rule the land. I would like to go too, but I cannot. Stay here and keep me company, for I'll need a friend. I'll be quite lost without Gemma. I need you around to keep me cheerful. More than that, Tabitha will be having her kittens any day now. I'm sure you want to get back to her.'

Fleabag grimaced. 'The last place I want to be is home. I adore my Tabitha, but she's always so cross when she's had kittens. She tells me to clear out because I'm in the way!' He stood on his three legs, arching his back into a long stretch. Then without a backward look, the cat jumped down from the windowsill and stalked out of the room.

Fleabag was tired and he *did* feel unwell, but he was determined not to be left behind. Gemma needed him. He whispered to Cleo to investigate Rowanne's baggage to see where a respectable cat like himself might hide without too much discomfort. Cleo slipped past the maid with a purr and an appealing look, and jumped onto Rowanne's kit bag. She tried her claws on it. It was stuffed full. No room even for one of her elegant paws in there, let alone the whole of her large, comfort-loving father. The golden cat cast around for other possibilities. Ah, on the dressing table was a basket of the delicacies that Rowanne liked to eat: dried fruit and sweet pickles. Cleo smirked. Just what she needed!

When Rowanne left the room for a moment, and the maid had her back turned, Cleo said, very clearly, imitating Rowanne's voice almost perfectly, 'Oh, fetch another basket, and put it next to my kit bag, will you? I have a few more bits and pieces to take.'

The maid did not turn around, instead she just curtsied, said, 'At once, Madam,' and scurried away, looking just a little surprised as she met Rowanne coming in the door. Cleo gave the princess a sweet, innocent smile, and ran to where Fleabag was catnapping.

'Dad, Dad,' she prodded the older cat with her nose.

'Avast, ye dreaded rats. Have at you!' The black cat was obviously dreaming great deeds. Cleo prodded him a little harder. 'Dad, hurry! I've got you a passage on board ship, but I think you'd better come now!'

Fleabag opened one golden eye, then the other. 'Good girl!' he grinned, and followed her down the corridor. As they turned into Rowanne's room, they could see that the heavy kit bag had already been collected, but the maid had found a large wicker basket and left it by the bed. Cleo whispered, 'In there! Quickly!' Then she trotted over to Rowanne and miaowed to be stroked. Rowanne, who realized she *almost* liked cats, obliged, saying, 'Send my regards to your father, will you? Sorry he's not well enough to travel, but tell him I'll catch him a fish.'

Fleabag took the opportunity of the distraction and slipped into the very commodious hiding place. With his teeth he grabbed a night-gown from the end of the bed and pulled it down over himself. Inadvertently he left his tail hanging over the side, so Cleo gave it a quick nip as she went past. Her teeth were needle-sharp, and Fleabag had to bite his tongue to prevent himself calling her every dreadful name under the sun. Cleo ran away chuckling, but a little jealous that she wasn't included in the jaunt.

Fleabag heard Rowanne's voice calling out to the maid not to forget to give the men her basket, and the girl picked it up and handed it over. The cat kept his ears low and his tail tightly wrapped around himself, lest a whisker betray his presence.

Cleo, being every bit as inquisitive as her father, could not resist following the man with the basket down to the quayside to see the ship off. She sat primly next to the ship, watching the loading, and made sure the Princess' belongings were all handed down the hatch to the small cabin that Rowanne had decided was hers.

Cleo grinned as Fleabag's hiding place was bumped and shaken on the way. 'Never mind,' she thought. 'It might knock some of the rudeness out of him!'

But scarcely had her father been safely stowed when a strong, brown hand caught Cleo under her belly and held her up for inspection. 'A ginger cat!' boomed Captain Marcus' deep voice. 'Just what we need! You are the young lady who gave me such useful information in the King's study. Would you like to come along and keep the rats well mannered and polite, eh, puss? Are you a ratter?'

Cleo looked into Marcus' black eyes and decided that not only would she very much like to be on the same ship as Fleabag and keep an eye on him, but it would be a fine thing to be a ship's cat and have adventures with the handsome captain. Cleo opened her delicate pink mouth and gave her new friend a wet, raspy lick, right down his cheek. 'It's a deal!' she purred. Then she draped herself around his big, comfortable shoulders and smirked.

The *Flora* had been at sea for two days before, as far as Rowanne was concerned, disaster struck.

Up until then, the water had been calm. But now the storm Domnall had created, by throwing his scrying bowl, was spreading all across the eastern seas. Captain Marcus had skilfully caught the winds, guessing the direction in which the tide would have swept Gemma's little boat. But the suddenness of the storm caught everyone unawares.

The *Flora* was far enough away from the eye of the storm to escape the worst of the winds. It was a rough ride, but not a dangerous one. But Rowanne, who had never been to sea before, was horribly sick.

Until this happened, she had been moderately pleasant to everyone, not wanting to reveal that she was very apprehensive. She was a warrior, not a sailor, and the feeling that her feet were being tugged from under her, while her head was left somewhere completely different, again and again, hour after endless hour, was more than she could stand. Her stomach protested strongly and Rowanne had to hang her head over the side in case she was sick. But worse than the discomfort was the thought that anyone should see she her in this state. The embarrassment was more than she could tolerate.

When Captain Marcus ordered her below, she refused to go. But he was not used to being disobeyed. The last thing he wanted was a sick hand on deck. 'My Lady, if you don't go below then I swear, Princess or not, I will have you clapped in irons for the rest of the voyage.' Then he turned away from her and smartly began to climb the mast, to help furl the mainsail before another squall took it away.

Rowanne leaned over the rails and was sick at last. Then she did as she was told.

It was only when she lay in her hammock, which swung dizzily with the rocking of the boat, that she realized she was not alone. A small, black mop of fur slithered stealthily from behind her kit bag. Rowanne sat up as best she could in the ever-moving, ever-sagging hammock.

'Rats!' she hissed as she threw a well-aimed boot at the lithe shadow.

'Hey!' moaned Fleabag indignantly, 'Don't do that! You might ruffle my fur!'

Rowanne buried her head in her arms and tried to turn over. 'Oh, it's you! I thought you'd been told to stay home and keep well away from the sea!'

Fleabag put up a paw and tapped his right ear. 'Sorry,' he said, 'I didn't catch that. I've been a bit deaf since my wetting. I find I miss a lot of things people say.'

Rowanne groaned. 'I hope Phelan skins you for a fur collar when you get back. He's probably worried sick about you.'

Fleabag sat up and began to wash. 'My Lady, you have threatened that for years, but you will never catch me. Neither will he. Anyway, he won't be cross, he'll guess where I've gone.'

Just then a clatter at the door heralded the cabin boy with a tray of stew for Rowanne. She groaned at the smell. 'I'm going to throw up again!' she wailed and fell out of her hammock to droop her sore head over a bucket.

But Fleabag only had eyes for the dinner tray. 'Oh goody, can I eat your dinner? I've only had a couple of mangy rats since I took berth in this fair vessel, and I'm famished!'

'You'd be doing me a favour if you did,' Rowanne moaned.

The stew was excellent. It was much better than seafaring rat, which is nutritious but tough, and has a distinctly over-salted taste which Fleabag did not entirely like. Cleo had, of course smuggled him chunks of steak and chicken from the galley but, as far as he was concerned, they didn't count and he wasn't going to let on about them. The role of half-starved stowaway suited him better. It evoked a more practical sympathy.

When Rowanne had righted herself again, and had washed, she sat on the edge of her kitbag and surveyed her old friend. 'So, what are you doing here? I thought you were at the palace.'

Fleabag licked a small drop of gravy from his paw and grinned. 'I've come to help you out, of course.'

Rowanne was puzzled. 'How do you mean, "help" me?'

'By eating the food which you are unable to eat because you haven't got your sea legs yet.'

Rowanne was about to swipe him for his cheek, when the ship suddenly gave a great lurch to starboard, sending the cat, the Princess, the kit bag and the dinner into a great, gravy-covered heap in the far corner of the little cabin. 'Yuck!' bewailed Rowanne, plucking at the long coils of her dark hair which were now liberally bathed in stew.

'Allow me to assist,' Fleabag offered, trying to nibble one of the bigger lumps of meat from behind her ear.

But Rowanne was in no mood to be 'assisted'. She pushed the cat aside and stumbled out of the door. Scrambling up the steps as fast as she could, she clung onto the railing at the top, unable to move for the tossing of the ship. From there she bellowed at Captain Marcus who stood on the bridge, Cleo draped adoringly across the back of his neck. Despite her encumbering presence, the Captain was standing solidly at the wheel, keeping a steady course. He ignored Rowanne as she ranted and raved at him for what she called his 'bad steering'.

However, as Fleabag approached, the Captain looked down. 'Aha, another cat, and indeed, one that I might have mistaken for a pirate, with that great golden earring, had I not already seen you in the King's study. I hope we have enough rats on board to satisfy you both.'

Cleo stretched gently around the Captain's neck and whispered, 'Oh, throw him overboard, Marcus. He's just a flea-infested old stowaway. Hang him from the yard-arm, make him walk the plank!'

Fleabag looked up and sneered. 'Is that all the thanks I get for my bravery, coming on board despite my life-threatening illness? I had to make sure my daughter, whom you are presently wearing as a scarf, was safe, and to offer you my experience and wisdom on this adventure. The noble Fleabag, at your service, sir!' and he bowed, or tried to. But just at that moment the ship lurched, Fleabag lost his balance, toppled over and slid down the sloping deck with all his three paws stuck up in the air.

He hated losing his dignity, so immediately started to wash. But then he spotted Rowanne who had managed to let go of the railing and was staggering across the deck, glowering and red in the face, furious at being ignored. For once he decided she could have the limelight while he slipped down below to clear up some of that excellent gravy. Purely to help out, of course.

Rowanne now stood squarely in front of the Captain. He nodded curtly to her, without taking his dark eyes off the sea. 'Are you feeling better, my Lady? How can I be of service?'

Rowanne clutched the rigging and hung there like wet washing. 'I came to see what the matter was! You're driving this thing like a maniac—can't you take it any slower? You have passengers aboard, or had you forgotten?'

The Captain looked at her for a moment. He hated bossy landlubbers. He turned his attention back to his wheel. 'Madam, the wind is, as you call it, driving the ship. I merely steer it. We go as fast as the wind goes, and if the wind chooses to play games and buffet us a little, we have to go with it. I recommend you go below and try and get some rest. By the look of those bluish clouds on the horizon, we are in for a long night.'

12

On Spider Island

The storm did not abate that night. Captain Marcus took short rests, preferring to be at the helm himself. His crew of fifteen men worked almost as hard as he did. There was no thought of steering any sort of course; all they could do was to try to avert disaster. Dawn broke, but still the wind did not lessen. High above, blue clouds rose and spread, blocking out the stars and the sun, leaving everything in a dull haze, day and night.

After a few days the Princess had found her sea legs, and was actually enjoying the work of sailing. She was as strong as any man, and her sword-trained arms could haul a rope without any trouble.

The captain spent hours peering at his compass; he could not use the sextant without a clear sun. He looked worried. His tall frame stooped over the brass compass housing as he shook his head. 'I don't see how it is possible, but we seem to be going round in circles,' he told Rowanne at last.

She looked out to sea. The unnatural blue pall overhead gave the ocean a dull, thick, turquoise colour. With monotonous regularity, the waves rose and lifted the *Flora's* bow, then slapped her down again into a deep valley between the watery mountains. Rowanne was good at orienteering on dry land, but she conceded that sea navigation was beyond her. 'How can you tell we're going in circles?' she asked.

'Look, we've been swinging through the points of the compass at an even speed for two days now. If I didn't know these seas better I would say we must be caught at the edge of an enormous whirlpool.'

Rowanne stared at the compass, then out to sea again. Marcus had gone forward to talk to one of his men. He never elaborated on anything, but he left Rowanne with a cold feeling of apprehension creeping down her back.

And she was not the only one feeling odd.

Neither Fleabag nor Cleo were quite themselves. The strange sense of 'something' had come back. All day, and long hours of the nights as well, the two cats found they could not rest. Every time they closed their eyes their whiskers twitched, and their dreams were full of blue shadowy flames that reached for them.

Fleabag was worried. He guessed that the approaching blueness meant that Domnall or some power of Porthwain was near at hand. It also probably meant that they were nearing Gemma. Whatever happened next would be important. He tried to collect his thoughts, but every time he sat in a quiet corner to think, he found he couldn't. As soon as he began to concentrate on what to do, he simply *had* to jump up and chase and leap and fling himself this way and that. He had to catch, or even better, kill whatever was pestering him. Only there *was* nothing there.

Very soon, both he and Cleo were quite worn out. Their coats were unwashed and had lost their sheen, and they were getting thin. They were both so obsessed with the 'somethings' they even left the rats in peace. Not that the rats would have been difficult to catch. They were acting very oddly themselves and almost flung themselves into the cats' paws, so blindly were they leaping.

The humans did not seem to be affected in the same way. They did not have the same sensitivities as cats. But what could the animals *do?* Fleabag wished Gemma or Phelan were with them—they understood the Ring Fire (although Gemma did not think she did). They needed that flame now to give them some wisdom and perhaps just to be a steady light as they sailed through this endless and ever-thickening blue.

Fleabag sat in a corner, with his back wedged between the luggage and the wall. 'Nothing is behind me, and nothing can *get* behind me,' he told himself, 'so I must not jump around, however much I want to. Neither the King nor the Fire Wielder are here,' he told himself firmly. 'I may be only a cat, but I am just going to have to sort this out for myself. Now I must concentrate,' and he closed his eyes and imagined the Ring Fire, small and steady, a tiny golden fire within the King's opal, then tall, majestic and glorious in Gemma's hands as Phelan was proclaimed King by the old Fire Wielder. In his mind, the Flame burned so steadily and strongly that Fleabag soon began to feel better in this terrible, dark place.

But he could not concentrate. His whiskers tickled again. He ignored them for a long time, but at last the feeling was so insistent, he opened his eyes. There was Cleo, curled up next to him, her ears flat against her head, looking very worried.

'Marcus says the circle we are in is getting tighter. Each circuit we make is taking less time to complete. We are being sucked into something.' The marmalade cat snuggled up to her father. 'I'm scared. Tell me again how Gemma burned the Ring Fire to save Phelan from the wolves.'

In his study at Porthwain, Domnall peered into his scrying bowl. It was badly dented, so the image he saw was distorted. He did not have time to make another bowl. This one would have to do.

Gemma was alive, he could tell that much. She was on a small island with two domed hills, one large, one small, so it looked like a huge spider. It even had several long outcrops of rock stretching out to sea like giant legs. The girl was sitting in a dark place. She was cold and miserable, but fed and alive. Good. She was safe. He knew the King had sent a search party to fetch her, but they stood no chance. He had all the power of the Order of Wizards at his finger tips; they did not even have a weather-maker on board.

He turned his gaze to watch the little ship tossing in the blue maelstrom. He stirred the water and laughed as the ship spun around once or twice and he heard cries of terror from the crew. He stretched his hand out and searched the minds of the sixteen men and one woman on board, finding mostly fear and dread. The Captain was strong-minded, but he did not know where he was going. This 'rescue party' was no threat.

Domnall did not bother to observe the cats. He simply threw them something to chase, and left them to their own devices. They were fun to torture, that was all.

His work now was to concentrate on making a great wall of magic around the island, blue and impenetrable. Gemma was caught in his trap. Perhaps he should make it a web, as this was Spider Island. He laughed a little as he raised his spells around the dented edge of the scrying dish, constructing a great twisting wall of blue, leaving everyone within the wall at his mercy. And those outside the wall? Well, they didn't matter. He frowned as he considered the dents in the rim of the silver bowl; they would make the wall of water weak in places. But no one in their right mind would even attempt to sail through. He would be quite safe.

His plan was to surround Gemma with the full force of the blue flames, then slowly tighten the ring until she was consumed. Then he would be waiting to capture the fleeing Ring Fire. She obviously had no control over it, so he would have to chase it out, and be ready…

Fleabag spent several hours remembering the Ring Fire, how it looked, how it felt, and how good it was to be near it. Several times he felt it was speaking to him, but heard no words. But by the end of the morning, the idea forming in his head was so strong, it was almost a shout.

Suddenly it came even more clearly than before. It made Fleabag jump, waking Cleo. 'Quick!' he ordered. 'Run to the Captain! You climb quicker than

I can. Tell him to head for the centre of the storm. Do it *now!*'

Cleo sprang to her paws instantly. She wanted to ask what on earth her father was talking about, but the look in his eyes brooked no argument. Immediately she fled out of the cabin and leaped up the steps, her paws scarcely touching the rungs of the ladder.

'*NOW!* Tell him the Ring Fire says he's got to do it *NOW!*' Fleabag bellowed as he struggled behind her on his three legs.

Cleo caught the urgency and sprang with a flying leap right onto the Captain's shoulder, her claws digging into his right arm so that his hand slipped from the wheel and the ship turned sharply to port. Blood welled in hot streaks as Marcus swore and struggled with the cat. But the turn had been made. Already behind them a great wall of water was rising, pulling the ship into a whirling frenzy of white and blue waves.

'All hands on deck!' the Captain bellowed as a great rocky outcrop suddenly loomed, huge and jagged, out of the blue ahead of them.

Gemma had been put to work the morning after her rescue. Aidan had brought her twine and nets to repair. He was not a good teacher, but during her years as a Fire Wielder, Gemma had not forgotten how to use her fingers. She quickly learned how to twist the string and pull it tight to repair the holes in the huge nets he brought. At noon he gave her bread and water.

The wind was howling and the rotten hulk was

scarcely any protection against the weather. Aidan let Gemma gather moss and driftwood to caulk some of the wider cracks. But he would not let her light a fire. He said it was in case the ancient hulk burned down. As he could not put to sea in the wild winds that were whipping frantically around the island, Aidan sat next to Gemma and watched her working.

He still hoped that she might be the daughter of a rich merchant and perhaps worth a reward. On the other hand, she was very good at her work and had been worth rescuing; he could not decide whether it would be better to keep her or not. What was more advantageous? A good worker around, perhaps for life, or a great deal of money?

His indecision was made worse by her inability to answer his endless questions about who she was and where she had come from. All she knew was that she had been adrift for several days, and that a man had put her in the boat. But why, she did not know. She still could not remember her name, so Aidan still called her Ahanet—the hard worker.

He fed her as well as he could in case she proved to be worth exchanging for a reward. He did not want her to say she had been mistreated. Thankfully her memory was so hazy that she did not even miss her golden chain and her heavy ring with the emblem of the Ring Fire on it.

One day she was sitting sewing, in the bluish light at the entrance to her little home, when she realized she had a white band of skin around her middle finger where the Fire Wielder's seal had been. 'I wonder why I have a pale mark there?' she asked Aidan, who was sitting with her. For a second his heart missed a beat. He shrugged and said nothing. She forgot it and went on with her work.

Another time she was standing, looking out to sea when Aidan brought her daily food. 'Another day of no work,' he said, miserably. 'I'll be ruined if this strange weather doesn't change soon.' His sparse fortune from selling the gold chain had almost gone, and the endless wind was keeping traders from the island. He could not sell the ring to another islander. It was far too precious; and besides, too many questions would be asked about it.

Gemma took her ration of bread and bit into it. 'Is everything always this blue here?' she asked.

Aidan shook his head. 'No, only since you came. What's it like where you come from?'

Gemma found she could remember that, 'Oh, blue skies. But a nice blue, not a heavy, threatening blue like this. And green hills, and I can remember a city. And I can remember a fire. I'd like a fire; I'm cold,' she added, pulling her stiff sailcloth cape more closely around her.

'No!' he snapped. 'It's too dangerous in there.'

'How about one out here then?'

Aidan was adamant. He did not want anyone from the village seeing the smoke. If they did, his parents would take his precious servant from him and set her to work for them. But something else occurred to him… they might well put her to death. For the heavy blue clouds and terrible winds *had* come when she had. Perhaps she was a sorceress who brought the evil eye with her. The villagers were malicious gossips, and would convince themselves that their imminent ruin was Ahanet's fault. There would be nothing he could do to help her... No, he had to keep her a secret.

He wasn't superstitious. And Gemma did not *look* like a sorceress. The storms would pass.

'No fire!' he ordered as he turned to go. Then he looked back at her. 'If you light one I'll whip you; then you'll be sorry.'

Gemma looked down at her hands. They were scarred from where something had hurt her palms before Aidan had found her. Her fingers were sore from the hempen twine she used on the fishing nets and sails she was given to mend. Her skin was too soft for this sort of work, although there had been calluses on her hands once, she was sure of it.

Where, when? She knew she didn't belong here, but where did she belong? And why did she dream every night of sitting by a lovely fire? She shrugged. Probably because she was cold.

She dragged the pile of nets she was working on inside. She lay down on her sackcloth and straw bed and closed her eyes. All she could see before her eyes was fire. Not a great roaring blaze, but a steady, gold-red light.

13

Gemma Remembers

Gemma awoke colder than ever. 'Does that wind ever stop blowing?' she wondered as she left the old upturned boat, once again in search of something to try and fill the gaping spaces between the shrunken boards.

She returned with armfuls of bracken and moss, but as soon as she had pushed the wadding into the cracks, the raging wind tugged it all out again and infuriatingly tossed everything away.

After a while, Gemma gave up. She had no time for this; there were so many nets to mend. She guessed that Aidan was getting her to repair other people's as well.

Something kept making her shiver and look around. It wasn't the cold, it was a feeling… a feeling of something, some*one*, watching her. It made her uneasy, so she crawled back inside on her hands and knees, and sat cross-legged near the entrance with her nets. The light was poor, but she could just about see. As she worked, she found herself singing. It was a song about the hope each season brought and a fire that burned at the centre of all things… She stopped and thought for a moment. Who had taught her that song? She closed her eyes and put her head on one side.

Someone not like her at all, but someone nice. A friend. A man or a boy, not the one who had put her into the boat, someone with dark, golden-brown skin and thick black curly hair, and was there a beard? Someone very untidy and smiling, looking contented. Who was he, and why that image of fire again?

Fire, fire, what fire? She was so cold she would have given anything for a fire at that moment, even if Aidan did whip her for it. She was so cold! Even inside, the wind kept wrapping her hair around her face. It was a mousy brown, with a red tinge which came off on her hands. The colour must have been dyed. Why should she dye her hair red? The colour of fire...

She tried to put the thoughts out of her mind. She had work to do, and Aidan would be angry if it lay unfinished when he came. Bending her head over her task, turning the nets so they caught the mean, blue light from the entrance, Gemma tugged at the twine, twisting and knotting it, hour after hour until the morning was over. Aidan would be here with food soon. When he had gone, she *would* light a fire, just a small one. She had to have warmth and solace.

Fire seemed to be important to her; she always seemed to be thinking about it. Perhaps if she saw a flame, it might give her a clue as to who she was and where she belonged. She had to find out the truth soon, for at the back of her mind there was an urgency she could not push aside. The wind was blowing harder. Her fingers grew too cold to work. She put her needle down and began to rub her shoulders and arms to try and revive some warmth in them.

And warmth came. Suddenly she felt very warm indeed. In fact, her hands were hot. She held them out to see what had caused the change, and she screamed—for there was fire in her palms!

Hurriedly she pushed the nets away from her and tried to scramble outside. The nets caught fire from her hands, and tangled around her feet. In terror she tried to kick free as she staggered a few steps up the nearest dune where she fell face down, filling her mouth and eyes with fine, pale grains of sand.

But the flames did not go out.

Far away, Aidan's voice was calling, half scolding, half terrified. Gemma tried to answer so he could find her, but she had too much sand in her mouth. Behind her the hulk was fiercely aflame and the crackle of the wood drowned out her terrified whimper.

Unheeding, Aidan stood helpless, looking at the flames. There was no way for him to get inside and rescue Ahanet. He realized suddenly that he had quite liked her. She was quiet and did as she was told, and he enjoyed being with her. She would have made a good wife, he was sure. Now he felt very sad. The villagers would soon come to investigate the smoke, and when they found a skeleton in the burned-out wreckage, there would be questions asked. Questions he did not want to answer.

There was nothing for Aidan to do now but to wait for the flames to die down. He sat down heavily, at the bottom of the dune where Gemma lay. She kicked sand down on him, making him turn around.

'Help!' she spluttered, spitting sand, 'Help! I'm on fire!'

Aidan heard her this time, and scrambled up towards her. 'No you're not!' he said, pulling a small gutting knife from his pocket so he could cut the net from her feet. 'That's a good net you've ruined! Anyway,' he scolded, 'what were you thinking of? I told you no fires!'

Half of him was so angry he wanted to carry out his threat and whip her, and the other half was relieved she was unhurt.

'Why aren't I on fire?' Gemma asked, looking at her hands, 'I was a few moments ago.'

'You put it out by rolling in sand. Best thing to do.'

Gemma held open her hands. They were hot and, although it was difficult to see in the daylight, a tiny flame burned in each palm. She closed her fingers quickly. Suddenly, she knew what that burning feeling meant. Terrible danger was near. She knew what the Fire was. She knew who *she* was.

Gemma grabbed Aidan by his sleeve. 'You have got to help me find shelter! Quickly! I know who I am and what I've got to do!'

'I've *got* to do nothing of the sort. If anything, I've got to give you a thrashing for disobeying me!' Aidan replied, taken aback at Gemma's sudden boldness and change of character.

'Oh, don't be silly!' she replied urgently. 'There's no time. If you won't help me, I'll help myself, but you are in almost as much danger as I am. Will you help or not?' Gemma had pushed her hair back and stood staring up at her rescuer—or was he her captor? Her clear eyes challenged Aidan, but she wasn't bullying, like his parents. This girl who had once been timid and obedient, suddenly had dignity and presence. In her mind she had ceased to be the submissive kitchen maid, and become once more the Fire Wielder she actually was.

Aidan did not understand any of this. He swallowed hard as he looked at her. In an odd way she seemed almost to have grown several inches since that morning. She must be from a good family, used to ordering servants around. He would play along with her; the reward could be better than he had even imagined. But she mustn't think she could boss him around just like that. He crossed his arms and shrugged his shoulders. Then with his head on one side he took a step back and looked her up and down. 'All right then, who are you?'

When she told him, he laughed and shrugged again. 'They're only in stories!'

Gemma did not have time to argue. She could sense the presence of Domnall all around her. The Fire in her hands was burning. As the flame grew in strength, the wind was whipping up, whistling around, tugging her hair every which way. Blue lightning started to crack across the skies.

Gemma threw off her stiff, cumbersome cape, leaving her arms free. She raised her burning hands to the blue clouds and called clearly, 'Lord Domnall—or should I call you Chancellor of All Wizards—I hear your challenge and I answer you. I, Gemma, Fire Wielder of this Land, servant of the

Fire Giver, will meet you and do battle. I will no longer believe your lies and deceits. You have held sway long enough. Whether or not I am sufficient for my office no longer matters. The Ring Fire is here!'

Domnall stood back from the scrying bowl, watching the tongues of flame rising from Gemma's hands with full strength and authority.

He rubbed his well-shaven chin. 'Well, at least I know she still has it, but she seems to have grown in strength. I wonder where *that* came from?' he mused. 'So she will not surrender the Fire, and now she summons me to battle; then battle it is!' He leaned over the scrying bowl and breathed on the water.

At the same moment a thick blue mist covered Spider Island. 'He has heard me,' Gemma said quietly. 'Now, I need that shelter, please. I must make my preparations for what is to come.'

Confused and frightened by the blue mist and Gemma's sudden change, Aidan stammered, 'C-come this way, but stay close, you will lose me very easily in this fog.' Running this way and that through the dunes, he led her down a rocky path and onto the shifting stones of the beach. He said nothing. This girl was definitely a sorceress. She had powers. He didn't want anything to do with this sort of thing. He was a practical lad, and he kept magic and the stuff of legends firmly at arm's length. Above all, if she was really what she claimed to be, what would she do to him for the way he had treated her?

But despite that, he still liked her and hoped she won this challenge, whatever it was. Deep down he was certain that whatever she was, she was on the side of good. He must give her shelter, then leave her to her own devices as quickly as possible. The sooner she forgot about him, the better.

After a short walk across the noisy pebbles, the air suddenly cleared, and Gemma found she was standing in a small, damp sea cave.

Aidan was standing in the cave entrance, dark against the eerily swirling mists. 'At this time of year, the tides don't reach this far up the beach. You ought to be safe,' he said. 'But given how strange things have been since you came, I won't guarantee anything. Watch the tides, and get out quickly if you see the water coming in. The path is to your right. Follow the bottom of the cliff and you'll get to it. Goodbye, Gemma or whatever your name is. Thanks for mending the nets. I...' he hesitated. 'I hope there're no hard feelings?'

Gemma smiled. 'None. Thank you for saving me.'

Aidan stepped backwards, deeper into the mists. 'You're not going to put a spell on me or anything when my back is turned, are you?'

Gemma smiled again. 'No, why should I? Anyway, I don't do spells. I am not a sorceress. I only carry the Ring Fire. I am the servant of the Fire Giver. *I* have no powers. I simply challenge evil with what is true.' And with that she held out a hand with a small clear flame burning in it.

Aidan opened his mouth in amazement at the clear calm beauty of the little light. 'You, you didn't bring the blue clouds and the strange wind then?'

'No. That's none of my doing, but I suspect that it *is* here because of me. There is an evil wizard called

Domnall who wants to take this Fire from me and rule the land with magic and spells for ever.'

'You're not going to give it to him?'

'It's not mine to give. But if you can help me find my boat so I can get back to King Phelan on the mainland, I suspect the blue evil will follow me and leave your island in peace. Will you help?'

Aidan stepped further away. Even now he was too scared to turn his back on this strange girl. 'I'll bring you food, and I'll give you back your boat and ring, but I sold the necklace to feed us both...'

Gemma nodded. 'That's fair, I prefer to pay for my keep. But where is my boat?'

'It's beached just along a bit in a small cove, but you'll not get anywhere in it—the waves are too high. You would drown in minutes.' He looked at her sidelong, wondering, perhaps, if she would be able to ride the craft, skimming over the tops of the waves like the magical creatures in legends.

Gemma glanced out of the cave towards the raging sea. 'You could well be right. I know nothing about seafaring. I'll stay here for a while and listen to what the Fire says before I decide what to do. By the way, don't bother to return the ring. Sell it and buy us both food and warm clothes. You can keep the change for another boat if that's what you want.'

Aidan was about to say, 'I'll do my best,' when there was suddenly a terrible crashing sound, followed by screams and shouts.

'A ship on the rocks,' Aidan said, and ran down to the sea.

14

Abandon Ship!

Gemma's first instinct was to rush out and help rescue any survivors. She might be able to use the Ring Fire to give light to the rescuers, or to guide the struggling crew to land.

Yet she knew the Ring Fire wanted her to leave that to others. Instead it was telling her to sit quietly and listen. There were other islanders to help, maybe the crew of the ship were safe. Whatever the reason, she knew what she had to do.

Silently she sat on a cool, damp rock at the back of the cave. She was hungry and thirsty and worried about the poor souls at the mercy of the sea. Gemma surrounded whoever might be in the shipwreck with the glow of the Ring Fire to keep them safe until help came, as she had done when Phelan faced the terrible monster on the scaffold at Beriot. Then she turned her attention to the Fire itself.

The sweeping of the angry waves had impaled the *Flora* on one of the rocky arms of Spider Island. The ship had been driven so hard between two huge, granite boulders that she was held quite firmly.

'Abandon ship!' Marcus bellowed. 'We're on the rocks! Over the starboard side, quickly. It's too misty to see properly, but I think you'll be able to scramble to land, or at least be safe until help comes!'

Calmly and carefully, Marcus took Cleo from his shoulders and lowered her over the side into the arms of the first mate. The ship shuddered as wave after wave battered the sides and slapped across the decks. Soon all the crew were safe, but Rowanne hesitated.

'I can't see Fleabag!' she yelled down to Cleo. 'Is he with you?'

The ginger cat winced as another breaker drenched her. 'No, he was just behind me last time I saw him.'

Rowanne spun around. The decks were awash with swirling sea water. 'I can't see him... just a minute, what's that?' She staggered across the shuddering planking, clinging to ropes and rails at every step, trying to stop herself being swept overboard by the pummelling waves.

A small, pathetic, black shape was peering out of the aft hatch. 'Fleabag!' Rowanne yelled, springing forward. But as she let go on the gunwales to grab at her friend, a huge wave broke across the ship, sweeping her off her feet and swirling Fleabag into the hold below.

Without hesitating, Marcus heaved himself back over the side. Cleo had climbed onto his shoulder again, and was yowling for her father.

Rowanne leaped blindly into the pitch-black hold, landing knee-deep in a tossing torrent of baggage and water. How could she ever find her friend in all this?

Just then, a sharp set of claws embedded themselves desperately in her thigh.

Rowanne scooped up Fleabag's sodden body and grabbed at the ladder. As she stepped on the first rung, Marcus bellowed down, 'Hurry, the ship is breaking up!' And with that a thunderous wave caught the *Flora* amidships and tugged her groaning and creaking hulk so badly that Rowanne was thrown back into the hold.

Fleabag clung onto Rowanne's neck and shoulders with all his claws. His little dagger points were agonizingly sharp as the friends tumbled together into the shuddering darkness. Rowanne gritted her teeth and, holding onto the terrified bundle of black fur with one hand, she stood and tried the ladder again. The seas pounded the ship relentlessly, each wave hitting the vessel without mercy.

'Quick!' Marcus ordered, putting his hand down to pull Rowanne up.

Cleo was standing on the gunwales howling at her father to hurry.

'Jump!' Fleabag ordered. 'Don't wait for us!'

Just then, with a terrible cracking and groaning, the stern of the ship broke away, swept off into the raging depths as if a giant hand had ripped it asunder. As it did so, the swirling sea swept into the shell of the forward section, scooping out goods and luggage and equipment like a great, hungry tongue.

Marcus grabbed Cleo, flung himself overboard, and landed on the rocks beyond. He leaned over and tried to grasp Rowanne's fingers. 'Grab my hand! I have a good foothold, I'm firm!'

But Rowanne could not hear him. The roaring of

the engulfing waves filled her ears and eyes and throat. The last words she heard as they were swept away from the ship were Fleabag muttering, 'Oh no! Not again!'

Rowanne lay exhausted on a stony shore. She was not too bruised or battered, but she could not see where she was, for a thick, blue mist hung like a heavy blanket over everything.

Rowanne managed to right herself. Then, spotting Fleabag a few steps away, she picked him up, almost kindly. 'You all right?' she spluttered.

The cat coughed seawater and groaned. 'Yes. I suppose I have to say "thank you" now?'

'It's not so hard, is it?' Rowanne laughed. 'Never mind, at least I got to wear your pelt as a fur collar as I always said I would. But you're right, I didn't like it. You pricked!' Rowanne pulled her shirt back from her neck and felt the bleeding scratches gingerly with the tips of her fingers. 'Ouch!'

'Serves you right!' Fleabag grinned. 'I always said I wouldn't suit you—now you know why. It'll teach you to treat me with the respect I deserve! Flinging me over your shoulders like that, I ask you. Is that the way to treat a royal cat?'

Rowanne playfully tossed a small pebble at him. 'Ungrateful animal, I was saving your life!'

Fleabag began to wash himself to get the sticky salt out of his fur. 'OK. I'll let you off this time, but next time you attempt anything like this, I require at least two servants to fetch my best basket and carry me out properly, with a royal guard, a marching band and everything. Being rescued, like everything else I do, has to be done with style and dignity.' Then he stopped washing, and rubbed his nose against Rowanne's hand. 'But thanks anyway,' he added quietly. 'And I'm sorry I hurt you.'

Rowanne could hardly believe her ears. Suddenly she laughed and picked Fleabag up and hugged him. But when a flea jumped onto her face, trying to escape the wet fur of the bedraggled cat, Rowanne put her friend down again, very quickly. 'Let's not overdo this, eh?'

Fleabag shook himself and licked a few more hairs. 'Just what I was thinking myself. But what we really should do is to see if the others are safe.'

'I should think they'll be all right. They were on pretty solid rock. Even if they are cut off, they'll be safe until we can get a boat to them.'

'If we can find a boat, let alone get it through these waves... and the mist... where *are* we?'

'I don't know, but there's a something that could be a boat beached over there,' Rowanne slipped and climbed up the shingle until she reached a long, low shape, upside down at the foot of the cliff. 'It's a boat all right. Look, it's got something scratched in the side, "V" and a circle with a teardrop shape in it.'

Fleabag, who was a lot nearer the ground than Rowanne, twisted his head around. 'It's not a "V", it's an A upside down, and that circle pattern is... could it be? I don't believe it!'

'What?' demanded Rowanne impatiently, crouching down low. 'What are you talking about?'

'Turn the boat over quickly,' Fleabag said. 'Look, Rowanne, it's the sign of the Ring Fire! I don't know what the "A" stands for, but Gemma's been here, I'm sure of it!'

15

The Cats and the Ring Fire

The excitement of the shipwreck meant that none of
the islanders noticed Gemma's burning boat. Now
that Aidan knew that she was safely away from there
he was not so worried. If anyone asked, he'd say the
hulk had been struck by lightning.

But for now he had to take a look at what was
coming ashore. It had been a well-provisioned ship,
judging by the good quality of the wreckage. Shouts
from Aidan's left meant that there were survivors on
the rocks. They would get to land easily enough
from there. He spotted some good clothes and barrels of dried fruit and started to pull them clear of
the water. Then he left them in a heap while he
thought.

Good-quality cargo meant wealthy people, and
that meant handsome rewards! Perhaps it would be
better to leave the salvage and guide the people to
safety first. But he would make it look difficult and
dangerous on the way, to impress everyone with how
brave and courageous he was.

But his delay made him too late. Already the dark
figure of Captain Marcus was stepping down from

the rocks onto the pebbly shore. He was followed by his crew and the lithe Cleo.

Marcus bowed slightly to Aidan. 'Good sir! If you can find lodging for myself and these people, you will be repaid handsomely. We are from the King's ship, the *Flora*, run aground not far from here, and His Majesty does not forget those who do good in his name.'

Aidan was impressed with this speech. His quick mind was also thinking that he could slip Gemma in amongst them and get good lodgings for her as well. Soon he would be a rich man indeed! He grinned quietly to himself. 'I will do my best for you, sir.' Aidan replied, bowing deeply in response. 'Come and rest in this small cave while I run up to the village for you. Another lady is also sheltering there. Are you all saved, or is anyone still in the sea?'

Marcus looked pleased. 'Indeed, we were missing another lady. I am relieved to find she has come ashore so quickly. Was a black, three-legged cat with her?'

Aidan led the way towards the cave. 'I don't think this is the lady you are hoping to find, sir. She came ashore a few days ago, but like you she is stranded and in need of proper lodging.' He trudged ahead of the men up the shifting shingle to the cave mouth. 'Lady Gemma,' Aidan called, 'may I bring in the people who survived the wreckage?'

Gemma was about to be cross about the interruption, but as she turned from the flame that burned steadily in her hands, Marcus and his men immediately knelt at her feet. 'My Lady,' he said, 'we have been searching the high seas for you. I thank the Fire Giver you are safe.'

Gemma allowed the Ring Fire to settle back to a tiny flame in her hand. She looked at the kneeling sailors. 'Do get up, please. Is anyone else with you?' she asked.

Marcus glanced around. 'All my men are here, my Lady, but the Princess Rowanne was swept out to sea, along with the three-legged cat.'

Gemma went pale. 'Is the King with you?'

'He had to remain in Beriot, my Lady.'

Gemma stepped decisively towards the cave entrance, and stood there contemplating the swirling mists. 'Aidan?' she called over her shoulder.

The boy ran to her side and tried to kneel as well. 'Oh do stand up,' she chided. 'I hate all that nonsense. When the Ring Fire is burning, that is one thing, but now I am just like you. Tell me, is there a chance that anyone else could have been washed ashore?'

Aidan was nervous. Gemma was obviously a greater personage then he had imagined, maybe even a Fire Wielder as she claimed. But he had to keep calm and concentrate. His future comfort was at stake. 'Ordinarily, anything would come to shore away to the east,' he waved his hand to the right. 'But the tides are strange at the moment...' he added lamely as Gemma went crunching down the shingle as fast as she could run in her bare feet. After a moment the others followed.

It was not long before Gemma spotted the dark figure of the Princess treading the stones as she made her way inland. Behind her trotted an ungainly three-legged black cat. Gemma called out, running and stumbling across the noisy pebbles, flinging herself at her old friend with a bear hug. 'Rowanne! You're alive, and Fleabag! I'm so pleased to see you! There is so much I have discovered. There is a terrible danger hovering above this island, greater than anything we have ever met before!'

Marcus' voice boomed through the heavy mists, 'This lad has promised to find us lodging. When we are snug in a hostelry with a meal inside us, we can all swap tales. But let us get out of this mist first.'

Aidan guided the party up the cliff path towards the village, looking nervously over his shoulder every few minutes. He half expected Gemma to be putting spells on him. He had heard tell of the Fire Wielders, of course, but they were always strange, mystical figures from stories. They were never real, let alone someone almost his own age, skipping along, carrying a flame-red cat in her arms with a tatty black three-legged one at her heels, talking nineteen to the dozen to a Lady Knight.

It was all odd. Very odd.

The little port lay on the south side of the island, where the two dome-shaped hills met. It was a ramshackle place built of ship timbers, which were added to every time there was a wreck in the area. The only inn was similarly built of huge, curved beams and roughly dressed stone, but it was warm and welcoming enough, especially when Marcus presented the landlady with gold. She was pleased to have the custom. Sailors and merchants usually stayed there, but it had been empty since the coming of the strange winds which had kept the usual trading ships well away.

Seated around a roaring fire with plenty of good stew inside them, the travellers told their tale to Gemma. She sat quiet and still. She had bathed and dressed herself in a gown she had bought from the landlady, a long green dress with a wide skirt and huge white buttons down the front. It was big enough for two Gemmas and swamped her in copious folds of material. But she did not mind. She was grateful to be warm at long last.

Marcus and Rowanne both had cat scratches on their shoulders and necks. The Captain's were worse by far. 'Why did you leap at the Captain's shoulder so viciously?' Rowanne asked Cleo as she gently pulled the blood-soaked shirt away from his wounds.

The red-gold cat stretched luxuriously in front of the flames and purred. 'Fleabag told me to. I always do as *he* says.'

Fleabag got up and cuffed his daughter's golden ears playfully. '*Cleocatra*! How dare you! I told you no such thing, I simply asked you to request the Captain politely to change course very quickly indeed.'

'But why so *violently*, Cleo? Why didn't you just *ask*?' Marcus asked, wincing as Rowanne began to dab an ointment onto the wounds.

But before Cleo could answer, Fleabag jumped up onto the Captain's knee and peered at the ten little lacerations on his upper arm. 'Um. Nasty. Well, I had been thinking about the Ring Fire to cheer myself up, you know like Gemma does, then suddenly I just knew what we had to do. The Ring Fire wanted us to go right into the eye of the storm, and we had to do it immediately.'

'But could Cleo not simply have discussed the matter with me?' Marcus shrugged his shirt on again.

'No time.' Fleabag jumped down. 'The Ring Fire told me. We had to do it *then*.'

Gemma nodded. 'It must have been about then that I challenged Domnall and he tightened his spells very suddenly. If Cleo had stopped to ask Marcus nicely, the wall of sea would have risen to such a height you would have been crushed beyond all help. By turning at that instant, you were probably saved.'

'Does this mean that even a *cat* can hear the Ring Fire?' Rowanne was genuinely shocked, and rather put out. However much she longed to serve the Ring Fire, it always seemed to speak to others, never to her. She could only ever comprehend battles and stratagems, sword thrusts and armour. At times like this, she felt hurt and excluded. To make matters worse, this time it wasn't just another human who had heard the Ring Fire speak, but a *cat*, and the mangiest, scraggiest, worst-mannered one at that! The Princess folded her arms and glowered menacingly at Fleabag as he stretched himself on the hearth.

Gemma could tell Rowanne was upset. 'Why shouldn't Fleabag hear the Ring Fire speak? *You* might hear it if you listened and watched and tried to put warfare out of your head sometimes! In fact, one day the Ring Fire will be there for everyone, and you won't need a Fire Wielder.' There was an uncomfortable rustling in the room, as Gemma's listeners shifted and murmured apprehensively. They were shocked and confused. What *was* she talking about? But Gemma ignored them. She didn't know where that idea had come from, but she knew it was true.

At the back of her mind she felt the familiar urging to surrender the Ring Fire. But that was something different. That was what Domnall wanted her to think. Today she was still the Fire Wielder, and she was still needed. For better or for worse, she had to carry the Ring Fire as best she could until people learned to listen for themselves, or until someone took her place. Everyone was relying on her, and she mustn't let them down.

Gemma stood as tall as she could and started to speak again. 'You will all see what I mean in time. But for now I must explain what is happening. I suspect that Lord Domnall is the successor to the old Chancellor of All Wizards that Fleabag and I saw die in Porthwain, and he is attempting to take the Ring Fire from me. In past months, I have not been listening to the Ring Fire as I should, and Domnall would have won his battle to steal the flame if it had been mine to give it up. But the Fire Giver chooses who holds the Ring Fire, and,' here she smiled and opened her hand towards the disreputable black furry lump on the hearthrug, 'the Fire Giver also chooses who hears its wisdom. It is not for us to make rules that contain the Fire and where it may or may not burn.'

Everyone in the room was silent, looking at Gemma in her too big green dress, standing next to the fire, hands behind her back, almost like a schoolgirl reciting her lessons.

Gemma looked out of the little window. The mist had blown away, but night was falling, leaving the little island deep in the deadly blue of Domnall's spells. Everything in the firelit parlour at the inn seemed cosy and safe, but the small party of sailors led by Marcus and Rowanne was as tense as a new bowstring as they listened to the Fire Wielder's words.

16

Fire Cat

'The Ring Fire has challenged Domnall to meet him and do battle,' Gemma said. It will not be a battle with swords and spears, but one between the Fire Giver and the forces of magic and sorcery that Domnall has at his disposal. Soon I will meet him. I am only human, and can be killed, but even if I die, the Ring Fire will go on.

'I had hoped to be able to leave the island and join the Ring Fire with the King's Ring. By doing that I would draw this terrible blue magic away from the islanders. But it cannot be done. The winds and sea around the island are too strong for any boat. The battle will be fought here, and soon.

'While I am fighting Domnall, you must all do as Fleabag did, and look to the Ring Fire to protect yourselves and to help me. I cannot tell you what you must do, but I need you all, whether you are a cat, a princess, a sailor or a fisherman. Meanwhile, we must all get some sleep, for I do not know when Domnall will call me—or any of us—to the battle. Goodnight.'

And she turned to go to her room.

She left a shocked and silent group of friends behind, but Rowanne rushed after Gemma and caught her arm. 'Look, we can find weapons here; there must be knives I can sharpen. If we beg and buy all the pots and pans we can, I can reforge them into armour. There's a lot we can do with very little, you'll see! You aren't alone. We'll go into battle together. Give me a few days and I will be ready for any army…'

Gemma reached her bedroom door and turned towards her friend with a smile. 'No, Rowanne. Thanks, but—I don't know how to explain this to you—it's just not going to be like that…' Then she shut the door, but not before the two cats had slipped through as well.

In the dark of her room, Gemma sat on her bed and let the Ring Fire glow within the pink goblet of her fingers. Fleabag jumped up beside her and sat, tail neatly turned around his paws, as he contemplated the soft, strong light. At their feet, Cleo, who felt a little shy, sat and looked up. The neat, white triangle on her face stood out clearly in the gentle light.

Gemma looked a long while. Then her shoulders shook a little, and tears began to flow down her cheeks.

'Don't cry, we're with you,' Fleabag assured her, licking the back of one of her hands.

Gemma sighed and placed the Fire on the table next to her bed, like a comforting nightlight. Then she turned and hugged her old friend. 'Oh, Fleabag, I know you are, you dear, faithful thing. And I owe you an apology, I think…?'

'An apology?' Fleabag scratched a wandering flea under his chin. 'What for?'

Gemma picked the offending creature from the cat's fur. 'You've been trying to tell me something for weeks, and I didn't want to listen... And I didn't want to listen because I knew what you were going to say, and I didn't want to hear it because I knew it was true!'

'Do Fire Wielders always talk like this, Dad?' Cleo whispered to her father. 'I can't understand a word she's saying.'

Fleabag glowered. 'Cheeky kitten! Be quiet or I'll send you to bed with no mice on toast!' Then he hesitated and raised his whiskers questioningly. 'All right, Gemma,' he said, 'we both give up. *I* don't understand a word of what you said either!'

Despite her sad mood, Gemma couldn't help but laugh as she scratched the cat behind his ears. 'In the garden, that day of the blue storm, you must have seen me reach for the window to shut it against the rain...'

'Yes...'

'And you saw the Ring Fire was burning in my hands?'

'Yes.'

'Then you saw how the rain put it out... At that moment, Lord Domnall's rain was more powerful than the Ring Fire... probably because I had been ignoring it, not listening, not watching the flames. It was pretty scary. That was when I realized I would have to find a new Fire Wielder. I came on this so-called "holiday" in the hopes of thinking of someone else I could appoint, then go off on my own

somewhere. I knew I had let the Ring Fire down—
I'm not the right sort of person to carry it.

'I realize now it will always be burning somewhere; its strength does not depend on me... But I
still want to find a replacement as soon as this is all
over. Perhaps the time of everyone carrying the Fire
for themselves is close. Who knows? But I was
wrong not to discuss it with you and Phelan at the
time. I should have faced the truth and not run away
from it.'

The deep velvet brown and black shadows shifted
as the Ring Fire danced. The light gleamed on
Fleabag's earring like a tiny flicker of flame in his
black fur.

There was a long silence. At last Fleabag said:
'But that wasn't what I wanted to say at all.'

It was Gemma's turn to look bemused. 'What *did*
you want to say, then?'

Fleabag climbed onto Gemma's lap and rolled
upside down so she could rub his barrel-like tummy.
'I wanted to warn you that I had seen blue forks of
lightning searching for you in the storm. When you
reached out to shut the window, and the Ring Fire
was burning in your hand, the flame went out. But it
wasn't because of the blue magic or the storm or anything else proving stronger than the Ring Fire...'
The cat paused and stretched a front paw up. 'Just
scratch there, please...'

'But what *did* put it out then?' Gemma was so on
edge she stopped scratching completely.

'If you stop, I can't think!' he moaned.

Gemma resumed the thorough rubbing and ruf-
fling of Fleabag's tummy fur. 'Sorry.'

'I should think so too!' Fleabag closed his eyes, as if he were watching the whole scene happen again. Then he said very slowly, 'The Ring Fire put *itself* out. Whatever was searching for you through the blue lightning came very, very close. Too close. The Ring Fire ceased to show itself in order to protect you. Burning as it was, it was like a beacon in the storm, saying, "here she is!" By ceasing to burn at that second, it probably saved your life!'

Gemma lay back on the bed and closed her eyes. 'You're right, of course, you irritating old ratter. I'd have seen it too if I'd let myself. I suspect I wanted an excuse to give up. I was so weary. I let Domnall convince me that I was damaging to the Ring Fire, that I wasn't good enough to carry it. I'd forgotten how simple and beautiful the Ring Fire is. It's not a matter of being good enough or not, it's just a matter of allowing it to burn.'

She opened her eyes again and watched the steady golden flame for a few seconds. 'I have been so stupid!'

Fleabag put his forepaws onto Gemma's shoulder and licked her face. 'Well, we're all together with the Ring Fire again, and that's what matters. Now, what can we do to help?'

Gemma leaned over and reached out to stroke Cleo on the floor. 'Sleep up here with me tonight, then I won't feel so lonely. I'd like that.' The ginger cat sprang up onto the bed and stretched. Gemma smiled as the light from the Ring Fire caught the soft, luxuriously shiny golden fur of her back. 'Your daughter is beautiful, Fleabag. She looks like a Fire Cat!'

Fleabag stiffened. 'Hush!' he snapped. 'Who told you? You must never repeat that! Come, Cleo,' he snapped. 'Curl up and go to sleep as you've been told.'

Cleo began to knead the covers and purr before turning around several times and settling down.

For a little while, Gemma lay still, worrying. Why had Fleabag snapped like that? Of course: 'Fire Cat' must be Cleo's real name. Cats were especially careful about not using their real names in case spells were put on them by evil-minded people like Domnall. 'Sorry,' she murmured, reaching out to touch the cat's ginger fur as she went to sleep.

17

The Dreams

Far away, in Porthwain, Domnall was preparing his spells to take to Spider Island. He would have to go in person to take the Ring Fire from this stupid girl, who not only frustrated his plans, but then had the gall to challenge him. *Him!* The Chancellor of All Wizards, the destined King and Fire Wielder! How dare she!

His preparations were intricate. His shade would not be powerful enough to make the spells hold, or to grasp the prize as it slipped away from the child at the end of the battle. He would have to face her himself.

But first he needed dreams for the islanders... dreams telling everyone for certain that a tall, freckle-faced girl with mouse-coloured hair was to blame for the terrible blue clouds and strange winds. The dreams promised riches and glory for those who helped to defeat her. The images were powerful enough to last for several nights and even to linger during the days.

At last, Domnall spread his arms and shivered in delight as his silk gown shimmered, darkened and became the smooth blue-black feathers of a crow. He turned his head and preened the soft down around his neck. Even when he shape-shifted he liked to look immaculate.

The night was getting dark as he rose up towards the stars. He would scatter the dreams over the islander's dwellings as he flew past. By dawn he would be on Spider Island, and by sunset the Ring Fire would be his.

Gemma did not need a scrying bowl to know what Domnall was up to. The Ring Fire told her all she needed to know. She slept badly, knowing that all the time the evil wizard was on his way.

As another unnatural blue dawn broke, Gemma rubbed sleep from her eyes and sat up. What was that dreadful clanging noise outside?

She stood by the window and looked out. Walking towards her down the street, was the familiar figure of Rowanne, her dark hair tied back severely, and her arms full of pots and pans. Behind her, Aidan struggled with more of the same. Rowanne grinned up at Gemma's window and tried to wave, but succeeded only in dropping a large stewpot that clanged like a dull bell as it hit the cobbles. 'Look what we found on the town's rubbish heap!' she called, delightedly. 'We'll have good armour made in no time. We're off to the forge now!'

Gemma stepped back and shut the curtains. 'Oh no!' She shook her head. 'How can I make Rowanne understand?'

Aidan had insisted on arranging accommodation at the inn. When everyone was settled, he slept in the stables all night as a self-appointed servant to the newcomers. At first he did it to ingratiate himself and be certain of a reward, but he found he actually liked the strangers and wanted to help them. He was fascinated by all this talk of the Ring Fire, which had never meant anything to him before. He had, after all, actually *seen* it, which was more than anyone else he knew.

Rowanne had summoned his help at dawn. Now he was struggling down the road behind her, carrying scrap iron, thrilled at being asked to help yet again. They dropped their clattering burden outside the forge, and Aidan hammered at the door.

The smith was still in bed, but flung the windows wide and peered down into the street below.

'This is the Princess...' Aidan began.

But the smith did not let the lad finish. 'I know who they are—troublemakers from the mainland. I'll not have any of them in my forge!'

Rowanne stood firmly, her muscular hands gripping a large ladle, and briefly considered bashing the man's brains out for his insolence. She put her head back and bunched the muscles in her jaw. But when she saw his face, she changed her mind. He was not just being difficult; there was real fear in his eyes. *Something* had terrified him.

She decided to try a gentler approach. 'There is a great evil threatening your island. I am a soldier of the King's Guard, and a warrior of many years' experience. If you let me use your forge to make swords and armour, we can help you defend your home... Furthermore, we can pay you well.'

But the smith did not wait to hear. He slammed

his window shut and would not answer Rowanne's persistent thumping at the door.

Just then, another door opened across the street, and Gemma and the cats stepped out from the inn and crossed the cobbles to greet their friends.

'You're up early,' Rowanne remarked.

'We've been thrown out like last week's rotten fish,' Fleabag replied indignantly.

'What did you do? Criticize the landlady's breakfast?' Rowanne laughed.

'Didn't even get to taste it,' Fleabag replied. 'She said she had a dream last night that we were the cause of the evil weather and were come here to bring destruction on the island.'

Gemma looked around worriedly. All the doors were shut, except for the inn, where fifteen bleary-eyed sailors were also being evicted. Marcus shook his head. 'Even the baker won't serve me. It seems the whole village has had the same dream.'

'Domnall!' Gemma whispered. 'He's here at last, I know it.'

Marcus looked across at Aidan. 'You, lad, will you help us, or will you go to your people? No one will blame you if you want to stay with your friends and family. It would be understandable. You and the islanders will be in no danger from us. Our quarrel is with Lord Domnall and his magic. We will leave your island as soon as we can.'

Aidan blushed and stepped forward. He glanced around at the tightly shuttered windows and barred doors. He guessed they were being watched through every crack and keyhole. If he went back to the villagers he would be treated with suspicion and what was there to go back to? He had not had a particularly happy life. These people from the mainland were different from anyone he had ever known. He liked them: they seemed to be fair-minded, and they might offer him a way out of his narrow, miserable existence. But would they want a lad who had made the great Fire Wielder mend rotting nets?

Aidan decided he had nothing to lose. 'I too had a dream last night. I dreamed you were the cause of all this evil, and I would gain great riches and power if I betrayed you. But it didn't make sense. I knew it wasn't true. I may be a bit of a thief and out to make my life easier, but I hope I know what is wrong and what is right... or at least...' he hesitated, giving Gemma a sideways look, 'at least, I think I'm learning. I am with you, if you'll have someone like me.'

Gemma smiled and went to shake his hand. 'I'm glad, Aidan. Without you I'd have been lost. But what about your parents, won't they be upset?'

Aidan blushed at Gemma's thanks. He felt he didn't really deserve it. 'I'm sick of being beaten and half starved. My parents don't need me. They don't even like me.' Then a thought struck him and his face brightened. 'The Captain promised I'd be rewarded if I helped you...'

'Yes, indeed you will. In the King's name I give my word that if we get home, you will be rewarded.'

Aidan plucked up his courage. 'Well, can my reward be to go with you... if we win this battle?' he asked doubtfully.

At this Rowanne clapped an iron pot on the boy's head to look like a lop-sided helmet. 'You work hard,

Aidan. I need a good squire—I haven't had one for quite a while.' She grinned at Gemma, remembering what a useless squire the girl had been on their quest for the Ring. 'If you'll work hard—and *honestly*—' she added with emphasis, 'I'll take you with me.'

Aidan grinned under his improvised armour. 'I will, ma'am. I will!'

'Then that's settled,' Marcus said. 'Now we have to think what we are going to do next. We will get no more help here.'

'I know how to get bread for us all... *honestly*,' Aidan volunteered. 'May I borrow the black cat?'

'Ask him yourself. He has a very good tongue in his own head!' Rowanne laughed, handing the boy a fistful of coins.

Aidan led Fleabag towards the baker's shop. The two whispered a little before going in. Then Fleabag sprang up onto the counter.

'Let us hope they've never heard a talking cat before,' Aidan muttered.

18

Preparing for Battle

The baker was astounded when Fleabag walked
sedately along the top of his counter, looked him up
and down and pronounced very clearly, 'Nineteen of
your best loaves, please. Now!' he added when the fat
little man hesitated.

Sweat dripping as he shook and trembled, the baker
stuffed the loaves into a canvas kit bag that Aidan
handed him. At last he stood back, staring in horror at
the pile of money Aidan pushed across the counter.
'Take it, there's more than enough there!' the boy said.

'You… you won't put a spell on me, will you?' The
little man shook his flab and his eyes bulged. You
won't turn me blue? The dreams… the dreams said…'

'What do you think, cat?' Aidan raised an eyebrow at Fleabag as he slid from the counter, landing
awkwardly on his three legs.

'No,' Fleabag replied, yawning widely. 'We won't
do anything if the bread's good.'

The little man hastily filled a large bag with cakes
and pushed them across the counter. 'With my com-
pliments, no need to pay,' he squeaked, his voice
rising with his panic.

Rowanne, standing in the doorway of the shop, pushed a large silver piece across the counter. 'Thank you, but we would rather pay for the cakes. And remember, if anyone turns blue around here, it will be none of our doing!' She took the heavy kit bag and slung it over her wide shoulders, leaving the poor little man staring at the silver coin as if it was about to bite him.

Rowanne ordered the sailors to carry the pots and pans, and the company walked out of the little port and across the dunes to where Aidan's burned-out hulk lay in ashes. The boy led past the blackened ruin and pointed to a small patch of scrubby bushes and bent trees just a little further on. 'There is a stream nearby, and we will be in a dip there, sheltered from this awful wind.'

Aidan dropped his share of the ironmongery on the marram grass. 'Can you really make armour out of this rubbish, Your Highness?'

'Of course!' Rowanne answered as she turned some of the pieces over with her foot. 'Every squire learns how to make and repair armour for their Lord or Lady. If you are ever knighted, you must teach your squire the same. Now, to work. Without a proper forge this will be very makeshift, but we must do our best. Gemma has a great battle to fight. We must be prepared. She thinks I don't understand what she needs, but I do. She knows about the Ring Fire, but I understand about battles. I know what I am doing.'

The Captain sent his men down to the beach to salvage all they could from the wreck. Soon torn sails were being patched and spread over broken spars and planks to form three large tents. Bread, cakes and dried fruit were handed round, and everyone began to feel better.

In the ashes of the old boat, Rowanne had built a small hearth of flat stones. Then, selecting charcoal from the remains of the burned-out hulk, she built up a furnace, walling it in with stones and mud. Aidan worked with improvised sailcloth bellows to blow the fire to a good heat, then the work began.

For hour after tedious hour, the bellows wheezed and Rowanne clattered away with a small, bent hammer that she had found amongst the scrap iron. The white-hot metal was folded and shaped, dipped in the stream and then heated again before it was layered with mud to slow the cooling and strengthen it. The princess was determined that however odd their weapons might look, nothing would shatter. After a while everyone, especially Gemma, began to develop a headache from the noise.

In the blue afternoon, Gemma slipped away, followed by the two cats. She wandered over the dunes until she found another small, wooded hollow, almost out of earshot of the camp. There she sat and dabbled her feet in a pool between the trees. The cats sat like guards on either side. Marcus, watching from a distance, made sure she was safe, then left her alone.

Gemma was cold and tired. Indoors, the dress the innkeeper's wife had sold her was warm enough, but the strange, biting wind still pervaded everything. She shivered, and hugged the cats, one under each arm.

No one spoke for a long time, but when the light began to fade, Gemma brought the Ring Fire to life, and put it gently on the ground where they could all look into its glow.

'It doesn't look like something that would defeat an evil wizard, does it?' Cleo asked timidly.

'You'd better believe it!' Fleabag said quietly. 'The Ring Fire burns in so many strange ways, you're never quite sure what it is going to do next.'

'Ssh!' Gemma put her finger to her lips and looked anxiously up into the darkening sky. There was a new noise, a booming. It wasn't Rowanne's perpetual hammer strokes, but a deeper, more threatening sound, like the depths of the earth cracking. Gemma looked up as a flicker of black crossed the dull blue sky. High above, a crow circled and landed on the tree behind her.

Then came silence. There was no sound or movement. The whole world seemed to be holding its breath.

'It's beginning!' Gemma shuddered. Then of its own accord, the Ring Fire flickered and rose higher and stronger, spreading the golden glow into something that resembled a camp fire, warming and heartening, yet without burning anything.

'Would you mind if I asked you to stay with me?' Gemma asked the cats. 'I'd be frightened on my own.'

Cleo crept into Gemma's lap and curled up small. 'I'm too frightened to go away,' she mewed, and hid her head under a ginger paw.

All night the lightning cracked and sparked. The thunder rolled and shook the ground with its noise.

At the main camp, Marcus, Rowanne and the men sat silently, watching the terrifying storm. They felt helpless and small against the terrible blue powers swelling and throbbing around them. It was as if they were being swallowed into a deep and terrible throat, with only the steady golden light of the Ring Fire to cheer them.

Peering down from between the leaves of the tree, Domnall in crow form watched his adversary. It was almost dawn, and they would do battle when the sun rose. He had to learn what spells and incantations she used to control the Ring Fire so, when he pulled the ring of blue magic tight, the elusive flame would not escape him.

But soon Domnall began to find the light of the Ring Fire intolerable. He flew a little further away where he could watch but not have to look into that terrible light. It burned him. It occurred to him for the first time that he might not be able to carry the Ring Fire. If that happened, he would have to extinguish it and rule by the destruction of the blue flames. He was disappointed. That meant he would not have the adoration of the whole world for ever: for in the end the blueness only killed. Without the Ring Fire he would be the monarch of everything that existed, but eventually there would be nothing left for him to rule. He would be alone... and that was his only, terrible, dread.

But it might never come to that. He might be able to control the Ring Fire—it was probably a matter of time and finding the right spells to subdue it to his will. He could not see or hear what gestures and incantations the girl was using. The terrible flame seemed to burn without the slightest command from her. She must be more powerful than he had guessed.

Still, all was not lost. He had time on his side. Ultimate destruction was a long way off. Anyway, the Ring Fire was destructive too. Look how it pained him to be near it! Surely *that* was the real threat to the world! He would do humanity a favour by destroying it and smothering it into oblivion.

He considered the approaching morning with pleasure. He would be the saviour of the world, the destroyer of the Ring Fire! With smug satisfaction, Domnall preened his crow-feathers. This would be the day of his coronation as King and Fire Quencher!

Meanwhile Gemma and the cats sat by the Fire in the little wooded dip. The Fire Wielder remembered how she had surrounded Phelan with the Ring Fire as he went out to face the monster of Beulothin. Now she did the same for her friends just a little way off, then for Phelan waiting anxiously at Beriot. If she were killed in this fight, he would have to rule as King *and* Fire Wielder until someone else could be found.

Gemma did not know whether Phelan enjoyed being King. She knew he disliked having people asking him what to do all the time, and bowing and scraping to him. What would he think about being Fire Wielder as well? Perhaps it would not happen. But while Phelan was surrounded with the Ring Fire, he would be safe. If he had to take on the role, things would sort out if he just watched and listened for the Fire's guidance. One by one she thought of all her friends, and the people she served in the land, then of the people of Spider Island. It was not their fault they had been deceived by Domnall. She held them safe in the Fire as well. She hoped they would not be hurt by the storms or by any of Domnall's doings.

As dawn broke, the thunder and lightning subsided. The winds and the heavily oppressive blueness still buffeted and smothered everything. Gemma was glad the battle was coming. None of them could take much more of this.

Flying away, Domnall came to land on the crown of the larger of the two domed hills that made up the island. Then, reaching out to Gemma's mind, he called out to her:

'Come, *child*, I accept your challenge. Are you still willing to face me?'

19

Battle Commences

Gemma found she had slept. Had she dreamed the trumpeting call of Domnall's challenge resounding across the island? What had really woken her was a clattering noise coming down into the dip behind her. She sat up quickly. Above her the sun was struggling to peer thorough the heavy blue clouds. It was a warm day, but the dry, endless wind still battered from all directions at once.

There, coming triumphantly towards her, were Rowanne and Aidan with a large wheelbarrow loaded with all sorts of strange objects. 'Look what we've got you!' Aidan shouted. 'Didn't we do well?'

Fleabag was perched on top of the pile, grinning widely under his whiskers. 'You're going to *love* this, Gemma!' Then he sprang down and trotted over to his friend. He clambered up into her lap and whispered, 'Be nice to Rowanne; she and Aidan have been up all night making this stuff. Personally, I think it's going to make you look like an unopened tin of dog food, but never mind, she meant well!'

Gemma's heart sank at Fleabag's warning. What *had* the Princess been up to? She got to her feet and brushed twigs and grass out of her dress and hair. Gemma could accept that Rowanne and the men would want armour, but they had not *really* made some for her as well, had they? Holding her windswept hair back, Gemma stepped forward to see what Rowanne was so proud of.

As she approached, the Princess grinned as she held up a pot-like iron helmet, a breastplate that looked suspiciously like a roasting tray, and a sword which might have been several carving knives beaten together. Rowanne was smiling broadly. 'It looks a little odd, I know, but it'll hold, I'll stake my life on it!'

'Why, Rowanne, it's…' Gemma could not think of the right words, but Fleabag purred and rubbed against her legs, whispering, 'magnificent!'

'Why, it's magnificent!' Gemma declared, grasping the breastplate. As she took it, the blueish light caught a device hammered into the centre. It was the emblem of the Ring Fire, a circle with a small flame in its centre. Standing a little behind the Princess was Aidan, blushing slightly. Gemma guessed it had been his handiwork.

'Why Aidan, what a lovely idea to put the sign of the Ring Fire in the centre! How skilfully it's been done!'

'You will wear it, won't you?' he blushed again. 'We've made ourselves some too; not as good as yours, of course, but we're going with you.'

Gemma felt a lump rising in her throat. How was she going to tell him she couldn't possibly wear this sort of thing? They must have worked until they dropped. Aidan and the Princess looked quite exhausted; they were black with soot, and stank of sweat and iron.

'Help me strap it on!' she smiled. After all, she thought, the battle might be between powers and forces which could neither be seen, nor attacked with a weapon, but what harm would it do to please her friends by wearing their gifts? It might well raise their spirits.

Soon Rowanne had Gemma strapped and buckled in every conceivable place, as piece after piece of bent, black iron was tied around her body. She knew she looked stupid and vulnerable. The skirt of her long green dress billowed and flapped around her legs, and she felt as if she was struggling to keep afloat, just as when she had fallen into the sea.

But she did not have any time even to think about such things. She kissed her friends and thanked them for their gifts, then turned towards the higher of the two hills. Something told her that was where she had to go. She felt terribly alone. Although she knew her friends were going with her, Gemma sensed the battle would be between herself and Domnall.

Around the crown of the hill flapped a huge, blue-black crow, calling hoarsely in the wind. No words were spoken, but Gemma could hear the challenge ringing out again, clear as a bell.

'Time to go,' she said quietly, and slowly clanked away, the others following just a little behind.

Fleabag was by her side in an instant, with Cleo not far behind. 'Want a tin opener Gemma?' he asked cheekily.

'I may well,' Gemma muttered from behind the

heavy visor which looked as if it had been cut from a colander. 'Do you think I'll taste good?'

High up on the hill the crow landed. With a shimmer of blue light the wizard resumed his human form. Domnall could hardly contain his laughter. What did the girl think she was up to? She would take all morning to reach him at this rate, and he had planned to be at Harflorum for his coronation feast by evening. With a long-suffering sigh, he waved a hand and sent a small whirlwind to scoop the party up. But apart from a blustering and battering, nothing happened.

Irritated, Domnall drew back his hand and threw the spell again, this time harder. For a few seconds Rowanne was taken off her feet and dropped a little way off.

Fleabag threw back his head and shouted through the wind to his companions, 'He can't put a spell on us! He doesn't know our real names. The old Chancellor knew Rowanne's, so she might be at risk. When magic is involved, it's anyone's guess what secrets are known! Clear your minds, everyone, don't think of who you really are!'

Cleo stood still and sank her ginger head between her paws. 'I keep being asked my name; he keeps demanding I tell him! What do I do, Dad?'

'Fight it!' Fleabag growled, teeth bared and fur blown flat by the wind.

'Think of a brick wall!' Aidan suggested. 'Keep imagining it, count the bricks... There's ivy on the wall...'

'And spiders!' squealed Gemma. 'Huge grey and purple ones with... Oh, I can't keep this up. I don't *know* my real name, but he's demanding, so loudly I can't think of anything else. I remember, I remember my mother. I could never think of her face before. She died when I was very young. I can see her leaning over my cradle and talking to me. What's she saying? She's calling my name…'

Suddenly Fleabag started singing, a painful experience for everyone listening. The raucous caterwauling distracted Gemma for a few seconds. 'But my mother was beautiful,' she pleaded. 'I want to see her again…'

But Cleo sprang into Gemma's arms and started singing too, so loudly that Gemma could not but listen. She sang better than her father, and the words of the riddle-song were heart-warming:

> 'First came a burning bright:
> the peerless one in darkest night
> And then into a golden ring,
> The second in a tiny thing.'

The tune was so strong and insistent that Gemma soon found she had joined in and was singing the song again and again; they all were. Flat and noisy the chorus rose into the blue wind as the five friends bent their heads into the blast and began to walk towards the hill.

After a little while, Fleabag added another verse, and the others picked up the words. Gemma wondered what the song meant. The words seemed familiar and strange, all at once.

> 'From milky stone came clearest sight
> a wisdom that was crystal bright.

142

The third in stone and fire and gold,
the strongest story ever told.'

But as she sang, she found she could hold the thought of the brightly burning Ring Fire before her eyes, and she felt more courageous. She would have liked to remember her mother's face. But was it really her mother, or just an image Domnall was using to mislead her? It didn't matter.

What *did* matter was remembering that Domnall had no power over her while he did not know her real name. More importantly, he could not cast spells on her while she remained within the Ring Fire.

As she struggled up the hill in her clanking armour, Gemma vaguely wondered how he had managed to get her so deeply asleep and into the boat the night she had been kidnapped. Probably the servants had drugged the food. She had been so far from the Ring Fire that night, Domnall could easily have influenced her. Perhaps he had hypnotized her. She had a vague idea that she might even have been quite willing to get into the boat: she remembered thinking that if she was gone, the others would *have* to find a new Fire Wielder.

Who knew? But she must not let it happen again. She was who she was, until the time came for things to change. The Ring Fire was not unkind; there would be a way through all this. She would have a long talk with Phelan and Fleabag when she got back.

Head down she trudged on, hot and out of breath as she climbed the hill. As best she could, she tried to walk in time to the rhythm of the strange song.

But the makeshift armour was making her very sweaty and uncomfortable. Blisters were rubbing under her arms where the straps of the breastplate chafed. She felt she could hardly breathe under the heavy helmet. She longed to take it all off, but it occurred to her that it might be wiser to keep it on, at least for a while. If Domnall could not defeat her by magic, perhaps he might try using a sword?

She kept singing.

Far behind her, Gemma could hear shouts and jeers from the islanders who were gathering at the bottom of the hill. They were gathering to cheer Domnall on.

Whether they won or lost this battle, any of Gemma's friends who survived would be torn to shreds by vengeful islanders. Fighting for the Ring Fire there were nineteen humans and two cats. Fearsome battle cats it was true, but still no bigger than ordinary mousers.

Suddenly Gemma tripped and sprawled in a most ungainly, clattering way on the ground. Rowanne sprang to her side and helped her up. From below the sound of derisive laughter echoed around. Gemma was glad for a few seconds that she wore a helmet to cover the blushes in her cheeks.

'Get up,' Rowanne said kindly but firmly. 'We're almost there.'

'I'm going on alone,' Gemma said. 'If I fail, you'll still be alive to fight. There's no point in us all dying at once.'

Rowanne knew better than to argue, but the cats followed Gemma closely, pretending they hadn't heard.

On the crown of the hill, Domnall stood staring down at his adversary as she approached. Dressed in a badly fitting woman's dress, with bits of home-made armour strapped all over her, the girl looked derisively funny.

With a few more steps she stood before him. She was hot, sweaty, out of breath and had the lower ground with no flat place for her to stand comfort-ably, leaving her off balance. Good. Domnall stroked his clean-shaven chin as he looked the Fire Wielder up and down. She was young, and even under the makeshift helmet was visibly scared. She looked neither strong nor awe-inspiring. It had been the same when they had met at Harflorum. Gemma had been heavily made-up and swamped in trappings.

He jerked a thumb at her. 'Why do you always hide behind so much *stuff*, my dear girl? Are you afraid to meet me properly, face to face?' He spread his hands wide. 'Look, I don't have as much as a pocket knife on me. You come so… dauntingly arrayed to challenge an unarmed man. It is hardly fair, is it?'

Suddenly, Gemma made a decision. She lifted the helmet from her head and threw it to the ground. Then she dropped her sword and unbuckled her breastplate. Kicking them aside, she turned to face Domnall.

'No,' she said. 'I wore them out of loyalty and love for the people who made them for me. I had no real intention of wearing them for the battle.'

Domnall was surprised. He had expected her to clutch her armour more tightly around her, like a timid tortoise in its shell. But she was obviously

145

stronger than he had guessed. The way his spells had bounced off her worried him too. But he would find a way. Victory was his destiny, after all. 'Look,' he said, pointing down the hill. 'We have company.'

Gemma's heart missed a beat, for not only were her friends valiantly trudging up the slopes towards them, armed and arrayed in their own makeshift gear, but the islanders had decided to move in for a closer look as well. They were in an ugly mood, shouting and waving their fists, carrying swords, knives, billhooks—anything that might inflict damage.

'They think you brought the blue clouds and the endless wind. They think you are a sorceress who has angered the seas. Perhaps I should give you and your friends to them. Then they can pull you all apart, limb from limb. It would save me the trouble of fighting you... Not that it'll be a *fight*, really...' he paused and inspected his fingernails in a leisurely way. 'More like a cat playing with a mouse before he eats it!'

Fleabag tutted. 'Tsk! I never play with my food before eating it. Do you, Cleo?'

'No, Dad,' she replied primly. 'Mother would be deeply shocked if I did that.'

Both cats turned to glower at Domnall with their gold-lamp eyes. The wizard was discomfited by their stares, but pretended they were beneath his notice.

Gemma unstrapped the rest of her armour piece by piece, and tossed it down towards Aidan and Rowanne. 'They might need it; I don't,' she said simply.

'Oh no? Domnall jeered, his pale face looking

146

almost moon-like in the eerie light. 'So what are you going to use for armour?'

'The Ring Fire is all the armour I need,' Gemma replied curtly. She felt small and stupid, looking up at the grey willowy figure sneering down at her from his advantageous position. She folded her arms and put her head back, meeting him with a cool, freckle-faced stare, straight in the eye.

Deep inside she was still the timid, uncertain girl she had always been. But more importantly, she knew that this was the Ring Fire's battle, not hers. She could believe in that, even when she had no faith in herself.

Domnall shrugged. 'The Ring Fire your armour? But you don't even *like* carrying the Ring Fire! You told me yourself how wearied you were by it.'

'I was carrying it badly.'

Domnall laughed. 'I'm astounded they even made you Fire Wielder. Why, if you had been any good at all, you would have known months ago how strong my powers were growing... Ever since you murdered my father in the Great Hall of Light at the University, I have been planning this day. But I cannot imagine why the Fire Giver (if there is one, which I doubt), chose *you* to carry the flame. It shows how few *real* sorcerers there are in the land. A mere child who doesn't even know how to handle the simplest little fire trick!'

Domnall had stepped closer to Gemma during this speech and was holding out his right hand to her. Although he was speaking out loud, he was silently putting words into her mind:

'Give me the Ring Fire. Give it to me! I will

quench it and you will be free from your terrible burden for ever!'

Through gritted teeth she muttered, 'I am not a sorceress. I do no magic. I cannot give what is not mine to give.'

But this time Domnall's demand came from even deeper inside her mind. 'Give me the Ring Fire! Where is it?' he demanded. 'Give it to me!'

20

Death to the Blue Sorceress!

'I don't think much of your Ring Fire armour!' Domnall jeered. 'I'm right inside your head! I suppose it works like the rest of the Ring Fire... it is only any good when you carry it properly? Well, you're a lost cause then, aren't you? You never *did* do it right. You're hopeless. You forgot the Ring Fire, you didn't bother to look into it, you allowed these poor islanders to be put in danger because you didn't see me coming. Oh my, what a brilliant choice *you* were for Fire Wielder!

Gemma felt her heart sinking. All her old fears and feelings began to flood back to her. He was right. It *was* all her fault. But she must not let him get to her. She clenched her jaw.

Domnall came closer and put his wide, pale face next to hers. 'Oh dear, did I upset you...? Well, it's true, isn't it? You are useless. The so-called Fire Giver chose a failure in you! Remember...' He passed his right hand in front of her eyes and Gemma saw the times she had ignored the Ring Fire—the times when she had not just been too busy, but simply couldn't be bothered to go and watch and listen. Then she had been officious, and had ordered servants around unnecessarily, becoming like the sort of arrogant courtier she had always despised...

Gemma turned her head away and ground her teeth. Deliberately she bit her tongue. The pain jerked her back to reality. She was *not* going to be sucked once more into Domnall's trap of being overwhelmed with worthlessness and shame. He had almost defeated her that way once... Not again! The Ring Fire loved her, and that was what mattered.

But before she could answer him, he reached out and passed his hand in front of her eyes again and her vision blurred. 'Why do you fight me? Everything you see is all true. I'm only showing you what is inside your own head. I'm not putting anything in there which didn't happen.'

Then he laid one finger on her right temple. 'Show me how you became Fire Wielder,' he commanded.

Gemma closed her eyes and smiled. This time she felt happy. This was something she *did* want to see again. Domnall wanted her to experience shame and failure. But Gemma knew that she could use this moment as she chose. He wanted her to feel bad and guilty. She could use it to remember how glorious it had been and be heartened by it. So she welcomed the images that came flooding back into her mind...

Soon she was remembering that evening when she had stood with Phelan and the old Fire Wielder in the Hall of Light at Harflorum. The old man had grown so weary and thin when they had come to him at last with the Royal Ring. Phelan was made King, and Gemma swore to carry the Ring Fire well. She remembered that the Fire had suddenly flamed up in her hands to fill the evening-darkened room with a glorious light. 'All homage to the Ring Fire,' the King had said, 'in which we live and move and have our being!'

As she recalled that moment with delight, Domnall reeled back, calling out as if in pain. He had failed.

Gemma opened her eyes in surprise. The wizard was crimson in the face. 'Don't you ever do that again, or I will slay you on the spot!' he threatened, coming close to her again, then beginning to pace around her in an anticlockwise direction.

'Do what?' Gemma asked, wishing she knew what she had done to make Domnall stagger so.

'You know, you impudent child!' Suddenly Domnall stopped behind her and whispered in her ear: 'Give me the Ring Fire, as the old Fire Wielder gave it to you!'

'But he didn't give it to me!' Gemma replied. 'I've just shown you that. You saw the pictures in my mind as clearly as I did! No one gave it to me—it just appeared of its own free will.'

'Give the Ring Fire to me now!' Domnall demanded. 'I am tired of asking you. The time has come. Give it to me!'

'I cannot.'

Domnall came to face Gemma again and seized her. 'You may have some magic that prevents me from casting spells on you, but I can still hurt you!' he jeered, giving her arm a painful twist. Gemma knew the Ring Fire rarely came when bidden, so she was just as amazed as Domnall when the Flame momentarily roared out at him, burning his silk robe and scorching his face.

In fury he slapped her. Gemma fell sprawling on the rough grass at his feet. Domnall cradled his burns. 'You think you are so clever, don't you?' he scoffed. 'That was a child's trick. My patience has run out.' Shaking with fury the wizard pointed downhill at the awe-struck spectators. 'They will put you to the death you deserve. As soon as I raise my little finger they will come up the hill and destroy you and your so-called friends for bringing this terrible weather to their island.'

Gemma breathed deeply. Instinctively she knew the truth was more important than anything. She plucked up all her courage and struggled to her feet. 'It is true—I *am* a failure, and I have let many good people down. But the Ring Fire has never let anyone down. Getting the islanders to kill me won't mean you escape the torment of the Ring Fire's brightness for one second of your life. Now you have seen it and touched it, it will never let you go. It will burn you for ever. There will be no escape.'

Standing tall, Domnall raised his arms and bellowed as loudly as he could. 'Hear this, good people of Spider Island. This sorceress accuses me, Lord Domnall, your future King and Fire Wielder! She says that *I* brought this terrible torment on your island. What do you say?'

The islanders bellowed in reply: 'Death to the blue sorceress! Let us deal with her!' and the braver amongst them took a few steps up the hill, waving their billhooks and scythes menacingly.

But Domnall was not finished yet. He stretched

out a calming hand towards the crowd. 'You will have her soon, I promise you. But of course,' he faced Gemma again, 'it *was* you who brought this evil. If you had paid attention to the Ring Fire, I would never have been able to come this close. Your negligence summoned me here!'

Gemma looked around at the anxious faces peering up from below. She felt sorry for them. They were only ordinary people who understood nothing about the strange battle on their hilltop. They did not deserve this. Between her and death were Captain Marcus and his fifteen men. They stood facing the islanders, defending her.

The Ring Fire did not need to be protected. The sailors had come across dangerous seas to help *her*. Even though she could not see their faces, she could feel their fear and their longing to be home. She did not deserve their faithfulness. She hardly knew them, yet they were steadfastly risking their lives for her.

'In a way, this *is* all my fault,' she said to herself. 'The things I am facing are my own responsibility. I certainly shouldn't be asking this of them.' She felt herself sagging at the knees. Why were so many lives threatened because she had failed? Men, women, children—people who worked hard against severe odds, trying to earn a living.

Once again she felt the great longing to pass the Ring Fire on. The blue magic was Domnall's, but *she* had allowed it to grow and to come here endangering so many others...

She sank back to the ground and buried her head in her arms. Fleabag and Cleo rushed over to her and began to lick her face with their rough, warm tongues. 'Don't listen to him, Gemma. It's not like that!' Fleabag urged. 'We're all here to help in the battle; it's *everybody's* battle, not just yours. If Domnall hadn't fought us here, he'd have done it somewhere else. And if you weren't the Fire Wielder, someone else would be feeling just as awful as you!'

Gemma said nothing. Suddenly she felt so tired. If only there *was* someone else to bear the Ring Fire... This battle had wearied her beyond belief.

But Domnall had not finished. He stood over the little group of friends and crossed his arms, a look of pure contempt on his face... 'And that so-called king of yours, he is a common thief, and deserves to be hanged, not crowned. Born at the back of a junk shop, the son of criminals, and a criminal himself. What sort of a society has a convict as a king? No sensible, civilized community would give such a man the crown!'

Then he turned his attention to Fleabag. 'And what sort of land allows black, mangy cripples like this to advise their kings and princes? Eh?' And he hooked his foot under Fleabag's belly and tried to toss him in the air.

That was his first mistake.

21

Spells and Promises

Fleabag twisted as he was tossed in the air and landed on his attacker's leg, all claws firmly caught in the man's flesh.

Domnall howled and buckled in searing pain, but before he could throw a spell at the cat, Cleo had clambered onto his back and perched herself on his head. There she sat, her claws firmly caught in her victim's scalp, purring deafeningly in his left ear.

Slowly and steadily, Fleabag crawled up Domnall's front, taking each step deliberately and carefully, sinking in each claw as far as possible before putting his weight on the next paw. When he reached Domnall's neck, he smiled sweetly, twitching his whiskers in the man's eyes. 'I suggest you sit quietly while we explain a few home truths to you. If, on the other hand, you so much as twitch one eyelid, Cleo and I may momentarily mistake you for a large grey rat… purely accidentally, of course.'

Cleo stretched out a glistening talon and inspected it. 'That *would* be a shame—especially as I've just sharpened my claws.'

Fleabag looked up to grin encouragement at his

daughter perched in Domnall's ruffled hair. The cat-warrior's golden earring reflected the glow of the Ring Fire that hovered above Gemma's slumped form. As the gleam of light caught the wizard's eye, he winced and shrank away, causing the cats to dig their claws even more deeply into his flesh.

'Get off!' he howled as he shrank to his knees. 'I can't negotiate if you are causing me such agony… I'll come to an agreement. What if you become Prime Minister when I'm King? What do you say?' The dishevelled young man looked cunningly into the fish-breath face of the cat, only a finger's breadth from his own nose.

Fleabag pretended to consider the option. 'What do you say, dear? And you'd be a princess, of course.'

'Oh, at least,' Cleo purred, curling up on Domnall's head like a huge ginger hat, pinned carefully in place with needle-like talons.

Domnall turned his eyes from Fleabag's insistent stare as he desperately tried to unhook Fleabag, claw by claw, but as he pulled each talon away, the last one was replaced more firmly than before. All the time the infuriating cat purred.

This made Domnall so furious he flung a spell at Fleabag. But the cat heard the muttered incantation and saw the wizard's fingers flicking. In the blink of an eye he scrambled over the man's chest and onto his shoulder. Consequently the spell missed completely, slipped past the cat and caught Domnall in the face, turning him into an enormous toad. There he sat on the top of the hill, swallowing air and looking quite confused. He was a very ugly toad indeed—fat and lumpy with slimy green-grey skin, covered in brown warts. His eyes bulged round and pus-yellow with fury. Domnall blinked, narrowed his gaze and looked down at his green, pad-tipped fingers, then at his huge webbed back feet. He tried to move and found he could only hop. The suddenly jerky movement meant that Cleo and Fleabag had to dig their claws into the toad's smelly, mucous-covered skin even harder.

Domnall gulped air again. Then, hissing with pain and sheer malevolence, he let out a loud 'ribbit' as he changed himself back into human form.

'You missed!' Fleabag announced gleefully as he clambered further up the wizard, to where he could drape himself comfortably around Domnall's neck. There he hung languorously, closely resembling the black fur collar Rowanne had always coveted.

Domnall smiled sarcastically, showing firmly clenched teeth. 'Maybe. We'll see,' he growled. This time, he spun a spell by his waist, flicking his fingers in time to his incantation. With the final flourish a great snake appeared, wound several times around the wizard's middle. It was a heavy, smooth boa con-strictor, with millions of minute rainbow-oiled scales. At Domnall's command it writhed and heaved its weight upwards, and opened its jaws to devour Fleabag. But the cat hissed and scratched the snake on the nose so hard that it twisted away and slithered to the ground, allowing its heavy body to flow away like a muscular river towards a large rock behind which it hid.

Domnall swore roundly at his failure. Once again, he tried to tug and pull at the entwined cats, but they were there to stay. He would have to try a different approach. 'What more could you *want*, dear creatures?' he wheedled.

Fleabag and Cleo exchanged glances. 'What about you making my Dad handsome and four-legged again?'

'Anything, anything, just let me go!'

Fleabag stuck his nose in Domnall's ear and whispered, 'What about you making my daughter obedient and good?'

'I'll try, but that might be difficult.'

'Difficult! It's impossible!' jeered Fleabag. 'That proves you're an impostor.'

'In fact it proves you're lying on every point!' Cleo added gleefully, kneading her claws in and out of Domnall's head. 'I will never be a good little cat, and Fleabag will *never* be handsome and four-legged. We are what we are, and we're proud of it!'

'And Gemma is what she is!' Fleabag added. 'And she may not always have got things right, but it isn't whether we think she's a good Fire Wielder or not, but whether the Fire Giver wants her to be one that matters. You may be telling the truth about her past, but what is gone is only half the story and it doesn't count any more.'

The wizard looked as if he wanted to interrupt, but Fleabag didn't give him the chance. He pushed his smelly face in front of Domnall's mouth so he couldn't speak. 'And most important of all,' he went on, 'none of us were dragged into this; we're all here because we want to prove you're a liar and a bully. And we're not making any deal with you!'

And with that, he sprang from the wizard's neck and landed awkwardly on the ground, followed closely by Cleo, who stalked away, her tail erect and proud.

Domnall, clutching his neck, flicked his left hand towards the cats, who just turned and stared at him in a supercilious way, then sat down to wash. The wizard looked in horror at his fingers, then made the gesture again, but this time he recoiled as the spell flew back in his face, turning himself into a rather moth-eaten tiger rug, with glaring eyes.

Fleabag walked across him, kneading his claws into the back of the rug-animal's head and smirked, 'Now *you* should know you can't put a spell on a cat unless you know its real name, and you certainly could not *begin* to guess mine!'

Domnall was so furious he shrugged himself free of the tiger shape, picked up a small rock and threw it with all his strength at the sniggering felines. 'Take that!' he roared.

They both leaped out of the way. 'Temper, temper!' chided Fleabag. 'That will get you nowhere. Now what was that you were saying about striking a bargain with us?'

'I'll not make a bargain with you two,' he muttered between clenched teeth. 'But I will crush you if it's the last thing I do!' With that, Domnall picked up another rock and threw it at Fleabag, catching him on his one remaining back leg. Howling, the cat sank to the ground and began to lick furiously at his wound. Domnall picked up another rock.

Cleo did not hesitate. She leaped in front of her father and stared wide and golden eyed at her attacker. 'If you throw that at my father I swear the Ring Fire will burn you.'

Domnall just laughed as he pulled back his arm, but he never threw the rock, for from behind him, he heard a noise. He looked round and saw the Fire Wielder getting to her feet. In her right hand the tongue of Ring Fire was rising.

Domnall dropped the rock and threw up an arm to protect himself from the pain of the sight. He swore again, for Fleabag and his daughter had succeeded in distracting him from his real purpose—that of either taking the Ring Fire from this stupid girl, or crushing her and quenching the Fire.

He glared at the cats. 'I'll see to you two later,' he promised. 'But first, I must complete what I came to do!' Then he raised his right hand, and for the first time, Gemma realized he carried the same ring his father had worn at the battle of Porthwain. It closely resembled the Royal Ring of the land, but at the heart of it, there was no glowing Ring Fire, but an ice-blue flame. The living fire of evil—the source of all his power.

22

The Fire Cat Runs!

Gemma ducked as blue flames flashed across her vision, leaving her feeling icy cold. She stood again and met Domnall's glare with a steady gaze. The wizard seemed to have shrunk and aged in the last few hours. The constant shape-changing was sapping his strength deeply. He was hunched thin, grey and fearsomely angry.

Domnall twisted his lips into a devastating sneer. 'Well, my dear, have you had a nice little rest while I played with these charming little puss-cats? Have you thought about things? Are you ready to see reason now? It is surely time to stop endangering your friends and give me the Ring Fire.' His eyes were wild and unfocussed. 'He's quite mad,' Gemma thought. 'But he's dangerous too. I must be careful.'

Out loud she said: 'I've let the Ring Fire down in lots of ways, but I still love it, and it still loves me. I will not and cannot give it to you. Anyway, it would destroy you: look!' And she thrust out her hand which held the clear, steady flame in the palm.

Domnall recoiled, shielding his eyes from the

unbearable glare. 'Kill her!' he bellowed to the silent islanders, waiting at the bottom of the hill.

But none of them dared to move. From where they stood, they could see nothing for the thick blue cloud hanging heavily above their heads. From time to time they heard shouting, as gold or turquoise lightning flashed from the cloud, and terrible thunder rolled.

Not so far away, Rowanne and Aidan waited with the faithful sailors. The princess and her squire were still clad in their cooking-pot armour, makeshift swords in their hands, and deadly looks in their eyes. At the call for Gemma's death, they ran uphill, yelling and screaming battle cries, determined to plunge their swords into the wizard. But he was too quick for them.

With a flick of his long fingers he threw a spell in their direction, but the glow from the Ring Fire that Gemma had given them before the battle caused Domnall's curse to slither harmlessly to the ground and dissolve into millions of slimy white maggots.

Gemma did not hesitate. She was furious that Domnall dared to attack her friends! She stooped down and called Cleo. Gently she laid the living flame on the back of the golden cat, making her the Fire Cat she really was. 'Run!' Gemma ordered. 'Give a little to all our friends.'

Swiftly Cleo darted hither and thither like a lithe sun flare, bringing each of the company a small portion of the light to hold, until the Ring Fire made a great circle of renewed, steady brightness that wrapped everyone in its golden light. The sailors all moved into a circle around Gemma and Domnall, then one by one, they began to sing the song the cats had taught them.

But Rowanne did not join in the song, nor did she try to find her sword. Instead, she stood and stared, open-mouthed at what she held in her hands. She had always felt so far from the Ring Fire; now she was actually *holding* it, and it was not slipping away from her like mercury between her fingers.

In the middle of the circle of Ring Fire, the blue cloud darkened, thickened, and recoiled. Domnall howled in rage and flung back his head, uttering terrible words that Gemma did not understand, although in her bones she could feel the hate and malice. She stood still, and watched, and waited, as Domnall brought his hands down to wrap his opponent in the dreadful spell of final desolation.

23

The Spell of Desolation

Gemma put her head on one side for a moment and listened to the cruel, cracking syllables of Domnall's spell. Then she stepped forward and tapped him on the arm.

'Excuse me,' she said. 'Excuse me...'

He slapped her aside, and glowered at her, but the interruption made him stumble over his words. He raised his arms again and repeated the complicated gestures and syllables.

Gemma shook her head. 'I've got to get his attention, Fleabag; there's something very important I've got to say to him.'

Fleabag grinned and nodded to Cleo. The two cats opened their mouths and began to sing. Not a special, tuneful song this time, but they howled as gleefully, loudly and badly as possible, making Domnall put his hands over his ears. As soon as they saw the spell was interrupted a second time, the cats stopped their noise. Fleabag then put on a prim face and coughed politely, 'Lord Domnall, sir, the lady wishes to speak with you. Please be quiet and listen to what she has to say...'

Domnall rolled his eyes and spat at the cats, then he started his incantation again, so again the cats began their racket. This time, to make it special, Cleo sang a rather splendidly out-of-key descant she had composed only a moment before to honour the occasion.

At last Domnall stopped the spell for a third time. 'Well, what *is* it? It's very dangerous to interrupt mid-spell. Anything could happen,' he snapped.

Gemma shrugged. 'That's what I'm trying to tell you, Lord Domnall. I suspect that what you are saying is a very dangerous spell indeed. If you finish what you are doing, then everything will be destroyed... You will be alone.'

Then she turned on her heel and began to walk away from him.

Domnall made a noise in his throat that sounded as if he were choking. He pounced on Gemma and grabbed her by the shoulder. 'And *you* will be the first to die!' he snarled, shaking her hard.

Gemma shrugged. 'So? What does that matter? Everything will be dead... except you. You will be completely alone. There will be nothing for you to have sway over, it will just be you floating through the nothingness for ever!' And she continued her walk down the hillside.

Domnall stamped with rage and exasperation. 'The aloneness won't come for many years,' he bellowed after her. 'I will have time to create a race of slaves to entertain me.'

Gemma had a hunch. She turned back, just as Domnall was trying to complete the spell again. 'By the way,' she shouted, 'I suspect you *won't* have time on your side. If you finish that spell, everything may be destroyed very quickly; it may be that everything will happen faster than you think.'

Domnall was incensed. He shook his fist. 'How dare you presume to advise me? What do *you* know about magic? Come back here and fight me properly! Don't just walk away from me! You're a coward running away. You're scared the Ring Fire won't win, aren't you? Well, it won't. I can tell you that now...'

Gemma looked back over her shoulder. 'No. I'm not a coward, but you are just a bully, and there is no reason for me to stay here and take what you are doing. If you want to destroy everything, go on, do it. But I think you will not enjoy your eternity of aloneness.' And she stooped to pick up the helmet Rowanne had lovingly made for her, and walked down the hill.

Domnall climbed back to the top of the hill and breathed deeply, but as he tried yet again to utter the spell of desolation, he faltered and hesitated. He had forgotten the words, and mismatched the intricate gestures. He knew the spell was going wrong... it was not what he had intended it to be at all. Domnall went pale and cold, and looked around for help, but he was alone within the seething, dull blue evil, as it tightened around him, closer and closer.

Sweating with fear, he tried again, but his eyes were staring wildly as he cast around for something to give him comfort or confidence. At last, shaking and breathless, the terrified wizard finished the final words—but were they the right ones? Had he forgotten a phrase, or missed a vital movement?

Domnall lost his balance and began to sway. He felt as though he was slipping down a slope. He glanced at his feet; they were still planted firmly on the rocky hillside... but the feeling was getting faster and faster, and it was not a controlled slide. Blue winds rushed past his face and caught at his clothes as he spun downwards into the nothingness. In terror he called out, but there was no one to hear him.

Suddenly the blue that had lain everywhere became indigo, then as blue-black as ink. Slowly, malevolently it heaved and swelled, smothering, swamping, intense and so heavy it suffocated itself everywhere it lay.

The blueness was collapsing in on itself like a dying star. Suddenly there was a brilliant burst of blue light, then it was gone.

Far below at the foot of the hill, the islanders screamed and fled. Gemma, who was still quite high up the slope, was caught and lifted by the spell, suspended in nothingness: no earth below, no sky above.

But in the all-consuming silence that seemed to quench all life, the Ring Fire burned on, golden and life-giving, dissolving the blue as finally as ice melting on a glorious spring day.

24

The Way Home

Only a small, infinitely lonely sigh of wind disturbed the grassy hilltop, sending a last puff of blueness out across the sea.

At last, a soft, westerly breeze blew the final strands of the blue mist away. Far below, the sea fell back into its own tides again with a soft roar.

Gemma did not waken for several days. The tidal wave from Domnall's spell had knocked her unconscious. She lay oblivious to everything for two whole days. When she awoke, she and her friends were far out at sea in a fishing boat.

High above, Cleo was in the crow's nest—or as she preferred to call it, the cat's nest—keeping a look out for a shoal of fresh fish for supper, or maybe a few pirates to bring to justice. As she scanned the horizon, the ginger cat was singing 'North-west Passage' with a good pair of lungs, while her father snored loudly on a bed of folded sails below.

Gemma sat up and rubbed her eyes. 'Where am I? What happened?'

Rowanne brought a cup of water. 'The battle is over. Domnall is gone and we are on our way home.'

'But how did we get here?' Gemma tried to sit up, but felt very weak and sank back onto her mattress again.

Rowanne loved to tell of great battles, and this was surely the greatest ever fought! All the more so because the Ring Fire had rested in her own hands. She would never forget that moment!

Gemma smiled as Rowanne embroidered the tale as only a warrior can do. But at the description of Domnall's end, she shook her head. She found Rowanne's words distressing. She didn't wish a terrible death even on someone as evil as the wizard had been.

'What happened next?' she urged, eager to get past that bit.

Rowanne hugged her knees and her eyes glowed. 'Well, then the blue clouds parted, the strange winds dropped and the sea returned to normal. Of course, once the blue mist had lifted, the islanders realized that it was Domnall who had caused things to go wrong, but they still thought you were a terrible sorceress, one greater even than Domnall! I think they were ashamed of the way they had treated you—well, all of us, really—and they begged us to leave the island. They gave us this boat, food and water, and couldn't get rid of us fast enough. Perhaps they thought you would punish them for backing Domnall; I don't know. Still, we're well on our way now. Marcus reckons if this wind holds we'll be back by noon tomorrow. Talking of which, I had better go and do some work.'

Gemma heaved herself upright and leaned over the side. She stared into the reassuringly green waters, breathed deeply and looked around. The boat was an open craft, with no separate deck. Above, a huge, wide-footed single sail had a full belly of wind, making the vessel slip along at a great rate of knots. The boat was cramped, but adequate. The weather was fair, and everyone seemed in a good mood.

Fleabag sprang up onto the gunwales and walked carefully along the narrow edge to greet his friend. Gemma smiled and reached out to stroke him. 'Hello, you disreputable doormat!' He put his untidy black head up to be scratched. He roared a delighted purr.

Despite the way things had worked out, Gemma felt worried by something. 'Is everyone all right? Did anyone get hurt?' she asked.

Fleabag thought for a moment. 'Rowanne got a speck of something in her eye that went a bit nasty, but we washed it well and it cleared up. No one got *hurt* as such, not anything Rowanne would consider a proper injury worth a song or tale. As you so kindly noticed, *my* fur is intact, and that is all that matters really.'

Gemma laughed, then looked serious. 'Have I been intolerable lately?'

'Oh, totally!' chided the cat.

'You deserved it!' Gemma grinned.

Fleabag sat upright and looked offended. 'How now?' he demanded.

'For being right most of the time, I expect,' she laughed. Then she looked around. 'Is Aidan on board?'

'Indeed he is. Rowanne is already teaching him bad manners to cats. He actually refused to give me his supper last night when I said I was still hungry after I had eaten my own.'

'Shocking!' Gemma laughed. Then she looked serious again. 'I suppose this was all my fault. I should have known it was coming. If I had been doing my job, Domnall would never have got as close to me as he did.'

'But it was his choice to try to take the Ring Fire. You didn't ask him to, did you?'

'I almost did.'

'But if he had not found this means of attack, he'd have found another... Someone else, somewhere else. He would have endangered people whatever he had done. He was like that.'

'Rowanne said Domnall was just a pile of blue dust now...'

'That's right. Not a very pretty blue either, a sort of thick, sickly colour, if you know what I mean.'

Gemma leaned on her hand and stared out to sea, watching the gulls diving and swooping in their wake, hoping to catch leftovers of food thrown overboard, or small fish churned up by the boat's passage. 'What happened to that dust?' she asked, suddenly realizing what had been bothering her.

Fleabag frowned under his long whiskers. 'It blew away in the last of the blue wind. It was so fine there was nothing we could do to sweep it up. I am sure it could still be dangerous, but with any luck it's all blown away over the sea by now.'

'I hope so,' Gemma said thoughtfully. 'I really hope so.'

At the quayside Fleabag leaped ashore first. 'I'm not a sea-cat like my daughter,' he announced. 'I am now returning to life as a confirmed land-lubber.'

Cleo sprang gently onto Marcus' shoulder, and held herself there by twisting her tail around the Captain's neck, and gently pushing her claws just a little way into his thick leather waistcoat. 'If you're going back on land, may I have your pirate's earring?' she begged.

Fleabag was shocked. 'Indeed you may not! When you are knighted for some great deed, King Phelan may see fit to give you your own, but I doubt it. You are far too wilful a cat to get an honour as great as mine!'

Cleo looked crestfallen, 'Oh *please*! Marcus is going to take me to sea on every voyage for ever!' she announced gleefully as she was gently but firmly disentangled and put down.

'Only as long as you continue to catch rats!' Marcus said firmly. 'This last voyage had rather too many nibbles purloined from the galley and too many rodents left loose for my liking!'

Cleo flashed a row of pointed white teeth at her father. 'He loves me really,' she grinned. 'It was he who did the "purloining" of the titbits for me.'

'I should hope so!' Fleabag rejoined. 'The thought of a daughter of mine left to feed on sea rat for the rest of her life is more than I can stand.'

'I will do my best to feed your daughter like a queen,' Marcus laughed. 'But for now, please excuse me; I must be about my business.'

Just then Phelan ran across the quay, arms wide to hug his friends. His dark eyes twinkled as he laughed out loud to see them all back safe and well.

He took Gemma and Fleabag to the nearest inn, and ordered a meal. While they waited for the food,

Gemma told him all that had happened, and everything she had felt. Then she tried to explain why she had not told him the truth about her fears. 'It wasn't that I didn't trust you; it was just that I wanted to protect everyone from suspecting that their Fire Wielder no longer knew how to carry the Flame. I had hoped to find a replacement quietly, without anyone knowing they had ever been in danger.'

Phelan nodded and rubbed his hands through his black, curly hair as he thought. 'I can see your point, but wasn't it more dangerous *not* to tell Fleabag and me, at least?'

'Yes, it was silly of me. I'm sorry. But I still feel as if I don't want to go back to Harflorum.'

Phelan looked dismayed. 'But everything has turned out so well, why ever not?'

Gemma shrugged. 'Perhaps not everything I have been thinking lately has been wrong. I still have a hankering to go to the cottage in the rocks. I don't know if it's just for a holiday, or to live. But if I'm not so tied up in ceremonies and duties, then perhaps I can learn to listen to the Ring Fire without distraction. I know the old Fire Wielder used to live somewhere quiet with his wife and a few friends. He would only come to Harflorum when he was needed... when he really felt he had something to say.'

'Then I think that's a good idea, if that's what you want to do, Gemma. Who will you take with you? I will make sure the cottage is rebuilt and waterproof, and well stocked of course. But it's not safe for you to be all alone up there.'

'If there have to be guards, can I at least have the cottage all to myself? Really I'd just like a couple of goats… and Fleabag, I wonder if any of your talking offspring would like to join me?'

Fleabag was about to open his mouth and indignantly protest that *he* hadn't been invited, when a fat, brown tabby ran across to them. 'Excuse me for butting in, old man!' he miaowed in cat language. 'I've been looking all over for you… You'll never guess!'

Fleabag eyed the other cat suspiciously. It was Prince Tomas' butler's cat, a nice enough fellow but a bit slow in the rafters. He was waddling as fast as his fat legs could carry him, obviously bursting with some vital news.

'I give up,' Fleabag chuckled. 'Tell me what I'll never guess, then I'll know whether I could have guessed it or not.'

The fat cat blinked at him, looking rather lost and bemused. 'Um. Yes. Quite. Well, the day after you left, a rider came from the royal palace at Harflorum. Your lady wife has produced six kittens. Three daughters and three sons. Congratulations, sir! You're a father!'

Fleabag, who was fairly experienced at being a father, just nodded and said, 'Thank you' politely, and translated the news for the humans in the room.

At that moment Rowanne came across the room with flagons of mead and just caught the end of the conversation. 'Do I take it you'll be needing a lift home post-haste, old friend? You can travel in my saddle bag tonight if you like.'

'I suppose so,' Fleabag replied reluctantly, sad at the thought of missing out on a few weeks in the mountains with Gemma. He knew she would not hear of him staying when his wife Tabitha might need his help. 'But I'm not looking forward to going back,' he grumbled. 'I adore my wife, but she's so grumpy when she's just had kittens. It'll be "hold this one, lick that one, take this one for a walk and box that one's ears." There'll be no sleep for months and then when peace starts to reign again, last year's kittens will be bringing *their* kittens home for Granny and Grandpa to look after. No, I'm not looking forward to this at *all*.'

Suddenly his eyes lit up at the sight of Captain Marcus crossing the quay with Cleo swaying like a huge, golden parrot on his shoulder. He climbed onto the back of a chair and called out of the window: 'Hey, Marcus, I've changed my mind about going to sea. Might you have a berth for one more on board your next ship?'

'No,' Marcus shook his head. 'One cat is quite enough, especially when that one cat is as much trouble as your Cleo!'

'Nothing for it,' Rowanne teased. 'You'll have to hop onto my shoulder and pretend you're my fur collar.' The Princess stretched out a strong hand to grab Fleabag by the scruff of the neck.

'No, thank you,' he laughed as he sprang out of reach. 'I miss my Tabitha too much, and apparently one of the boys is just like me—with four legs of course! Much as I'm honoured to be asked to be your fur collar Rowanne, I think I'd rather go home and face the mews-ic!'

All Lion books are available from your local
bookshop, or can be ordered direct from Lion
Publishing. For a free catalogue, showing the
complete list of titles available, please contact:

Customer Services Department
Lion Publishing plc
Peter's Way
Sandy Lane West
Oxford OX4 5HG

Tel: (01865) 747550
Fax: (01865) 715152

CW00778800

CRIME TIME 2.2

PUBLISHER
CT PUBLISHING
PO BOX 5880
BIRMINGHAM B16 8JF

DISTRIBUTION
Turnaround

PRINTING
Caledonian International Book
Publishing, Glasgow

EDITORIAL
Editor
Barry Forshaw
Advertising, Founding Editor
Paul Duncan
**Reviews Editor, Designer, Founding
Editor**
Peter Dillon-Parkin
Audio
Ellen Cheshire

EDITORIAL ADDRESS
Crime Time, PO BOX 5880, Birmingham
B16 8JF
Phone: 0121 454 3031, Fax: 01582 712244,
E-mail: ct@crimetime.demon.co.uk

ADVERTISING
Please fax or phone Paul Duncan (01203
315864) for rates, or write to the editorial
address.
SUBSCRIPTIONS
Crime Time Subscriptions, 18 Coleswood
Rd, Harpenden, Herts AL5 1EQ

LEGAL STUFF
Crime Time is © 1998 CT Publishing
ISBN 1-9020020-5-9
All rights reserved. No part of this
book may be reproduced, stored in or
introduced into a retrieval system, or
transmitted, in any form, or by any means
(electronic, mechanical, photocopying,
recording or otherwise) without the
written permission of the publisher.

COVER
Peter Mann portrays Mr Freeze, in a
typical moment, from Mark Timlin's *Dead
Flowers*

EDITORIAL SUBMISSIONS:
Send us your stuff! Sample reviews
should be 150—250 words. *Crime Time*
cannot accept responsibility for any loss
of material submitted, as the Post Office
is in league with the makers of *Ultravio-
let*. Submissions should be typed &
accompanied by an SAE. We reserve the
right to ~~weep pitifully at your terrible
work~~ amend submissions for publication.

DISCLAIMER
The views expressed by contributors are
not necessarily those of the publisher. Hey,
who knows what the publisher thinks.
Perhaps he dreams he's a butterfly. Perhaps he dreams he's a butterfly dreaming
he's a publisher. Who knows? Or, indeed,
cares? Oh, we're a philosophical lot round
here...

Contents

Tirade

TRADITIONALLY, A NEW editor uses this space to say *"we'll take the magazine you know and love in a whole new direction..."* So, allow me to spike that cliché: for a start, Peter Dillon-Parkin is still very much around. His credits (fiction & reviews editor , as well as general éminence grise) are on the frontispiece, and the look and tone of voice of CT are largely his creation (building on the inaugural work of himself and Paul Duncan – also still on board). I started writing for the magazine precisely because of these factors, and I'm a great believer in the "if it ain't broke, don't fix it" school. And when I was handed the poisoned editorial chalice (moving on from my features editor duties), my ground rules involved Peter staying on. After all, he has bugger-all to do, and needs to fill his evenings.

So—expect continuing in-depth coverage of every possible crime genre, from Woolrich to Batman, from Fritz Lang to Tarantino and from Sax Rohmer to James Ellroy. And we'll always try to find a new approach, with nit-picking detail a speciality.

Expect opinionated writing. Expect rude writing (I've persuaded the great Mark Timlin to contribute a column... he'll be writing in that quaint Home Counties style of his). We've got the noted crime fiction correspondent Adrian Muller, and many new writers and journalists. More interviews, more features more reviews. You'll disagree with us as often as not – but isn't that why you've bought CT in the past?

Barry Forshaw

WHEN I FIRST SUGGESTED the idea of *Crime Time* to Paul Duncan, in the seemingly now naïve belief that it would make our fortune, I didn't intend I would ever edit the magazine. How naïve *that* now seems. I've now actually edited more issues than anyone else, and haven't run from the building screaming yet, although that may be due to the heavy duty restraints.

This column is a bit of a tidying up job then. All of you whose work isn't in this issue (lack of space), who are waiting for a reply from me (lack of time) or have any other unanswered query or proposition—bear with me, you'll hear soon.

Meg Chittenden, who writes the wonderful Charlie Plato series (which no British publisher has picked up, but someone really should) writes to worry that CT won't be as witty (I think she means sarcastic, but is too nice to say so) without me. Don't worry I still design the thing. And do the reviews and fiction. And am interviewing for it. Meg's books (*Dead Men Don't Dance* and *Dying To Sing*) are set in a Country and Western Tavern which runs line dancing evening (I can almost *feel* Mark Timlin bristling), which would ordinarily put me off, I'm ashamed to say, but are witty (not sarcastic), first rate mysteries and great fun. You can probably get them in the UK from the usual suspects – they're published in very handsome editions by Kensington.

Which brings me to my last beef. This hard-boiled/traditional battle. I recently saw CT criticised for 'pushing hard-boiled fiction on to us'. Duh! I don't think I've made any secret of the fact that my preferred type of crime fiction is traditional, and the duller the better. I *have* an exciting life, and I like to relax with crime fiction. This doesn't stop me enjoying all the other variant of the genre—hard-boiled, historical, thrillers—add your own. Or from reading history, science fiction, horror, children's books, comics or the backs of cornflake packets? What's the matter with these people—do they eat cornflakes from dawn to dusk, only wear one colour of clothing

and listen to one record? Again and again?

If we have had more hard-boiled material in CT it's quite simply that the hard-boiled enthusiasts have, well, been more enthusiastic. If you want more of something else, contribute, don't complain. What makes it more galling is that the complainant in question was, indeed, approached to do an interview, and didn't have the courtesy to reply.

Finally can I thank all the contributors past and present without whom CT just wouldn't have been here. Well, alright, it would, but I'd have had to write it all. This issue's highlights include a story from Fred Willard that should make the years 'best of' lists, Gary Phillips' essay into the graphic arts and as strong a raft of features, reviews and fiction as I've seen anywhere since, well, since the last issue.

I hope everyone will welcome Barry as the new editor, and I thinkt that his touch is evident in this issue (well it is to me—he does all that 'correcting' business on his bits. Hey, Barry, wanna proof mine?)

See you in 90 days with even more good stuff, including a horror/crime crossover (yes, something more to complain about), a Raffles story and a sinister tale of an ex-magazine editor turned serial killer.

Ooooh, *creepy*!

Peter Dillon-Parkin

DROP DEAD PROMO

Bonkers value—£2.99 each or 4 for £10 inc P&P!!!
Cheques, PO's payable to Oldcastle Books Ltd.
Visa, Mastercard, Switch, Delta accepted.
Original prices as shown.

Drop Dead Promo (CT2.2), 18 Coleswood Rd, Harpenden, Herts. AL5 1EQ

1874061378	HAPPY BIRTHDAY TURK	JAKOB ARJOUNI	£4.99*
1874061289	MORE BEER	JAKOB ARJOUNI	£4.99*
1874061297	ONE MAN ONE MURDER	JAKOB ARJOUNI	£4.99*
1874061475	BURGLAR WHO TRADED TED WILLIAMS	LAWRENCE BLOCK	£5.99*
1874061556	BURGLAR THOUGHT HE WAS BOGART	LAWRENCE BLOCK	£5.99*
0948353864	BURGLAR WHO LIKED QUOTE KIPLING	LAWRENCE BLOCK	£5.99*
1874061793	TWO FOR TANNER	LAWRENCE BLOCK	£4.99*
1874061866	TANNER'S TIGER	LAWRENCE BLOCK	£4.99*
1874061262	LITTLE BOY BLUE	EDWARD BUNKER	£5.99*
1874061610	FADE OUT (Brandstetter 1)	JOSEPH HANSEN	£4.99*
1874061653	TROUBLE MAKER (Brandstetter 3)	JOSEPH HANSEN	£4.99*
1874061599	FALLING ANGEL	WH JORTSBERG	£6.99
1874061157	KILLING SUKI FLOOD	ROBERT LEININGER	£5.99*
1901982017	SUNDAY MACARONI CLUB	STEVE LOPEZ	£5.99*
1874061343	FALSE PRETENSES	ARTHUR LYONS	£4.99*
0948353961	OTHER PEOPLE'S MONEY	ARTHUR LYONS	£4.99*
1901982157	DOUBLE TAKE	JUDY MERCER	£5.99*
1874061963	THE MONKEY'S FIST	WILLIAM D PEASE	£5.99*
1874061750	VIOLENT SPRING	GARY PHILLIPS	£6.99
1874061769	PERDITION U.S.A.	GARY PHILLIPS	£6.99
1874061637	BLACK HORNET	JAMES SALLIS	£5.99
187406170X	THE WAY WE DIE NOW (Moseley 4)	C. WILLEFORD	£4.99*
1874061300	MUSCLE FOR THE WING (Shade 2)	DANIEL WOODRELL	£5.99*

NO EXIT PRESS

Bullets
by Adrian Muller

Murder One

At Murder One in August, owner Maxim Jakubowski (together with authors, customers and staff) celebrated the first ten years of Britain's first bookstore to specialise in crime fiction. Before the evening party, it was open house at 71-73 Charing Cross Road, and customers mingled with all the authors who had shown up to sign stock, socialise and complain about their agents.

Sujata Massey

The first published winner of the US Malice Domestic convention writing grant, Sujata Massey, is an author to look out for. As yet, the British born writer is unpublished in the UK but Massey, who now resides in the USA, is going from strength to strength across the Atlantic. Her first novel, *The Salaryman's Wife*, is set in Japan and introduces her series protagonist Rei Shimura, a young American woman of Japanese extraction. Published last year, it has won the Agatha award for Best First Mystery, and has been nominated for Anthony and Macavity awards. The most recent instalment, *Zen Attitude*, is again a paperback original, but next year's *The Flower Master* and future books featuring Rei will be released in hardback first. Contact advertising specialist bookstores for imported copies of *The Salaryman's Wife* and *Zen Attitude*.

Red Herrings

The Crime Writers' Association's monthly magazine, *Red Herrings*, has traditionally only been available to its members. However, to celebrate the 500th issue, a limited number of copies have been made available to the general public. Featuring an interview with CWA/The Macallan Diamond Dagger Winner Ed McBain (not in the same league, of course, as the CT interview...), articles by Natasha Cooper, Peter Lovesey, and Val McDermid, and a quiz by Mike Ripley. Readers interested in obtaining a copy should contact crime fiction bookstores listed below New British Publications.

Dead on Deansgate

Dead on Deansgate, the new British crime fiction conference organised by Waterstone's Booksellers (with the full backing of the British Crime Writers' Association) will take place in Manchester over the weekend of the 23rd, 24th, and the 25th of October. The conference hotel will be the Ramada International (£70 a night); the Travelodge next to the Ramada is available for those seeking budget accommodation (£45 a night for a room sleeping a maximum of four).

Authors expected to attend include Robert Barnard, Kate Charles, Ruth Dudley Edwards, John Harvey, Joe E. Lansdale, Edward Marston, Val McDermid, Susan Moody, Ian Rankin, and many, many more. The registration fee for the whole weekend is £55, which includes two Author Breakfasts. There will also be an optional Dead on Deansgate Dinner on Saturday night (cost and guest speakers to be announced). If all goes well, Waterstone's hope to make this an annual event and the European showcase for crime fiction. For registration details and more information contact Dead on Deansgate, Waterstone's, 91 Deansgate, Manchester M3 2BW, United Kingdom. Tel: +44-(0)161-832-1992. Alternatively you can e-mail David Lovely, Waterstone's crime fiction buyer, on dave.l@bigfoot.com.

(Talking of big conventions; for those planning to attend the Bouchercon World Mystery Convention in Philadelphia in October there have been a few new updates to the website. Check out:

www.geocities.com/alecwest/bouchercon/philly.htm)

Val McDermid

The Manchester author is very active at the moment. Not only is there a new Kate Brannigan book, *Star Struck*, out in September, but BBC radio also adapted a McDermid book that same month. The adaptation of *Clean Break* was broadcast on Radio Four (fingers crossed for an audiocassette release). Currently working on a psychological suspense thriller set mostly in the early sixties, Val is also toying with a third instalment in the series featuring policewoman Carol Jordan and criminal profiler Tony Hill. If the idea ever reaches the page, the duo will find themselves collaborating with Europol on a series of killings across Europe. Collectors might be interested to know that The Poisoned Pen Press will be the first to publish McDermid's *The Wire in the Blood* in the United States. This US edition, the second in the Jordan and Hill series, will have a print-run limited to 300 copies. Val has written a new foreword, with an introduction by fellow writer Michael Connelly; all 300 copies will be signed by both authors. Costing approximately $50, the publication date is expected to be September, as with the new Kate Brannigan. To reserve a copy, contact advertising crime fiction bookshops or The Poisoned Pen Press, 6962 East 1st Avenue, Suite 103, Scottsdale, AZ 85251, USA. Fax: (602) 949 1707, e-mail: susan@poisonedpenpress.com.

Baronesses of Crime

Appearing at the Royal Geographical Society in London recently were the two Baronesses of crime fiction, P. D. James and Ruth Rendell. The subject of the discussion between the Baroness of Holland Park

(James) and the Baroness of Babergh (Rendell) was 'The Art of Writing Crime Fiction'. Benefiting from the event was the Limegrove Appeal who will help finance a hostel for homeless people in west and central London with the proceeds. Following on from the latest Dalgleish television adaptation, *A Certain Justice*, viewers have new episodes to look forward to of James' PI Cordelia Gray, again starring Helen Baxendale. Fans of Rendell have a new novel in store for them: *A Sight for Sore Eyes* is published by Hutchinson in September.

(To support the Limegrove Appeal contact: Notting Hill Housing Trust, Grove House, 27 Hammersmith Grove, London W6 0JL.)

The Queen of Crime

In November HarperCollins will publish a new Hercule Poirot novel by Agatha Christie. A new Poirot? Well, yes and no. Following the publication of newly discovered short stories by Christie last year, *Black Coffee* is a novelisation by Charles Osborne of one of the Queen of Crime's plays. If the publication proves successful, no doubt Christie's other four original plays will receive the same treatment. There are also numerous short stories that became the bases for plays.

Kate Ross

Fans of the historical crime series featuring Julian Kestrel will be saddened to hear that his creator, Kate Ross, died earlier this year. Days be-

fore dying Ross completed *The Unkindest Cut*, a short story written especially for *Past Poisons*. This short story collection, edited by Maxim Jakubowski, was conceived as a tribute to the late Ellis Peters, creator of medieval sleuthing monk Brother Cadfael. Other contributors include Lindsey Davis, Laurie R. King, Edward Marston, Anne Perry, and many more. *Past Poisons* will be published in November by Headline.

Diana Rigg

As Uma Thurman hits the screen as Emma Peel in the cinema adaptation of *The Avengers* (undemanding fun or dire travesty, depending on your point of view), news came that Dame Diana Rigg, the actress who originally played John Steed's sidekick, is to play a sleuth in a new BBC series called The Mrs Bradley Mysteries.

John Harvey

A much loved series came to an end with the September publication of *Last Rites*. It is the final instalment of John Harvey's Charlie Resnick series. However, the Nottingham policeman went out with a bang at a jazz party to launch the book. The party also celebrated the new autumn publications of Harvey's publishing company Slow Dancer Press. New crime titles include: *Blue Lightning*, a collection of jazz-inspired short stories by a variety of authors: Neville Smith's *Gumshoe*; and *New Orleans Morning*, the first in Julie Smith's superb series featuring policewoman

Skip Langdon.

Kate Charles

Best known for her clerical mysteries featuring Lucy Kingsley and David Middleton-Brown, Kate Charles has temporarily abandoned the series to write a number of stand-alone novels for Little, Brown. Fans of ecclesiastical crime novels need not worry, Lucy and David will return, but in the meantime look out for *Unruly Passions*. Out in October this is the first of Charles' non-series novels, and the psychological thriller is about a woman who for the first time encounters something she cannot have...

And finally:

New British Crime Novels
Author—Title (series character), Publisher, Price

September

Eliette Abecassis—The Qumran Mystery (debut crime novel), Orion, £9.99/£16.99

Jane Adams—Fade to Grey (DI Mike Croft), Macmillan, £16.99

Robert Barnard—The Corpse at the Haworth Tandoori, HarperCollins, £15.99

Brian Battison—Mirror Image, Constable, £16.99

Jay R. Bonansinga—Head Case, Macmillan, £16.99

Fiona Buckley—The Doublet Affair (Ursula Blanchard), Orion, £16.99

Andrew Coburn—Birthright, Simon & Shuster, £14.99

Denise Danks—Phreak (Georgina Powers), Gollancz, £9.99

Frank Delaney—Desire and Pursuit, HarperCollins, £17.99

Michael Dibdin—A Long Finish (Aurelio Zen), Faber & Faber, £16.99

Kate Ellis—The Merchant's House (Wes Paterson—new series), Piatkus, £17.99

Janet Evanovich—Four to Score (Stephanie Plum), Macmillan, £16.99

Ken Follett—The Hammer of Eden, Macmillan, £16.99

Dick Francis—Field of Thirteen, Michael Joseph, £16.99

Ray Harrison—Draughts of Death (Bragg & Morton), Constable, £16.99

John Harvey—Last Rites (Charlie Resnick), Heineman, £16.99

Carole Hayman—Greed, Crime, Sudden Death (Warfleet Chronicles), Vista, £5.99

Keith Heller—Man's Loving Family (watchman George Man), Headline, £16.99

Judith Jones—Baby Talk, Constable, £16.99

Joe Lansdale—Rumble Tumble (Hap Collins), Gollancz, £9.99

Sam Llewellyn—The Shadow in the Sands, Headline, £12.99

Sara MacDonald—Listening to Voice (debut crime novel), Headline, £16.99

Val McDermid—Star Struck (Kate Brannigan), HarperCollins, £16.99

Susan Moody—Dummy Hand (Cassie Swann), Headline, £16.99

Robert Newman—Manners, Hamish Hamilton, £10.99

Julie Parsons—Mary, Mary (debut crime novel), Macmillan, £16.99

Ruth Rendell—A Sight For Sore Eyes, Hutchinson, £16.99

Gavin Robertson—Thousand (debut crime novel), Headline, £12.99

Veronica Stallwood—Oxford Blue (Kate Ivory), Headline, £16.99

Elise Title—Chain Reaction (Dr Caroline Hoffman), Little, Brown, £9.99

Fred Willard—Down on Ponce, No Exit Press, £6.99

Margaret Yorke—False Pretences, Little, Brown, £15.99

October

Lawrence Block—Everybody Dies (Matt Scudder), Orion, £16.99

Belinda Brett—Mother, Piatkus, £17.99

Gwendolin Butler—A Grave Coffin (John Coffin), HarperCollins, £15.99

Jon Cleary—Five Ring Circus (DI John Scobie), HarperCollins, £16.99

Ethan Coen—The Wrestler (short stories), Doubleday, £12.99

Anthea Cohen—Angel of Retribution (Agnes Turner), Constable, £16.99

Patricia Cornwell—Point of Origin (Dr Kay Scarpetta), Little, Brown, £16.99

Margaret Cuthbert—The Silent Cradle (debut crime novel), Simon & Shuster, £9.99/£16.99

Emma Davidson—Who's Been Sleeping In My Bed, Orion, £5.99

Paul Doherty—The Mask of Ra, Headline, £9.99/£16.99

Daniel Easterman—Incarnation, HarperCollins, £16.99

Ron Ellis—Mean Streets (Johnny Ace), Headline, £16.99

James Ellroy—Crimewaves, Century, £15.99

Allan Folsom—Day of Confession, Little, Brown, £16.99

Reg Gander—Mother, Son & Holy Ghost (Alan Rosslyn), Faber & Faber, £9.99

Jonathan Gash—Prey Dancing (Dr Clare Burtonall), Macmillan, £16.99

Robert Harris—Archangel, Hutchinson, £16.99

Peter James—Denial, Orion, £9.99/£16.99

Quintin Jardine—Murdering the Judges (Bob Skinner), Headline, £16.99

Philip Kerr—The Second Angel, Orion, £16.99

Andrew Klavan—The Uncanny (horror), Little, Brown, £15.99

Bill Knox—Death Department (Thane & Moss), Constable, £16.99

Janet Laurence—Appetite for Death (Darina Lisle), Macmillan, £16.99

Jessica Mann—The Survivor's Revenge, Constable, £16.99

John Milne—Alive & Kicking, No Exit Press, £10.00

Margaret Murphy—Caging the Tiger, Macmillan, £16.99

Kem Nunn—Dogs of Winter, No Exit Press, £6.99

James Patterson—When the Wind Blows, Headline, £16.99

Manda Scott—Night Mares (Kellen Stewart), Headline, £16.99

Cath Staincliffe—Dead Wrong (Sal Kilkenny), Headline, £16.99

Grant Sutherland—East of the City, Headline, £16.99

Peter Tonkin—Hell Gate, Headline, £16.99

Minette Walters—The Breaker, Macmillan, £16.99

David Williams—Suicide Intended (DCI Merlin Perry), HarperCollins, £15.99

David Wishart—The Lydian Baker (Marcus Corvinus), Hodder & Stoughton, £16.99

Various (Maxim Jakubowski—editor)—Past Poisons: An Ellis Peters Memorial Anthology, Headline, £9.99

November

Geoffrey Archer—Fist of Fire, Century, £15.99

David Baldacci—The Winner, Simon & Schuster, £9.99

T.R. Bowen—The Death of Amy Parish (debut crime novel—new series), Michael Joseph, £5.99

Simon Brett—Mrs Pargeter's Point of Honour (Mrs Pargeter), Macmillan, £16.99

Jane Brindle—The Hiding Game, Headline, £16.99

Agatha Christie (& Charles Osborne)—Black Coffee (Hercule Poirot), HarperCollins, £15.99

Elizabeth Corley—Requiem Mass (DCI Andrew Fenwick—new series), Headline, £16.99

Liz Evans—JFK is Missing (Grace Smith), Orion, £5.99

John Francome—Safe Bet, Headline, £16.99

Kinky Friedman—Blast From the Past (Kinky Friedman), Faber & Faber, £9.99

Ann Granger—Running Scared (Fran Varady), Headline, £16.99

Peter Guttridge—Two to Tango, Headline, £16.99

Sparkle Hayter—The Last Manly Man (Robin Hudson), No Exit Press, £10.00

Juliet Hebden—Pel is Provoked, Constable, £16.99

Tom Holland—The Sleeper in the Sands, Little, Brown, £15.99

Michael Jecks—The Leper's Return (Sir Baldwin Furnshill), Headline, £16.99

Anthony Masters—The Good and Faithful Servant (Daniel Boyd—new series), Constable, £16.99

Jennie Melville—Stone Dead (CS Charmian Daniels), Macmillan, £16.99

Richard Montanari—The Violent Hour, Michael Joseph, £5.99

Bill Napier—Nemesis, Headline, £12.99

Frank Palmer—Final Score (Phil 'Sweeney' Todd), Constable, £16.99

George Pelecanos—Nick's Trip (Nick Stefanos), Serpent's Tail, £7.99

Sharon Penman—Cruel as the Grave (Justin de Quincey), Michael Joseph, £15.99

Richard Pitman—No Place to Hide, Hodder & Stoughton, £16.99

Candace Robb—A Gift of Sanctuary (Owen Archer), Heineman, £10.00

Barrie Roberts—Sherlock Holmes and the Royal Flush (Sherlock Holmes), Constable, £16.99

Laura Joh Rowland—The Concubine's Tattoo, Headline, £16.99

Paul Thomas—Guerilla Season (Tito Ihaka), Vista, £5.99

Marilyn Todd—Wolf Whistle (Clau-

dia Seferius), Macmillan, £16.99
Martyn Waites—Little Triggers, Piatkus, £17.99
Various (Otto Penzler—editor)—Criminal Records (short stories), Orion, £9.99/£16.99

For further information on the above titles, or to order books, contact:

Crime in Store, 14 Bedford Street, Covent Garden, London WC2E 9HE.
Tel: +44-171-379-3795, fax: +44-171-379-8988.
E-mail: CrimeBks@aol.com
Website:
http://nt.pleasuredomes.co.uk/crimeinstore.htm

Murder One, 71-73 Charing Cross Road, London WC2H 0AA.
Tel: +44-171-734-3483, fax: +44-171-734-3429.
E-mail:
106562.2021@compuserve.com
Website:
http://www.murderone.co.uk

The Mysterious Bookshop, 82 Marylebone High Street, London W1M 3DE.
Tel: +44-171-486-8975,
Fax: +44-171-486-8953.
E-mail:
MysteriousLON@compuserve.com
Website:
http:/www.MysteriousBookshop.com

Post Mortem Books, 58 Stanford Avenue, Hassocks, Sussex BN6 8JH.

Tel: +44-1273-843066,
Fax: +44-1273-845090.
E-mail:
ralph@pmbooks.demon.co.uk
Website:
http://www.postmortembooks.co.uk

All the above are available from the Crime Time website at:
http://www.crimetime.demon.co.uk

US News by Peter Walker

Gary Phillips

...has a new book on the way, the third outing for hip and totally right on the button Ivan Monk. Did you know that Robert Crais taught a mystery course and one of his pupils was... Gary Phillips? On the subject of LA mystery writers look out for new writer, EM Cosin, who's written what looks like a pretty good opening few chapters of a novel about a female eye in Los Angeles. A bit more earthy than some females PIs, this one hangs out in a pub! It's due out in the States in September(and you can check out her work on *The Thrilling Detective* site in the near future as well).

Vintage Crime/Black Lizard has just re-issued the three novels Carl Hiaasen and fellow journalist Bill Montalbano published with Atheneum between 1981 and 1984.The titles are *Powder Burn, A Death in China* and *Trap Line*. Incidentally, Carl Hiassen is the American guest of honour at Bouchercon.

James Ellroy, so rumour has it, has a new book on the way (well, it wasn't a rumour but a posting in the e-mail list rara-avis, but rumour sounds better). Tentatively called *Crimewave* it is due out in Feb 1999. Is this the next book in his American Tabloid trilogy? Be sure *Crime Time* will get round to telling you sooner or later.

The July issue of *Ellery Queen's Mystery Magazine*, in its new, larger format, features a new Nameless story by Bill Pronzini, and a story by Loren Estleman on his film detective Valentino, a series exclusive to EQ. As well, Jon Breen reviews several of the latest PI books in his column. The July/August *'Special Summer Double Issue'* of *Alfred Hitchcock's Mystery Magazine* features a new tale about Puerto Rican P.I. Carlos Bannon. The Summer 1998 issue of *Mary Higgins Clark Mystery Magazine* is out, with new stories by Rick Riordan, Marcia Muller and Edna Buchanan.

The Summer 1998 issue of *New Mystery* is out, with an overview of black mystery novels, and fiction by Gary Phillips, James Sallis and Richard Torres.

Books worth a mention (well, I think so...)

Anthologies and Collections;
A hard-boiled anthology called *The Cutting Edge*, edited by Janet Hutchings is worth a look. So is *Lethal Ladies II* about *'private janes'* edited by Robert Randisi and J Matthews. Also well worth checking out is a collection of new pulp called *Murder for Revenge* featuring Mickey Spillane, Max Allan Collins and various other authors.

Comics and Graphic Novels:
Max Allen Collins' *Road To Perdition* is a graphic novel which pits an eight-year old against gangster Al Capone.
The Bogie Man by John Wagner and Alan Grant is a graphic novel reprinting two rare, full-length adventures of Francis Clunie, AKA the Bogie Man.

Reference:
Ed Gorman's *Speaking of Murder* (Berkley Prime Crime), which he edits along with Martin H. Greenberg, has interviews with Stephen King, Mickey Spillane, Sue Grafton and others. Not to mention interviews conducted by our own Crow Dillon-Parkin and Paul Duncan.

General
Daniel Woodrell has a new book coming out called *Tomato Red* . Looks like Woodrell is ready to hit the big time. Ang Lee (*Eat Drink Man Woman*, *The Wedding Banquet* and *Sense and Sensibility*) is set to film *Woe To Live On*. *Give Us A Kiss* has also been optioned by Fox.

A related bit of news—though not strictly crime—is that the *Richmond Review* (www.demon.co.uk/review) have two brilliant short stories—one from James Kelman, the other from Frederic Raphael. The Raphael, previously unpublished, is one *"of the finest examples of the short story form we've ever seen and a must read for any fans of Nabokov/Lolita"*.

And finally a bit of TV news. The fifth season of the excellent *Homicide: Life on the Street* has just ended in the States and a few of the major characters obviously aren't renewing their contracts. The Emmy nominations have just been released and once again Homicide wasn't nominated for Best Drama. Without a shadow of a doubt it is one of the most consistently intelligent, provocative and well-acted programmes on television. Over here this kind of thinking is reflected in the fact that we have to content ourselves with series 4 re-runs which, once again and for no apparent reason, don't include the first two in the series.

The Thrilling Detective Web site

One of the many advantages to visiting this excellent and well organised site is the fact that I write for it! But don't let that scare you! The basic premise is to collate listings for every Private Eye ever created. This rather daunting task reflects the incredible knowledge and enthusiasm of the sites creator, Kevin Smith. Not only are there selected comments on PIs but there are also extensive notes and lists on the characters books, shorts stories, TV and film appearances. No small task and one which, in its enormity, opens the way for you to offer your very own contributions positively encouraged by Kev, a true web democrat. In addition to all this the site offers some amazing resources: great links, trivia, incredible book searching links, a monthly P.I. Poll, news and hopefully soon, some featured showcase writings. All in all, well worth pointing your mouse at. The site is at:

http://www.colba.net/~kvn-smith/thrillingdetective/

And a big thanks you to Kev Smith of *Thrilling Detective* site for his newsgathering.

Writers in London

RM Eversz

Jack Higgins

Richard Price

WHETHER THEY ENJOY a bagel from a New York bakery or a butter-basted lobster on the isle of Jersey, writers on the publicity trail usually end up sampling the culinary delights of London. The hard-pressed hack trying to interview New York's Richard Price, Jersey's Jack Higgins and RM Eversz (Prague, out of L. A.) all on the same day, finds himself tracking down his beleaguered authors on their way to meals. The laconic, street-wise chronicler of urban low-life, Price (with a new novel from Bloomsbury, *Freedomland*) is grabbing a snack in the luxurious surroundings of Brown's Hotel, while the wealthy Higgins is on his way from a penthouse suite at the Dorchester to a black-tie dinner. Eversz is reading in an Islington bookshop, before sampling one of that area's well-known cluster of eateries.

The personal styles of all three men could not be more different. Price, with his brooding looks and mop of curly hair, may be showing the effects of his publicity schedule,

by Barry Forshaw

but remains a raw, punchy and prickly interviewee. Higgins, by contrast, is the practised interviewee to the point of smooth perfection – the interviewer has to quickly abandon any agenda they may have (or struggle bloody hard to get back on the rails). Eversz is witty, articulate and urbane.

Price enjoyed considerable success with his last book *Clockers*, and is reconciled to the fact that more people know it through Spike Lee's movie (about which Price has very mixed feelings), than via his original novel. His acerbic, knowledgeable narratives make salient points about the lower strata of life in LA, and he's struck by the similarities between the racist events of *Freedomland* and the Stephen Lawrence case enjoying much coverage during his visit (both life and art have a sympathetic black man eloquently trying to persuade black special interest groups hijacking a miscarriage of justice for their own ends).

His first answers to questions are monosyllabic and tired-sounding, but one is soon aware of a sharp and incisive intellect which, combined with his remarkable literary panache, has made him a writer to be reckoned with.

Critics have likened Price to Nelson Algren, the latter finally enjoying long overdue reappraisal as the definitive American chronicler of blue-collar life, but Price only knows of his work through the Sinatra movie of *Man with the Golden Arm* – which he concedes, is hardly a way to judge a writer's work. And Price knows about screenwriting. Although he underplays his contribution, movies such as Pacino's *Sea of Love* and the Scorsese adaptation of Tevis' *The Colour of Money* owe much to Price's powerful screenplays, even though they enjoyed the usual strip-mining on the way to the screen. But he's philosophical. His philosophy is: if you've been fucked several times, there's no use pretending you're a virgin.

While denying that he is a crime writer, he acknowledges the centrality of crime to his genuinely epic narratives. And his every word reflects the unsentimental, tough version of social realism his books trade in. If his conversation is rough-hewn, this is absolutely of a piece with his writing.

The contrast with Higgins in his even more well-upholstered surroundings could not be more marked. Even before the pleasantries are exchanged and the tape-recorder's turned on, Higgins, checked into the Dorchester under his other writing name (and real name) of Harry Patterson, has a new thriller from Michael Joseph, *Flight of Eagles*. He's also holding forth with fascinating anecdotes about the filming of the book that really made his name, *The Eagle has Landed*. And he's telling you about the Hollywood legends he's met, from Mitchum to Connery…so it's with difficulty that one gets him back to his writing. The supreme self-confidence he casually displays could be off-putting, but somehow isn't. After all, he's noted for the ingenuity of his plots, and if he's the first to point this out, it's difficult to argue with him. The line from Sapper and Buchan (often invoked in connection with his name) is clear enough, but there's no anti-semitism here – although Jewish elements in a recent book prevented it being filmed for complicated reasons.

Unlike many a writer, Higgins is more than ready to reveal carefully-constructed plot developments in forthcoming books – not to be repeated here – but is at pains to point out that his books are character-, rather than plot-driven. And the physicality of his books is mirrored in the pride he feels in wearing his considerable years so lightly.

It's hard to find out quite why Higgins has remained so prolific: financial considerations are clearly not an issue. The Protestant work ethic, he wryly concedes. And after several more well-turned anecdotes, the interviewer finds himself in the lengthy and tastefully upholstered corridors of the Dorchester, trying to find a door that resembles a lift.

A bookshop on Islington Green is a suitably cosmopolitan setting for a reading by the even more cosmopolitan crime novelist R. M. Eversz. Speaking to him in an upper room (formerly the site of England's last musical hall, Collins), the urbane and good-looking Eversz gazes out at the treetops and talks about his own odyssey from Los Angeles to Prague (where he lived for some time). The con-man hero in his tortuous and witty *Gypsy Hearts* (recently published by Pan) was inspired by Eversz's meeting with a florid businessman on a Prague-bound train. Eversz tells how his assumptions that the businessman was on his way to open new wine markets were quickly confounded by the latter's real motive: the sexual availability of women in that country since the collapse of Communism. His novel's reptilian but attractive hero meets an equally duplicitous woman who takes him for every cent he's got, with the result that he falls desperately in love with her. And while Price had earlier made clear that he didn't consider himself a crime novelist, Eversz is happy to have that sobriquet affixed. Ironically, his writing is every inch as 'literary' as Price's (if not more so), but he points out his immense love for the genre. Even the clichés attract him, he tells me, and he's happy to subvert these. The subsequent reading to an enthusiastic audience proves how resoundingly he's able to do this: a description of a clumsily executed killing grips the audience by the throat. And despite Eversz's initial nervousness, he soon demonstrates something highly unusual for an author reading from his own work – an actor's ability to hold the audience with a glittering eye. After the usual pressing of the flesh, those trendy bistros beckon, where Eversz and his publishers no doubt hope for the kind of success that this pithily written tale undoubtedly deserves.

Back Issues

Crime Time 1 Our debut issue contains interviews with John Harvey, Martina Cole, Derek Raymond, Andrew Klavan (*True Crime*). Plus, features on *Cracker*, Colin Wilson, Griff, Dannie M Martin, and our notorious reviews section.

Crime Time 2 Sorry, sold out.

Crime Time 3 We interview Robert Rodriguez (*Desperado*) and Michael Mann (*Heat*), investigate the transvestite hitman fiction of Ed Wood Jr, talk the talk with Elizabeth George, Elliott Leyton, and Lawrence Block, give the low-down on German crime fiction, and feature an article by Booker prize nominee Julian Rathbone.

Crime Time 4 'The Violence Issue' Reservoir Dog, ex-con and writer Edward Bunker tells us how it is, Ben Elton takes the piss out of it, Joe Eszterhas exploits it, Morgan Freeman abhors it. Plus *Mission: Impossible*, *Heaven's Prisoners* (Phil Joanou), *Curdled*, Kinky Friedman, *The Bill* and *The Verdict!*.

Crime Time 5 Female Trouble! Interviews with Patricia Cornwell, Michael Dibdin, James Sallis and William Gibson. *Feisty Femmes And Two- Fisted Totty* gives the lowdown on women PIs, Ed Gorman talks about Gold Medal books of the Fifties, Hong Kong filmmakers Wong Kar-Wai & Christopher Doyle discuss *Fallen Angels*, and Michael Mann (*Heat*) is examined.

Crime Time 6 The Mean Streets issue contains interviews with writers James Ellroy, Gwendoline Butler, Sara Paretsky and Joseph Hansen, and film directors George Sluizer and Andrew Davis. Articles include Post-War Paperback Art, Batman, Crime Time:The Movie, and Steve Holland's excellent Pulp Fictions.

Crime Time 7 Val McDermid, Hong Kong Cinema, Phillip Margolin, Molly Brown, Ian Rankin, Michael Connelly, Daniel Woodrell and a cast of 1000s in this special 96 page issue!

Crime Time 8 Fantastic! Homicide, Faye and Jonathan Kellerman, Mark Timlin, Anthony Frewin, Gerald Kersh, Gwendoline Butler, Chandler on Celluloid, James Sallis on Chester Himes, The Payback Press and the biggest review section yet!

Crime Time 9 We *Got Carter*, with *Get Carter!* director Mike Hodges writing about making the film and Paul Duncan profiling the man who wrote *Jack's Return Home*. This plus scads of good stuff and the inimitable review section...

Crime Time 10 *Sin City*, Ed Gorman interviewed, Lawrence Block in the Library, Stella Duffy, Lauren Henderson, Sean Hughes, Denise Danks, Jerome Charyn and a cast of squillions...

Crime Time 11 Shut It!!! *The Sweeney* cover feature with those cheeky chappies Regan and Carter, Colin Dexter, Sparkle Hayter, David Williams, Gary Phillips, Janwillem Van De Wetering and the Great Grandam of kid's crime Enid Blyton.

Crime Time 12 The Last Time! (In floppy format anyway!) Joe R Lansdale, Simon Brett, Jay Russell, Steve Lopez, James Patterson, *Black Mask* magazine and the late Derek Raymond on Ted Lewis.

Each issue is £3.00 post paid in the UK (please add £3.00 p&p per order overseas and Southern Ireland). Make cheques payable to 'Crime Time' and send your orders to: Back Issues (Dept CT2.2) Crime Time, 18 Coleswood Rd, Harpenden, Herts AL5 1EQ.

Subscriptions
Free Book Offer!

So, you like getting free books? No? Well tough luck, 'cos we've a barrel load to get shot of, and your only evasion tactic is to choose the one you'll least dislike.

When you subscribe to the new format Crime Time—more pages than you can shake a stick at for £4.99, you'll receive five issues of Crime Time for fourpence more than the cost of four and, you can obtain a major contribution to work literature free! Choose from *The Crime Time Filmbook* (voted *the* book to heave by your side in case of a dispute on the formal aspects of the crime film) or *The Third Degree* (the soul of a writer and/or writers stripped naked). Printed on long lasting 'paper'(TM), these books form a valuable addition to any pile of other books.

Marvel! As John Ashbrook proves that mobile phones really *are* annoying with a galaxy of film professionals!

Watch and wonder! As Derek Raymond (*"It's gin, darling!"*) explains the intricacies of the 'Black Novel' (not to be confused with the Black Novel).

Make a loud oohing sound! As Patricia Cornwell, Elizabeth George, Lawrence Block, James Ellroy and a cast of millons join in! Watch as anyone who's anyone in crime fiction opens their mouths!

Simply send a cheque for £20, made payable to '**Crime Time,**' to: **Subscriptions Dept, Crime Time (Dept 2.2), 18 Coleswood Rd, Harpenden, Herts AL5 1EQ.**

Remember to include your name, address and the title of your free book. Don't forget that last bit now!

Overseas Subscriptions: One issue £6.00/four issues £24.00 and you're not eligible for the free book offer due to copyright restrictions—sorry!

Please phone 01582 712244 and pay by VISA or Mastercard.

NOTHING PERSONAL
by Jason Starr

Praise for Jason's Starr's first novel, Cold Caller:

"*Well crafted and very scary.*"—The Times

"*Cool, deadpan, a rollercoaster ride to hell*"—The Guardian

"*Tough, composed and about as noir as you can go. Starr is a worthy successor to Charles Willeford*"- Literary Review

"*Tough, dark, elegant, pure 90's noir*"—Ed Bunker

"*Darkly brilliant noir of the old school.*"—Richmond Review

"*At the cutting edge of the revival of classic American noir fiction*" - Daily Telegraph

Jason Starr is just 30 years old and lives in New York. Former playwright, perfume, computer and state of the art, unrippable panty hose salesman, now self declared expert on horse racing, gambling, American Football and baseball, he is still selling his very soul in telesales.

ISBN: 1 901982 05 X PRICE: £6.99

A NO EXIT ORIGINAL PAPERBACK

THE DOGS OF WINTER
by Kem Nunn

"A profound study of skill, courage and the human psyche."—Robert Stone

Heart Attacks is California's last secret spot—the premier mysto surf haunt, the stuff of rumour and legend. Down and out photographer, Jack Fletcher, hitches up with surfing legend, Drew Harmon, active men past their prime, formerly heroic figures still trying to catch the perfect wave. Harmon's wife, Kendra is on an obsessive search of her own to find the murderer of a local girl. Quests converge and events play themselves out in ways that are both inevitable and surprising and provide an epic homage to the ragged nobility of wounded man.

"Nunn explores the consequences of failure, the demands of courage and the healing powers of penance. A serious, richly satisfying novel infused wi

"As if Elmore Leonard and Cormac McCarthy had teamed up to write a surf novel."—Village Voice

"This is the greatest novel ever written about surfing."—Newsweek

ISBN: 1 901982 35 1 PRICE: £6.99 Pbk
ISBN: 1 901982 50 5 PRICE: £12 Hbk
(500 copy Limited edition—100
copies signed & numbered)
A NO EXIT ORIGINAL

Most Wanted

Writing about crime...

McQueen and Me
Charles Waring

TO ANYONE UNDER THIRTY, the name 'Steve McQueen' probably doesn't hold any magic or mean a great deal. But in my early teens, there was no doubt that Steve McQueen was God. My friends and I all had push-bikes, and out of school hours we could usually be found down at the old recreation ground, attempting to emulate McQueen's daring feat in *The Great Escape*, as we sought to jump and wheelie our way across the banks of a small brook.

As awkward adolescents attempting to grapple with our own raging hormones and a frustrating sense of sexual inadequacy in that nebulous twilight world between childhood and adulthood, McQueen was everything we aspired to be.

He was effortlessly cool and made inarticulacy an art form. He didn't say much and often didn't do much, but he was the ultimate cool hero. For recalcitrant teenagers who despised authority, McQueen was an inspiration. Yet despite the fact that he was always a rebel, you instinctively knew he was a good guy.

Of course, when I saw *Bullitt* for the first time in the early seventies on TV, the iconic reverence and awe we held McQueen in grew even more. Here was a man who could not only throw bikes around in the most spectacular fashion, but cars too! It didn't matter that he was playing a cop. He was still cool and still a rebel. He was still Steve McQueen.

And this was the movie that captured the enigmatic essence of McQueen.

Bullit—The Background

Thirty years, let me tell you, is a lot of time. It's almost half a human lifetime, and many people will find it hard to believe that *Bullitt*, the film that catapulted American actor, Steve McQueen, to superstar status at the box office, celebrates its thirtieth anniversary this year.

The public's interest in the film has recently been re-awakened by an expensive (60 grand, so I'm led to believe) car ad which appeared on our television screens at the tail-end of last year. Utilising Lalo Schifrin's exciting original theme from the movie, the advert cleverly used seamless computer editing to intercut and superimpose old footage of McQueen so he appears to be at the wheel of a brand new vehicle. Very stylish and very effective, but despite the arresting visuals, one doubts whether McQueen would seriously consider getting inside the vehicle in question!

More important, however, was the fact that a new generation were getting a taste of *Bullitt* for the first time. The ad no doubt boosted the credibility of the Ford Puma (there, I've said it!) and probably accounted for increased sales but it also was responsible for resurrecting the original movie, which reappeared as a widescreen video as part of a Maverick Directors series. The soundtrack too, benefited from exposure on the small screen, resulting not only in the re-issue of the full score but the release of the main theme as a CD single (contemporary remixes and all), which notched up sufficient sales to register in the lower echelons of the top fifty!

So, not a bad result from one (all-too-brief) thirty second sequence of celluloid. I should think Warner Entertainment laughed all the way to the bank, which is ironic, really, when you consider that they didn't even want to make the movie in the first place, regarding it as a potential flop!

But then, so had Steve McQueen at the outset. He had always regarded himself as an outsider, a rebel. In real life and on film, he was an anti-authority figure. When he was approached to consider the idea of movie based around a police detective, he found the notion almost repugnant: *"No way am I playin' a cop. Those kids call 'em pigs, man. What are you trying to do to me?"*

His early objections seemed rooted in his own bad experiences at the hands of the law when he was a juvenile. But, as history shows, of course, McQueen eventually relented and changed his mind about the project. McQueen was worried about alienating his own fan-base. He was, after all, supposed to be the quintessential authority-hating rebel. After serious deliberation, McQueen thought that the film had the potential to help change his public's perception of the police by presenting a picture of the contemporary cop that was realistic, down to earth and someone they had more in common with than they realised.

In fact, the extent of McQueen's change of attitude towards the police is borne out by the tale of his being stopped for speeding. Legend has it that when the cop realised who he had pulled over, he became embarrassed and deeply apologetic. But, as was McQueen's wont, rather than use his star status as a lever to gain favour and reduce his punishment, the actor was insistent that he should be booked. He apparently was heard to utter afterwards "...*those guys aren't so bad, you know. Some of them are OK*"

This was the first movie that McQueen's own production company, Solar, was involved in. They had a contract with Warner Brothers to deliver five movies. *Bullitt* was to be the first. As a result of his increased responsibility, McQueen had a big say-so in the hiring and firing of staff for the movie.

The screenplay was written by former lawyer, Alan Trustman (who had also written the script for McQueen's previous movie, the dazzling crime-caper *The Thomas Crown Affair*) and Harry Kleiner, based upon the novel *Mute Witness* by Robert L Pike. The screenplay went through several mutations until one that was deemed satisfactory by all parties was arrived at.

McQueen was urged by a friend to see the British movie *Robbery*, directed by Peter Yates. It was only Yates's third film and starred Welsh actor Stanley Baker (he of *Zulu* fame) in a plot that was loosely based on the Great Train Robbery of 1963. Among other things, this hard-boiled suspense movie featured a heart-stopping car chase. After seeing *Robbery*, McQueen was adamant that Yates was the man to direct *Bullitt*.

For the relatively unknown Yates, this was his first taste of the Hollywood big-time. As such, he was unaware of McQueen's reputation as a "*difficult*" actor to work with (directors Don Siegel, Norman Jewison and Mark Rydell had all experienced acrimonious on-set disputes with McQueen). Yates, however, established a creative rapport with the movie-star, remarking that McQueen was a "*delight*" to work with and "...*incredibly supportive at all times.*"

The supporting cast was handpicked by McQueen and Yates. But some of the recruiting was not easy. Robert Vaughan, for example, was not initially enamoured with his proposed role as Chalmers. In fact, he turned down the part three times before finally accepting. He was associated with altogether lighter parts (such as Napoleon Solo in *The Man From Uncle* series) than the one he ended up playing in *Bullitt*. For Vaughan and his portrayal of the Machiavellian slime-ball Chalmers, it was ultimately a brave move away from potential type-casting as a romantic leading-man. *Bullitt* was the vehicle that saw him move away from playing heroes to more shady characters.

But it was a gamble that paid off, as he later explained: *"All the roles I was doing were romantic, tongue-in-cheek, semi-humorous characters. The role of Chalmers set the pattern, which kept me employed for the next twenty years in terms of motion pictures and television."*

The movie's love-interest was provided by young British actress, Jacqueline Bissett. Like Yates, her British counterpart, the twenty three year old Bissett was relatively new to Hollywood. Frank Bullitt's detective partner in the film, Delgetti, was played by actor Don Gordon, an old friend and acting buddy of McQueen's (in only his first film role).

At the instigation of Peter Yates, McQueen and Don Gordon paid a visit to the San Francisco police department to research the background material for their respective roles. Certainly, both actors soon got an insight into the modern day role of a police detective. There is an interesting and humorous anecdote concerning McQueen's own background experience for his role of Detective Frank Bullitt. He was assigned to tag along with two officers who thought they'd give a cosseted movie star a baptism by fire as initiation into the work. They asked McQueen to meet them at the city morgue, of all places. Little did they know that McQueen himself was an arch tester of people's reactions and looked forward to the challenge. Characteristically cool, the unflappable McQueen turned up at the morgue nonchalantly munching on an apple as he was shown a succession of chilled corpses!

Despite this incident, McQueen's hostility to the police noticeably diminished, as was apparent in his words to journalists when promoting the film: *"We're trying to show what a cop could be like. Everybody dislikes cops till they need one."* It now seems apparent that the time McQueen spent with the San Francisco police department opened his eyes to the difficulties, frustrations and ultimately, reality of the job. Although it's hard to say exactly if McQueen empathised with the police, he did try to invest Frank Bullitt with a believable realism. He wasn't a hero. Just an ordinary man doing an extraordinary and often thankless job.

When the film began shooting in February of 1968, troubles with Warner Brothers were already on the horizon. A change of personnel at the company (having been taken over by Seven Arts) resulted in a series of mutual misunderstandings which ultimately precipitated distrust on both sides.

The first stumbling block in an already deteriorating relationship with Warner was the actual location for the movie. Warners wanted to cut costs and restrict the film to one of its studio lots where much of its television work was done. McQueen, however, was insistent that they shoot the movie on location in San Francisco itself: *"The theatre is the streets, where the people are. You can't stage it. You have to be there."*

The deadlock was broken by the timely intervention of the Mayor of San Francisco. He struck a deal with McQueen's Solar productions: the city would co-operate fully if extras were employed from the city's gangland areas (and paid at the going rate, according to the Screen Extras Guild scale). Solar also made a donation to one of the city's all-black areas in the form of a community swimming pool. Consequently, Warner, albeit reluctantly, ended their opposition to the idea.

As a result, the film set a precedent by becoming the first major movie to elude the studio's possessive clutches and be shot entirely on location with a bona fide Hollywood crew.

However, friction with Warner Brothers continued right through the making of the film. Mainly, the gripes were about money. Warners claimed that the film was over budget by one million dollars with costs escalating from a proposed five to six million dollars. The tension between the Hollywood studio and Solar productions reached boiling point when McQueen ejected all Warner/Seven Arts executives from the set. In this particular battle of wills, McQueen was not averse to using his star status to procure favours and ensure that things ran as smoothly as possible. Also, McQueen, who had a propensity for conflict with authority, projected himself as the focus of the disagreements, and according to Peter Yates, *"protected us like mad from the studio."*

Four months after shooting had commenced, *Bullitt* finally wrapped up in May 1968. Warner Brothers were so deeply pessimistic about the movie that none of their executives bothered to turn up and attend pre-screening showings of the film. At one of these performances, black American musician Quincy Jones, hired to compose the soundtrack, was heard to exclaim in regard of the film *"That's a motherfucker!"* Ironically, though, Jones, enthusiastic as he undoubtedly was about the project, was unable to commit himself to the film as a result of a burst appendix which hospitalised him two weeks before he was due to commence work. Argentinean jazz composer Lalo Schifrin received the commission and brought to the film a cool, stylish, jazz-flavoured score.

A somewhat bemused Peter Yates was told by one enthusiastic viewer: *"I don't think you quite realise what you've got here. This film is going to guarantee you another nine years in the business."*

On 17th October 1968, *Bullitt* was premiered at Radio City Music Hall in San Francisco. The feedback and reaction from the movie was phenomenal, both from an artistic/critical perspective and financial one. The film easily recouped the original finance invested in it, grossing an estimated 18 million dollars on the domestic front and 33 worldwide.

Bullitt was McQueen's fifth box-office hit in a row and for many of the other people involved in the film, the success of the movie acted as a springboard for greater recognition.

Bullitt—The Plot

Steve McQueen plays Detective Frank Bullitt, a taciturn but quick-thinking, pragmatic San Francisco cop. Bullitt has been assigned to protect a government witness over the weekend before taking him before a Senate sub-committee hearing the following Monday morning. The instigator of this is the politically ambitious Chalmers (Robert Vaughan), a slimy, morally questionable individual who manipulates by a mixture of charm and veiled threats. The witness is taken to the Hotel Daniels under Bullitt's protection. During the night, however, two hitmen break into the room and succeed in shooting the witness. He is taken to the hospital but dies. Frank Bullitt, however, suspects a conspiracy afoot and stalls Chalmers by moving the body under the pretext that the witness is still alive.

After many twists and turns, Bullitt is eventually vindicated to leave Chalmers with a tarnished image and egg all over his face, but not before a thrilling car chase and climax at the airport have sent adrenaline levels sky high.

Bullitt—Those famous stunts

That Damned Car Chase!

Or at least that's how the film's original director Peter Yates views it. For Yates, the film was a film that unlocked the gates of Hollywood, as he acknowledges: *"That was my first film in America and without it, I wouldn't be here now."* Unfortunately, though, as well as a talisman, the film has become a bit of an albatross around his neck: *"It's annoying at times, because people talk more about* Bullitt *than any other of my films. I've had two films nominated for an Academy Award (*Breaking Away *and* The Dresser*) and they still want to talk about that damned car chase! That's Hollywood for you."*

Amazingly, the celebrated car chase almost never happened. Peter Yates had just done a car chase in *Robbery* and wasn't, in his own words *"up to another chase."* McQueen, similarly wasn't altogether keen on the idea as he was preparing for the film *Le Mans*. In fact, it wasn't until filming was well under way that the suggestion of a car chase was proposed. The stunt driving occupied the last scheduled two weeks of filming.

Of course, at the heart of McQueen's mythology and appeal with the public was the notion that he did all the stunts himself. In fact, as with McQueen's celebrated motorcycle jump in the 1963 movie *The Great Escape*, nothing could be further from the truth.

The stunt sequence for the film was co-ordinated by Carrie Lofton, who had a long association with McQueen which stretched back into the nineteen fifties. McQueen regarded Lofton as the best in the business. Lofton, however, while respecting McQueen as a *"good driver"* believed that *"there's a difference between a good driver and a stunt driver."* McQueen, though, regarded his own driving skills highly (he actually finished second behind racing star Mario Andretti in the 1970 Sebring 12-hour race!)and had begun doing the stunt driving himself. It was patently obvious to onlookers that McQueen had none of the control and expertise to pull off the shots that were needed. To the alarm of those present, he succeeded in crashing and spinning the car on several occasions. In desperation, Lofton contacted an old friend of McQueen's, Bud Ekins, stunt motorcyclist and a motorcycle shop owner. Lofton's advice to Ekins was uncompromising: *"Get him out of the fucking car. He's going to kill somebody!"*

The major difficulty with the chase sequence was the fact that for the first time in movies, the cars would be travelling at genuine high speeds (in excess of 100 m.p.h.). Given the fact that the movie was shot entirely on location on San Francisco's hilly, winding streets increased the potential for real hazard and danger.

With safety paramount in the eyes of Lofton and Ekins, on the day of the most difficult and perilous stunt, they arranged to do it without McQueen's knowledge. In fact, McQueen received a late wake-up call, engineered for the specific purpose of keeping him out of the way and out of the action. McQueen's friend, Bud Ekins was already throwing the car in dramatic fashion over the city's hills when the irate movie star arrived on set. At the completion of the stunt, McQueen rushed over to the car to find Bud Ekins inside. Legend has it that McQueen furiously demanded where Ekins had learned to drive like that. Ekins, somewhat sheepishly, replied: *"I don't know, Steve."*

Ekins, of course, was the man who did the thrilling motorcycle stunt in *The Great Escape*, jumping the bike over the prison-camp fence to freedom. Most moviegoers were under the misapprehension that it was McQueen on the bike, doing his own stunt. McQueen confessed, albeit reluctantly, to Ekins's involvement on the Johnny Carson Show. The thought that he was being upstaged again rankled him as is evident in what he allegedly said to Ekins: *"You fucker, You're doing it again. The Great Escape, right? I had to go up in front of the whole world and tell them I didn't make that jump over the fence and the same thing's gonna happen all over again. I'm going to have to go on the Johnny Carson show and tell him I didn't do it again!"*

Beginning on the rolling, hilly streets of San Francisco, McQueen's green 390GT Mustang pursues the two bad guys out onto the freeway, reaching speeds of over one hundred miles an hour. As Bullitt closes on the other vehicle he dramatically dodges gunshots as they attempt to force each other off the road. The chase culminates in an explosion at a petrol station when the car Bullitt is pursuing careers off the road out of control.

His part of the sequence represented the most expensive shot of the whole movie and had to be done in one, perfect take. However, according to Peter Yates, the car in fact *"overshot the gas pumps"* but no one realised this because of some ingenious back-room editing.

Chase at the Airport

"I did it and walked away and I don't want to do that again." These are the words of stunt man extraordinaire, Loren Janes. He was referring, of course, to the end sequence of *Bullitt* which involved another celebrated but potentially fatal stunt. This is the scene where Frank Bullitt chases original witness turned killer, Johnny Ross, across a busy airport runway at night. While in hot pursuit of Ross, Bullitt has to duck under a moving Boeing 707 passenger jet. Apart from being run over, the main hazard was being incinerated by 240 degree heat blasts from the jet's engines. Add to this scenario some unpredictable crosswind gusts at the time of shooting and you can understand why none of the pilots or the Federal Aviation Authority wanted to be involved with the project in any shape or form. One pilot, however, after much persuasion re-considered, thereby giving the scene the green light.

In one breath-taking, life-threatening shot, Loren Janes ran across the path of a moving plane and positioned himself to fall on the runway tarmac between its undercarriage as the plane passed over him. Scary! And he only got paid five thousand dollars for it.

Bullitt—A Final Evaluation

Bullitt, with its tough, uncompromising anti-hero pays homage to the crime movies of Bogart's era, but brought cops and robbers into the modern age with McQueen's reticent performance and realistic portrayal of the moral ambiguities that invest both heroes and villains.

Although McQueen found himself wrestling with his instincts by playing a cop, the personality of the actor is ultimately indistinguishable from the character he plays. You always feel that McQueen is being himself. To all extents and purposes, then, McQueen is Frank Bullitt, a perfect picture of cool under pressure, still shaking off the shackles of authority even when on the right side of the law. A rebel to the end.

Although the epic car chase is the undoubted centrepiece of the film, unlike many of today's action thrillers, there's nothing gratuitous or irrelevant about it. It is a key part of the story and not there merely to titillate.

The film may seem tame to those used to today's over-blown empty Hollywood exercises in screen pyrotechnics but it is a film which still thrills and gives a value-for-money, white-knuckle ride.

In a sense it is a celebration of the motor car. Much of the background noise in the film is provided by cars: the sibilant hiss of passing freeway traffic, the deep guttural throb of McQueen's Mustang, the screech of brakes and tyres, the sound of metal on metal... Whether intentional or not, it is a movie reflecting the ubiquitousness and dominance of motor car culture in late twentieth century life. Something that is a fitting testament to a car fanatic like McQueen.

It is not really surprising, then, that the film should be used as the basis for a car advert in 1997.

Thirty years down the line and the film still holds us in its thrall. It's perhaps surprising how little it has aged. Sure, the cars look a little strange and archaic to us but the film has transcended time and fashion to become a classic.

This seminal movie exerted a huge influence on so-called action thrillers and it made an icon out of Steve McQueen. With his minimal acting style, he says even less than the Arnies, Slys and Bruces of the present, but McQueen as Bullitt still captivates with his charismatic on-screen persona.

At a glance: ten things you never knew about *Bullitt*

- The first McQueen movie in which the word *"bullshit"* was uttered!
- The film received two Academy Award (for Film Editing and Sound)
- The first and last time McQueen was to play a cop.(McQueen was offered the roles of both Dirty Harry and Popeye Doyle in *The French Connection* afterwards but turned them down.)
- The scene in which Bullitt and Delgetti discover a suitcase which might shed some light on the murder is a one-take ad lib.
- Original music for the film was to have been written by Quincy Jones but he fell ill prior to the scoring date.
- The first Hollywood film to be made entirely on location in San Francisco.
- Robert Duvall in one of his early screen roles plays a taxi-driver

who is curiously viewed only from behind in most of the shots he appears in.

- Convinced the movie would be a failure, Warners/Seven Arts cancelled their five deal contract with McQueen's Solar productions mid-way through the picture.
- Most of the really dangerous driving stunts were executed by McQueen's motorcycle pal, Bud Ekins.
- First Hollywood movie for British director Peter Yates.

Bullitt; —The Soundtrack

It's hard to imagine any music other than Lalo Schifrin's accompanying the film, let alone consider the idea that jazz luminary Quincy Jones was originally hired to provide the score.

Like the movie, Schifrin's cool, jazz-influenced music has aged well despite its thirty years, remaining remarkably fresh to the ear. Schifrin, an Argentine, pipe-smoking jazz musician achieved international fame with his theme and incidental music for the TV series *Mission: Impossible.* His other famous themes include *The Cincinnati Kid, Dirty Harry, Enter The Dragon* and *Starsky and Hutch.*

Sources:

Steve McQueen: Portrait of an American Rebel by Marshall Terrill, Plexus 1990

Steve McQueen: The Unauthorised Biography by Malachi McCoy Signet, 1975

The Films of Steve McQueen, by Casey St.Charnez, Citadel Press, 1984

BOX NINE
by Jack O'Connell

"A dark and visionary talent"—Richard Shephard—Waterstones, Hampstead.

"A surrealistic noir epic that's part David Lynch and part Brett Easton Ellis"—Booklist

"The most electrifying debut crime novel you are likely to read all year"—GQ

A stunningly original nightmare novel about the impact of a new synthetic drug—Lingo—on the depressed New England factory town of Quinsigamond, where it was secretly developed. Besides offering a potent high, Lingo also delivers a shot to the brain cells governing linguistic comprehension and verbal skill. Until murderous rages and babbling insanity take over, this mind-expanding feature makes the drug dangerously seductive to the unusually literate cops, scientists and dope dealers competing to find its distribution source. Written in the cranked up style of Lingo, Box 9 shows a noir vision of a city that has become a virtual war zone between warring multi-ethnic drug cartels. The narrative shifts from one head case to another but never loses sight of Detective Leonore Thomas, an undercover officer addicted to speed, rough sex, heavy metal and the feel of her .357 Magnum.

A dark, disturbing book that speaks with a fine fury about the yearning for forbidden knowledge and the langauge to articulate the mysteries it unlocks.

ISBN: 1 901982 27 0 PRICE: £6.99

A NO EXIT ORIGINAL PAPERBACK

Imagine... paperback books so cheap you can read them on the train and then throw them away if you want... hold on...!

Métro-Police
Brad Spurgeon

Olivier Breton

PARIS — When Edgar Allen Poe set a genre-creating short story in the Rue Morgue he could hardly have imagined that a century and a half later France would be continuing the tradition with crime stories not only set in Paris's streets, but sold under them in vending machines in the Métro.

While the imaginary landscape of the French mystery short story is stronger than ever in the 1990's, the marketing techniques are just as original. Since last year commuters have found not only chocolate bars and breath mints in the Métro, but mystery chapbooks selling in the candy bar distributors for the same price as much of the candy: 10 francs (97 pence).

Métro-Police, the idea of publisher Olivier Breton, and crime writer Gérard Delteil, the editor of the collection, has worked so well (each of the more than 30 volumes has sold out their six thousand copy print runs) that boxed sets are now available in bookstores.

But the Métro collection is only one of many original ways the French are feeding mystery short stories to a hungry public. Stories are also popping up as inserts in newspapers — notably in the national dailies *Le Monde* and *Libération* — and on France's mystery writing Internet site, Polar Web (www.mygale.org/00/polar), and in a slew of thematic chapbooks sold for less than 20 francs.

Le Monde's idea was born in autumn 1995 when the top French mystery line, La Série Noire, an imprint of Gallimard, celebrated its 50th anniversary. The newspaper inserted a short story, that by best-selling author Maurice Dantec. The insert was made of the same newsprint of the newspaper, but when pulled out and cut with scissors along a dotted line it became a chapbook with the famous white-framed black covers of the Série Noire books. It was such a success that the newspaper ran mystery stories in the same format throughout the following summer, featuring such popular writers as Didier Daeninckx (who is published by Serpent's Tail in England), Thierry Jonquet, Daniel Pennac, Marc Villard and even France's resident American, Jerome Charyn.

Bertrand Audusse, who was deputy literary editor of *Le Monde* and in charge of the project, said, *"At first I thought of doing a collection of stories from several different genres, since I was afraid just one genre might be boring for the readers."*

But he settled for running only his passion of crime stories.

"As a journalist," he said, *"I decided to have examples of the many different styles in the genre, except for the puzzle mystery. It was definitely all in the noir style."*

They were later sold as an anthology, and the next summer *Le Monde* ran another series, but featuring French women mystery writers Andrea H. Japp, Brigitte Aubert, Fred Vargas, and foreigners Ruth Rendell and Elizabeth George. This summer *Le Monde* ran short story inserts during the World Cup, each one using that event as a theme.

Le Monde's summer mystery story innovation developed imitators, and jealous neighbours. A regional newspaper, *Sud-Ouest Dimanche*, in the south of France, also ran a series by many top writers, and they were compiled by a small publisher called Zulma, into an excellent collection, *Neuf Morts et Demi* (*Nine and a Half Deaths*). *Libération*, the left-wing national daily, apparently decided that it was not to be upstaged by *Le Monde*, its staid voice-of-authority competitor.

This summer *Libération* commissioned 17 writers of the *Série Noire* to write crime stories using short news reports published in the newspaper as their point of departure. For three weeks in July a short story by a top French crime writer adorned the central pages of the newspaper and was illustrated by ink drawings.

The newspaper's marketing director, André Gattolin, had at first wanted to publish a chapter a day of a crime novel, but he never found anything that he felt worked in that format. It was in speaking to Franҫis Mizio, *Libération's* cyber writer and an upcoming crime writer, that he decided on the formula of using short news reports as a point of departure.

Mizio had, last March, developed and judged a contest in an Internet discussion group devoted to the French mystery story, that worked on the same principle. Members of the discussion group were given a report from Agence France-Presse about a Japanese businessman who had arranged his own murder in order to give his family the insurance money. The contestant were told to fabricate a crime story using that as their starting point. They were given a few weeks to do so before a group of crime writers and specialists judges voted on the winner. All the stories were posted on Polar-Web, and the winner was to be published in a fanzine called *Caïn*.

Indeed, mystery short story contests are sprouting up all over the country, as part of mystery writing festivals, fanzines, or even major publishers' efforts at promotion. The top publishing house Editions du Seuil is sponsoring a contest for mystery short stories that closes on 30 October this year. The winners will be published in an anthology, and winners and runners up will receive the 79 crime novels from the publishers' mystery collection.

Most publishers large and small are jumping on the short mystery bandwagon. Fleuve Noir last year assembled a collection of 12 stories by top French writers, called *Douze et Ameres*, and recently came out with another; Le Masque published one by Fred Kassak and this year by its leading French woman writer, Japp; and Maud Tabachnik, another leading woman crime novelist, did one at Editions Viviane Hamy.

The chapbook rage has been exploited not only by the Métro editions, but by several small publishers, including one called *Mille et unes nuits* (*1001 Nights*), with a collection called, *Dix Petits Noirs*, that included a story by the aforementioned Mr Poe. Editions Baleine, a prolific new mystery press, created a line of chapbooks selling for 19 francs, called *Tourisme et Polar*. 'Polar' is a word for a crime story, and each one also reads like a travel account. For instance, *L'Egarement*, by Michel Lebrun, the late writer, translator and critic, paints a vivid picture of his neighborhood in Paris around the Place de Clichy.

Lebrun also compiled the 1995 anthology, *La Creme du Crime* (*Cream of the Crime*) along with Claude Mesplède, an anthologist and encyclopedist. It is a thousand page volume of the best mystery stories by French writers from Alphonse Allais (1854 - 1905) to Marc Villard, today's consummate nouvelliste.

The golden age of the mystery short story in France, said Mesplède, was from the 1940's to the 1960's, when the *Ellery Queen Mystery Magazine* and *The Saint Magazine* were published here.

"After that," he said, "it was difficult to find places to publish short stories. I think we always had short story writers, but the problem was that no one could — or wanted to— publish them. They'd say that the French don't like short stories.

Which always puzzled me. Maupassant is a master, after all, and we still read him."

Mesplède agrees that the short mystery has never been healthier in France than today, with some writers, like Villard, who *"are better with short texts; and others, like Pascal Dessaint, who are as good in both novels and short stories."*

Villard's stories are typical in that they fall decidedly in the noir category, and do not often depend on a strong plot. Rather they illuminate epiphanic moments in their characters' lives, that are usually linked to crimes. As in the story, *Quinze ans (Fifteen Years Old)*, where a girl of fifteen who lives in a poor suburb wants to go out into the world. This, we discover, means going out and stabbing someone to death. Where Villard's stories are atypical is that their main characters are frequently young women (who are not all murderers). In the mostly macho world of French crime writing, this is a refreshing change.

"When I go to the poor suburbs outside Paris to readings and whatnot," said Villard, *"I notice that it's the young women, either French or of north African origin, who are often very attentive to the work of the writer, and who ask the questions. And I noticed that in these poor areas that are hit by drugs, violence, and gangs, that the people who have the strength, the energy, and the desire to break out of that world are frequently the young women. While the boys have a tendency to fall into the gangs and violence or just desperation."*

Villard has published 10 novels and 10 collections of short stories since 1980. The 1990's have seen a wave of young writers who excel in both the long and short forms. Many are published by a small press called Editions La Loupiote, based in the Atlantic coastal town Le Poiré sur Vie. Run by a school teacher named François Braud, the house was founded on the short story after Braud went to mystery festivals for years and discovered that there was much excellent short mystery fiction out there, but that it was homeless.

The collection's first books were called 'Zebras', as each volume consisted of two short stories, one by a well-known writer, one by an unknown. Some of the unknowns have since come into their own, like the aforementioned Françis Mizio. After publishing a Zebra last year Mizio then published his first novel at La Loupiote, and a collection of short stories, *Le Pape de l'art Pauvre (The Pope of Poor Art)*, in January 1998. Mizio had been submitting stories to contests for a decade, and winning most of them. This fall he is leaving his job at *Libération* to write fiction full-time, having recently sold novels to the mainstream publisher Flammarion, and to the Série Noire.

Jean-Hugues Oppel, 40, who has written mystery novels since 1983, also published an excellent collection at La Loupiote in January, as did the aforementioned Dessaint — both writers' novels are published at Editions Rivages, where the Mystery Writers of America's 1997 Ellery Queen Award winner François Guérif is editor. The Loupiote's line was inaugurated by a collection by the pope of today's French mystery writers, Jean-Bernard Pouy.

Mizio and Dessaint stories are often spiked with black humor, like many of the best French stories. Tonino Benacquista's, *Pizza d'Italie*, appears in his collection at Rivages, and in the *Cream of the Crime* anthology. It was originally commissioned for an anthology of stories taking place around the Place d'Italie in Paris. It is an outrageously funny tale of a serial killer whose victims are pizza delivery boys on motor scooters. Police start to figure out the killer's motive when they find that the victim's pizza boxes are always empty.

Collections such as that based on a theme or a place are very popular, and many were born from regional crime festivals. The biggest such festival, at the Atlantic port of St. Nazaire, has several short story contests, including ones for local school students. Last year for the 10th anniversary of the festival they created a miniature boxed set of the 10 winning stories of the main competition for each of the festival's years. The southern town of Villefranche-de-Rouergue is the theme of *Villefranche, Ville Noire*, a collection put together for that town's first festival, and published by Zulma.

Braud, who has been to almost every edition of the St. Nazaire festival, is also publisher of one of the top fanzines, *Caïn*, that features short stories in every issue. Rivages publishes the top mystery review, called *Polar*, that also contains short stories. Many others have been short-lived, such as *Nouvelle Nuits (Short Story Nights)* and *Ecrivain* magazine, that was run by Villard and his wife Christine Ferniot. Currently *Nouvelle Donne* is devoted entirely to the short story, with a leaning toward the mystery.

This summer financial realities took their toll on La Loupiote, however, and it has temporarily ceased publication while Braud deals with losses incurred through his association with a problematic distributor.

When Braud was asked why he would publish something as apparently suicidal as collections of short stories, he said, somewhat taken aback, *"Because I like them! It's a genre where there's quite a lot of experimentation, where a writer may with a single idea, a single ambience, a single snippet make you see, surprise you, or make you laugh."*

Not to mention you can read one on a single Métro ride too.

Mitch has a dream ... and it involves lots of very hilly streets...

The Streets of San Francisco
Mitch Rice

WHERE TO HOLIDAY THIS YEAR? In imagining the perfect getaway I'm assailed by images of far away places, of different climates, different landscapes and shopping opportunities! We all form mental maps about places from the TV, radio, talking to others, images and of course reading. How we view a geographical location is the essential framework for all our modes of thought. For me, things occur or exist in relation to space and time; without an understanding of where I am the rest of the puzzle doesn't easily fit into place.

Many authors have been known as saying that without the strong sense of the setting of the novel there is no novel, that from the place comes the story. Teri Holbrook, creator of the Gale Grayson books, professes to know more about the setting in her books than she does about the characters, believing that people are born of a place. She wants to understand the land beneath her character's feet before she can actually think of how those feet will travel. For her, the place suggests a story. How characters react to that place develops the story further—adding much more to the novel than an atmospheric backdrop. Living in an 'inner city' environment I am aware, sometimes in only a small way but occasionally significantly, that the language of the environment around me shapes not only what I do but how I react and think. This powerful external process is something I think attracts me to living where I do. It has a language that I understand and rules that I am prepared to live by—for me green fields, open spaces and country coffee mornings instil the fear of God in me. If I was forced to make that move I think I'd leave behind a significant part of what it means to be me.

Elizabeth Daniel Squires is of similar mind. In wanting to concentrate on the plot and characters of her novel she has set her Peaches Dann series in the mountains of North Carolina, an area she knows well. Being familiar with the land, the smells, the details and the customs, the ground beneath

Peaches' feet was drawn effortlessly on to the page. And out of this place the characters grew.

Without making that commitment to change my life beyond recognition I can escape. Travelling in the safety of my own armchair (which is free from plane delays, turbulence and lost luggage), I can explore places I've ever only dreamed of being able to be part of, through the magical world of books. First I'm off to the second most densely populated city in the USA. (I'm definitely magnetised to the urban!), with 700,000 residents crowded into an area of 47 sq. miles, situated at the tip of a hilly peninsula, overlooking the Pacific Ocean- San Francisco.

San Francisco, by modern standards, is a small city. With its physical boundaries of sea on three sides and steep hills inland, urban sprawl is somewhat defeated by geography. The compactness of the city has produced very distinct districts in the city that have a particular and cherished personality. In *The Naked City*, Ralph Willett sees each zone, whether culturally, ethnically or socially, as a miniaturisation of the political and social condition of the USA. This is a strong element in the fiction based in San Francisco. Each particular part of the city has a very symbolic identity that is fixed and identifiable.

The city is overflowing with great novels that explore its many distinct sections and factions. An obvious place to start- Julie Smith's *Tourist Trap*, featuring her lesser known series character Rebecca Schwarz, the Lawyer-sleuth on the hunt for a serial killer targeting tourists in order to somehow punish the city. The city is victim, streets are unerringly empty at night, sidewalks only supporting a hesitant, fearful crowd. The life of the city seems to be draining under the fear the killer has cultured.

Pier 39 plays centre stage to one of the killings. As opposed to an appealing, entertaining tourist's haven, the most visited tourist attraction in the entire country (according to the guide book!), Smith paints a rather different view. One that doesn't have me rushing on to the next cable car to the waterfront. I see instead a hideous crowded ensemble of waterfront kitsch, described beautifully by Smith 'The place makes my skin itch as if it's turned to polyester'. The sad, tacky essence of the place is captured for me, stripped of glamour, the surface paint peeling to reveal a rather shoddy, empty, money making venture. She isn't so harsh on Ghirardelli Square, an old chocolate factory, now a mini-mall enterprise. It fares somewhat better than the fast decaying commercial version of an old, quaint New England fishing village of bygone days that is Pier 39.

As Rebecca fearlessly races towards the climax of the book, with her lover's life dependent on her quick thinking and anticipation, she goes under-cover in the Tenderloin area, a place where mugging is rife and the vision of an urban utopia is far from evident. I salute Rebecca in these closing chapters as a woman of great courage (or stupidity?); she's embarking on a journey into the dark underworld, into the belly of the monster. A place where street corners are over populated with junkies, alcohol soaked depressives, desperate and alert individuals looking for a make. The smell of Thunderbird and urine lift from the page as I reluctantly follow in Rebecca's shadow, taking care where I tread. The picture painted is so real I get the feeling the place suggested the story, rather than the story looking for an area to be anchored to. As Teri Holbrook said "I don't think I could convincingly create characters without first understanding the land beneath their feet". It seems to me that Julie Smith has trodden in the rot many times.

No visit to San Francisco would be complete without a visit to the great, 'founding mother of the contemporary female hard boiled detective novel' (quoted by Grafton), Marcia Muller. Sharon McCone is deeply rooted in the city, which provides the arena in which McCone both lives and works. She operates from one of the huge Victorian fancy houses that give the city many a postcard opportunity. The essence of the city is sought through the weather. The drifting tendrils of fog, swooping in from the bay at just the right time to cloak the city in a dense, mischievous cloud transports me swiftly into the chaos of the city. I almost feel like Sherlock Holmes (disguised as a London cabby, of course), lost in the fog of the East End on the tail of a notorious criminal.

Of course fog is not the most pressing natural threat to disrupt life in the city. Hiding behind the bravado of McCone (who was, as would be expected, single-handedly pulling grateful souls from the wreckage), I've felt the violent tremors of the 1989 earthquake. I have seen the mighty bridge collapse and crush, witnessed the plaster rain from the sky rendering all that seemed invincible-not and been part of that community panic to search for and rescue survivors of the blasts.

In a more positive mood, McCone also takes us to Pier 39. She weaves us around the tourist traps, avoiding the glitz and tack and finds us a nice quiet bench and lets us gaze out along the shoreline in a quite contemplative manner. The calming sea, the incoming fingers of fog (!) and the proximity of the best seafood restaurants in town all provide for a deeply satisfying evening. What more does one need but good food, a gorgeous bottle of superb Californian wine and the sound of waves lapping in the distance? One passage from Muller works quicker than any other relaxation aid I know. And of course it's all followed by a good chunk of sourdough!

Food is the centre around which all else orbits for my next character that is to show me the delights of San Francisco. The food columnist Angie Amalfi, created by San Francisco native Joanne Pence, uses the city's culinary connections to weave mysteries that are full of suspense, farce and romance, three ingredients that rarely mix so harmoniously. And of course her boyfriend (conveniently a Homicide Detective in the SFPD!) adds not only the spice to the books but the insider information Angie needs to go off on her crime busting sprees across the city (which I'm told is not normal for food columnists).

In no other city than San Francisco could you orientate yourself after being abducted, gagged, knocked unconscious and dumped on the floor of a car by the steepness of the incline at which the car is travelling. The city was a very obvious location for Alfred Hitchcock"s *Vertigo*. It must be Telegraph Hill if the car is at such a steep angle—a good time to jump ship and head for safety. And if that's not enough, once free from the car Angie uses the uphill climbs to slow down her wounded attacker. The Streets of San Francisco literally save our heroine's life!

Pence obviously knows and loves her city well. In the opening six pages we've had fog, a mention of the city's great restaurants, the Giants, The Chronicle, cable cars, parking problems and the Marina! San Francisco in a nut shell—obviously a relief for the time limited traveller! Yet however pushed for time you are, a fog experience at least every few chapters is obligatory!

The fog here has us in an almost Hitchcock like grip, the moist shroud adding a menacing B movie feel to the stalking executed by an unknown mystery assailant.

Not put off by this, in fact drawn because of it, my flight is booked- San Francisco here I come! My reading has built up a collage of images in my head that, for me, mean San Francisco—from the span of the orange web-like bridge to the wafting smell of the local Italian Trattoria. I already feel on intimate terms with the city.

Next time you're feeling in the mood for travel, put those Sunday Supplements to one side, ignore the overly enthusiastic travel shows aimed at the uninspired comfort-seeking tourist and shelve those dusty fact and map filled books. Instead, turn to crime!

If you fancy more of San Francisco search out -
Dianne Day- Historical series featuring Fremont Jones
Laurie King- SFPD homicide detectives Kate Martinelli &
Alonzo Hawkin
Lia Matera - Laura di Palma and Willa Jansson books
both with law connections
Marcia Muller-The infamous Sharon McCone
Julie Smith - Rebecca Schwarz, defense attorney
Gloria White - Ronnie Ventana, the Anglo-Mexican PI daughter
of cat burglars

Mitch has another dream... and this one involves crime...

A Beginner's Guide to Crime
Mitch Rice

NOT ALWAYS have I felt so comforted by my addiction. For years I suffered alone, friends and family pushed to their outer limits, my passions unrequited! What does this crazy lady lament I hear you cry, my addiction and passion to crime fiction of course. But... there has been considerable light on the horizon: it has never been such a good time to share in the wonderful world of Crime Fiction. My life is so busy, my mind so racing with enthusiasm, my desk so cluttered with post-it notes of jobs to do, people to contact, books to read, that I need to give up the day job really!

I've been a fan of female detective stories for many years, the history of which I can trace back to the Famous Five! But about 3 years ago I'd got to that awful stage of having read all I thought was out there that I liked (well, all that my local chain store bookshop had in its crime section at least). Then I took my first visit to the States. Needless to say the lid was lifted from my world (as well as the bottom taken out of my suitcase as I tried to drag my book filled suitcase through the Departure Lounge). I discovered a whole new arena of great women, writing fantastic stories to keep me turning pages well into the night. On returning home, disillusioned with UK booksellers, but re-enthused with Crime Fiction, I found my way to *Crime Time*. A whole magazine of the stuff! That means there must be a large body of people out there with similar tastes to me; funny, I've never met one! The magazine has been great. It's widened my reading habits and been a useful place to find advertisements for small, dedicated bookshops. I've loved every issue of the magazine, reading it hungrily as soon as it arrives on my doormat, and then regretting my haste as the next publication is always too far away.

Living in London I've absolutely no excuse now. I don't have to worry about expensive airfares or reinforced luggage; a £1.20 bus ticket into the West End puts me in touch with every title I could ever want. Now with three exclusively crime bookshops, don't we feel spoilt! Murder One, on the Charing Cross Road has got to be the best stocked, most densely packed of them all. Although what they lack in range, Crime In Store in Covent Garden has got to be said to more than make up for it in the quality of its staff and the luxurious atmosphere. There's isn't anything they don't know, can't find or recommend. And all of you with less than willing partners in tow, you can happily deposit their weary bones on the deepseated, inviting sofa. The newest addition to the London scene is Mysterious Bookshop, part of the American chain and warmly received this side of the Atlantic. They've been very active in their first few months, taking on board the American feeling that they're more than out to take your money! They've got a comprehensive Bi-monthly catalogue up and running, had a hugely enjoyable 'How to write a crime novel in an hour' workshop, lead by Annie Ross and Alison Joseph. And most exciting of all, are putting together a Crime Addicts club on the first Monday of every month.

Sadly though it does seem you must live in London to sustain your habit. But don't despair out there in the Home Counties; all three bookshops do mail order and be inspired- bug your local bookshop to enter the 20th Century, stock what you want to read and take some initiative in organising book related events. Waterstone's are brilliant for this, they run reading groups at their Earls Court and Eastbourne branches and have hospitality rooms in many of their branches for you to make use of. At their Manchester branch, late October time, there's a weekend of crime fiction related events called Dead On Deansgate, call them for more details (0161 8321992). I've found the staff to be very helpful and actually enthused about making books an active experience

Nearly a year ago now a group of people got together at Crime in Store to do just that—share their enjoyment of books. Thus the Crime in Store Reading Group was formed! It's a brilliant group and I wouldn't miss the meetings for all the chocolate at Cadburys! We meet about once every six weeks on a Thursday night after the shop has closed (it's a great opportunity to browse and spend money painlessly as well!). One person introduces a chosen book that we've all read in advance and then the conversations just flow and flow, around the book, the author, similar books, what we're reading etc., etc. It's a wonderful forum for sharing ideas, being introduced to new authors and making new friends with similar interests. We're interested in all things Crime Fiction related- so we've also gone out to see 1940's classic B&W Hitchcock-like movies and stage versions of the classic whodunit variety. We're open to all suggestions!

A contact from the Reading Group led me to my other group that I feel very passionate about—Mystery Women (only one vote short of being Bloody Minded Babes!). This is a newly formed group of readers, writers and general enthusiasts who aim to promote women in the field of Crime Fiction. The Mystery Women, based loosely on the American 'Sisters In Crime', read and discuss books by and about women, as well as having guest speakers, workshops and pizza! And it's not based in the capital! At the moment the group meets in Waterstone's in Cambridge on a Sunday afternoon about every six weeks. Its gorgeous surroundings are enough to make a day of it. Members come from all over, some as far away as Birmingham and Leicester.

Having just been initiated into the 20th Century myself (and not willingly I might add) with the purchase of my first computer (although I still refuse to have an answer phone!) I know don't know how I lived without the Internet! Those of you who relish the thought of leisure time intricately bound up to the warmth and comfort of home will appreciate the overwhelming amount of Crime Fiction related sites on the Internet. From being able to buy discounted books from the Barnes & Noble in New York, to participating in murder mystery games, to reading the latest reviews, to participating in themed discussions it's all there at the click of a button. And it really is that simple or else I wouldn't have found it!

Here's a few of my favourites—

TheCase.com — check this out for a wide range of discussions to get involved in: http://www.thecase.com/thecase

Tangled Web — the best, British online Crime Fiction magazine: http://www.twbooks.co.uk

The Mysterious Home Page — a comprehensive American magazine with a host of connections and pointers to other sites of interest; http://www.db.dk/dbaa/.jbs/homepa@

*[…err can we mention **Crime Time**, now with the reviews from issues 5 to 2.1 (200,000 words) sorted by author at www. crimetime.demon.co.uk]*

It does seem there never has been such a good time to get out and get involved with Crime Fiction, may it continue forever!

You can contact the Crime in Store Reading Group via Thalia at the shop on 0171 379 3795 and Mystery Women via Mitch at 90A Greenwood Road, London E8 1NE, new members always welcome.

For Crime Time readers living in Birmingham Erdington Library has a regular and thriving crime fiction group. Recent visitors have included Lawrence Block, Chris Niles, Jane Adams and Mike Ripley. You can contact the group at the Library. CT's own Peter Dillon-Parkin is running a reviewers workshop there in October.

If other readers belong to groups they'd like to see publicised send information to the editorial address, and we'll start a diary feature.

ED GORMAN
CAGE OF NIGHT

TWENTY-ONE-YEAR-old Spence returns to his home-town after two years in the Army and falls in love with Cindy Brasher, Homecoming Queen and town goddess to a long line of jealous men. A string of robberies put Spence at odds with his obsessive love for Cindy. One by one Spence's rivals are implicated in horrific crimes. Spence wonders how much Cindy knows, and why she wants him, like her past boyfriends, to visit the old well in the woods...

"The book is full of Gorman's characteristic virtues as a writer: sympathy, humour, commitment to the craft of storytelling, and a headlong narrative drive. A real writer is at work here and there aren't many of those to go around."

—DARK ECHO.

"Cornell Woolrich would have enjoyed Cage Of Night."

—LOCUS.

"A book that combines romance, sex, violence, madness and an almost oppressive degree of grief, Cage Of Night is one of the most unique noirs ever written."

—PIRATE WRITINGS.

"Gorman is defining noir for the nineties."

—CEMETERY DANCE.

Available from all good bookshops, or post free for £4.99 from: CT Publishing, PO Box 5880, Birmingham B16 8JF

email ct@crimetime.demon.co.uk

CT Publishing

Murder One for all the Pulp Fiction your heart desires.

Murder One where you can find all the Usual Suspects. If it's in Print, in English, we have it. If it's not in Print, we might well have it too. The **ultimate** mystery superstore. **Mail Order** all over the world. **Catalogue** on request.

Visit our spanking new, criminal website at www.murderone.co.uk **and** e-mail:106562.2021 @compuserve.com

Britain's Only Major Mystery Bookstore

71 -73 Charing Cross Rd, London WC2H 0AA, Tel 0171 734 3483 Fax 0171 734 3429

The Third Degree

People with criminal intentions talk...

Stuart Pawson
Anne Artymiuk

I've always wanted to ask a writer not, why do you write? which is something I understand, but how do you justify spending the time writing your first book when you don't know if it will be published or not?

I was in a lucky position. I'd been made redundant and so I found myself wanting to do something to fill in the rest of the time—something creative. The idea of spending hours on the golf course reducing my handicap by two didn't appeal. I'd have liked to paint, but most of all I'd have liked to be a song writer. The thought of writing 3 minute songs does appeal to me ...

... as opposed to a 200 page book?

Yep! I'd dabbled a bit once; I went out with a folk singer and I wrote some stuff for her, which she scoffed at. And unfortunately I'm tone deaf! So I thought I'd have a go at writing a book. I had a computer sitting idle. I'd bought it to type job applications and do a nice CV. Years ago I worked for a guy who did one of these correspondence courses in writing, and he used to ask my advice. So I knew you didn't need a degree in English Literature or anything to write a book. Anyone could do it. It took me 18 months part time to write the first one, and while I was trying to get it published I started on the second one. My target was to write two books and it they didn't get published, well tough! I would have them bound myself and let anyone who wanted to, read them. They'd always be there. So that's how I justified the time to myself.

And did you try crime for the hoary old chestnut of a reason, that it supposedly comes with a ready made structure?

Well, I do believe in that. I have all these old fashioned ideas about poems rhyming and books having a beginning, a middle and an end. Although as that film producer said once, "Not necessarily in that order". But actually I think the reason that I chose crime was because I didn't know how to hook the reader. I couldn't grip a reader with an opening paragraph about a couple of people living in a pit village. There's "Call me Ishmael" which is supposed to be a great opening, but I have to say has never sounded terribly gripping to me. So I decided that the easiest thing to do would be to kill somebody in the first paragraph and hopefully that would work. The only place I could do that was in a crime novel, and in the event I didn't kill him, but I did shoot my policeman in the first line.

You did, and in fact going back to what you were saying before, that is almost the end of the book, right at the beginning. With a couple of exceptions you write mainly in the first person. Was that deliberate, or was it just how it came to you?

No, it was the biggest cock-up I ever made. It's like an albatross around my neck now. I read somewhere that writing in the first person is a sign of a first time writer. And actually it suited the style of the first book, and you do get much more involved if you're writing in the first person. But when you come to write the second book you're hamstrung. There are only so many ways a policeman gets information. And you can only show things from one point of view. It's limiting. If you write in the third person you can show the same scene from several points of view and to be honest apart from anything else it helps with the word count.

In *The Mushroom Man* and *The Judas Sheep* you alternated first and third person narrative, which actually I thought worked very well. I assumed that was the way things would carry on. But you reverted to first person only narrative and I wondered why?

It's just how it comes really. When I finished *Mushroom Man* and realised what I'd done I thought it would be thrown back at me. But no-one seemed to notice. One reviewer pointed it out, but he said it worked well.

Since it is largely first person narrative the obvious next question is How much of Charlie Priest is you, and how much is he a made up character?

He's taller than me!

Ye-e-s! But apart from that?

Very little, to be honest. His humour is mine of course, but that's because I'm not clever enough to write a different sort. Some of his tastes are mine but that's a matter of convenience. If I'd made them different then I'd have had to write them down and then refer to it every time. It's easier if we share tastes. So odd things like that are me, but basically he's a totally different personality.

A lot of crime writers claim to get bored with their series characters? Are you bored with Charlie yet?

Not so much bored. I fear that I might be running out of ideas. The first two books just came out of the ether. The third one I had to really sit down and work at; I was really pleased when I did it. And that was the same with books four and five. I was really pleased that the second book was probably better than the first since a lot of writers write one good book and then flop with their second one. And despite the struggles with the later books I think the improvements have been steady and I think I've maintained the standard. And I'm proud of that.

If you ever did run out of ideas for Charlie would you stop writing or would you try writing something else?

I'd have a go at writing something else to start with. I'd like to try doing an international thriller—so I could do all the research in America!

I wasn't going to ask if that was the motivation. I thought it would sound rude if I suggested it was so you could go to glamorous places and have the trip tax deductible!

I also read a book recently by Keith Waterhouse about his childhood in south Leeds which is where I came from. I'd love to write something similar, but it would be a bit of a steal of his idea.

Turning back to the books you have written, when we were setting up this interview I intimated that I wasn't 100% happy with what you have done in the latest book to Charlie's long term girlfriend Annabelle. And you said 'They told me to do it' or words to that effect, and I wondered who this mysterious 'they' might be?

Well… I'm wondering how much I can say without putting my foot in it. I work for two masters, an agent and a publisher and I think it was a suggestion from my editor at the publishers. It wasn't a concrete suggestion; we have very little conversation. I'm just left to get on with it. She said something about *"maybe doing something about Annabelle, and dropping the E-type Jag"*. Actually I'd already dropped the Jag once and then resurrected it, and I had every intention of dropping it again, as it had become an embarrassment. I started writing in 1993 and I wasn't aware of Morse at the time. Obviously I should have given Charlie a blue Triumph Stag or something. Anyway, going back to Annabelle, I think it was a very tentative suggestion from the publisher, with which I agreed.

Well, we don't want to let any cats out of bags, so I'll just say that whatever it was you did to Annabelle I almost cried. That might get a few people hooked! So you don't actually get much interference from 'them' then?

No. I'm struggling a bit with the next book and the publisher offered to look at it. But I said no, I was going to finish it and then she could take it or leave it, but at least I would have fulfilled my part of the contract.

I wondered it we could talk a little bit about John Harvey, because in

some ways his books are very like yours and in other ways they are very different. To begin with, he uses Nottingham very minutely, even to having people meet in front of Boots or whatever. You set your books in Yorkshire and use some real places such as Leeds and Bradford—and of course the Pennine barrier to keep out the barbarian hordes! But Heckley itself is fictional and I wondered why you made somewhere up rather than use somewhere that already existed.

I don't really know. It just sort of suited the first book, to have places either side of the Pennines. When I look at the map, Heckley is probably Huddersfield to be honest. Maybe I just didn't know Huddersfield well enough, so I made it semi fictional and called it Heckley.

And where did the name come from?

A mixture of Heckmondwike and Batley.

Thank goodness for that. I had this awful feeling you were going to say it developed from 'eeh by heck!' To go back to Harvey, he is very bleak, and if anything getting bleaker with every book he writes. He makes some terrible things happen in his books, but there are some things just as awful that happen in yours. Yet yours come over as a lot more optimistic in tone. You do of course have a lot of humour in your work, and that's a quality Harvey isn't really noted for. Is that what makes the difference?

Yes ... but it might also have to do with the fact that they aren't set in a big city, but in a small market town. I think generally the levels of violence aren't so extreme. A serial killer of course can just as easily live in a small market town as a big city, but the general level of nastiness is lower. I live quite close to somewhere like that and although you do get plenty of people going round late at night drunk and wearing nothing over their T-shirts even in February, there's no threatening atmosphere like I assume you'd feel in Leeds.

Where do your jokes and the humour come from?

I invent most of them. Occasionally I resurrect really old ones. Sadly on a couple of occasions people have said to me *"I really like the bit where..."* and then quote back the old jokes, thereby picking out the only bit that isn't original, which upsets me! But mostly I make them up, although I struggle sometimes.

Well I thought the Siamese twin joke in the latest book was a classic! I must say reading the jokes and the banter between your police officers, reminds me of when I was at work and you get this sort of developing banter when you have a lot of bright people penned together doing a job that has a lot of routine to it. I have to say it is the one thing I really miss about working!

It's what I miss actually. I don't try to write funny books, I try to write realistic dialogue and all the people I've ever worked with have been would-be stand-up comedians. My policemen friends are the same—you know they'd do anything for a laugh. I daren't put some of the things they do and say in the books—they'd get fired!

Mentioning horrible things, which we did a moment ago, I'm usually quite blasé about horrible things in crime fiction, because I resent the attempt to manipulate my emotions that is implicit in having someone in the book torture a cat or whatever. But the swan incident at the opening of *Last Reminder* I found quite horrendous. Did you really dream that up, or had you read about something like that happening?

I dreamed it up.

Really!! I shall look at you quite differently from now on, because it really is horrible. Much worse than say someone poisoning a dog.

It came to me while I was suffering from a migraine. I get some of my best (or worst) ideas while I have my migraines.

So you don't suffer in vain then!

No, I suffer to the advantage of my work. Actually I'm suffering a lot less from them these days—maybe that's why the ideas aren't coming!

You're not on medication for it are you? Then you could stop taking it for a while, just until you get some new ideas.

No, unfortunately not.

When I went back to to reread the books before you came, I was quite surprised to realise how much they, and the character of Charlie, has changed. The pace is a lot less hectic now, and Charlie's not quite the maverick in *Deadly Friends* that he was in *Picasso Scam*. Has he changed, or have people had a quiet word and said that the police just don't act like this anymore?

Nobody's commented on it actually. In *Deadly Friends* he does try to get Darren to implicate himself. He throws him those gloves and the implication is that he wants Darren to try them on so that he can then send them to forensic, and get them to tie Darren and the gloves together. I don't know if that came over or not?

Yes, it did. Unfortunately for Charlie, Darren was too wide-awake to fall for it.

I haven't been back and read them myself but I have wondered about this. I had noticed myself that he has changed, but I excused it—or explained it by saying that in those early days he was a bit of a novice with those sorts of major crimes and now he isn't.

Also when I reread I was quite surprised at the amount there is about guns in the books?

Is there?

Yes. In a lot of detail. But you don't come across as someone who feels that using a gun is the only way to validate your personality. Do you know all this stuff or do you have to look it up?

Oh, I look it all up.

And the forensic stuff too? Or do you have a man you can ring up?

Well, I have two police inspectors who help me a bit, and one of them got me a day with a Scene of Crime team. And one of them knows a bit about guns and he finds things out for me. So I do have contacts but I've never spent the day with a firearms unit. I think I just have the average man's knowledge about guns.

There's this bit in *Deadly Friends* about the noises that all the different guns make ...

Oh, I invented all that.

Oh, right! But isn't that a bit dangerous? One of the things that I was going to ask about forensic was that nowadays it's so important isn't it, to get it right. Otherwise someone in some little one horse village in the Home Counties with nothing better to do with their time will write to you and tell you you've got is all wrong!

Well, I invented it, and I took it to one of my policemen friends and he rang the firearms group and read it out to them over the phone! And he's sat there saying "...*And the Kalashnikov goes ker... chink...*" and this chap at the other end is saying "...*Ker-chink. Well, yes, that's about right.*" And then he would say things like "*it's more a ker-kluck than a ker-click*" and things like that.

So most of your forensic and firearms stuff is researched. I sometimes wonder, you know, if this is why historical crime is getting so popular; because you don't have to do any forensic research, because there wasn't any forensic science to speak of. So you have to rely on the dropped yellow hanky or whatever.

I think actually that a lot of the historical stuff is bogged down with other research though—I'm surprised they find time to do the writing. But going back to my police contacts, I do want to stress that they are both amazingly generous with their information. They don't resent me writing about their jobs at all, which surprises me. I thought they would have got tired of it by now.

When I read *The Mushroom Man*, to discuss the strand of the plot where the little girl goes missing, I was very suspicious of the father, because experience of real and fictional situations like that leads everyone to suspect father/stepfather/Mum's current boyfriend or whatever. But when I read the book I honestly didn't realise that Charlie and Gilbert had the father fingered for something right from the off. When I re-read it I could see that they were keeping tabs on him and were certain he'd engineered it all. Now, was that skilful writing or was that mean being stupid? Or maybe that's not a fair question to ask you?

I suppose it was deliberate, but not overtly. You find out towards the end what it is the father has done. Charlie suspected him from some little detail of his behaviour at the press conference, plus in 80/90% of these cases it is someone in the family, as you say. I think as a writer you just need to subtly justify what Charlie and Gilbert are doing in such a way that the reader doesn't exactly realise what's going on. I'd like to say that it's deliberate ...

... I was going to say, you should just have said that of course it is down to very skilful writing....

... but I honestly can't remember!

Are we going to see Charlie on the television?

Write to your friendly neighbourhood TV company and ask!

There are so many cops on the box at present, I sometimes think too many, but then it all depends on which cop really. I just wondered it you'd been approached.

No, although they are with somebody at the moment. But quite honestly I think I'm five years too late. Especially since they're set in Yorkshire. There's been a plethora of these things set in Yorkshire..

Reg Hill, Heartbeat ...

Yes, and then there was one called... it was set in a little town ... oh yes Wokenwell. I ...

[both simultaneously] only watched the first episode!!

And that was exactly where my books are all set!

But it wasn't really cops was it. I think surreal was the word that everyone was bandying about when they tried to talk that one up. I don't think it's coming back anyway, thank goodness.

No. And the Jag's old hat, as we already said. Calling him Charlie was the biggest mistake , everyone on TV seems to be called Charlie these days. So I'd do things slightly differently it I were to start again. It would be based in Suffolk or somewhere.

Can't do that! PD James sends Dalgleish to East Anglia sometimes. I don't know where's left really. Lincolnshire? But it's very flat. I think you do well to stick to Yorkshire; it's God's Own County after all.

Well I shall cross my fingers that they turn up on TV sometime,—and that they get the casting right. And meanwhile I look forward to Charlie's next adventure.

Caleb Carr
Barry Forshaw

Photo: Robin Saidman

SOME AUTHORS may toil ceaselessly for years before achieving a modicum of success. Others may be catapulted into the limelight after only a couple of books. Caleb Carr is of the latter breed: the remarkable acclaim that greeted The Alienist *two years ago looks set to be followed up by similar attention for* Angel of Darkness, *recently published in this country by Little, Brown. Carr's speciality is a canny synthesis of the Holmesian novel of deduction, a Thomas Harris-style pursuit of a serial killer, and the detailed topography and historic verisimilitude of Doctorow's* Ragtime. *While Carr's preternaturally brilliant detective/alienist Laszlo Kreizler is at the centre of the books, there is a shrewd strategy at work in allocating the peripheral characters their share of the limelight in successive books. Speaking to Carr in a Knightsbridge hotel, I found him a curious mixture of the engaging and the eccentric. He has no false modesty about his achievements, but (unlike many a crime author) is not upset by what he perceives as negative criticism.*

You're talking to movie types at present over options for *The Alienist*. Who's going to play your female protagonist Sara Howard – Sharon Stone?

I favour Gwyneth Paltrow. If, that is, it ends up as a star vehicle. There are many lesser known actresses who'd be fine, but the producers might be determined on this issue.

And Anthony Hopkins as the eponymous alienist?

He's too old now. However, if he expressed an interest, I'd certainly be happy. And what about Ralph Fiennes? I'm battling with the producer who wants to turn it into a love story. But there isn't a love story in the book, and that's what people like about it. Classic Hollywood nonsense, of course.

So you're ready to be royally screwed by Hollywood à la Faulkner, etc?

I'm already being screwed like William Faulkner, in that I worked in Hollywood for some time. I'm actually being screwed in a fully participatory fashion, rather than from afar.

The essence of your books lies in the immense accumulation of detail. Although this will indirectly help the look of any movie, it will surely lose your tone of voice.

Well, ironically, they are saying to me that it's so much trouble to adapt my books because of the detailed description. And I reply that the actual story isn't, essentially, that difficult to translate. Often, I purposely chose to describe buildings that are still there in New York. You can easily shoot the Flatiron Building, and with what George Lucas and Industrial Light and Magic are now doing, it is possible to window-dress it with marvellous period detail.

I don't want to sound like a dog worrying a bone, but surely you can concentrate your description on a very specific aspect of period detail, whereas a movie has to, perforce, show the entire scene and lose that focus?

Yes, I hadn't thought of that. Well, the viewers will just have to catch it as they can. I feel, anyway, that whatever I can impart to people through the books is all to the good. Do you know that Random House didn't want to call the book *The Alienist?* They said, *"Nobody will know what the hell an alienist is".* My reply to that is, *"So what? When people read the book they'll realise that an alienist is an early form of psychologist and they've learnt something".* I'm never intimidated by the fact that people don't know things. They can learn things, can't they?

You have a sense of mission as a writer – and here's an example of it. Are you a frustrated educationalist?

No! I feel a writer has two jobs: to educate and to entertain. I'm not interested in being treated as a serious novelist, but I am interested in what I think writing should be doing now. Too much of the autobiographical, introspective style of novel being written today is really a dead horse that's being mercilessly flogged. It's a cliché, I know, but people are still desperately thirsty for stories. And in America, where educational standards are falling, I think there's a real importance in the concept of accessible books that teach something. You have to do it in a way that is entertaining to readers. I'm not claiming that I do this quite as well as I'd wish; there are some historical details in my books that seem to me, in retrospect, a little stuck on.

It's essential that this sort of thing is organic to the narrative. Maybe I haven't mastered that technique yet.

You're leery of wearing a literary mantle on your own shoulders, but there are more passages of literary description in your books than one is likely to find in anything other than a nineteenth century novel.

Well, I don't see a contradiction there – I see my descriptive passages as purely functional. I don't tend to wax very rhapsodic in my use of language – I go for language that is strictly utilitarian. I think that certainly since Hemingway (and certainly since my father's old friend Jack Kerouac), everything that can be done with language HAS been done. All the experiments you can perform with language have been tried. I do try to keep the description as straightforward as possible – it should serve a function.

You said that you wished to reinvent the serial killer novel. How is it possible to do that when the genre is in danger of (you'll forgive the pun) overkill?

Well I began with the concept of a psychiatrist and a killer who had certain things in common. But I appreciated that this sounded like a hundred other books, and I thought to myself, *"What am I going to do to make this distinctive?"* So I went for something which wasn't quite a thriller and wasn't quite a historical novel – hopefully it was a new departure. My publishers, of course, said, *"What are we going to do with this?"* So it was decided to present this as part of a new genre: the psychological/historical thriller. To my editor's credit, she was right behind this idea, but the marketing people were deeply unhappy. They said, *"We can't do this – this is too new!"*

Surely nobody would say anything like that in publishing, would they?

I had a battle with them – they came around in the end.

Locales are crucial for many writers, but there are few who make a city quite as significant in their narratives as you do New York. Why did you take this approach?

Well, for a start, it's where I grew up. I was born and raised there, and I spent a lot of time on the streets of New York. It's the only city in the world where, for me, if I were homeless it wouldn't be too much of a challenge. And New York IS a character. You could view it as being like in an abusive relationship. You have a relationship with the city: it's not just a place where you live. And you HAVE to have this relationship: it may be love/hate or hate/love, but everybody has some kind of a relationship with the city.

An interesting metaphor. And you mention abuse, which is a significant factor in your books.

Yes, part of the reason I wrote the books was because I was getting so tired with hearing people say, *"New York's gotten so rough – it was so charming in the old days, the gay 90s, the golden age..."* And I'd look at them and think, *"Come on – the city's always been a sinkhole of corruption and crime and absolute degeneracy."* That's what I try to address in the books.

Some years ago, one of the broadsheets here ran a piece of reportage about how awful London had become: crime, mugging, not safe to walk the streets, etc. And the joke was that they'd merely made a few cosmetic alterations to a piece written by Charles Dickens about his London. Plus ça change.

Exactly the point I'm trying to make!

You also, of course, present this refraction of the past through a contemporary vision – the use of rent boys, for instance. Unacceptable territory for a nineteenth century writer.

I do have the advantage, as a modern writer, of being able to tackle the things which did exist in that era but couldn't be talked about – certainly not in the novels of the day. And, in the new book, *Angel of Darkness*, I play with the idea of the "unpublishable" (in the terms of that era) manuscript. And that would have been the case – you would have gone around with a manuscript telling that story and people simply would not have been prepared to touch it.

It's interesting, of course, how in this country people became conscious of the world of male prostitutes and so forth because of the Wilde case. In that buttoned-up society, the unsayable finally became the sayable. In *Angel of Darkness*, you inaugurate a change of narrator, moving one of the characters in Kreizler's circle centre stage. I must admit I was a bit disconcerted by this, as I like the Watsonian narrator of the first book. But you see the books as having a cluster of narrators?

That was the original idea: that the narration of each book would shift from person to person to person, with each narrator telling the story that was most significant for them. I chose Moore in the first book, as he was the most accessible of the group. He was modern in some ways, and I felt that people would have the least trouble with him. Stevie, the narrator of the second book, was much more of a challenge: not as articulate as Moore, not a professional man, and so forth.

But don't you have to cheat with Stevie? In *The Alienist* you have an intelligent, articulate narrator, whereas in the new book you have someone who was essentially an urchin, although he's now educated.

Yes, but that's just a question of attitude. Stevie's viewpoint and attitude is just as valid. I didn't have Moore's attitudes myself, so you could say that I had to cheat with him as well. This is really to do with language: the way Stevie views the city is not slumming. He's been there, he has lived in the lower depths, unlike Moore. To a degree, this reflects my background: I lived in an area where it was a question of slumming for the rich kids when they came to buy drugs and act disgracefully, before going back to their well-upholstered homes.

Your books are absolutely the last kind of thing one would expect from someone who's a second generation child of the Beat generation.

Well, I'm the reaction. For every action, there is an equal and opposite reaction. And that's me.

Were people like Jack Kerouac and Nelson Algren habitués of the family household when you were a child?

It was Kerouac and Allan Ginsberg and that whole crew. But I had my interest in history back then – their world never interested me. I started off on the traditional boy's stuff: King Arthur and the Knights of the Round Table, that sort of thing. I actually read a lot of British fiction, and English history is a specialist subject of mine. I was more interested in English than American history. In this country, just sitting under the statue of General Gordon for the first time was a tremendous thrill for me.

Teddy Roosevelt is utilised by you in a very clever way as a major character. With the decline in educational standards that you talked about earlier, aren't you worried that some of your readers nowadays might not even know who he was?

Like I say, people learn. I have to admit that at readings in the States people have asked me questions like, *"Is that where Dr Kreizler really lived?"* They have difficulty sorting out the historical from the invented characters. But in the States, because of the name Roosevelt, people might not know exactly who he was, but they're pretty sure he was real. But in the first book, all the gangland figures were real. And in the second book, I use Clarence Darrow as a character, and people have assumed that I created him. It's sad that people don't know who Clarence Darrow was. What kind of job is being done in American schools?

But some people would make the same accusation of British educational standards – kids were recently asked in a survey who this country fought in the Second World War and most of them came up with the Russians. It really is prehistory to them.

A recent survey of American schoolchildren demonstrated that 80% of them couldn't say in which century the American Civil War took place. Of course, I try to *"freight in"* a little history in the books: Roosevelt, for instance, has made his career leap from one book to the next. And by making Sara a kind of proto-feminist, I still ensure that she's not unrealistically ahead of her time. People are not aware of how many professional women there were in the United States at that time. These women had to give up having husbands and children and the reality was often very different from the view that people have of women then. Many people's attitudes are conditioned by their reading Henry James and Edith Wharton, who only cover a fraction of the reality. There were a lot of women like Sara who worked hard at a job.

You've written about the US government's obsession with secrecy...

I have! That really interests me, as it ties in with my idea that all history is really psychology. National character IS national psychology: all historical questions are biographical and sociological in nature. I don't believe in the Marxist economic theory of history, in social forces being more important than human forces. People make history. If you examine in detail most periods of American history, you can find out why things happened as they did by looking at the neuroses and psychoses of the key figures involved. Take our most awful institution, the CIA. This whole organisation was put together by a man who was a certifiable paranoid schizophrenic, James Forrestal. He ended up hanging himself, after running through the streets naked shouting, *"The Russians are after me! The Russians are after me!"*

Sounds like he would really have got on well with J Edgar Hoover.

Hoover looked like a well-balanced man compared to him! All Hoover did was dress up in women's clothing and mooch around in other people's lives. All this is the kind of thing that interests me, within the context of historical thrillers. Hopefully, the movies of the books (if they ever get made) will ensure a continuing interest in what I'm doing – although, in all modesty, I seem to be building up a faithful following anyway.

Caleb Carr Bibliography

Casing the Promised Land (1979)

First novel by Carr is, by all accounts (well, all those we can find) a tad flavourless.

America Invulnerable: The Quest for Absolute Security from 1812 to Star Wars (1988) (with James Chace)

The Devil Soldier: The Story of Frederick Townsend Ward (1991)

Carr's first book as an a historian was a thorough but dull biography of Frederick Townsend Ward, whose career in the 1850-60s in service of the Chinese emperor allowed him unusual influence and status in the closed society of China. Ward shot from being a mate on American clipper ships to become the commander of the Ch'ing dynasty in its struggle against the Taiping Rebellion (1851-64). Ward's company of foreign irregulars were swiftly trained and thrown into battle, but the results were a vicious defeat while assaulting a rebel-held city near Shanghai. Ward changed tactics, recruiting the Chinese and drilling them in Western military methods. He soon enjoyed success, and was internationally famous as the commander of the Ever Victorious Army. His place in Chinese military history was assured by the time he fell mortally wounded in battle in September 1862.

Carr's meticulous and scholarly biog debunks myths as much as possible but isn't a compelling account. Solid but disappointing was the general verdict at the time of publication.

The Alienist (1994)
In 1896 New York, psychologist—or in period terminology, an alienist— Laszlo Kreizler joins forces with journalist John Schuyler Moore to track a vicious serial killer.

The Angel of Darkness (1997)
The second case for the team of Kreizler et al holds the interest from page one. Better written than *The Alienist*, with the characters (who came over as rather flat in the first book) more fully-developed. The use of Stevie as narrator in a switch from the first novel adds considerable flavour and melancholy to the book. The descriptions of late nineteeth century New York are fascinating, and as well executed as in the earlier novel.

THE DOGS OF WINTER
by Kem Nunn

"A profound study of skill, courage and the human psyche."—Robert Stone

Heart Attacks is California's last secret spot—the premier mysto surf haunt, the stuff of rumour and legend. Down and out photographer, Jack Fletcher, hitches up with surfing legend, Drew Harmon, active men past their prime, formerly heroic figures still trying to catch the perfect wave. Harmon's wife, Kendra is on an obsessive search of her own to find the murderer of a local girl. Quests converge and events play themselves out in ways that are both inevitable and surprising and provide an epic homage to the ragged nobility of wounded man.

"Nunn explores the consequences of failure, the demands of courage and the healing powers of penance. A serious, richly satisfying novel infused with sad wisdom"—GQ

"As if Elmore Leonard and Cormac McCarthy had teamed up to write a surf novel."—Village Voice

"This is the greatest novel ever written about surfing."—Newsweek

ISBN: 1 901982 35 1 PRICE: £6.99 Pbk
ISBN: 1 901982 50 5 PRICE: £12 Hbk
(500 copy Limited Edition—100
copies signed & numbered)
A NO EXIT ORIGINAL

Lee Child
Barry Forshaw

Photo: Ruth Child

IT'S A BRAVE WRITER who opts to set all his books in a country not his own: in the days when Englishman James Hadley Chase set George Orwell's least-favourite book No Orchids for Miss Blandish *in the States (which he'd never visited), a less sophisticated reading public would not be scrutinising the text for errors of detail. Not so in the 1990s, and Lee Child's considerable success with his two US-set books* Killing Floor *and* Die Trying *(both published by Bantam) is based on a flavoursome verisimilitude that makes it hard to believe Child is not a native of the States. Meeting the fit-looking author in a hotel room somewhere in the clouds above Broadcasting House, it's quickly apparent from Child's measured and focused method of speech that this is a man who knows exactly what he wants to achieve and exactly how to go about it.*

You've written two very assured thrillers in which the American locales have a real authenticity. Why did you decide to take the Americans on at their own game?

There were a lot of reasons, all of them pointing in the same way. I can't say that I weighed things up and made a decision; first of all, there were plot considerations. The size of the plot I wanted to tackle lent itself more to the sense of space that America has to offer, much more than Britain. I'm a big admirer of much British crime writing, but it can all be a little tight, a little claustrophobic, and certainly too psychologically oriented for my taste. I was looking for something more wide-ranging and that certainly had more sense of space geographically. This pointed me towards the US. And, of course, when you're writing fiction you're making something of a leap out of the real world and into a created world. And, to me, this logically pointed towards writing about a foreign culture.

And yet, your sense of locale brings to mind a very British writer: John Buchan. The traversing of landscape, the hero at odds with all around him, the impossibility of knowing who he can trust.

I think that may be accidental, although I'm happy with the comparison. Isn't that a common currency of thriller narratives anyway? Ironically, I found myself thinking of the Western as a presence behind what I'm doing. You know—the hero rides into town, sorts everything out, and rides out. This is your classic Zane Grey territory.

Would I also be right in suspecting a commercial imperative in your choice of locale?

Oh, sure: you have to think about relative size of markets, and that sort of thing. It's relatively easy for a British writer writing about Britain to sell in America, but why give yourself one extra hurdle? After all, it's a fact that British readers read Americans somewhat more than vice versa. So I thought to myself: let's go where the big market is.

What about the American readers who are going to say, *"But you couldn't get from Union Square to Fifth Avenue in that amount of time"*?

Well, obviously, this is a crucial consideration. Every single detail had to be gone over with a fine tooth-comb in that sense. You can never relax and slip into complacency. Also, I have the considerable advantage of an American wife who's a demon at detail-checking.

Moving on to the actual style of writing, I didn't really perceive a British sensibility.

No, I don't think there is. And, for me, that's a good thing, because it shows I've been successful in completing the task I've set myself. People have said to me, *"You must know these places very well"*, but the truth is I haven't been to them. I haven't actually been within a thousand miles of Georgia. But I have a sort of philosophy or approach which says that it doesn't matter whether or not what you're writing about is real – it's whether or not the reader perceives it to be real. We're sitting here looking down on London, which is a city that people around the world have very specific conceptions of, and, for a writer, it's more important not to rupture those perceptions than to go for a kind of truth that may be more accurate.

You're very upfront about the commercial aspects of being a writer – you don't claim to be writing primarily for yourself, for instance. Would it be true to say that you see writing as a job rather than a compulsion?

Well, you make it sound a little naked when you put it like that. I really do enjoy writing. And to be able to do it for a living is something I regard as a tremendous privilege. After all, if you write what is loosely called *"genre fiction"*, you accept certain externally imposed forms, do you not? And these have existed for some time – you can't ignore them. Let's face it, this is a commercial form of literature. It always has been, since Wilkie Collins. If you don't take that on board, you're putting yourself in an invidious position. It's like saying, *"I want to go to the Olympics as a sprinter, but I don't really care whether or not I can run."*

And there are different rules for a writer of genre fiction than for a writer of literary fiction?

Absolutely. I have a great deal of respect for someone who tries something radical in literary terms that may fail now, but will be accepted in 50 or 100 years. But you can't look at popular fiction in that light: it has to succeed NOW.

What made you characterise your hero Jack Reacher in the way that you do?

I had a lot of things that I didn't want him to be – and this, to some degree, was in reaction to other writers. I didn't want him to be disfunctional, for instance. Or depressed. Or alcoholic. Or divorced. I think all this has been done to death, and I was keen to avoid those clichés. But my own situation at the time I created him was significant: I'd been made redundant and I was experiencing quite a lot of insecurity. I wanted him to be somebody who'd suffered through having his life turned upside down, but was a sort of positive example. His whole life has been in the army. But when he's 'downsized' out of the military, I wanted to show that it's possible to deal with this sort of thing constructively.

You take an interesting approach to violence in both *Killing Floor* and the new book *Die Trying*. I found myself thinking not only of John Buchan but Mickey Spillane. You describe terrible damage to the cartilage or whatever in the Spillane fashion, but I felt that you were also trying to be responsible in showing exactly what happens when violence is done.

Well, I wasn't really going for a kind of fantasy violence – I think that's a little irresponsible, in that it's wrong to disconnect the portrayal of violence from its effects. If you say, *"I hit the guy, and he fell over"*, that's a dishonest glossing over of reality. If you're going to do it at all, I think you're obliged to do it honestly.

But aren't you trying to have it both ways? After all, let's face it, we enjoy the violence in crime novels…

Oh yes, of course we're having it both ways. But the fundamental reason is that I couldn't bring myself to write a sanitised, superficial view of this subject.

It seems that women respond positively to Jack – why do think that is?

Well, first of all, let me say that I'm glad that they do. That was impossible to predict. I think that's a little like moving into a new town or a new block of flats – you can't make people like you. If you try too hard, you probably end up by achieving the opposite effect. So I hoped people would like Jack, and, thankfully, they appear to. Many of the books' biggest fans are women—in publishing itself, and the readers. But I really don't know why. He's tough and capable, of course, but he's also vulnerable and perhaps a little bit gawky. His appearance and his thought patterns aren't neat, and that has an appeal.

He's not a superhero, and you don't try to present him as one.

Oh, he's not James Bond. At least, not the James Bond of the movies: Fleming's 007 was much more human. Jack has led a narrow kind of life in the military. He has a small set of superb skills, but he's naïve and rather fumbling, and I think that comes across as appealing.

You spent some time working as an executive for Granada TV: did that affect the way you write?

I think that's been the fundamental influence on the way I write. My job involved presentation, which meant watching every second of the station's output. I was there for almost 20 years. And many of the thousands of hours I supervised were drama. I developed an instinct for the rhythm and pace of drama and mass-market entertainment until it became utterly ingrained. I didn't, however, write the books as blueprints for movies, even though they've been optioned. But there are real dangers in taking that approach: you can end up with both a bad book and a bad movie. However, I appreciate that both books are very visual and pacy. I'm also conscious of trying to keep a kind of intelligence at work behind things. I was very aware during my time at Granada of an encroaching stupidity. The effect of that has been that when an intelligent movie or programme appears these days, it's much more conspicuous than it once was. I do have a certain sort of nostalgia for the days when standards of aspiration were considerably higher. I did want to make the books intelligent. For me, it would be an unpleasant task to write for the lowest common denominator. Neither did I want to make it highfalutin'. It had to be accessible to a mass market, but not insulting to the readers' intelligence.

The new book makes some cogent points about America's home-grown militia and the Survivalist movement.

Well, I hope there's a certain ambiguity at work there. I know it's fashionable to dismiss these people as stupid rednecks, but the truth is more complex than that. They're neither wholly right nor wholly wrong. In a devil's advocate way, I enjoy arguing the alternative side of the case. The bad guys in this book ARE bad, but possibly in the sense that they are corrupting a worthy cause. And the good guys, while conventionally on the side of law and order, operate in a way which is rather oppressive.

Do all noble causes get corrupted in life?

I think they do – surely history makes that clear. By the same token, look at any corrupt or inexcusable cause, and there may be some merit in there somewhere.

There are three love stories in *Killing Floor*, which is unusual for a thriller.

Well, obviously Reacher has a relationship, but the plot acquired a kind of mirror aspect here. One of the love stories is in the distant past, one is in the recent past, and one is in the present. It became a stylistic exercise to parallel all three of them. That's the book that's been optioned by the producer of *Donnie Brasco* and *Rain Man*. I was hoping that by going with a producer who's more interested in character than just non-stop action sequences, the movies might end up with a touch more humanity and intelligence than the standard Hollywood product. In the end, however, it doesn't matter. The books are what count, and if I can give readers a good time with them, I've achieved my aim.

Ed McBain
Barry Forshaw

Photo: Dragica Dimitrijevic

He did it first. You think Hill Street Blues *inaugurated the group of detectives scenario, each with his own equally important agenda? No – Evan Hunter, aka Ed McBain, was responsible for this innovation in the remarkable series of 87th Precinct novels, which began with* Cop Hater *way back in 1956. With very few misfires, McBain has developed this rich, taut and stylish series of books into the* locus classicus *of the police procedural. Even in this country,* The Bill *is indebted to McBain's influence. But McBain has also enjoyed success under his own (adopted) name of Evan Hunter, creating the definitive juvenile delinquent novel in* The Blackboard Jungle *(the film of which memorably started riots to the strains of Bill Haley's* Rock Around the Clock*). As Hunter, he also produced powerful dramas such as* Strangers When We Meet *(although the latter tends to read as proto-soap opera these days). His finest hour using the Hunter sobriquet was probably the screenplay for Hitchcock's* The Birds *(maligned in its day, but now seen as a crucial element in a film finally recognised as one of Hitchcock's late masterpieces).*

McBain/Hunter was at the House of Lords as the first recipient of the CWA/Cartier Diamond Dagger award. In these august surroundings, he was not inclined to talk about his lifetime's achievement at length, so I cornered him at London's Mysterious Bookshop, where, plied by manageress Sabine Bessler's wine and sandwiches, he proved to be a fascinating interviewee.

So… receiving the Cartier award at the House of Lords! How did that feel?

Well, they had a guy there with the Queen's Seal, you know? I don't know what his title was, but he had the silver baton with which he'd announce people as they arrived. 'Sir Percival Denham' – just like the movies you saw in the 40s. Standing there with my wife (and Keith Miles and his wife), I have to admit it was quite an experience.

And you're the first colonial to receive the award?

The first colonial. I once came here to accept an award for Ellery Queen, but that wasn't quite the same. Incidentally, Ellery Queen's son is now my attorney – at least he's the son of one half of Ellery Queen.

And you've had a very successful series of novels featuring the attorney Matthew Hope running alongside your 87th Precinct books.

Well, *The Last Best Hope* is, as the title suggests, the last one.

The legal profession is held in a kind of contempt that people don't have for cops.

You're right, the legal profession IS held in very low esteem. But cops aren't liked either, and, you know the third most despised profession? Dentists. Of course, the image of the cop in the States is, for many, just a step away from the Storm Trooper. And this isn't just LA – Chicago has a similar problem.

The new book hasn't got a valedictory feel – why are you pensioning off Matthew?

It's difficult to write about a lawyer. You need to do an awful lot of research – I have to check it with two or three attorneys. I have to speak to a practising lawyer and a criminal lawyer.

But you presumably had to do similar research for the 87th Precinct books?

That became progressively easier, and I often wrapped up the books with a Q & A session with someone from the District Attorney's office. You need to know the procedure about cutting deals and so forth. But with the Hope books, it's always been difficult for me to justify an amateur solving crimes: someone hired by somebody to defend them. He has to be in there, for instance, at the showdown, which is not logical. You'd rarely find a lawyer in that position. In fact, you'd rarely find a police detective in that position.

You're widely regarded as the éminence grise behind the police procedural. You could either be said to have inspired the form, or have been ripped off by a lot of people. How do you see it?

In some instances I feel flattered, and in others I feel violated. I really don't think *Hill Street Blues* was an homage to Ed McBain, I think it was a rip off. Without even a tip of the hat – had the creators said somewhere that it was inspired by Ed McBain, I'd feel a little better about it. We are all inspired by what has gone before: none of us sprang out of the earth. But to use the

87th Precinct books as such a clear blueprint is something that goes beyond inspiration.

But most crime readers, when they saw *Hill Street Blues* instantly recognised it as an unacknowledged riff on your work.

Well, I'm not sure everyone recognised that, although I do hear that expressed a lot these days. But then it was "something exciting and new...first time on television..." and so on. Ironically, in foreign countries, it was recognised more quickly. In France, for instance, it was recognised he minute the series hit the screen. The French said, "Ed McBain comes to television!"

I don't think you should feel too maligned – certainly, in this country, there's a tremendous affection for you as a writer.

I've never been sure why the British took my very American work so much to heart: I know we have common roots, and we don't study German literature in our schools. English literature is what we're taught – there are these controversial moves to prioritise ethnic literature in American schools, but there's no denying the centrality of the great English writers. And Irish writers: James Joyce is still a great influence. And Shakespeare of course: the milestones of your literature. But one reason why my books may have caught on here could have been that they were so different from what you had. They were grittier, of course, and perhaps the British responded to the humour of the books. You have a very keen and dry sense of humour here.

There's also what might be called a peculiarly British-seeming irony to the books – and irony is possibly found less in American writers than British.

Well, Americans can be a little slower to catch on. And I sometimes wonder if Americans say Ed McWho?

How do you feel about the way your publishers sell you – both in this country and the States?

You ask any writer, and he'll tell you that he's not sold energetically enough. But I know they do try. Actually, I'm not that *au fait* with the situation in the UK. I know that as a writer you have to remain in touch with the things that readers want.

That leads us into an area which you've already discussed with this magazine's Peter Dillon-Parkin; the increasing violence of your books. You were always realistic in this area, but the books undoubtedly became increasingly graphic. Can you tell me why you moved in that direction?

That came because I was riding with the cops. I'd get out of a cop's car, you'd walk over to the kerb and there'd be a guy lying in the gutter with his brains all over the sidewalk. There'd be the police photographer snapping pictures, people crying or shouting in the background, blood splattered all over the brick wall. And there'd be brain tissue on a nearby parked car. As a writer, I felt you couldn't pull punches in this area. If you wanted your books to be authentic, then it was essential to tell the truth. As I saw more of just how tough things were out there, the books undoubtedly reflected this. It's not like it is in the movies – well, actually, it *is* like it is in the movies nowadays, rather than the discreet amount of blood you were allowed in the 40s and 50s. But what they don't do in the movies – and what I try to do in the books – is to represent the fact that when you get shot it *hurts*. I've started to close in more tightly on murder scenes now. In *The Last Best Hope*, there are several deaths that happen in the book. I had this curious feeling while I was writing it, that I was somehow an observer: that I was witness to it, watching it. I'm hoping that this sense of immediacy will be conveyed to the reader.

The deaths in the book are very vividly realised.

I hope they are. I'm hoping for a feeling of *cinéma-vérité*.

That could be said to be another area in which you've been pretty comprehensively ripped off. You were the first person to emphasise the importance of forensic detail. Now there are writers who've carved a whole career out of that single element of your work. How did you feel when you saw that catching on with other writers?

I don't know what to say about that. I can't honestly say that Patricia Cornwell read my books and said, 'Gee, I think I'll write something making the forensic elements centre stage'. On American television there was the character that Jack Klugman played – what was his name? Quincey! So those ideas were around in general: I can't lay exclusive claim to them. One thing I'm quite proud of is making a certain concept a part of crime writing: the fact that the 24 hours before a crime and the 24 hours after a crime are the most important. I labelled this the 24/24. I invented this phrase. Shortly after, I was reading a novel by a writer who quoted this virtually verbatim: he said, 'This is known in police jargon as the 24/24.'

I'm one of those people who'd actually read Evan Hunter before I'd read Ed McBain. How do you handle both careers?

Well, I think that's simplified by the fact that Evan Hunter is virtually unknown these days, don't you think? Certainly, my publishers have a harder time selling Evan to the booksellers than Ed.

I'd dispute that, at least in the case of the one great movie that Evan Hunter is really associated with, Hitchcock's *The Birds*. Although at the time there were criticisms of Hitchcock's lengthy dallying over his characters' relationships before the bird attacks began, that's been retrospectively perceived as a master strategy in lulling the audience into a false sense of security, or alternatively spinning out the viewer's anticipation to audacious lengths. And your screenplay (which only takes from Daphne du

Maurier's short story the concept of birds attacking people) is intelligent and thoughtful – as well as being able to deal with the apocalyptic theme of the film. And you inaugurated the revenge of nature theme that resulted in so many lesser movies. Your book *Me and Hitch*, which dealt with your working relationship, was very well received. And *Blackboard Jungle* is still very well known as both a movie and a book...

Well, for a long time *The Birds* was simply considered a Hitchcock movie. Hitch always downplayed the writer's contributions to his films, and sold himself as their onlie begetter. Which is fair enough, as he was undoubtedly the main reason for their greatness. But his best films ARE well written. You mentioned *Me and Hitch*: I always remember the story that I tell there in which one of my kids says to his classmates, 'We were just in California because my father was there writing *The Birds*', and his classmates reply, 'No, he didn't. Alfred Hitchcock wrote *The Birds*'. But most directors don't consider the writer really important.

You, of course, followed Raymond Chandler as one of Hitchcock's screenwriters. And Chandler was famously unhappy with the collaboration, feeling that he was there more to stitch the set-pieces together than to develop character. But Hitchcock was no fool, surely? He was aware that character is what makes his movies work so well, as much as the generation of suspense?

We began *The Birds* with only the title: Hitch told me, 'We're throwing away the Du Maurier story'. Ironically, that's still happening: Ruth Rendell recently commented in *The Telegraph* that Almodovar bought a book of hers, and *Live Flesh* had only the sketchiest connection with what she had written. Anyway, I went out with some ideas, and he had some ideas. I came up with the notion of doing a screwball comedy set against the terror. In my estimation, that never quite worked, because we didn't have Cary Grant and Grace Kelly.

But surely, *The Birds* is all the better for the fact that Rod Taylor and Tippi Hedren *aren't* Grant and Kelly: they're not such big stars, and the audience had fewer preconceptions about them.

That may be, but that wasn't the original intention: the comic timing of the earlier scenes simply didn't have what I was aiming for. If there's something else there which works as well or better, fine. But I didn't feel that there was any chemistry in that first meeting between them in the pet shop.

But the most accepted analysis of the movie is that it's about complacency – an attack on complacency. Surely that was your imput as much as Hitchcock's?

Maybe. But the scene in the movie that I feel is really mine is the scene in the restaurant with the ornithologist. There's the drunk at the bar, 'It's the end of the world'. The fisherman who complains that the birds are playing hell with his fishing boats… That whole scene is like a one-act play, and I really love it. I wrote that after I left California, and I sent it to Hitch. And he shot it without a moment's hesitation.

You'd worked together so well, it must have surprised you when you got dumped on *Marnie*.

It did surprise me, because I thought he'd recognise that I was right about a crucial thing in *Marnie*. That after the rape, you'd never get the audience's sympathy back for the lead character. I didn't know how to make a rapist seem likeable. Still, despite the crude back projection, that movie has a legion of admirers, so maybe I was wrong. I'm satisfied to have made one movie at least as Evan Hunter which will be remembered. And as long as people remember the 87th Precinct books, that'll be satisfaction enough for me.

Otherwise Known as
Ed McBain...

ED MCBAIN is the pseudonym of Evan Hunter, born in New York in 1926 as Salvatore A Lombino. Although McBain considers Evan Hunter to be 'who he is', he is undoubtedly best known as Ed McBain, the creator of the 87th Precinct.

In addition to the McBain pseudonym Hunter has written crime and mystery fiction under a variety of names, including Richard Marsten and Ezra Hannon.

Following his time (1944 to 1946) in the United States Navy, Hunter graduated from New York's Hunter College in 1950, a member of Phi Beta Kappa. He held a wide variety of jobs—lobster salesman, reader for a literary agency and teacher at two vocational high schools, the experience that lead to him writing his breakthrough novel, *The Blackboard Jungle* (1954).

The Blackboard Jungle, a powerful story of juvenile delinquency in an urban high school, established Hunter as a major contemporary writer, which was consolidated by a collection of short stories using same background, *The Jungle Kids*, appeared in 1956.

Although McBain considers the Evan Hunter name to be reserved for literary fiction (and has argued quite vociferously about this in the past), some of his output as Hunter would undoubtedly be considered to be crime fiction. Three early paperbacks prior to the creation of the Ed McBain pseudonym: *The Evil Sleep!* (1952), *The Big Fix* (1952), and *Don't Crowd Me* (1953) are undoubtedly crime fiction. Later fiction like *Matter Of Conviction* (1959) and two comedy-crime titles, *A Horse's Head* (1967) *And Every Little Crook And Nanny* (1972) can also be considered as crime titles. The political terrorism novel *Nobody Knew They Were There* (1971); and his fictionalisation of the famous Lizzie Borden case, *Lizzie* (1984) also have roots in the genre. When I talked to Hunter he told me that *Lizzie* had been a failure. I was surprised, because I had remembered it as one of his best novels, and remembered the large amount of publicity that heralded it in the UK (including a BBC documentary on Hunter).

Hunter also wrote more standard PI fare—with a typical twist. As Curt Cannon he wrote about a PI, Curt Cannon, (who appeared in one novel—*I'm Cannon, For Hire* (1958)—and a book of short stories—*I Like 'Em Tough* (1958) was homeless and a wino, drinking *"twenty-five hours out of twenty-four,"* but still able to solve a case. One of the most remarkable pieces of work by Hunter was the 1958 completion (as Ed McBain) of a book by the undoubted master (mistress?) of the screwball crime novel, Craig Rice. *The April Robin Murders* had been left unfinished at her death. Hunter completed it in superlative style.

Despite this work, and a huge body of work under his own name Hunter is best known for his work as Ed McBain and the creation of his most enduring fictional 'character', the 87th Precinct (see below for more information). The first 87th Precinct book *Cop Hater* (1956), introduced the members of the 87th precinct, set in the fictional city of Isola (New York). Steve Carella, Meyer Meyer, Andy Parker, and the other cops are seen tackling several cases simultaneously, and although McBain did not invent the American Police Procedural (that honour should go to Hillary Waugh) he certainly invented the multi-threaded, and often interwoven, plot structure for it used (or perhaps one should more accurately say stolen) so sucessfully by Stephen Bochco for Hill Street Blues, the best adaption of the 87th Precinct never to pay royalties to Hunter. Hunter is rightly bitter on this point, and none too happy with legitimate adaptions of his work such as *Fuzz* (1973). Perhaps the saddest outcome of Bochco's lack of even a credit for inspiration for Hunter is that the best two people to adapt the McBain books (Hunter and Bochco) will never work together.

The detectives of the 87th have not aged now over the course of four decades. McBain says, *"If I hadn't done that, I'd now have a precinct of doddering old men."*

The McBain version of police life is gritty, realistic and sometimes grim but the emphasis is 'realistic', not 'real'. Hunter has used the series to experiment with every kind of crime story, from comedy to tragedy and all points between.

In *Goldilocks* (1978) Hunter used the McBain name for a new series about Matthew Hope, a lawyer in Calusa, Florida. Initially each book in the series was named after a fairy tale, but this restriction loosened as the series progressed. Hope has never been as popular as the 87th—perhaps Hunter wandered too far from his inspiration in New York. He joked to me about the crackdown on crime by Mayor Giulliano that *"I hope he doesn't go too far—he'll put me out of business."* He wrote about another precinct in his unamed city in *Another Part Of The City* (1985), but although in it's own way a good novel, it wasn't the start of another series as some had hoped. The 87th is just planted too deeply in our souls. The Hope series has recently ended, and in *The Last Best Hope,* Matthew Hope turns to Steve Carrella of the 87th for help… Hunter and McBain are home.

In 1986, Hunter was named a Grand Master by the Mystery Writers of America, and this year he was awarded the Cartier Diamond Dagger award. There is no one more deserving of any award for crime fiction. Hunter has written at least seven of the very best crime fiction novels of the twentieth century. I asked Ed Gorman for his opinion of McBain, and he came back with this:

"Ed McBain's books offer us not only great entertainment but also the best writing course on popular fiction available anywhere in the world. Want to know how to set a scene? Study McBain. Want to know how to create a character through dialogue? Study McBain. Want to know how to skilfully juggle three different storylines at the same time? Study McBain. He's the master. A few of the McBains have gotten lost over the years. *He Who Hesitates* and *Blood Relatives* are two of his very best and yet they rarely get mentioned. The former gives us a new kind of killer, a dopey sort of guy who can occasionally be downright appealing. The latter gives us the diary of a young woman that proves to be a definitive and heartbreaking examination of romantic love. Or *Sadie When She Died*. One of the best mystery plots ever devised. "

"This isn't to slight his Evan Hunter books. *Last Summer* and *Nobody Knew They Were There* are flat out masterpieces. *Nobody* captures the early seventies, with all its talk of political revolution, better than any novel I've ever read, a particularly amazing feat when you consider that it was written by a middle-class middle-aged literary man. He got it right, all the sanctimony, all the narcissism, all the theatrical despair. I'm always eager for the next McBain because I know I'm going to be entertained, and I'm going to learn a lot of new things about writing."

The 87th Precinct Novels

"The city in these pages is imaginary; the people and places all fictitious. Only the police routine is based on established investigatory technique."

That disclaimer appears at the beginning of every 87th Precinct book, a signal to us that we are beginning our journey—sometimes a descent—into his unnamed city, which we know in our hearts to be New York.

Or rather it's New York rotated a little. Take a map and try it. Using a map and the books you can match up some of the references: Calm's Point (Brooklyn), Isola (Manhattan), Majesta (Queens), Riverhead (the Bronx), Bethtown (Staten Island). Why has Hunter decided to do this? Partly it's to allow him to use time and space as he wishes—no-one to say 'you can't get there from here in that amount of time', but partly it's to allow himself the luxury of doing whatever he want's (even if he often chooses *not* to do it). By doing this he has created a setting that is a recognisable microcosm of *all* urban life.

Although no single character is central to the books, Steve Carella, the ostensible hero of *Cop Hater* (1956), the first in the series, comes nearest. In the first book, we meet Steve's fiancée, Teddy Franklin, a beautiful deaf-mute. Over the course of the series, they marry and have twins who grow to school age. As noted above time is treated with more leeway than anything else in the series—Meyer Meyer, a bald, patient Jew and Carella's best friend and frequent partner, has been thirty-seven years old (and slightly older than Carella) for thirty years, *"and he always will be,"* McBain says, defiantly.

Other significant characters include blond Bert Kling. Introduced as a rookie patrolman in *The Mugger* (1956), he soon becomes a detective. Kling has possibly the worst luck in the world with women—one fiancée was murdered, one walked out on him, one was kidnapped; his wife cheated on him, another girlfriend was raped and blames him. Most recently (in *Romance*) he has been dating a black doctor—another relationship fraught with danger for the vulnerable Kling

Cotton Hawes is a huge New Englander, with a white streak in his red hair, and knows the city inside out. Roger Haviland, a brutal, bullying cop who was killed in *Killer's Choice* (1957), was resurrected six books later in *See Them Die* (1960) as Andy Parker, a lazy slob and a bad cop who demonstrates in *Tricks* (1987) that he *can* do police work. Hal Willis is a diminutive judo expert; Arthur Brown is black man with ferocious pride and very little patience. Overseeing the squad is Lieutenant Peter Byrnes, a bullet-headed man who has a special affection for Carella, who helped get his son off drugs. Fat Ollie Weeks of the 88th Precinct is a fat, sweaty, thick-skinned racist who loves police work so much he helps the 87th in his spare time and is frighteningly good at it.

Over forty-odd years McBain has used the form of the police procedural to write every known type of crime fiction, not to mention romantic novels (*Romance*), political commentary (*Hail To The Chief*, 1973), religious allegory (*And All Through The House*, 1988) as well as much social commentary (the lastest of which, a commentary on privilege and the mores of the night city, is *Nocturne* (1997)).

He has housed within the 87th Precinct a mini series that could have come straight from the pulps. Again and again the city is menaced by a master criminal known as the Deaf Man. The Deaf Man books (*The Heckler* (1960), *Fuzz* (1968), *Let's Hear It For The Deaf Man* (1973), *Eight Black Horses* (1985), *Mischief* (1993)) are black comedies of errors as the 87th does its best to stop their very own criminal genius. Although he is always foiled, it's usually a close thing and is accomplished as much by good luck as judgement.

The 87th has starred in eight feature films (three made for TV). *Cop Hater* (United Artists, 1958, directed by William Berke) starred Robert Loggia as Detective Steve Carelli (not Carella) investigating the serial murder of policemen by. The setting is clearly Manhattan. *The Mugger* (also United Artists, 1958, directed by William Berke) is also set in New York City. Kent Smith as a police psychiatrist replaces the 87th as the detective in this one, based on the second novel in the series. Tokyo is the setting for *Tengoku to jigoku* (1963, directed by Akira Kurosawa, also known as *High and Low, Heaven and Hell* and *The Ransom*), based on *King's Ransom* (1959).

Ten Plus One was adapted for *Sans mobile apparent* (also *Without Apparent Motive* 1972, directed by Philippe Labro); the film stars Jean-Louis Trintignant and Dominique Sanda and in the same year, Boston was used as the setting for *Fuzz* (1972, directed by Richard A. Colla), adapted by Hunter. Burt Reynolds played Carella, Tom Skerrit was Bert Kling, James McEachin was Arthur Brown, Jack Weston was Meyer Meyer, and Yul Brynner was the Deaf Man. Racquel Welch also starred. Despite having written the screenplay Hunter is not complimentary about the film, his main dislike being the casting.

Most recently Hunter (as McBain) has had a series of TV Movies adapted from the 87th Precinct under the general title of *Ed McBain's 87th Precinct*. The first, *Lightning* (1995), scripted by Mike Krohn and Dan Levine, starred Randy Quaid as Steve Carella, Alex McArthur as Bert Kling, Ving Rhames as Artie Brown, Alan Blumenfeld as Ollie Weeks and Ron Perkins as Meyer Meyer. *Ice* (1996) was scripted by Larry Cohen and starred Dale Midkiff as Carella, Joe Pantoliano as Meyer Meyer, Paul Johansson as Bert Kling, Andrea Parker as Eileen Burke.

Heatwave (1997) had essentially the same script team and cast as *Ice*. Let's hope this series is more to Hunter's taste, and has provided for some of that *Hill Street Blues* kudos.

Earlier there was an 87th Precinct TV series that ran for one season on NBC (1961) with Robert Lansing, Ron Harper, Gregory Walcott, and Norman Fell as the detectives and Gena Rowlands as Carella's deaf and mute wife Teddy.

The Books

Cop Hater (1956)
The Mugger (1956)

"Clifford thanks you, Madam", *The Mugger* says bowing from the waist, and then he vanishes into the night, leaving behind his battered and terrified female victim. He has struck fourteen times so far and the cops of the 87th Precinct want it to stop now. Then a beautiful young woman is found dead and the case of Clifford turns even uglier.

The Pusher (1956)
The Con Man (1957)

A trickster is taking money from an old woman for his own private charity, fleecing businessmen out of thousands of dollars, and he's also a lady-killer. If the 87th Precinct know every trick he's played why are the bodies still washing up on shore?

Killer's Choice (1957)

Someone killed Annie Boone, but was she an innocent victim or a hitman's target? Carella and Kling of the 87th precinct pick up the pieces of life and move relentlessly closer to the answers

Killer's Payoff (1958)
Killer's Wedge (1958)

Lady Killer (1958)

"I Will Kill The Lady Tonight At 8. What Can You Do About It?" The boys of the 87th have just twelve hours to find out who the crank letter writer is—and who he means by 'the Lady'.

Til Death (1959)

Death stalks the groom and the groom is about to marry Steve Carella's sister. Tommy and Angela's wedding party has become a deadly game of hide-and-seek for Steve and the 87th. Tommy is 'it' and Steve has only a few hours to find a killer and prevent Tommy from being tagged 'out' for good.

King's Ransom (1959)
Give The Boys A Great Big Hand (1960)

The hand is a literal one, of course...

The Heckler (1960)
See Them Die (1960)
Lady, Lady, I Did It! (1961)
The Empty Hours (1962)
Like Love (1962)

It's obviously a lovers' double suicide, yet it seems too neat. A routine check turns up three suspects—but how can the 87th Precinct catch a cold-blooded killer and make him confess when they can't prove the victims were actually murdered?

Ten Plus One (1963)
Ax (1964)

Steve Carella, Cotton Hawes, and boys of the 87th Precinct know where, when, and how George Lasser died, but they don't have a clue as to who has 'given him the *Ax*'. And when the mad marauder strikes again, it's time to take the *Ax* to the grindstone.

He Who Hesitates (1965)

Outside the 87th Precinct a stranger stands in the falling snow. He knows he should go in and tell a policeman about what happened the night before, about Molly. Every second that he hesitates takes him one step farther away from the 87th Precinct station, as another second ticks away on an innocent woman's life.

Doll (1965)

She's a living Doll—until she's slashed to death. Detective Steve Carella wants Bert Kling on the case, even though Kling is making enemies of everyone. Finally even Carella has had it with Kling, but suddenly the detective is missing and suspected dead. The 87th Precinct go full throttle to find the truth. But what they really need is a little Doll—a little Doll with all the answers.

Eighty Million Eyes (1966)

Stan Gifford is America's most beloved comedian—40 million people watched the comedian crack his jokes. And those same 80 million eyes see him die on camera.

Fuzz (1968)
Shotgun (1969)
Jigsaw (1970)
Hail, Hail, The Gang's All Here (1971)
Sadie When She Died (1972)

Detective Steve Carella thinks he has an open and shut case. A killer has confessed, clear fingerprints, and a witness. But when the victim's husband seems less than mournful at her death, and her little black book turns up a record of her love life, Carella knows it's time to call in the 87th precinct.

Let's Hear It For The Deaf Man (1972)
Hail To The Chief (1973)

Even 13 years in the 87th Precinct haven't hardened Bert Kling and Steve Carella to such murders—six naked bodies, including an infant, and no one knows who any of them are. An anonymous phone call leads Kling and Carella to a private street war, and the two cops get caught in the crossfire of organised violence.

Bread (1974)

In the heart of the summer kids are playing in open hydrants. Water pressure is sinking, tempers are rising. The 87th Precinct knows that someone is fighting fire with fire. As usual, it's all about *Bread*. The bread in this case is money—lots of money. Money lost in a warehouse fire. Money gained in extraordinarily successful, important business. Money waiting in the cheque-printing machine of an insurance company. Carella and Cotton Hawes take over the arson case from indolent Andy Parker. But what they find behind a tale of fire and money is murder. Lots of murder.

Blood Relatives (1975)
So Long As You Both Shall Live (1976)
Long Time No See (1977)

They never saw their executioner. Because each victim was blind. Steve Carella is stymied in a hunt that began when a Vietnam veteran, his sight taken in war, was found with his head nearly separated from his body. As the bizarre killing spree goes on, Carella looks into the first victim's dreams and sees a panorama of war, sexuality, secrets, and torment — and one man's pure, blind rage…

Calypso (1979)
Ghosts (1980)
Heat (1981)

A dead man lies reeking of alcohol—no forced entry, no visible wounds, and an empty bottle of seconal. It all adds up to a simple suicide. Or does it? Why would an alcoholic artist, terrified of drugs, have ended his life with sleeping pills? It's up to Detective Steve Carella of the 87th Precinct to uncover the real story.

Ice (1983)

Ice coats the streets where the rapist prowls. Ice spills from the pockets of a dead diamond dealer. Ice runs through the heart of a cold-blooded killer and that of the players in a multimillion Dollar show-biz scam. And in the deep chill of winter, it is the 87th Precinct who must brave the winds of death to save a city frozen with fear.

Lightning (1984)
Eight Black Horses (1985)
Poison (1987)
Tricks (1987)
Lullaby (1989)

In the 87th Precinct Detectives Meyer and Carella find that their New Year has a macabre beginning when they must track down the brutal killers of a baby girl, smothered, and her babysitter, viciously raped and murdered, on New Year's Eve

May well be the very best of the 87th Precinct novels. It moves like a bullet train. —Joseph Wambaugh

Vespers (1990)
Widows (1991)

Not long after the brutal slaying of his sexy blond mistress, twice-married lawyer Arthur Schumaker is gunned down in the heart of the 87th Precinct, leaving behind dark secrets and unanswered questions.

Kiss (1992)

Someone is trying to kill rich, beautiful Emma Bowles. Is it her stockbroker husband? And can she trust the handsome private eye her husband has hired to 'protect' her? McBain's new 87th Precinct installment, less ambitiously multi-plotted than some recent entries, has just two very different narratives, delivered in alternating chunks. Meanwhile Steve Carella must suffer through the trial of the psychopath who killed his father in a holdup.

Mischief (1993)

Graffiti-writers are being knocked off at a frightening rate, there's an epidemic of 'granny-dumping' (abandonment of old people, usually senile) and the return of the Deaf Man, a master criminal who taunts the 87th detectives with advance clues to his schemes. Eventually the cops prevail, but not until the Deaf Man has orchestrated a huge, deadly diversion from his clever scam, after which the master criminal puts another one over on the 87th. Or does he?

And All Through The House (1994)
Romance (1995)

It's not a mystery, it's a story of survival and triumph. That's what some people say about *Romance*, a would-be hit play about an actress pursued by a knife-wielding stalker. Before the show can open, the leading lady is *really* attacked, outside the theatre. And before the detectives of the 87th can solve that crime, the same actress is stabbed again. While Bert Kling interviews witnesses and suspects ranging from the show's producers to the author. With a doctor. Who happens to be a deputy chief surgeon. Who happens to be a black woman. In the city of Isola, nothing is black and white.

Nocturne (1997)

The murder of an old woman makes the wee hours at the precinct anything but peaceful — especially when they learn she was one of the greatest concert pianists of the century. Meanwhile, 88th Precinct cop Fat Ollie Weeks is on the trail of three prep school boys and a crack dealer who spent the evening carving up a hooker.

The Matthew Hope Novels

Hope, transplanted from the North to Calusa, Florida, is a lawyer specialising in contract and real estate law. Which frequently leads to murders. Originally titled after nursery rhymes and fairy tales, the plots of the Hope books echo them. *Rumplestiltskin* (1980) has a rock band called Wheat that can spin gold records, *Cinderella* (1986) tells the story of a young woman who steals mob money and changes her appearance. Hope, unwillingly divorced, has romances with various women, but still loves his ex-wife.

The Hope novels have never really had the popularity of the 87th precinct novels, but it's an odious comparison. If they'd been written by anyone but McBain they would have been better appreciated. The trilogy that includes the last novel in the series—*There Was A Little Girl, Gladly, The*

Cross-Eyed Bear and *The Last Best Hope* are some of the strongest entries in the series, especially the bravura touch of having Hope in a coma throughout *all* of *There Was A Little Girl*

Goldilocks (1978)
Rumplestiltskin (1981)
Beauty And The Beast (1982)

Matthew Hope spots her on Saturday, exquisitely beautiful, strolling topless on the beach. On Monday, she shows up in his law office, beaten and bruised, ready to file for divorce. By Tuesday, she is dead—and her big, ugly husband is arrested for murder. But Matthew believes he is innocent; now, he has to prove it.

Jack And The Beanstalk (1984)

Jack McKinney decides he's going to turn a bankrupt snapbean farm into a paying operation, and hires Matthew Hope to push the land deal through. Four days later, Jack is dead—and there was no trace of the $36,000 Jack had promised to deliver for the farm.

Snow White And Rose Red (1985)
Cinderella (1986)
Puss In Boots (1987)
The House That Jack Built (1988)
Three Blind Mice (1990)
Mary, Mary (1993)

Defense Attorney Matthew Hope believes eccentric Mary Barton is innocent of murdering and burying three young girls in her lush garden. Although the evidence is over-whelming, Hope is willing to unearth long-buried secrets to gain an acquittal.

There Was A Little Girl (1994)

Hope spend his time in a semi-coma after being shot outside a bar on the seedy side of Calusa, despite his vow to avoid the criminal side of his law practice. Meanwhile, Hope's PI pals Warren Chambers and Toots Kiley, as well as police detective Morris Bloom, try to reconstruct Hope's previous week…

Gladly, The Cross-Eyed Bear (1996)

Lainie Commins, a designer of children's toys, engages Hope in a suit against her old employers, Brett and Etta Toland of Toyland over the rights to 'Gladly,' a teddy bear with crossed eyes. When millionaire Brett Toland is shot, things begin to spin out of control

The Last Best Hope (1998)

Jill Lawton approaches Hope for help in finding her missing husband, Jack, whom she intends to divorce. That night, a body with Jack's identi-fication is found, shot in the face and dead. It's not Jack Lawton, but Ernest Corrington, burglar and actor who part of a love triangle with Jack and a woman who goes by two names Melanie and Holly. Holly and Jack have also comprised an erotic trian-gle with Jill … and they have all par-ticipated in a criminal plot. McBain involves Hope and the 87th Precinct in a seamless and satisfactory whole

Non-series books as Ed McBain:

The Sentries (1965)

A hurricane is bearing down on South Florida, as is a storm of fanaticism and violence. Though the small Florida Key known as Ocho Puerto lies in the path of destruction, ground zero is some 100s mile to its south. It's all part of a scheme engineered by a rogue right-winger—a freedom fighter with his own private army. It's up to a courageous few to stop him.

Where There's Smoke (1975)

Benjamin Smoke is a retired police lieutenant who walked away from the job for one reason alone: he was bored. Bored of the criminals. Bored of the crimes. Bored of answers that came too easy, too fast, and too often the same. Now, working as an unlicensed private detective, Smoke finally gets his wish. Someone has committed the perfect crime — a perfectly senseless crime — by stealing a dead body.

Guns (1976)
Another Part Of The City (1985)
Downtown (1989).

Florida citrus grower Michael Barnes has his wallet and rental car stolen at a New York bar. Things go from bad to worse when the car turns up with a corpse in the trunk. Now he is hunted by both the cops and the mob.

Book as written by Curt Cannon:

I'm Cannon, For Hire (1958)
I Like 'Em Tough (SS) (1958)

Books as written by Richard Marsten, many later reissued as written by Ed McBain:

Runaway Black (1954)
Murder In The Navy (1955)
The Spiked Heel (1956)
Vanishing Ladies (1957)
Even The Wicked (1958)
Big Man (1959).

Book as written by Ezra Hannon, later reissued as written by Ed McBain:

Doors (1975)

Alex Hardy knows that Doors can always be opened—you just need the right tools. The rising young New York burglar is ready for the jewelry heist of his life. There's only one problem. A door has been cracked open. It's a door inside of Alex, a door of love for a beautiful and honest woman. She's the only jewel he can't steal—and the one most likely to cost him his life.

Collections of Short Fiction

The McBain Brief (1982)
McBain's Ladies (1987)
McBain's Ladies Too (1989)

'Genuinely chilling undercurrents, and above all that authentic page turning quality'
MICHAEL DIBDIN

Out in paperback in December

'Sheer good writing'
FRANCES FYFIELD

Also available in paperback *Every Breath You Take* and *Running For Shelter*

 ORION PAPERBACKS

Lauren Henderson
Adrian Muller

'Barbie is a slut' reads crime writer Lauren Henderson's T-shirt. Thinking of Mattel's lawsuit against pop group Aqua for their song 'I'm a Barbie Girl', I wonder if the toy manufacturer will be suing Henderson as well. Not if they know what's good for them: they wouldn't survive the hell she would give them in her novels! I am in Crime in Store, a London bookshop specialising in crime fiction, talking to the author who made her debut in 1995 with the acidly titled Dead White Female. *The book introduced Lauren's series protagonist Sam Jones, a sculptress with a fondness for recreational drugs and casual sex. In Sam's first outing she turned amateur sleuth after a close friend was found dead. Two books on, and numerous deaths later, Sam makes her fourth appearance in* Freeze My Margarita. *Published by Hutchinson in August, this latest instalment in the Jones series seemed to be the ideal excuse to find out more about the author and her creation.*

The thing that gradually came to me when reading Lauren Henderson's novels was that they were nothing like I expected them to be. From her bio I knew that the author had gone to a public school and had studied English at Cambridge. Then she went on to work for publications such as *Lime Lizard*, an indie music magazine; *The Observer*; and *Marxism Today*! So how did she come to write books that were so light and entertaining? Admittedly Lauren's protagonist, Sam Jones, starts off as a struggling artist and many of her friends live in squats. Whilst not being unaffected by the privileged lifestyle of her clients, she manages to keep her principles in perspective. However, I was expecting something a lot more… "Worthy?" Lauren prompts laughing. *"I've just never seen why being left-wing means that you can't have fun,"* she says, slightly exasperated. *"Sam has an absolutely strong left-wing sensibility but without being heavy or boring about it!"*

The author goes on to explain that the politics she favours are no longer burdened by the rigid ideology and political correctness once associated with socialism. This means they must have survived the Henderson test. *"My natural instinct,"* Lauren says, *"is to take the piss out of everything and see if it can stand up to it. Things have really changed. If some of my girlfriends are around on a Sunday evening we will rent* Showgirls *on video. It is just so stupid that it's hysterically funny. We're not particularly bothered about the large amount of female nudity—although, I have to say, it there had been the same amount of male nudity it would have been even better. You couldn't have admitted to this in left-wing circles ten years ago because men as well as women would have got on your case."*

Lauren's early days as a struggling journalist provided some of the background for her heroine. *"A lot of Sam's stuff comes from when I was living in London on a very tight budget,"* says the author. Yet, she has fond memories of those days, particularly of her time at *Lime Lizard*, a now defunct music magazine. It was an exciting time to be working in the music industry because the 'grunge' sound was just about to break through. Lauren saw many bands that went on to make it big, and she still caries around her ticket-stub from the first concert Nirvana played in Britain.

At the magazine she focused on sub-editing and also did some film interviews. *"I didn't really go in for music journalism, because it's a style of writing which is very over the top. The writing in the* New Musical Express *is very florid. It ruins you. It's like sugar, it eats into your teeth so you can never chew anything else again. I basically appointed myself to be the person who was going to tidy it up. I'm still quite strict about punctuation and grammar because I've edited for ages."* As for whom she interviewed, she casually mentions names such as Costa Gavras, the respected Greek director. *"I wasn't very good at doing interviews,"* she admits with a grin. *"I had to keep myself from writing the things that I thought they should be saying."*

It was only after both *Lime Lizard* and *New Marxism* folded that Lauren seriously started considering writing fiction as a full-time occupation. *"I'd always written fiction, but mainly short stories. I re-read most of them recently and I thought they were rather good—lots of sex and violence. Hopefully, they'll be published eventually."*

Returning to how her writing career unfolded she says, *"The magazines closed down, and there I was in London, having to decide whether I was going to try and get a job at* The Guardian *newspaper with everybody else. Instead I went off to Italy to write because I'd worked out that I was never going to be able to write in London. It just would have been too distracting."* Not that the move stopped Lauren from having fun in Tuscany as well, but she did start writing more lengthy material. So why crime fiction? *"Partly in an attempt to avoid writing the 'serious' novel that I've been working on for years,"* she says, smiling. *"But also because I really like crime fiction. And if you're interested in the role of women in society, crime fiction is a great way to be able to write about a strong female heroine. It is a brilliant way to have a woman who by definition is strong and independent, who is able to stand on her own two feet and be able to look after herself. That's what I wanted to write about."*

Has she always read crime fiction? *"I read everything,"* she says. *"crime fiction, romantic novels, science fiction. I only read fiction really. I tend to keep going back to the older writers like Raymond Chandler—even some of Georgette Heyer's fiction is very nice because it's well written. A lot of crime fiction nowadays is…"* she stops and thinks momentarily. *"Perhaps because it's not very well written, but once you've got through the plot there's no reason to pick it up and read it again. I like to re-read books if there is something to enjoy."*

It turns out that Lauren's first attempt at writing a crime novel was after getting drunk with a friend at a party. They decided there were virtually no contemporary female authors who wrote the kind of crime fiction that they wanted to read. *"At that time I was just voraciously reading crime fiction, and there were all these Virago titles with miserable heroines who couldn't get laid or, if they did, complained about it. Everything was so grey, bleak and depressing, and deliberately self-flagellating."* Lauren says she considers herself extremely lucky to be part of what she considers to be possibly the first guilt-free generation. *"It doesn't mean to say we are without responsibilities,"* she stresses, *"but there is less of the sense that there is someone looking over our shoulder, judging our behaviour. I think the women who were writing the crime novels that I was reading then still had a major chip on their shoulder about being female."* She suddenly stops and asks, *"Do you know a band called Aztec Camera? The guy who was the songwriter had this line 'They call us lonely when we're really just alone'. Women often get called lonely when they're really just alone, and one of the things I wanted to do with Sam was to have her be by herself without anybody feeling that she was being self-pitying, gloomily sitting in her studio thinking the world was having much more fun without her. That was what I often felt the heroines did in the books I was reading. Either that or the writers were trying much to hard to copy tough male behaviour instead of reinventing it for their heroines which is much more interesting."*

Lauren and her friend wrote a few pages together before it became apparent that a collaborative process wouldn't work out. As for why Sam Jones became a sculptress, most of the reasoning got lost in the alcoholic haze that she and her friend were in at the time. *"Maybe because I have friends who are sculptors,"* she tries to recall. Regardless, it turned out to be a good choice *"Because,"* Lauren explains, *"a sculptress is somebody who can whack large pieces of metal into shape, someone who's going to be strong and be able to use her body* well."

Sam's strength and cunning are put to particularly good use in moments of peril, possibly most memorably so in a fight scene in *The Black Rubber Dress*. "*Sam is a bit taller than me,*" says Lauren, "*but writing about a woman you have to be really plausible when you describe something like knocking down a six foot tall guy. One of the things I liked about the film* Bound, *which is this great lesbian thriller, is that when actress Gina Gershon is hit by the baddie she just stays down because she's not as strong as he is. They don't glamorise that, they don't try to pretend that it's going to be an equal fight. Likewise, Sam has to be sneakier, because I really wanted to make that fight believable for readers.*"

When I suggest that a central character often falls into one of two categories—the author's alter-ego or otherwise the fictional best friend—Lauren says, "*You're forgetting another big category which is women writers and their fictional detectives who they secretly fancy.*" Then, anticipating the question I was about to ask, she continues smiling, "*And now you're going to ask me how much alike Sam and I are, and I'm going to tell you that you'll have to work that out for yourself.*" Immediately disregarding her last statement she continues, "*'Alter-ego' suggests a degree of detachment from Sam... I suppose she is like me but more so. The big difference between me and Sam is that I am very domesticated, I bake a lot. Still, my friends always say it is eerie how similar the narrative voice is to mine—Sam's humour definitely is mine.*" And her daring? Modestly the author says, "*I don't know... She's me with the archetypal knob turned up. She's like Tank Girl. Somebody said to me that she was like a Panzer Tank of a girl, and she is.*"

And what about the blonde jokes? Despite the fact that Lauren went through a spell of dying her hair platinum blonde, Sam has cracked wise about that particular hair tone throughout the series. The author even called her second novel *Too Many Blondes*. "*I have a prejudice against the natural blonde,*" she admits with a barely suppressed grin. "*Everything kind of spiralled from my telling blonde jokes for a while.*" Pointing out her own blonde phase I put it to her that she presumably has less of a prejudice against bleach blondes? "*Not as much,*" Lauren agrees laughing. "*but being blonde is no so much a hair colour as a state of mind. I was a blonde, but I was still a brunette. Do you see what I mean?*" Fortunately she does not wait for me to answer. "*Sam has decided not to bleach her hair on principal,*" Lauren says. "*I made that clear at the end of* Too Many Blondes, *because I thought that we were getting too similar.*"

In her novels Lauren distinguishes herself by featuring characters who represent her generation, and she does so without the excessive violence and gore that is typical for many of her contemporaries in the new wave of British crime writers. Could her novels be considered 'modern' cosies? *"You're the first person to say that,"* she says, apparently pleasantly surprised. *"Everybody else has said 'Oh Lauren you're really trendy', and I don't think I am at all! My books are old-fashioned. I'm not remotely interested in cutting people up with chainsaws. I don't see why I should be. I call that the entrails tendency. You've got to very careful with splattering peoples' brains or shoving hands up their orifices, because it's really lazy. Unless you do it superbly well, it's not going to take you very far because everyone's going to get sick of it and you're going to get sick of it too. There's this ongoing debate about British hard-core vs. British cosy. God knows there are awful books on both sides of the divide, but I would rather read bad cosy than bad hard-core. At least a bad cosy isn't trying to be self-conscious about splattering people. One of the reasons I wanted to do a crime novel was because I wanted to do books about the way I and my friends were living in London, but I wanted a hook to do it with."*

Having chosen the cosy genre, how concerned is Lauren about her heroines continued success as a sculptress if people are being murdered wherever she goes? Surely, Sam's potential customers will be staying away in droves. *"Okay,"* Lauren says laughing, *"I have a strong line of defence for this. One of the conventions of the genre is: amateur sleuths always keep falling over bodies. Every writer does this, even authors with policemen or private eyes have their characters stumbling across bodies or their friends getting into trouble. They may have a better excuse but there are lots of cases where the 'professionals' go off on holiday and still come across bodies. The reason I actually didn't do a PI series in the first place was because I was worried of getting stuck into a formula. Someone hires the detective to find someone or something, and they go off and always do the same thing. It gets to be quite monotonous after a while. Obviously I have to deal with a lack of credibility, but the payoff is that Sam gets to go to all kinds of different places. And as long as people are prepared to take that leap of disbelief, then the books should be fun."*

Since the first instalment Sam seems to have been climbing up the social ladder. In *Dead White Female* she was still partying in squats, but *Too Many Blondes* saw Sam raising a sweat on the fitness scene, and in *The Black Rubber Dress* she was hobnobbing with merchant bankers. Is Sam in danger of losing touch with her roots? *"That's not going to happen,"* Lauren says firmly. *"When I started out I decided that she was not going to be one of those characters who was going to be fixed in the same location with the same group of friends around her. I've seen that happen in so many series that I liked. They seem to get ossified the further they develop. One of the good things about Sam being a sculptress is that she has a career that can move on, quite apart from being an amateur investigator. I don't want Sam to be a struggling sculptress in the fifth book. She's got to have done something with her life. She's got a lot of drive, so she would have pushed herself. Besides,"* she adds, *"you know how things are. Friends go away for six months, so they are not around when things happen to you. That, or they get a girlfriend, that is what happened with Tom,"* Lauren says, referring to one of the recurring characters in her books. *"He has a girlfriend who Sam doesn't get on with, so they are not seeing a great deal of each other."*

Increasing success might also become a problem for Sam, just as it has for the author herself. *"When I was living in this revolting, disgusting, squat in Camden there were about seven of us,"* Lauren recalls. *"Most have gone on to do pretty well, but the couple that haven't don't want to see any of us anymore. So it may well happen that, as Sam becomes more successful, she has to bully Tom into seeing her."*

The friendship with Tom is one of the few consistent relationships Sam has with men, mostly through her own choosing. It turns out that Sam's love life is one of the few grievances the author has about writing crime fiction. Lauren hates not being able to directly refer to how incidents in the previous books have affected Sam. In *Freeze My Margarita* for instance she found it difficult to write about how Sam comes to terms with the traumatic way in which the a relationship with a former lover ended. *"I'm trying to do it in such a way that someone who has read the fourth book, and then goes back to read the earlier ones, wouldn't automatically know what happened. Otherwise it would ruin the element of surprise."* Using a another relationship as a further example she says, *"What you end up having to write is 'There was this guy who wanted to take me down to meet his parents for the weekend, and that just wasn't on'."*

So is Sam ever likely to settle down? *"In the new book she's going out with an actor, and I think that one might last a bit,"* Lauren says. *"Sam actually says that of all the guys she has been with before she was the one who said the funny things. The guys always ended up being the foil and they became frustrated by it. Sam's new boyfriend is a lot more like her and she can't walk all over him like she did with some of the previous ones."*

What else does the author have in store for Sam in *Freeze My Margarita*? *"Well, she is doing some sculptures for a theatre set when a body is discovered in the sump. I foolishly I decided that the production Sam is working on would be A Midsummer Night's Dream because it's a play I know really well. I should have picked a Pinter, or a Beckett one woman show instead. It was too late before I realised that I'd picked a play with twenty characters!"* she concludes laughing.

Kem Nunn
Brian Ritterspak

When the great Robert Stone (of *Dog Soldiers* and *A Flag for Sunrise*) calls a book *"A profound study of skill, courage and the human psyche"*, the savvy reader takes note. Kem Nunn's *The Dogs of Winter*, his new book, is being received as his finest yet. Heart Attacks is California's last secret spot—the premier mysto surf haunt, the stuff of rumour and legend. Down and out photographer, Jack Fletcher, hitches up with surfing legend, Drew Harmon, active men past their prime, formerly heroic figures still trying to catch the perfect wave. Harmon's wife, Kendra is on an obsessive search of her own to find the murderer of a local girl. Quests converge and events play themselves out in ways that are both inevitable and surprising.

"As if Elmore Leonard and Cormac McCarthy had teamed up to write a surf novel", said the Village Voice, and the Washington Post enthused *"There is probably not an American novelist working today who is better at choreographing and describing physical action. The most accomplished practitioner of Californian noir writing today and the principal heir to the tradition of Chandler and Nathaniel West."*

Kem Nunn lives in Northern California and is also the author of *Pomona Queen*, *Unassigned Territory* and *Tapping the Source* (published by No Exit), which was nominated for the American Book Award's Best First Fiction.

Talking about his extraordinary new novel, Kem Nunn thinks movie makers might have trouble with what he calls his *"gnostic surf fable."* But not because the book lacks for gripping plot. *The Dogs of Winter* has enough story to keep a reader on the edge of his seat for days on end. *"The thing that will be tough for Hollywood types,"* says Nunn, *"will be figuring out who the hero is."* There is Drew Harmon, the legendary surfer who comes out of middle-age retirement to attempt the huge, cold waves at Heart Attacks, a secret spot on Indian land along the Northern California coast. Harmon's obsession and heroic stature are part of the book's central mystery, and his quest sets off a tragic chain of events. But Nunn thinks Harmon may be *"too dark; nobody will want to play him. And Jack Fletcher, an ageing surf photographer who hopes at the outset to recapture the party days of his youth but ends up knowing something about responsibility and recompense, may not be 'two-fisted' enough for Hollywood."* Then there is Kendra Harmon, Drew's young wife. She's kidnapped in revenge for Harmon's trespass, endures, then triumphs in a grim sort of way; but Nunn thinks it will be a rare actress who will wish to fill that difficult part. *"So you have this built-in problem,"* he says. Nunn has worked off and on as a screenwriter since he sold the movie rights to his highly acclaimed first novel, *Tapping the Source*. He has a sense of these things.

But Hollywood might have other problems translating this stunning novel to film. First there is the tone of the book. It is a book of big, dark moods. It has about it an electric gloom, part of which has to do with crimes and obsessions, and part with the vivid portraits of the decaying reservations and lumber towns and the cold, cloudy, jagged coastal landscape of Northern California. But most of which has to do with the hard specificity and sombre music of Nunn's prose.

Then there is the fact that the book is a novel of ideas. It may not actually matter for one's reading pleasure that the evil deeds that befall Kendra in the gloom of the forest hearken back to the first American storytelling genre — the captivity narrative. But once Nunn announces that this ordeal arises in part from his reading of Richard Slotkin's *Regeneration through Violence*, *"which talks about Puritans, Indians, captivity narratives, and the shaping of the first American hero myths,"* the haunting events of *The Dogs of Winter* take on new weight.

"There is the refrain in the book about surfers loving their heroes," says Nunn, who spent his youth in Southern California surfing and working on boats and did not go to college to study writing until he was nearly 30. *"People get lionised in a way that satisfies the myth. The culture does that. I was intrigued by the character of Drew. I wanted to explore what being elevated to that stature does to someone. Drew was this handsome young guy who did something very well and people cut him a lot of slack. But in the book he's at that point in life when all of that has run out for him. He's finally done something that he can't escape the consequences of, though he's still trying to. When Fletcher goes off to photograph Drew Harmon, he believes himself to be going off to photograph this legendary surfer. What is revealed to him is the man."*

So maybe there isn't a Hollywood hero in the book. Maybe this compelling, tragic, violent, and very American story will never reach the silver screen. Maybe *The Dogs of Winter* will remain just an amazing book. But…we'll see.

no alibis bookstore

83 botanic avenue, belfast. n.ireland, bt7 iji

crime, mystery & american studies

phone/fax 0044-1232-319607

e-mail david@noalibisbookshop.demon.co.uk

SPECIALISTS IN ALL THINGS CRIMINAL (OF A LITERARY NATURE, OF COURSE.)

AN EXTENSIVE COLLECTION OF BRITISH, AMERICAN, EUROPEAN AND IRISH CRIME FICTION

RECENT EDITIONS SIGNED COPIES OF ALL COLIN BATEMANS NOVELS INCLUDING HIS LATEST PAPERBACK "EMPIRE STATE"

SIGNED COPIES OF LAWRENCE BLOCK'S HITMAN NOW AVAILABLE £16.99

WE ALSO STOCK MANY OTHER IRISH CRIME TITLES AN ORDERING SERVICE IS ALSO AVAILABLE, WITH MAIL-ORDER FACILITIES. WE ARE ABLE TO SOURCE MANY, MANY TITLES FROM THE UNITED STATES, USUALLY WITHIN 2/3 WEEKS

CONTACT DAVID AT THE ABOVE NUMBER/EMAILADDRESS

Chris Niles
Adrian Muller

I SHOULD HAVE KNOWN BETTER: never judge a book by its cover. Well, not solely, anyway. Last year saw the publication of Spike It, *a debut novel by Chris Niles. The name of the author, together with the book's colourful jacket, suggested another laddish romp by a male writer. Regardless of whether this could be considered a plus or a minus, the cover had such an irresistible air of fun about it that I was compelled to pick it up and find out more. Inside the jacket the blurb appeared to confirm that the story—about a down and out radio journalist named Sam Ridley—would indeed be a great read. The author bio further revealed that 'he' was in fact a 'she', that Chris Niles was born in New Zealand, and that she was currently working in London for CNN, the twenty-four hour news network. Recently published,* Run Time *is the second instalment in the Ridley series, and in the following interview Chris Niles discusses her background and books in further detail.*

In hindsight it's probably not so strange that Chris Niles turned to crime writing: it could be seen as a continuation of her childhood activities. The young Chris grew up in a picture-perfect place called Lake Tekapo in the in the wilds of New Zealand's South Island high country. *"I used to spend my free time roaming the hills and lakes, making up terrible, derivative Enid Blyton stories."* With a slightly embarrassed grin, she continues, *"Memory has mercifully blocked out the details, but I seem to recall they always featured a tomboy whose name sounded a lot like George."*

After completing high school Chris studied journalism at a college in Wellington, then going on to work for a series of local radio stations where she did everything from making the coffee to reporting and reading the news. Of this time she says, *"I covered flower shows, council planning meetings, even kidnappings. It was a great time."* She learnt a lot and admits that fragments of some of the people she worked with emerge in the characters who populate City Radio, the radio station her protagonist works for.

She 'graduated' to Television New Zealand in 1984, but after a year she followed her then boyfriend to Australia. *"In Australia I worked for SBS, the*

Aussie equivalent of Channel Four," Chris explains. *"It was a station set up to report on ethnic issues—very important and well meaning. Unfortunately only a fraction of Australian households could receive the signal. We tried not to let it bother us as we went about our daily work,"* she adds with a smile.

She moved to London ten years ago and, in between freelancing and seeing the world, Chris met and married an American. She now divides her time between writing and her day job as a satellite feed co-ordinator at CNN. 'Satellite feed co-ordinator'?! Laughing she explains, *"It's what I call a cross between being a waitress and an air traffic controller. CNN sends most of its pictures around the world via satellite. It's not cheap but it's the most efficient way to do it, and I'm one of the people that helps those pictures get from A to B and if necessary on to X, Y and Z. CNN London is the network's biggest European bureau and we have a permanent satellite lease to Atlanta. We are the funnel between Atlanta and many of the other European, Middle Eastern and African bureaux."* Grinning she insists, *"It might sound like glamorous work but it generally isn't. I liken it to trench warfare: ninety percent routine and ten percent terror!"*

Chris first started seriously reading crime fiction after she moved to Britain. She cites Simon Brett as a favourite before going on to name further authors such as James M. Cain, Lindsay Davis, Sue Grafton, Ira Levin, Val McDermid, Simon Shaw, and Cornell Woolrich. *"One of my greatest regrets,"* Chris sighs, *"is that Michael Dibdin can't write books as fast as I can read them."* However, these days Chris only reads when she isn't writing crime novels herself, *"Because,"* she explains, *"I find the style of the book tends to bleed into my work."*

Is there a New Zealand crime writing tradition? *"There is now!"* she enthuses. *"It's just a shame there's such a large gap between Dame Ngaio Marsh, Stella Duffy and me. I used to think this was because crime writing is essentially an urban phenomenon. But what is probably the case is that New Zealanders take their literary traditions very seriously. If you think about becoming a writer of prose in New Zealand you think about Janet Frame, Keri Hulme, and Maurice Gee. Those guys cast very long shadows! For years, in my twenties, I believed I would never write because I had 'nothing to say'. The idea of writing a mystery book never occurred to me."* So what did inspire Chris to write crime fiction? *"It's more accurate to say who inspired me. And I have to place the blame firmly at the doors of Simon Brett and Andrew Klavan,"* she says.

It turns out that Andrew Klavan is a personal friend of Chris, and he and his wife Ellen have been her 'literary parents'. Explaining their parental role, Chris says this included, *"reading terrible first drafts, offering pointers, and gently telling me when I was way off base."*

In the early 90s Chris had some time off work due to illness. To occupy her time she would go to the library and bring back armloads of books by

Brett and Klavan and study them for their technique. *"Simon has a beautiful light touch, and nobody can beat Andrew for plotting,"* Chris states. *"When I was writing* Spike It, *and found myself getting stuck up the fiftieth blind alley of the day, I would re-read them for pointers on how to extricate myself."*

When writing crime fiction, the most difficult thing for Chris is the plotting. *"I find it incredibly difficult,"* she says. *"Some days I think my brain is going to burst from the strain of it all. I really envy and admire writers who can plot simply and cleverly, I'd give a major organ to be able to do that. I approach it full of confidence and bravado but quickly crumple into an indecisive, sobbing heap, so I suppose it's best to say I take an organic approach."*

She wishes that she could be one of those authors who works it out blow by blow in advance, but since she finds herself getting some of her best ideas whilst she is working, she tries to remain open to changes. *"Writing is a bit like making a sculpture,"* she says drawing parallels, *"you keep chipping away until you have something you're happy with. The fun part comes when everything's more or less in place and you can concentrate on making it smooth and funny because all the heavy work is done."*

As a published author, what has the reaction in New Zealand been from Chris' family and former colleagues? *"Well, my youngest brother is a big fan, he races through them and then calls to tell me he can't believe his sister actually wrote it. He sent me an ad for* Spike It *the other day. It was from the local rag in the small town where he lives. It had a picture of the jacket with beside it the rather bizarre sales pitch: 'This book was written by A New Zealand Woman!'"* Laughing, Chris says, *"I'm sure the whole town stampeded down to the store to buy a copy."* As for her parents, initially Chris was under the impression that, despite being proud of her literary achievements, they had not read the books because of their fundamentalist Christian beliefs. The author was touched when she recently found out that they in fact had read the books after all. *"They are busily spreading the Chris Niles gospel in deepest, darkest New Zealand. And,"* she adds, *"they keep calling with reports of strange places they've seen* Spike It *for sale."* Chris' former colleagues in the meantime have all turning themselves inside out to work out which of the motley crew at City Radio is based on themselves or people they know.

It seems curious that, with the wave of female crime writers writing about strong, independent female protagonists, Chris bucked the trend and created a male hero whose personal and professional life is a shambles. Was this a conscious decision? *"Well, I was thinking about writing what turned out to be* Spike It, *and I had a female reporter lined up for the protagonist,"* Chris confesses, adding, *"but when I started writing she wouldn't get off the page. So I went back to the drawing board and thought, 'why not a man?', and Sam came sprinting out of the starting blocks."* Describing Sam she says, *"I think he's a realistic hero. He is* hardly ever cool and in control. Some male writers seem to me to have protagonists who are walking wish fulfilments of their middle-aged fantasies. I don't think anyone in their right mind would want Sam's life. It is not glamorous nor particularly happy, and Sam can be a fool and a buffoon—there's usually a woman around who has to burst his bubble." With that description, how does the author explain why women appear to be so attracted to Sam? Chris laughs and says, "It's certainly not his dress sense! I think Sam's appeal is that of a roguish little boy. He's very stubborn and has a self-destructive and slightly self-pitying streak. But he can be funny and has bags of disreputable charm. He's good for a laugh and a couple of nights out."

Of the two novels to date, *Spike It* makes the most use of both Chris' and Sam's journalistic background. The incident that sparks off the novel has a drunk Sam stumbling across the body of a dead woman. As the first reporter at the scene of the crime he has a scoop on his hands, a scoop which the station supervisor then passes on to Sam's arch-rival as punishment for his unwittingly using the 'F' word on air. In the space of one morning Sam goes from crime and punishment to sex and shopping as he is demoted to researcher for the radio station's women's hour. Despite this, he manages to maintain some involvement in the case which he ultimately manages to solve.

Did Chris base any of Sam's blunders on her own experiences? "Let me tell you," she says smiling, "every mistake it's possible to make on air has been made by me. Although I've never said the 'F' word, once some comments I made to the control room engineer were broadcast to a less than eager public. I flicked the mike switch off, but it didn't go off. That was kind of the basis for the scene where Sam screws up big time at the beginning of* Spike It." Chris also remembers a similar, bur far more drastic anecdote. "I also heard this story about a horribly hung-over early-morning newsreader having to press the 'cough' button—which temporarily mutes the microphone—so that he could throw up in the waste paper basket." By now Chris' smile has giving way to full-blown laughter.

There have been some very likeable secondary characters in both of Chris' books, and Sam's run-ins with Felicia, the programmer of the women's slot, have to be fertile ground in further scenes in future instalments in the series. Can readers expect to get reacquainted with members of the previous supporting casts? "Yes, definitely! Felicia features quite strongly in the third book—she becomes more involved in Sam's life than he thinks is strictly wise. They are getting on better than they used to but are taking it very slowly; that is all I will say at this early stage! I'm not even sure myself what the outcome will be. As for the others, they'll probably all loop back in at some stage. The third book concentrates more on Sam's work, so there's more emphasis on the piranha-pit office politics than on Sam's life outside City Radio." The author likes the idea of having an ensemble of characters who drift in and out of Sam's life, adding, *"And let's face it, Sam needs all the mates he can get."*

In *Run Time* Sam finds himself in Australia where, instead of visiting his son, he finds himself hunted as the prime suspect of a murder. Putting a central character in a completely alien locale so early in a book series is extremely unusual. Also, considering Chris' nationality, wouldn't New Zealand have been a more obvious choice of setting?

"I'm very reluctant to write about New Zealand yet because I haven't lived there for nearly thirteen years. It's undergone a massive social upheaval in that time. So much so that, when I go back there, I feel as though they've swapped the country I grew up in for different one altogether. I'd need to go back and spend some time there before I could write about it with confidence. As for why I chose Australia, it was because I wanted to take Sam out of his milieu and put him somewhere he had virtually no support system. I wanted him relying totally on his wits. Sydney seemed the obvious place because that's where his son Simon lives." With a mischievous grin she adds, *"I also liked the idea of him being in a very glamorous location but not able to enjoy it. The whole city's having fun while he's in hell."*

Not having lived in Australia for some considerable time also, Chris felt slightly unsure about being able to find the right voice for the characters. *"I had a tough time with them to start with,"* she recalls, *"because I wanted them to be Aussie and yet not to fall into the trap of the stereotyped 'Ocker', which is very easy to do because of the distinctiveness of Australian slang. I desperately didn't want them to become caricatures."* Thinking of the possible response of her Aussie friends she says grinning, *"I haven't heard anything from them yet, so for all I know they could be having a whip-round to hire a hitman."*

With Sam's son living in Australia, and the vivid and entertaining use the continent as a setting, will make return visits in further instalments?

"That's a tricky question. I get oddly attached to all my characters, and when I began writing Run Time *I found I was missing the London characters like Lyall and Felicia, so for the third book Sam is back in London. However, I'm kind of tempted to take Sam back Down Under because Sydney seems like Sam's type of town. So I'm open to possibilities."*

The author's further writing projects include a possible non-series novel set in New Zealand, and she says that a recent nightmare gave her a wonderful idea for another stand-alone book set in Sydney. *"After I finish 'Sam 3', I'll take a few weeks off and have a good, long think. In the end I think it comes down to what I feel like the day I sit back down at my computer,"* Chris concludes.

Morgan Freeman
Alison Jones

AT THE AGE OF 60 *Morgan Free-man was dubbed sexiest man alive by Gwyneth Paltrow, former squeeze of Brad Pitt, who should know a thing or two about desirable men.*

He is the man to count on keeping his head in a crisis when all about him are, quite literally, losing theirs.

In fact he is so well liked that when he took a rare foray into villainy, in the water drenched thriller **Hard Rain**, *test audiences refused to let him die at the end.*

Crime Time *enjoyed a little Q & A with the king of cool when he slipped into town to promo the latest in his pro-digious output of work. (His co-star Christian Slater being indisposed due to incar-ceration.)*

The plot concerns master thief Freeman's attempts to relieve obstinate security guard Slater of the wads of cash he has just taken from the town bank. The twist is that said bank, not to mention the rest of the town is, rapidly becoming a modern day Atlantis, as it is flooded by torrential rains.

So what was it like working in enough water to sink a turn of the century transatlantic liner?

Very physically gruelling, though not for the actors. Actors are coddled in situations like that. It was gruelling for the crew. It required very long set ups and because we didn't have underwater equipment a lot of time was spent trying to keep the cameras dry and prevent them toppling into the water. The temperature of the water meant humidity was high so lenses kept misting up.

So not a holiday at Club Med, then?

I'm not much of a water person. It gets up my nose and seems to go all the way up into my head. When I go under and then come up I drip water for hours. I've gone scuba diving and hours later I'll bend over and water will just run out of my head.

Then why pick such a potentially soggy project?

It was an exciting script and the most interesting role was the one they wanted me to play.

A rare chance to play a villain, albeit one rather higher on the moral ladder than your average felon?

When I first read the script everything was in place except for the end. After they screened the original for the test audiences they seemed not to like it that I got my just desserts, so in the new one I get to sail off into the sunset.

Would he ever be tempted to play an out and out, dyed in the wool bad guy, or won't his many fans let him?

It is my sense the audience wouldn't get terribly involved with the character. It would require myself and the studio having the courage to go through with it, against stated audience wishes, and stick to being my being thoroughly bad.

But what *is* thoroughly bad? I'm not sure I would be able to accept a role that I had trouble identifying with. If you're gonna play a bad guy you want to find some quality that helps get you inside, that helps you sympathise with and like the person you are playing.

If I don't like the character I can't play the role. That's the deciding factor.

Was there ever any real danger on set considering the potentially volatile mix of fast boats, electrical equipment and millions of gallons of water?

In the first scene that involved me, we were doing a chase shot. I was in a little boat with a fairly powerful outboard motor. The shot involved the cameraman being in front of me and us having a fairly stable relationship.

So we set it up and rehearsed it a couple of times. Then we turned on the rain towers and boom, the jetski the camera operator is riding backwards on turned turtle. The driver, cameraman and camera all go kerblooee, into the water.

I had to stop the boat pretty much on a dime, which I did, because, immediately, up came the camera man looking for the boat. That was a pretty scary moment."

So why push himself into such situations?

The challenge of living requires more activities when you reach your 60s. I don't want to follow the old habits of assuming I should slow down because I am a certain age. I want to assume that I must keep going, maybe at an increased pace. I think if you slow down it's like with any group of muscles, when you stop using them you lose them.

Does the fact you had three films (*Kiss the Girls, Amistad* and *Hard Rain*) out in as many months, indicate you are a workaholic?

That's just because two of the movies were held back by Paramount from last year. The fact they've all been released at the same time makes me look like a workaholic when, in fact, I've been unemployed for six months.

Your participation is usually a guarantee of quality. It certainly leant credibility to the *Seven* similar *Kiss the Girls* (where Freeman plays a forensic psychologist tracking a kidnapper/killer who 'collects' young women).

I choose roles based on my response to the script, to the characters. I am not looking for any particular formula, just for something interesting to do.

What *has* grabbed his attention amongst the piles of material delivered to his door demanding an actor who combines the hip of Samuel L Jackson with the dignity of Trevor McDonald?

The next movie I have coming out is *Deep Impact* in which I play the President of the United States. It's a 'what if'movie. What if a comet was sighted and its trajectory indicated a collision with earth. What would our response be?

I also have a production company and one project I will crow about is an Arthur C Clarke story called *Rendezvous with Rama*. It's kind of a follow up to *Deep Impact* in that, after such an event, we would probably put a radar in space to catalogue anything coming our way before it becomes a danger. We do and we see something which turns out to be a spaceship.

Any chance of him reprising the role of psychologist Alex Cross again?

Never say never. I don't like to repeat things or do stuff over again. But if it comes up and the script is good enough I'll find it very difficult to say no.

Neil Jordan
Alison Jones

NEIL JORDAN *is a director who enjoys controversial casting. He raised questions by exploiting the androgynous looks of Jaye Griffith for* The Crying Game. *He raised eyebrows by convincing all American boy Tom Cruise to play the blonde bisexual Vampire Lestat in* Interview with a Vampire.

Now he risks incurring the wrath of religious activists by persuading picture-of-Pope tearing popstar, Sinead O'Connor, to play the Virgin Mary.

The once shaven headed singer appears in the visions of the disturbed Francie Brady, in Jordan's screen adaptation of Patrick McCabe's novel The Butcher Boy.

He defended his provocative decision in an interview with Crime Time.

"I thought Sinead was wonderful. She is quite religious. Only somebody who was would do what she did. You would have to care an awful lot to do something like that.

"She is a really good actress and had that profile I recognised from statues of the Virgin Mary when I was a kid.

"I wasn't trying to be anti-religious. It is just a film where these characters—statues, comic-strip people, B movie stars—happen to appear to Francie and speak to him in his own language, in a way he can understand."

And at least Ms O'Connor was more readily available than his first choice.

"Before we cast Sinead I was thinking of casting Marilyn Monroe as the Virgin Mary. It would have been appropriate because it would have been the image you'd have been seeing in the cinemas at that time.

"It would have been quite possible, technically, to do it. Taking her face, manipulating her and making her speak. But it would have been very expensive."

After the emotional epic that was *Michael Collins* Jordan deliberately downsized with his next choice of project.

The Butcher Boy, winner of the Irish Times award for literature and shortlisted for the Booker Prize, is a dip into the disturbed psyche of Francie Brady.

Product of, and outcast from, a small Irish town in the early 60s, the emotionally unhinged Francie, slips into a fantasy world after losing his mother, father and only friend.

Waging a one-boy war against a hated neighbour, his visions first comfort him, then goad him into an act of shocking violence.

"I bought the rights to it because I thought it was an extraordinary book," said Jordan.

"Originally I didn't intend to direct it because I wasn't sure I wanted to do another low budget film in a small Irish town.

"But after adapting it I found the voice of the boy just kept going through my mind. The way he talks about things and the way he sees the world became totally compulsive. The mental world he lived in is the centre of the film and as I wrote I felt I had to direct it myself."

Although McCabe is given joint screen writing credit, it fell to Jordan to come up with a workable translation of the apparently unfilmable.

"It's the paradoxical situation where the novelist is writing the screenplay and when he finishes you have to say 'thanks, but I'd rather like the book you wrote in the first place'.

"I've written novels myself and I know how hard it is to return to an emotion you had four or five years. Patrick came out with a huge amount of wonderful things, but they were variations on the original theme. They didn't have the connective tissue the book has, the sense of the voice running through the whole thing, like a stream of consciousness. I had to simplify it to get it down to a filmable level."

Critics have described the book as a cross between *Huckleberry Finn* and *Catcher in the* Rye, and Francie as Dennis the Menace turned Jack the Ripper.

The choice of young actor to play the part was crucial.

"If we couldn't find Francie we didn't have a movie," said Jordan simply.

"We searched round Ireland. The casting director saw about 2,000 kid. We found Eamonn (Owens) in Killeshandra, just a few miles from Clones (McCabe's home town which is fictionalised in the book). It was extraordinarily lucky, we found all the kids used in the film in this one little town."

The weight of the movie rested on the shoulders of a boy who had never visited the cinema and whose only experience of the spotlight was modelling for a local clothes shop when he was seven.

"Kids from country areas are generally quite shy, they are loathe to display themselves to the camera or any kind of adult. We needed a boy with all this life in him. Like he was driven by adrenaline.

"Eamonn was a natural because he knew all that stuff. He was a kid from a country town. His parents own the local vegetable shop. He knew every facet of the character he played. The brutality, the humour and the kind of weird optimism. His emotions were all in his face."

Despite immersing himself so convincingly in the character of the unbalanced, and ultimately homicidal, Francie, Eamonn remains psychological unscarred by the experience.

"Before we cast him I met the parents and asked them if they were worried about anything in the script and they said no. The boy is very bright. He is very believable but he play-acted the whole thing. He understood what was going on but he wasn't suffering the way Francie suffered.

"The odd thing is American parents are fare more concerned about what their kids will and will not do on screen and their kids are infinitely more messed up."

Co-starring with Eamonn, as Francie's dad and as the voice of the adult Francie, is Stephen Rea, a stalwart of Jordan's movies.

This will be their sixth collaboration together following *Angel*, *Company Of Wolves*, *The Crying Game*, *Interview With A Vampire* and *Michael Collins*.

"He is a wonderful actor and his subdued emotion just suited the part. What is refreshing about Steven is he is an actor who refuses to be a star because all he wants to do is act. He is the only person I know who has been directed by Samuel Beckett and Harold Pinter.

"He genuinely loves the theatre and refuses to take easy options."

Fans of Father Ted will also spot a familiar face in the form of Ardal O'Hanlon, Ted's simpleton sidekick, who crops up as a psychiatrist.

"I wanted someone with a kind face and I thought he was rather good," said Jordan .

"There is always baggage when you cast comedians. You don't want the audience waiting to go ha ha ha when they don't. But Billy Connolly gave a good performance in Mrs Brown and that wasn't exactly a laugh a minute."

Filming *The Butcher Boy* gave Jordan a chance to get backs to his film making roots, producing small, tightly controlled dramas. Featuring characters who play out their personal tragedies against the back-drop of far bigger issues.

"It's very comfortable making big studio backed films. Everybody gets very excited about it. There is a strange of comfort doing a big subject with a big star and a big press campaign behind it. Knowing that whatever happens your film will get a big release.

"But you are far freer if you chose to do a smaller movie, than if you get locked into that system of doing a massive movie once every four years with the fortunes of an entire studio resting on you. You get nervous and timid.

"You should always make movies for yourself. It's just difficult to abandon that huge support system and go to some rural backwater where nobody knows what you are doing."

Slow Dancer Press

Autumn '98 crime titles from Slow Dancer Press, run by
John Harvey, creator of the Charlie Resnick crime novels.

Blue Lightning ed John Harvey
Eighteen brand new short stories all inspired by music
from an outstanding selection of US and UK crime writers.
Includes stories from Liza Cody, Jeffery Deaver, Stella
Duffy, John Harvey, Walter Mosley, Gary Phillips, Ian
Rankin and many more.

ISBN 1 871033 43 8 £7.99

New Orleans Mourning by Julie Smith
The first British publication of Julie Smith's best selling
series featuring New Orleans policewoman Skip Langdon.
Edgar Winner for Best Novel, and over 200,000 paperback
sales in the USA.

"If you like your policewomen with balls, look no further."
—Liza Cody

ISBN 1 871033 45 4 £7.99

Gumshoe by Neville Smith
A funny and affectionate take on the private eye genre.
Eddie Ginley is a Liverpool bingo caller whose dreams of
being Sam Spade turn to nightmares when he gets caught
up in a real life murder.

ISBN 1 871033 44 6 £6.99

Special Crime Time Offer
Any two books for just £10 post free from Slow Dancer
Press, 59 Parliament Hill, London NW3 2TB. Cheques
payable to Slow Dancer Press.

Join our crime mailing list for news of publications and events.
Visit our web site at www.mellotone.co.uk

Crime Time

Meaty, beaty, big and bouncy...

We seem to have hit a real vein of sensitivity this issue (down at the back, Timlin!) with two of the most affecting stories I've read recently. Here's the first...

Lost
Russell James

THE FIRST THEY HEARD of it in the Deptford Arms was fifteen minutes before he arrived. Vinnie Dirkin had stumbled in, a wide grin across that smashed face of his, and had produced the photo from his trouser pocket. It had a creased and damaged look like Dirkin's face, and he flattened it out on the low counter.

"Have you seen her?" he asked. "There could be money in it."

Chippy Naylor was at the counter getting the drinks. "Where's the snap from, Vinnie—her mummy's photo album?"

Dirkin leant back. "There's a detective trying to find her."

"Detective? You ain't been narking, 'ave you, Dirkin?"

The man was outraged. "I never narked no one in my life. This is private—a private eye."

"Get off! In Deptford?"

"Honest. Geezer's trailing round the boozers, carrying a wad of these little snaps." Naylor picked it up. "You say there's money in it?" He studied the photo blankly. "I'll ask me mates."

"Give us the photo back," said Dirkin.

Naylor had paid for his round by now, and when he carried the tray of drinks to a side table, he kept the photo. The boys glanced at it and asked Vinnie, "What do you get out of it?"

"Nothing. The man's just handing out the photos."

"A cop?"

"No way."

"Who's the girl then?" Clyde asked. "A runaway?"

The boys squinted at the crumpled photograph, not because they really thought they might recognise the girl but because the idea of a detective—a private one—in Deptford was extraordinary, and quite flattering in a way.

Vinnie said, "There's an advert about her in the Mercury. He's carrying that around with him too."

Clyde held the photo to the light as if it might have been a counterfeit.

"So this detective will pay money for a lead on her?"

"Well, careful—they tried that on him in the Erin. When he finds her is what he said."

Naylor grinned at him. "What you doin' up the Irish pub, Vinnie—feeling brave?"

"Business," replied Vinnie grandly. "Anyway, one of the paddies tried to give the tec the runaround."

"And?"

"He's a big feller."

"That don't stop paddies."

"Hey," Clyde said. "D'you hear about those two paddies saw a notice—Tree Fellers Wanted. 'That's a shame,' says Paddy. 'Tree fellers—there's only two of us.'"

Chippy cackled.

"Anyway," said Vinnie, "I think they knew him."

"Oh, he's Irish? You didn't say."

"No, not Irish, but there was something. Someone knew him."

"He's a cop. I told you."

"That wasn't it. Can I have my photo back?"

Clyde was curling it between his fingers. "So if he's private, looking for a teenager, then her parents must be paying his fee. And you reckon they put an advert in the paper? Yeah, there could be money in it."

Chippy said, "Nah, that's just a schoolgirl no one ever saw. Give it back to him."

"All in good time." Clyde shielded the photo like a playing card, taking a peek at it on his own. "She ain't a school girl. Looks about eighteen."

"Don't get excited," Naylor said. "She's one of four million birds in London."

"Anyway," Clyde continued, still studying the photo, "she might be eighteen here, when the snap was taken, but you know how it is: she leaves school and this is the last picture her family's got."

Chippy Naylor turned to Dirkin dithering by his side. "I think Clyde's fallen for her. He'll pin the photo up by his bed."

"I'll pin his nose against his face."

Which brought a grin or two around the table—a fight was entertainment. Clyde sneered, then flicked the photo across the table as if throwing in a poker hand. "I wouldn't steal your woman, Vinnie. Dunno where she's been."

Vinnie started forward but banged his knee against the corner of the table. Chippy placed a hand on Vinnie's chest. "You want us all thrown out? Ignore him. Show your photo to someone else."

Vinnie scrabbled for it on the table. "You wanna meet me, Clyde? Just name the time."

From the other side of the table Clyde sneered again. "Look at the fuss you've caused. It's only a photograph."

The pub had been quiet for about ten minutes when Joe Venables finally walked in. He was a large gentle looking man with curly iron grey hair, and was wearing black. Something about the way he approached the bar suggested he had not come in to buy a drink. He muttered quietly to the landlord.

By this time Vinnie was in the rear with a bunch of kids, but at Chippy Naylor's table they didn't need Vinnie to tell them who this was. They watched Venables approach a young couple at the bar and show the photo. They watched him continue to a table near the door. By the time he reached them they had each rehearsed what they would say.

Clyde and Lucky Lennox leapt in at once. Clyde was saying, "Hey, I've seen that babe before," and Lennox: "Didn't she used to hang around the Duchess?"

Joe Venables smiled at them. "Now there's a thing," he said. "All night, not a single sniff of her, and now suddenly two people at the same table both recognise her immediately. And you, sir—" he was looking at Clyde "-you must be six feet from my photograph."

"I don't forget a face."

"But maybe you saw her picture in the Mercury?" Joe turned to Lennox: "And where might you have seen her?"

"At the Duchess," replied Lennox promptly.

"I can't believe my luck," Joe said, sitting down. "As you may have read in the Mercury, there is a reward if you help me find her, but—" he paused, "-a smack in the face if I get the runaround. Now, the Duchess, you said—"

"It's a little night club over—"

"I know where the Duchess is."

Lennox paused. "I didn't realise you was local."

Joe shrugged. "There are no border guards in Deptford."

Lennox glanced at this amiable but heavy man. "Well, you could try the Duchess. Look, if you do find something, do—um—I mean, how does someone get their hands on this reward?"

"Let me have your name."

When Lennox hesitated Venables smiled. "If your information was genuine I'm sure you'd want to give me your name. How about you, son?" This was aimed at Clyde.

"I ain't sure. She looks familiar, you know?"

Venables made a gesture with his hand, palm uppermost, asking for more.

Chippy intervened. "The thing is, we seen the photo earlier, so we had time to think about it."

"You mean that fellow in the back room—he showed it to you?"

"Oh."

"I noticed him when I came in. Never caught his name."

"He's Vinnie Dirkin," Lennox said.

Joe started to stand up. "I'll leave a photo. My number's on the back."

The men's eyes fastened on the snap as if it were a ten pound note. "There is a reward then?" Clyde asked again.

"If I find her."

"When a girl goes missing," Chippy remarked, "you should check the Albert."

"The black pub?"

Naylor nodded. "You know it?"

"That's my job," Joe told them. "But I'll finish here first."

The Royal Albert was so loud that Venables abandoned conversation; he simply thrust his way through the crowded pub and held the photo to people's faces. The music here had the deadening beat of an amplified heart. Lights were minimal. The air was full of smoke—some of it tobacco—and when men saw what Venables was engaged in they swayed aside to let him through. He was hot, his eyes were itching, and he understood why so many in the darkened hall wore shades. He saw a little guy dancing before him, grinning like a puppet, and when Joe tried to speak to him the man made as if either he could not understand English or the music was too loud for him to hear Joe's words.

The man mimed that the two of them should step outside.

On the cold pavement the music was so loud that Joe wanted to go back inside to turn it down. But the little guy brought his mouth close to Joe's ear: "Right, I've seen her, don't know her name."

"Recently?"

The man shrugged. "Not for several weeks. She went away."

"You know where?"

"No." The man brought his head back so he could gaze at Joe's face, then he leant forward again. "But I have seen her. She used to be around. You put her in the paper, didn't you? Are you her father?"

"No."

"And you're not a cop?"

"No. I'm looking for her."

"Relation?"

"If you help me find her, there'll be money in it."

"Are you managing her?"

"Her family has asked me to help. I'm a private detective."

The man leant back again, studied him, then let his face loosen in a smile. "No kidding—a private eye?"

"That's right."

"In Deptford? Shit." He shook his head at the incongruity.

Joe asked, "Well?"

"You're not her Daddy, then?"

"We've been through that."

The man was chewing an imaginary piece of gum, his head nodding to the music. "And you're not—well, no, you're not the kiddy's dad, either, right?"

"I told you—wait, which kiddy do you mean?"

"Hers, man. I mean, you knew she was pregnant, right?"

Joe's eyes gleamed. "It didn't say that in the Mercury."

"Ah shit, man, does this bring you grief? I'm sorry, right?"

"You knew she was pregnant?"

They were shouting this conversation in the street. The man took a step away. "Well, I ain't seen her recently, man. Expect she's had the kid by now."

"Hey, hey." Joe didn't want to lose him. "How did you know that she was pregnant?"

"Christ, man, she was enormous. She's probably dropped the thing by now."

Venables fumbled in his pocket. "It was definitely this girl here?"

The man took another step away. "I don't know. She looked like her. This was weeks ago. Hey, I'm through here, man. OK?"

"Where can I find her?"

"You're the detective." He saw Joe's face. "Look man, don't waste time hassling me. Try the Duke of Edinburgh."

Squashed in halfway down a road lined with terraced houses, the Duke of Edinburgh looked a quiet pub. Compared to the Albert it was quiet, despite the upright piano and the old boy with his hat angled at the back of his head, pounding out the favourites—East End music hall. A huddle of locals enthusiastically joined in the refrains. An old lady with a throbbing accent sang out the verse:

"The ballroom was a-filled with-a fashion's throng
It shone with a fousand lights
And there was a woman 'oo passed along
The fairest of all the sights."

And the ragged chorus, helped by the surprisingly resonant voice of Joe Venables, joined in:

"She's only a bird in a gilded cage

A be-eautiful sight to see

You may fink she is happy and free from care -

She is not, though she seems to be."

Joe moved closer to a table beneath the dart board where some youngsters seemed self conscious about joining in. Perhaps they didn't know the words.

"It's sad when you fink of her wasted life

For yoof cannot mate with age

And her beauty was sold for an old man's gold

She's a bird in a gilded cage."

As the song ended, Joe laid his glass on their table. "I'm looking for a young woman."

"You'll be lucky 'ere!"

"Pauline—Pauline Estobel. D'you know her?"

"Sorry."

He produced a photo. They shook their heads. He said, "She drinks in here." They shrugged. He said, "She's pregnant."

One of the girls at the table looked at him carefully. "You her Dad, then?"

"Friend of the family. She's not in trouble. If you do see her, my phone number's on the back. There's fifty quid for anyone helps me find her."

"Well, if she's pregnant she wouldn't come in here."

Joe smiled encouragingly. "Oh, but she did. She lived nearby."

"Where?"

"She moved away."

"Then she could be anywhere by now, couldn't she?"

Joe nodded again. He looked tired, human, the sort of man that you would like to help.

"I just need a start to help me find her. Her mother is frantic—you can imagine— she even placed an advert in the paper. You might have seen it? Look, I'll leave the photo with you. Ring anytime, no questions asked."

He was disappointed. Most of the pubs had been simply places to tick off his list but that little fellow outside the Albert had told him the Duke of Edinburgh was where she drank. And it was less than five minutes away from Endwell Road, where she had lived. No forwarding address, of course, just a suggestion that she had gone up west. But from Deptford most places were up west.

It was a pity that Pauline Estobel had not left a forwarding address. She had paid off her rent and disappeared as if she had always intended to vanish away. According to the landlord in Endwell Road she had returned from hospital while he was out and had immediately cleared her flat and left. The landlord said that, previously, Pauline had told him she would be living with the kiddy's father, but that did not accord with the fact that no man ever showed up at the house. No one helped her collect her things. Joe had checked with the hospital but, unfortunately, they had no record of Pauline Estobel. They had heard of her at the local ante-natal centre, and, yes, they did have her home address. It was the room in Endwell Street.

Two days later Joe called at Mrs Estobel's house to tell her that the trail was cold. In Deptford, one or two people had remembered Pauline but no one had seen her for about three months. None of her older friends from school days had heard a word. "The best we can hope," Joe said, "—and it's the likeliest explanation—is that after the trouble she caused at home she is making a new life for herself elsewhere. I could continue looking, of course, but with little to go on it will be expensive. Look, once she has settled down with the baby there's a pretty good chance she'll be in touch. I know this is difficult to accept, Mrs Estobel, but you may have to be patient and sit and wait."

That was what he had meant to say. The trouble was that Mrs Estobel was not easily deflected. She sat in her pastel drawing room, opposite a thirty inch commedia dell'arte embroidered clown in a wicker nursery chair, and she allowed him to get half way through his speech—to the word 'expensive'—which seemed a good place to interrupt, before she raised her hand and said, "Father Venables, you're not suggesting we should give up? It would be the death of me."

"I think it's wiser," Joe said. "And I'm not a Father now, as you know."

"A man like you is ordained for life."

Mrs Estobel had attractive eyes—sad sorrowful eyes on the brink of tears—eyes that would appeal to many men.

"I have a new vocation," Joe said, and smiled. "I think Pauline is bound to settle soon, and after that there's every chance—"

"She's had long enough. No, Father, my fear is that she's in desperate straits. She could be too frightened or ashamed to return home."

"Frightened?"

"Too proud, perhaps. It's silly, because we were the ones in the wrong. Patrick was upset, of course, which is why he reacted the way he did—when she told us she was pregnant. He was always … Patrick saw things in black and white."

"Well, perhaps—"

"I wish you'd buried him, Father. You were always … The man who came after you is too young, too insubstantial. He has no gravitas."

"Perhaps the job suits someone less substantial." Joe smiled and patted his thickening waist.

Pauline's mother sighed. She was a small, compact woman, burdened with what appeared a permanent sadness. She had lost her daughter, then her husband, yet her determination not to fold aroused Joe's sympathy. He wanted to help before he left.

She blinked. "Look, Father, I—"

"Joe."

"What?"

"Joe. Or Mr Venables, if you'd prefer."

She closed her eyes briefly and shook her head. "It does not come naturally, I'm afraid. I'd like you to continue trying to trace my Pauline. She's all that's left to me."

"Mrs Estobel, my advice—"

"No, don't." She waved a tired hand. "No sensible advice. I'm her mother. Since Patrick died I live in an empty house."

"I've explored all the obvious avenues—"

"The obvious ones."

"Her friends and school mates, the room she rented." He took her tiny hand into his familiarly comforting clasp. "Mrs Estobel, don't you think—"

"No."

"We've done all we can."

"You have." Her face was pinched.

"Yes."

She crumpled slightly. "I didn't mean that. We must go on searching, looking under every—"

"I've looked. Sometimes we—" He saw her head jerk. "—have to face the fact that someone we love has left us, and has chosen to make their way alone."

"I want her back."

Joe nodded. "Of course. And I'm sure she'll come back eventually. But for now—"

"Don't say that. Please, Father—Mr Venables—don't refuse to help. I'll pay you for your time."

"You've paid enough. I'll bill you for my time to date, but that will be my final account. I'm sorry."

She said, "I shall not stop looking."

She held out the photo. "This is my daughter. I'm trying to find her."

The two men seated at the pub table shook their heads. She said, "She used to come here."

"Never seen her," one of them mumbled.

The man behind the bar called, "Hey, missis! What you selling?"

Mrs Estobel looked strained as she proffered the photo. "I am trying to find my daughter. Perhaps you remember her?"

He glanced at the photo. "Oh, her."

"You've seen her?"

"I've seen her photo. Had a bloke in a couple of days back. You had that advert in the paper."

"That's right. I believe my daughter used to come to this pub. Perhaps she still does?"

"Nah."

"But she used to. Can't you remember? Please try."

He shrugged helplessly. "We get lots through here. A girl comes in once or twice— well, it don't register, you see?"

"My daughter was pregnant. Do you remember that?"

"Ah." He reached across the bar for the photo, gazed at it and shook his head. "Still don't register. You sure it was this pub?"

His tone was sympathetic, and the customers in the small pub listened silently. An old man said, "Better let us see it. You never know."

But she could tell from their faces that no one expected to recognise the girl. She added, "There's a reward for anyone who helps me find her."

The old man gazed at the snap with little hope. "Pretty girl. Yes. She run away?"

Mrs Estobel took a breath. "Yes."

The old man passed the photo to a thin girl who had moved across to stand close to them. He said, "Yes, they do that sometimes. Shame. I suppose you'd like to see her little baby?"

Mrs Estobel nodded, watching as the thin girl passed the photo on. "I'd like to see the baby and my daughter.—She has nothing to fear." This last was to the room at large.

The thin girl eased herself onto a stool beside her as Mrs Estobel announced in a trembling voice: "I've put my phone number on the back. Please phone—in absolute confidence. If anyone does know where she is … please tell her I only want to help."

Mrs Estobel had not realised how many pubs there were in Deptford. Outside some she hesitated, feeling that these were not ones her daughter would have entered, but she gathered her courage and plunged inside. And in one of the larger, more terrifyingly noisy places someone gave a glimmer of recognition—nothing definite, it didn't lead anywhere, but was enough to encourage her to go on. The larger the pub, she thought, the more people; and the more people, the more chance somebody might recognise Pauline. Mrs Estobel had handed out dozens of photos, and occasionally as she placed one in someone's warm hand she felt an unaccountable shiver of expectation, and she peered into that person's face looking for a sign. She would think, this is the one. But it wasn't. Outside in the cold night air she realised that the shiver of hope was no different to that felt by people buying their weekly lottery ticket: there's something about the numbers this week ...

The High Street was quiet. The Deptford Arms was dead, and the little corner pub, The Windsor Castle, did not look promising. But she went inside. Here, the few customers were older, less likely to have known Pauline, but she still showed the photo. At one table, drinking alone, was a girl who seemed faintly familiar—a thin girl—a school friend perhaps? Or she might have been in a previous pub.

She smiled cautiously at Mrs Estobel. "Not much luck then?"

Mrs Estobel was tired. "No, but I have to keep trying."

"You can sit here if you like. Take the weight off."

"Once I sit I won't be able to stand up again."

"Yes, you look like you need a rest."

The girl was urging her to sit down—and finally she did. The girl said, "I'd offer you a drink, but I'm skint."

Mrs Estobel ignored that. "I'll buy something in a moment."

"You don't have to buy anything in here. They don't mind if you just sit."

There was something waif-like about the girl that reminded Mrs Estobel of the sad child pictured in the posters for Les Miserables. She sat with her shoulders hunched as if she was cold.

"You'd think someone would remember her," said Mrs Estobel. "But I suppose people are wary of speaking to me?" She watched the girl. "There's no need."

The girl met her eye for a brief moment. "No questions asked?"

"None. And there'd be some money ... discreetly."

The girl was glancing around the pub. Mrs Estobel asked quietly, "Would you like to go somewhere more private?"

The girl pushed her glass aside as if Mrs Estobel had accused her of trying to pocket it. "Oh, I don't know. What for?"

Mrs Estobel kept her voice low. "So we could talk."

Nervously, the girl shook her head.

"Did you know my daughter?"

Mrs Estobel felt that the girl was rather too melodramatic. Though if something had happened to Pauline that required this caution—and if no one but the thin girl would admit to even recognising her—then perhaps her worst fears might be justified. If her daughter had become involved with some south London gang … But that was ridiculous—Pauline was an ordinary middle class girl who had fallen pregnant and run away from home. It was odd that she should have chosen this unsavoury area, but for Pauline to mix with unwholesome characters was stretching likelihood too far. Yet this furtive thin girl had asked Mrs Estobel to go out of the pub on her own and to walk to the burger bar along the High Street and wait for her there. Mrs Estobel had chosen a table away from the window, where the girl would see her only after she came in. If she came in. She had seemed so nervous she might easily bolt.

Mrs Estobel sagged in the plastic chair. She was weary after trudging round noisy bars and now, in this brightly lit, aromatic fast-food cafe she felt small and alone. When the waitress appeared with notebook and smile, Mrs Estobel said, "Just a coffee for the moment. I'm waiting for a friend."

"Cappuccino, Espresso, Speciality?" The waitress pointed to the laminated menu.

"Just ordinary, if I may."

"Standard or extra large?"

"Standard. We'll order when my friend arrives."

While waiting for coffee and the thin girl Mrs Estobel continued to brood about her daughter. Pauline had definitely lived in Deptford when she first moved away because Father Venables had found the room she had rented in Endwell Road. Earlier today Mrs Estobel had called there herself, but the landlord could tell her no more than that Pauline had moved out once her child had been born. She hadn't left any forwarding address. She hadn't any visitors, no friends. Could it really have been like that? It was horrible to think of her own daughter living alone in this hard unfriendly area, waiting for her baby to arrive. What had happened afterwards? All anyone could tell her was that Pauline had quit her rented room, had given birth and disappeared. As if deliberately. For the several months she had lived in Deptford she had been noticed by almost no one, and once she left, no one remembered her.

When the waitress arrived with her coffee Mrs Estobel thanked her and glanced to the door. "I'll order in a moment, if you don't mind."

Perhaps it was not surprising no one remembered Pauline. As her pregnancy had progressed she would have become increasingly housebound and despite her parting words to the landlord Pauline did not appear to have had a boy friend. She would have had to cope with the child alone.

Earlier that day Mrs Estobel had retraced the same path as Joe Venables: the few local shops, the Well Woman Clinic, the neighbouring houses made into flats. People responded to her queries warily. Some had already been approached by Joe Venables, others were simply suspicious of anyone asking questions. One woman refused to believe that she was really Pauline's mother. Tomorrow, she decided, she would bring a second photo of Pauline and her together.

She glanced up to see the thin girl slip in through the door.

As the girl wolfed down her food Mrs Estobel grew impatient. The girl was visibly ravenous. Presumably she had suggested they meet in here so she would be bought a meal. She sat opposite Mrs Estobel, spearing chips and sausages with stooped concentration, cramming them into her mouth so she could not speak. Though it was late—ten o'clock at night—she had asked for the Giant All Day Breakfast. "You can eat hamburgers any time."

Mrs Estobel tried to extract answers before the girl finished her food. All she had learned so far was the thin girl's name. "Now Charlotte, where can I find Pauline?"

The girl stabbed the last piece of sausage and gulped it down. "I dunno where she's living now. I didn't say I knew that, did I?"

"You haven't said anything much."

Charlotte took a large bite from her soft granary bap. "I dunno if she'd want me to tell you."

"When did you last see her?"

Charlotte swallowed some bread. "Must've been … oh, two weeks ago."

"Where?"

Charlotte glanced around as if someone might have been listening. "At my place. She came to see me."

Mrs Estobel leant forwards. "You're a friend of hers?"

Charlotte shrugged. "So-so. Are you having a pudding?"

Mrs Estobel gazed at her steadily. "I think you should tell me something first."

"You're not trying to bribe me with a pudding?"

"You could earn more than a pudding, Charlotte."

"Yeah, it said that in the paper."

"You saw my advertisement?"

Charlotte licked her lips. "Well, I knew it was her immediately."

Mrs Estobel remained unsure whether to believe the girl or not. "Her name was in the advert."

"Right—but I always called her Polly. That's what she called herself— Polly, not Pauline."

"Polly?" Mrs Estobel frowned. "You said she came to see you a couple of weeks ago. Why?"

Charlotte shrugged. "Friends. You know."

"Do you think she'll come again?"

"I expect."

"Will you give her a message from me?"

"Of course—if I see her." Charlotte stared at her. "Can I have a pudding—please?"

Mrs Estobel nodded impatiently. "Tell her, when you see her, that… Tell her that her Daddy died suddenly in an accident. That's important, you see—she doesn't know he's dead. Tell her that I want to see her again, very much."

Charlotte glanced away then back. "And her baby—you want to see it?"

"Yes, I— Have you seen … the baby? I don't even know if it's a boy or a girl."

"Oh, it's—" Charlotte smiled. "It's a boy. He's very nice." She waved the menu to attract the waitress. "Death By Chocolate, with cream and ice cream." She glanced across at Mrs Estobel. "Anything for you?"

She shook her head. "Another coffee, please."

When the waitress had left them, Charlotte asked, "Did she tell you who was the baby's father?"

Mrs Estobel paused. "No, she wouldn't. That made it all so much worse."

"You must have … made a guess?"

"Pauline kept herself to herself. Perhaps you found her to be like that?"

Charlotte shrugged. Then Mrs Estobel suddenly asked, "Tell me, then, about the baby— what's his name?"

"Jamie."

Mrs Estobel repeated the name softly. "What is he like?"

Charlotte grinned. "Like—you mean, is he black or white? No, you don't have to worry—he's white, all right. D'you think he wouldn't be?"

Mrs Estobel did not answer, so Charlotte pressed further: "Did Polly ever have a black boy friend?"

"No."

"Well, then. Don't look like that. The baby's white, healthy—well, quite healthy— brown hair, blue eyes… I think they're blue."

"What d'you mean, quite healthy—is something wrong with him?"

The waitress arrived with the Death By Chocolate and another coffee. Charlotte took her first mouthful of sticky dessert before saying, "Well, he had a bit of a cold last time I seen him." She took a second mouthful. "He did seem a bit run down, but Polly looks after him as best she can." A third mouthful was poised upon her spoon. "Is Jamie your first grandson?"

"Pauline was our only daughter." Mrs Estobel blinked. "I mean, she is our—she's my only … " She raised her napkin to her lips.

"Yeah. Sorry about your husband." To cover any embarrassment, Charlotte scooped some more chocolate fudge into her mouth. When she had swallowed it she said, "Still, at least now you can try to get in touch with her again. Wouldn't he let you?"

Mrs Estobel sat upright in her chair. "Is that what Pauline told you?"

"She seemed a bit … You know how uptight she could be." Charlotte filled her mouth again.

Mrs Estobel sighed. "I suppose she told you that it was Daddy who turned her out?"

Charlotte nodded sagely.

"He was ridiculously old-fashioned about … her predicament—partly because she wouldn't tell us who the father was, and partly because, well, Patrick was a deeply religious man. Afterwards, of course, he was most awfully upset."

"Even so, he wouldn't have her back?"

"He was very proud. Strong minded."

Charlotte scraped the last chocolate smears from her glass dish. "You never thought it might be his baby?"

Mrs Estobel jerked back from the table. "What a terrible thing to say! Pauline surely didn't tell you that?"

"It's not unusual. I mean, him throwing Pauline out—didn't it make you think?"

Mrs Estobel exhaled. "That's quite enough of that. There is no question of it."

"All right, all right. I didn't know, you see. No need to get all shirty. I'd better go."

As she stood up from the table, Mrs Estobel rose too. "No, don't go. Can't you tell me where Pauline is?"

Charlotte glanced towards the door. "I don't know. She'll probably be in touch."

"And you will tell her?"

"Oh, sure. D'you want me to give her anything?"

"Money, you mean? No, I—"

"You don't trust me, do you? Well, I've got your phone number. So long." She began to leave.

"Look, Charlotte, please—"

"D'you want to see the baby—shall I tell her that?"

"Of course."

Charlotte paused. "Right. Thanks for a lovely supper."

She was gone.

On the evening of the third day plodding around Deptford, Mrs Estobel sat alone in her drawing room, tired feet propped on the pale camel stool, television chattering in the corner, a smeared tumbler at her side—gin and tonic finished, wet slice of lemon lifeless at the base—when the telephone rang. She reached slowly for the handset. A week ago, when the advertisement had first appeared in the Mercury she had had twenty calls a night, but now they had diminished to one or two. Some held promise, most were instantly dismissible, none told her what she wanted to hear.

"Mrs Estobel? I said I'd ring."

"Who's that?"

"You know, when I heard from her again."

"Who am I speaking to?"

"Charlotte. You know, we met in Deptford?"

"Charlotte."

"In the Windsor. We had a meal."

"I remember. Have you seen Pauline?"

"Well, not exactly."

"Oh."

"I've sort of seen her. You haven't seen her yourself, Mrs Estobel?"

"No. Why—did she tell you she'd get in touch with me?"

"Well, no."

"I see. What d'you mean—you've sort of seen her?"

"Well, it's awkward."

"Awkward?"

"You know, speaking on the phone. Um, could I see you?"

"Of course. Where had you in mind?"

"You could come to my place. I can't get out, you see?"

"To your flat?"

"Yeah, you know, any time—well, no, sometime soon."

"Tomorrow?"

They arranged to meet the following morning. Evidently the girl had no job. She gave an address—hesitantly—but would say no more about what she wanted to talk about. At least she didn't want to meet in a restaurant.

The flat comprised two meagrely decorated rooms separated by a plain panel door. A corner of the front room had been crudely modified to form a kitchenette, and the furniture included a general purpose dining table and several chairs. Only the television set looked new.

Charlotte sat Mrs Estobel in a repellent soft armchair and placed herself in a wooden chair opposite. The door to the second room remained closed.

"No luck then?" began Charlotte.

"Not yet."

"I've put the kettle on."

"Fine." Mrs Estobel had decided not to ask questions; the girl had brought her here to reveal something and would be better at her own speed. For a few moments they stared at each other. Then Charlotte glanced over her shoulder to the kitchenette.

"It's nearly done," she said. "Coffee or tea?"

"Coffee," replied Mrs Estobel. "One sugar. Black." She doubted the freshness of Charlotte's milk.

As the girl tinkered with the cups they rattled on their saucers. "Polly says she's sorry, you know? She couldn't come."

"Why not?"

Charlotte sniffed. "Doesn't want to face you, I suppose. It must be awful for you. I mean, you're the grandmother."

"Yes."

"And you've never even seen your grandson."

"No."

She wanted to ask when Charlotte had last seen them, but she made herself stay quiet.

"Well, I dare say you'll be seeing him soon," Charlotte said. "It's boiling now. No sugar, right?"

"One sugar."

"Oh yes, you said."

Charlotte poured hot water into the cups. When she lifted them in trembling hands some coffee slopped into the saucers. Charlotte glanced from one rattling cup to the other like a nervous actress on first night. "I'll bring them one by one."

She put down the cup with most coffee in its saucer and approached Mrs Estobel with the other clutched in both hands. Half way towards her she was halted by a sound from the other room—the reedy, waking cry of a baby. Mrs Estobel did not turn round, but gazed instead at Charlotte's face. The girl stood motionless, her thin shoulders hunched over the coffee cup, an abject expression on her face. The baby cried again, more vigorously.

Mrs Estobel stood up. "Give me the coffee, Charlotte, while you go and see to the baby."

"No, it's all—"

Mrs Estobel took the cup. "Once they start they don't give up."

Charlotte dithered another moment, then scuttled past to the other room. Mrs Estobel came behind to peep inside. It was a bedroom in semi-darkness—the mother's single bed, the tiny baby in a cheap carry-cot. Charlotte leant over, scolded softly, then picked it up. There was no one else in the darkened room.

Mrs Estobel sipped her coffee. "So you've got a baby too, Charlotte? Let me have a look."

She couldn't see the baby properly because it had its back to her, its face buried in Charlotte's neck. The girl stared wide-eyed as if Mrs Estobel might want to take it from her. "He'll be all right. He's just woken up."

Mrs Estobel remained patiently a few feet from her, and spoke in a calm voice: "He wants his breakfast, I suppose. Do you breastfeed?"

The thin girl hugged the child more closely. "I can manage. I know what to do."

She showed no sign of it.

"Well, don't stand on ceremony," urged Mrs Estobel. "Put his milk on the stove to warm and we'll talk later."

"He's my baby."

Mrs Estobel looked at Charlotte sharply. "What's his name?"

Charlotte busied herself with the baby, and seemed reluctant to leave the bedroom. Mrs Estobel sensed that she had not been brought here by chance. Neither perhaps had the baby. Of course, it was possible that the baby did belong to Charlotte and that the girl was behaving oddly because she was ashamed of her own fatherless child. Perhaps she really had not meant Mrs Estobel to know of it. Anything was possible. Mrs Estobel went back into the living room and sat on a wooden dining chair. The armchair had had a musty smell.

Charlotte emerged. "I'll make the milk then."

"That's right."

Holding the baby in one arm, Charlotte crossed to her kitchenette. Mrs Estobel stood up. "Let me hold him while you warm it."

"No, stay away. The baby's mine."

Mrs Estobel did not say anything. She watched as Charlotte used her one free hand to run water into a saucepan and place it on the electric ring. From the shabby fridge she took a pre-filled bottle and slipped it into the water so it could warm.

Mrs Estobel sniffed pointedly. "I suppose you'd better change his nappy."

"Afterwards."

"Don't you change it first?"

"No." Charlotte peered into the water.

"I always liked my baby to be clean before it ate. Clean nappy, clean botty, then some food. That's what I did with Pauline."

"No point," muttered Charlotte. "Put him in a clean one, he messes that. He might as well do everything in one."

"Fashions change," said Mrs Estobel. "But I didn't like to hold Pauline smelling of poo. It didn't seem right while she was eating."

"I know what I'm doing. I'm a good mother." Charlotte lifted the bottle from the water and tested it against the back of her hand. The baby whimpered.

"You are his mother, then?"

Charlotte dropped the bottle in the water. "What d'you mean? Course I'm his mother. I'm—Oh, you …"

Her face crumpled, became small and pinched. For a moment she stood quivering in the kitchenette, then with a small cry she rushed to the armchair and sat the baby in it. He immediately began to cry.

Charlotte shouted, "You want to take him—I know you do!"

"Why should I?"

"Because you— Well, you can't have him. He belongs to me."

Mrs Estobel felt strangely calm. "Is that Pauline's baby?"

"I didn't steal him."

Charlotte grabbed the baby and held him close.

"That's why you invited me here, isn't it?"

"I didn't steal him."

"Oh, Charlotte."

"She gave him to me."

"Gave?"

"She did, she did. She left him here."

"Pauline left my grandson here?"

Charlotte collapsed into the armchair and the baby gave a startled scream.

"Oh, feed him, for God's sake, Charlotte—feed the poor little thing."

The following morning, when Mrs Estobel arrived carrying baby blankets, two cardigans, bright coloured hoops on a plastic ring, she half hoped to find her daughter with Charlotte in the flat. After a surprisingly good night's sleep Mrs Estobel still could not believe what Charlotte had finally told her the day before—that Pauline had never bonded with the baby, had resented her, had constantly found fault, and had then abandoned her to her friend. It did not seem credible. Pauline could not behave like that—no mother could. Perhaps she was using Charlotte to re-establish contact—had lent her the baby, as it were, to give her mother a chance to see the child. Last night, as Mrs Estobel had journeyed home alone, she had imagined Pauline returning to the flat to hear from Charlotte how she had been. Perhaps Pauline had seen the advertisement in the Mercury. It must have been a shock for her to read that the parents she had walked away from, who had thrown her out, were now advertising to bring her back.

"Polly hasn't been here," Charlotte insisted. "She never comes."

Mrs Estobel smiled and shook her head. "Of course she comes—don't start that again."

"She doesn't."

"I'm not stupid, Charlotte, I understand."

"Huh!"

"Was it because she saw my advertisement?"

"I don't know." Charlotte was jigging the baby on her knee. His face was wet. In one pink and wrinkled hand Jamie held a ring of plastic discs which he was trying to slide into his mouth.

Mrs Estobel tossed back her head. "Yes, she must have seen it."

Charlotte shrugged.

"Did you tell her that—her father is dead?"

Charlotte shrugged again.

"Well, you must."

"I never see her now."

Mrs Estobel frowned. Charlotte was being tiresome. "No, Charlotte, you saw her this morning—when she left the baby with you again."

The child was stroking its face with the plastic toy. Charlotte said, "I don't think she's still in London."

"Oh, really—why do you say that?"

"I haven't seen Polly for weeks. All it is, well, there was a couple of times a parcel arrived. They was just left here—for the baby."

"A parcel—nothing else?"

"No."

Charlotte adjusted the baby on her knee. Though he still clutched the plastic rings, they seemed to have lost their appeal and he was concentrating on something else. "She never left me no address. I reckon she used to wait till I went out."

"I don't believe you, Charlotte."

"It's true. Because of Jamie—she didn't want to see him. It was easier for her, you know?"

"Oh, come on."

"You never saw her in those last weeks, Mrs Estobel. She wasn't right inside her head. She blamed the baby for—oh, I don't know. I expect she'll come to her senses one of these days."

"And then she'll want her baby back?"

"No!" Charlotte glared at her. "Anyway, she don't even send parcels any more."

"You mean she has disappeared?"

"Pretty well. But a couple of weeks ago she posted me some money in an envelope."

"So she's still …"

"But she didn't write. I don't suppose she knows what she wants to say."

"Was there a card?"

"No."

"Then how did you know it came from her?"

"Who else could it have come from? Anyway, it wasn't much."

Charlotte dipped her head and rested it alongside the baby's. "That means you're mine now, you little darling. Isn't that right?"

Mrs Estobel could not stay away. On each of the next three days she deliberately arrived at different times, hoping that she might catch Pauline on a secret call. It seemed that Charlotte, in her slovenly way, was at least trying to be a mother, though she had a regrettable habit of silencing Jamie's whimpering by filling his mouth with something else.

"I have to," she explained. "Or I'll get complaints. I don't want the landlord to turn me out."

Mrs Estobel could not—would not—accustom herself to the idea of her grandson being raised, temporarily, she hoped, by an amiable slattern in a rented basement. She began to wonder if she could snaffle the child away. In one of her fantasies she took Jamie for a walk, called a taxi and disappeared. She had as much right to him as Charlotte had—more. Jamie was her flesh and blood. He was her heir, her link to Pauline. Though even so, mused Mrs Estobel, did she really want him for her own—without Pauline? Did she want to rear the child? She was approaching fifty now. To regain her daughter would be a glory, but to bring Jamie up could not be contemplated. She could hire a nanny, of course, but if somebody else was to look after the child, as seemed inevitable, then why shouldn't that somebody be Charlotte?

Mrs Estobel studied the thin lank-haired girl. Today, with Jamie asleep in the other room, Charlotte seemed at a loss to know what to do. She sat awkwardly, picking at her fingernails in her lap.

"Perhaps you should look for a better flat. It's hardly an ideal place to bring up a baby."

Charlotte suddenly grinned. "Well, at least he can't fall off a balcony." She scratched her head. "I've got to leave here anyway. I can't pay the rent." She sniffed. "You see, 'cos of Jamie I had to chuck my job."

"What are you living on?"

"Nothing much—you know how it is. If you chuck your job you don't get Social."

"But surely, with a little baby—"

"He's not my kid, is he? I mean, I love him like he's my own, but what am I supposed to tell them down the Social—I'm looking after him for a friend? No, I'll have to take the kid and do a bunk."

"You can't. Where would you go?"

"Who knows? Get away from here. Somewhere else, you know, some other town where they wouldn't know me. Then I could tell them Jamie was my kid."

"That would never work."

"What else am I going to do? Don't worry, once we've settled—well, if we get settled—I'll send you a card one day with our address. Maybe I'll send a photo when he gets older."

"You must stay here, Charlotte. It's the only address Pauline knows. And I need you here to help me find her." Mrs Estobel paused. "But I suppose you don't really want to find her?"

"And lose the kid, you mean? Oh, she wouldn't want him back." Charlotte smiled a strangely empty smile. "No, Jamie's got to stay with me. It's like I'm his mother now." She snorted and shook her head. "Like I've become your daughter."

Mrs Estobel closed her eyes. "I want my Pauline."

"Well, I'd like to help, of course. But I'm afraid I can't."

A week later, at eleven in the morning when the doorbell rang, Mrs Estobel rose from her pale pink armchair and entered the hall. She opened her front door to a tremulously sunny day, and was surprised to find Joe Venables standing politely on her step.

"I've come to make a final report, if that's all right."

She ushered him in to her pastel sitting room, still uncertain how to address him: first he had preached to her from a pulpit; now he had returned as a tradesman. On her hearthrug they waited for each other to sit.

Joe said, "I found the clinic where she had the baby."

"Mr Venables, would you like some tea?"

He seemed surprised to be diverted: "No. No, thank you. I had tried the general hospital—"

"The case is closed, I'm afraid."

Joe stared at her. Then she threw her head back and explained, "I have found the baby."

Joe nodded. "I know you met Miss Morrissey."

"Who?"

"Charlotte Morrissey."

Mrs Estobel was nonplussed. "Have you spoken to her too?"

He nodded again and licked his full red lips. "When Pauline ran away from home she tried to arrange an abortion. Did you know?"

Mrs Estobel did not answer him directly. "She may have tried to, perhaps, but she did not go through with it, I'm glad to say."

"Her pregnancy was too far advanced."

The corners of Joe's mouth sagged, and for a moment she could see the priest again. He said, "She was given lots of sensible advice—the kind I might once have approved of."

"Once?"

He looked tired again. "Nowadays I am not so sure. Am I telling you anything you don't already know?"

He leant forward, and for a moment she expected Father Venables to lay a comforting hand upon her knee. But he only smiled at her. "Pauline carried her baby to full term under an arrangement in which the baby would be immediately adopted. Once it had issued its first cry it was whisked away. She never saw the child again."

"No."

"They recommend immediate separation to ensure that the mother doesn't form a bond. It's the most humane course for the longer term."

"That is not what happened."

Joe sighed. "It isn't what Charlotte Morrissey told you, but it is what happened. When a girl goes to that kind of agency, the procedure is invariably the same. She is persuaded to deliver the child—literally to deliver it, be relieved of it—then is free to go. Once she has rested, she gets out of bed, gets dressed and leaves. Puts the whole thing behind her. Hopefully she will learn from the salutary experience. That's the idea. Some people would say that the whole experience should be a kind of punishment. If only you hadn't got into this mess in the first place, they would say."

"Pauline didn't have the baby adopted, Mr Venables. Perhaps she ought to have done, but—"

"The worst thing about my job is that I don't bring people what they want to find. The baby that you saw in the flat was Charlotte Morrissey's. She was conning you—extracting money from you."

"Not at all."

"You have paid the rent."

"Well, yes—"

"Three months in advance. And you paid money towards the house-keeping."

"Charlotte has no job—"

"But she draws her money from the state—not a lot, but it does include a child and rent allowance. I hear you offered to help her find a better flat?"

"She resisted that."

"Then let you 'overcome' her brave resistance. She is not a professional grifter, Mrs Estobel, but she played her cards quite well. Had the game continued, she might have taken you for quite a haul, as people say."

"It isn't the money."

"No."

For a short while they remained silent. Then she asked, "Was Pauline part of this?"

"No, Charlotte never knew her. You were just someone she overheard in a pub."

"But …" She was silent for a moment.

Joe said, "It was nothing personal."

Mrs Estobel took a deep breath and looked him in the eye. "Do you know where Pauline is?"

"No."

Joe sighed.

"Isn't there anything I can do?"

"Not now, I'm afraid. It's too late."

"But I'm alone here," she cried. "This whole house—empty. You must help me, Mr Venables. I'll pay anything."

Joe seemed to withdraw inside himself before he replied. "I'm afraid I can't do that. There are some things that when you lose them you can't buy back."

His voice was faint and distant, as if drawn from a soul in torment. They stood in her blush-pink room, staring at the carpet.

To lighten things up a bit (if 'lighten' is the word I'm looking for) here's a piece of black humour from Charles Shafer... boiled so hard you could use it to crack granite.

Trust Me
Charles Shafer

THIS IS THE WHOLE TRUTH, Chief. So help me.

They'd been jacking me around all damned day. Was after dark before the warden finally escorts me to the main gate. He gives me a shove, saying, "You're the kind that'll be back. No doubt in my mind."

I make sure I'm outside the wall, and say, "Remember that time you got leaked on off the third tier and locked us down for over a week? You're looking at the leaker." And give the old fart a one-finger salute.

You should'a seen him trying to run me down. Was like one of those Laurel and Hardy movies. Me being Laurel of course, skinny like I am. The warden yelling, "I get you back, I'm gonna rip that caterpillar looking thing off your face. We'll be calling you Nobrow instead of Eyebrow."

With my gangly legs I ditch him easy and head for the bus stop. Feeling good too, knowing it ain't gonna be long I'll be with the old gang. Not that I plan on going back to the wild side. Hell, no. Fifty's too old. Plus one more rap and I'm in for life.

And I hear, "Hey, roomy. Wanna ride?"

That voice I know, and spin around, seeing Georgie Sparks sitting behind the wheel of a brand spanking new Trans Am. I say, "What're you, nutty? Showing up at the County Jail in a hot ride."

He gives me that gurgle kinda laugh of his. Makes you all weird inside. Does me, anyhow. And you'd think I'd be used to it, knowing Georgie since third grade.

"Gotta catch me first." he says, swinging the door open.

Georgie's gotta point 'cause he's about the best wheel man ever. Could'a been anudder Mario Andretti, some say. And what's the ride up to the old neighborhood? Five-ten minutes at the most. So I get in.

Georgie lays rubber, saying, "Wait 'til you see what I got planned."

"A party, huh? Everybody gonna be there? I can't wait."

"Yeah, a party. Only don't go all blurry eyed just yet." And he opens the glove compartment. "Lookit my new toy. Cool, huh?"

I freeze, staring at a thirty-eight special.

"Go ahead on," he says. "See how it feels."

"No way. I just got through doing a year for carrying concealed."

He pulls it out, saying, "Chrome finishes I love. Smooth, like silk. And the smell of spent gun powder. Like roses."

Believe me Chief, when I tell you I can see where this is going. So I'm holding tight to the door handle, ready to jump. Only not getting a chance 'cause Georgie's on the side streets, genuflecting at stop signs, gunning on to the next one. Then he says, "I gotta score you ain't gonna believe. Trust me, it's worth thousands."

Trust me. Words to live by, but not coming from Georgie Sparks, and he flips a turn, goes down by the river.

I say, "We gonna hijack us a tugboat, or what?"

Anudder gurgle, and Georgie pulls up next to a dilapidated boathouse. Who walks out but Dumpy Carpo, the local bum. Lives in alleys, stuff like that. Anyway, its like Dumpy's been waiting for us, and he hollers "Hey, bro," going up to Georgie.

"Hey, yourself," and Georgie pulls a halfpint from under the seat, hands it to Dumpy.

Who takes a pull, saying, "You're a pal, you are. Coming down here last couple'a nights. Talking the old days."

"Any time," Georgie says, and throws an arm around Dumpy's shoulder. Takes him over by the river.

Up to no good too, 'cause he's looking over his shoulder, seeing if the coast is clear. But that ain't my worry, and I'm about to cut a choggy outta there when Georgie shoves Dumpy over the bank.

Hey, I admit it, I'm a wrongdoer from way back, but killing ain't my style. Well not so's it shows, so I run over, see what I can do for old Dumpy.

He's doing okay, dog paddling and all, and looking up at Georgie with one of those, 'why me', faces.

Can you believe it? Georgie's pointing the special at him. Biting his tongue, one eye squeezed shut. Like that Dirty Harry guy.

I yell, "No!" and pop goes the weasel. Georgie caps Dumpy square in the noggin.

There I am, not an hour outta the hoosgow, an accomplice to a damn murder. And I says, "You're one vicious bastard, you are."

Georgie, all satisfied. "And I'm gonna go on being a vicious bastard. Right up until I'm a dead vicious bastard."

Dumpy's bobbing around like fish bait, and I don't wanna join him. So I say, "Spoze this got something to do with that great plan you got worked out."

"C'mon, I'll show you," and Georgie gets back behind the wheel. Don't even give Dumpy a second glance. Acting like he's stepped on a bug, or something.

But hey, what'm I gonna do? So we're off, and pretty soon heading up Division Street. Georgie saying, "You remember old man Starski's grocery, don't ya?"

"Yeah, sure. When I was about eight, he caught me pocketing a pack of Marlboros. Beat me half to death."

Georgie does his gurgle thing, and says, "I remember. When your old lady found out. She did an Irish jig on your chest."

"Yeah. Fond memories. So what's this about Starski?" Then it dawns on me. "You gotta be goofy, cooking up a score in the old neighborhood. I mean, everybody knows us."

Georgie pulls over, and pointing, says, "Not to worry. Starski croaked while you was at the naughty boy's home and some big shot outfit bought the store."

He's right, 'cause what used to be a mom-and-pop kinda place now takes up half the block. I ain't convinced though, and say, "Somebody's still libel to recognize us. I mean, we growed up right across the alley."

"That's why we waited 'til closing time. Looky, nobody's around."

He's right again, and says, "After closing, Dumpy's been doing clean up for this place. And that's where you come in. All you gotta do is tell the boss Dumpy's all snookered tonight, that he sent you instead."

"And why would I do that?" Only I got me a pretty good idea.

"Simple; I been casing this place. They make a bundle, and while Dumpy's cleaning up the manager locks herself in the office, counts up the loot. You leave the back door open. I'll do the rest."

"Sounds good," I say, and get out.

Chief, getting away from Georgie is almost as good as leaving the County. And once I'm inside, I got plans on scooting out the back. Leave him high and dry.

Only when I get to the door a crowd of ladies come from inside, hollering, "See you tomorrow, boss." And, "Yeah, have a good night."

Hell, I know half of 'em. One's even my cousin Colleen, and I gotta duck around the corner. Colleen don't see me. But still, I'm ready to go back and strangle Georgie when I hear, "You have to be Georgie's buddy."

"Huh?" I say, kinda stumped, and look around. Some broad in a ponytail is holding the door open. No movie star, but a good body. You could tell, even in one of those grocery store outfits. You know, white shirt, blue trousers, a bow tie.

She drags me inside, saying, "He's gonna kill you, you know?"

"But…" Is all I can get out, 'cause how'm I spoze to know what's going on?

She pushes me into the office, closes the door behind her. "The plan is, as soon as you let Georgie in, he shoots you dead. I'm supposed to tell the cops there was two of you. That the other guy, who I can't identify of course, shot you and got away with the cash."

I collapse in the office chair, and looking up at her, "How come you're telling me this? I mean, thanks and all that, but — well, what's in it for you?"

Hands on those sweet hips, she says, "I got to thinking what's to stop Georgie from shooting me after he does you?"

Makes sense, and I tell her, "You did the right thing. So show me the back door and I'll be down the road."

She puts a hand on my shoulder. Makes me tingle all over. I mean, Chief. Seems like the last time I was next to a broad they had nickel candy bars. And she says, "That's what he's got you figured to do. Believe me, he's back there right now waiting with that crazy laugh of his."

"You know him all right," and I reach for the phone. "Spoze our only hope is to call the cops."

Her hand switches to the phone. "Go ahead," she says, "Only you're forgetting one thing. According to Georgie you're on parole. If that's right, they'll send you right back to jail. Consorting with known criminals, they call it, right?"

"Hell yeah, right. But I'll take the cops over Georgie any day of the week," and I start dialing.

Then she shows me this shopping bag. Can you believe it? The ting's chocked full'a cash. Like confetti, only green. I stop dialling, and say, "Uh, how much?"

"Lots."

"I can see that, but…"

And she pulls a four-five auto outta her desk. "Soon as you open the door I'm going to blast him."

I've seen lots of folks *talk* about shooting, few who really got the sand for it. And say, "That's a big piece, lady. You sure you can handle it?"

"Just watch me."

"That's the point. Am I gonna be watching you shoot Georgie, or Georgie shoot me?"

"I don't see you having a choice."

This broad's cool. Almost too cool, and I say, "What about afterwards? I mean, the cops are still gonna stick me back inside."

"That I got planned out too. You beat it. Call me tomorrow and we'll divvy up the cash. Trust me."

There it was again, that trust me stuff. But who cares? All I want is to get outta there with my skin attached. Okay, maybe some of that cash too. So I say, "Okay, whatever."

She grabs the shopping bag and takes the lead. I don't know what I'm watching more, the shopping bag or those hips flicking side to side. The hips, I'm pretty sure, 'cause the Chicago Philharmonic could keep time to those things.

Soon enough we're in the back where there's aisle after aisle of cardboard boxes, tin cans, freezer lockers. "That's it," she says, pointing at a steel door, and drags this flood light out, points it at the door. "When you open up, Georgie won't be able to pick out either of us."

"Not a bad idea," I say, and grab the door. Only I'm edgy. A whole lot edgy, you wanna know the truth, 'cause I can feel Georgie outside ready to plug me up. And looking over my shoulder, say, "You ready?"

"Ready," she says, legs wide, arms stretched out, the four-five twitching at the end of her hands.

"Hey," I says. "This ain't no Arnold Schwarzenegger flick, so forget the pose and get the job done."

She rolls her eyes, saying, "You want to do this before or after the cops show, dammit?"

The way she's flipping that gun around I'm ascared it's gonna go off, splatter me before Georgie gets the chance. So I yank the door wide, quick press myself against the wall.

I'm telling you, all hell breaks loose. Like one of those war movies, guns blazing, bullets flashing back and forth. I end up on my butt, head curled between my knees. Got my hands on my crotch. You know, just in case I happen to live through this ting and those whores are still operating up on North Avenue.

Then everything goes quiet.

I peek outside in time to see Georgie go to his knees, a nasty hole in his chest. Squirting blood. He gurgles, only not a laughing gurgle, and says, "Hadda be the broad's idea, 'cause no way a cluck like you comes up with something as good as this."

Anudder blast thuds into his belly. He flops backwards. Laying still. Kinda gory, but at least he ain't squirting blood no more. Yuk. Can't stand the stuff.

Anyway, I turn to Ponytail. The flood light's shot out and she's looking at her thigh where blood's oozing. "You gonna be okay?" I say, crawling outside, "'cause it's time for me to beat it outta here."

"Just a scratch," she says. And raises the four-five.

I run, flinching as a round whizzes past my ear. Which puts me into high gear, and zigzagging like one of those Bear halfbacks, actually see anudder flash between my legs. I'm sure the next one's got my number, and dive behind a dumpster. Two more zing close, and I'm saying my prayers 'cause no way I'm living through this one.

That's when this cop car comes screaming into the parking lot. Wouldn't you know it, Billy Dowd jumps out. About the crookedest cop on the Chicago PD. And mean. Like a junkyard dog, drooling all the time, the ape-looking bastard.

But beggars can't be choosers and I come out. Making sure he's between me and Ponytail, I say, "Billy, you ain't gonna believe it, but that broad over there, she kilt Georgie. Trying like hell to do me, too."

"Be with you in a sec, Eyebrow," he says, and goes by Ponytail.

"Didn't work out exactly how we planned," she says, holding her thigh.

I don't mind telling you, Chief, I about swallow my tongue, especially when he says, "It'll do," and pulls out his gun, snaps one off.

Ponytail's neck spurts blood. She plops on her behind. Jaw's hanging loose, a surprised look on her face. Coughing.

I wanna run, but where's there to go? So I'm waiting my turn, mumbling, "Mother of God — Mother of God."

Billy laughs, and puts his gun up to Ponyail's forehead, saying, "Never should'a trusted me, babe."

And boom. Only instead of Ponytail's head exploding, Billy gets lifted off his feet, comes down on his back all spreadeagled. Like when we was kids, making angels in the snow.

Ponytail, she points the four-five at me. I know I'm a dead duck. Then she gasps. Topples sideways. Eyes fixed.

Lights are coming on up and down the street. Worse yet, cop sirens are blaring, getting close too. I pull myself together and head for the Tranzy. Then stop, 'cause why not? Run over, grab the shopping bag. It's taking an awful chance, but no way am I gonna leave ready money laying around.

I get away clean. For the time being anyway, 'cause with Georgie back there, him and me old partners, it's only a matter of time before a warrant's out on me.

So I'm running scared, trying to figure a place to hide. Finally jump a freighter. End up on some South Sea island. We're tied up alongside one of those excursion boats. You know, like Gilligan and all that. Gives me an idea, so I spruce myself up and take a walk over.

This dude comes out, tanned like some movie star, probably hasn't worn long pants in all his life. I say, "That right what you hear? There's a hunert islands out there, and a guy could get lost easy?"

"More like a thousand," he says. "A charter runs five-hundred a day," and he's eyeing my shopping bag.

Yeah, I'm still using it, 'cause where else am I gonna keep a load like that? I mean, banks — not an option, and I say, "I was thinking more buying the ting. What you say to that?"

Now he's really scoping the shopping bag, and says, "What's the matter? Don't you trust me?"

That's it, and when he turns around I grab the nearest oar, bash him over the head. Dump him in the drink. Feeling bad about it. Yeah, right. For maybe two minutes. Way I look at it, it's either him or me.

Somehow I get the boat going, and I'm off. Where to I don't know, just go. Bouncing off one island then the next. Finally run outta gas. Go to drifting. How long, I couldn't tell you. Hit this storm, which about turns me upside down a couple'a times, finally washes me overboard.

"You know the rest, Chief. One of your boys finds me drifting in the surf, half dead. Lemme tell you, when I come to, lay my eyes on yous guys, I about jump outta my skin. No offense, but walking around half naked, blowguns and all — whatta you expect?

"You can't understand a word I'm saying, just sitting there like always, smiling, letting me blow off steam, but I wanna thank yous for taking me in, making me feel part of the family. Only been here, what? About a month, and the way you're feeding me I must'a gained a good thirty pounds.

"Hey, I see the pot's boiling. Wonder what's on for tonight."

The Chief licks his lips, and says in perfect English;

"It'll be good."

"Trust me."

Charlie served 28 years on the Chicago PD, mostly as a detective. Retiring 3 years ago he and his wife Betty now live in a small Southern Illinois farming community where he plays 200 rounds of golf each year, and bangs away on the keyboard. Charlie was first published in Blue Murder Magazine *due to the perspicacity of editor David Firks. Interested parties can contact Charlie at cshafer@chipsnet.com*

This is definately a 'push-the-envelope' sort of issue. Steve Aylett, author of The Crime Studio *and the forthcoming* Slaughtermatic *contributes a tale of a boy, a girl and a gun in the city of Beerlight...*

The Siri Gun
Steve Aylett

'WHAT WERE YOU DOING IN WASHINGTON, ATOM?'

'Visiting my rights.'

'Wiseguy, eh?'

'Where were you on June 16?' asked the second cop.

'Hiding a pod in the basement.'

'Wiseguy,'muttered the first, nodding.

Nice day—sunny outside and I hadn't bled much. I was sat in a yelling cell as a bullet lost its flavour in my leg. The two stooges had me jacked to a polygraph. I'd breezed the Wittgenstein controls and we were fronting off to beat the band.

'I get a phonecall? Need to send a singing telegram to my rabbi.'

'You keep mouthin' us Chief Blince'll tear you a new asshole.'

'I need a new asshole—how soon can he get here?'

'You got a gun called a Glory Hand, Atom?'

I rolled a nicotine patch and lit it up. 'Okay fellas, you got me.'

'I'll tell it like it happened. Now let's see.'

And I spun the following, beginning with my habitation of an office on Saints Street and nothing doing. People think my business is all swapping the clever with rich clients bathchairbound in a hothouse of flycatchers and septic orchids. Missing daughters and like that. In fact I was just sat in contemplation when the phone rang. Siri Moonmute sounding wired.

Siri explained that she was now wanted for everything. She had never been into the perfect crime as she didn't go for Gautier's principle of virtue in correctness of form. I knew a girl could be perfect because of her flaws. The whole thing was subjective.

Siri was into purity—this it was possible to quantify. A pure crime Is like a diamond in which no facet or depth is clouded by legality. It's criminally saturated, every move from start to finish creating a breach in legislation.

This was a headcrime Siri had pondered increasingly of late and with laws entering the statute books at a rate of thousands per year, it was getting easier all the time. So she'd done it, packing as many offences as possible into each second. Her name smeared the copnet like a rash.

Siri started in on how the difficulties of evading detection were no longer an inducement and she'd been hurting for a new challenge, at which I remarked if she wasn't careful she'd be sat cod-eyed in a bodyvan. Siri spoke in awe of the particle-science phenomenon of the *singularity*, a point at which all known laws broke down. If a substance was supposed to expand, in a singularity it contracted. If light was meant to bend, in a singularity it was stiff as a board. Where laws were created to explain behaviour these squirls occurred every few months; but where laws were created to prevent behaviour—like among people—they happened many times per second. The latter laws were patently inaccurate, and a pure crime was a statement of unmixed truth.

'Siri,' I stated, 'don't you understand that the cops will stick it in and break it off at a speed which will surprise everyone? Such pristine behaviour as you display is the sole preserve of a mutant in a belfry.'

Siri remarked that I had failed to gauge the full extent to which she was gung-ho. She was chock full of that quality and would express it at the drop of a hat. 'There was a point there, Atom, I'd set things up so that I was committing several hundred offences in one instant, and I could feel the very atmosphere change—it was as though my misdemeanours had reached such a superdensity that they began to implode.'

'Like a black hole, collapsing in on itself?'

'Exactly.'

'How do you feel?'

'Like God. Could you come over?'

By the time I got there the area was under containment by the cops. Behind them a hole in space spiralled like the water spinning down a drain, a tornado of light sucking scraps of paper and nuggets of masonry out of view. The trooper boy Marty Nada was stood at the cordon tape yelling through a bullhorn so I went to ask him the deal. He didn't bother to lower the bullhorn.

'Oh hi Atom. Ah it's a singularity of some kind, its gravity so powerful not even lies can escape. We've lost five officers going near that thing.'

'How'd it happen, they know?'

'Still guessing. Pun gun misfire? Etherics? Eschaton rifle'd do it, right person.'

'Uh, okay thanks Marty.'

'Sure Atom.'

Well, another day another dollar. But it has a bearing upon what happened the following afternoon when I got an out-of-town yell from the Caere Twins. These bottle-bald cuties were crime stylists who got off on the coining of new offences. They weren't after some benign act fallen foul of a legislation twitch or an old trespass enhanced to the fashion, but a wholly new and original template, outside the seven sins. They were camped out in Washington with the theory that a target moved least at the axis. I split the border to face with them in an apartment so small they had to sleep in the mirror. The place really served as a digital gun foundry. Forcing the gun scene from industry to desktop. the Crime Bill had freed it up for limitless configuration. The Twins were among the many who innovated firearms on the fly.

'Siri sent an "eyes only" letter,' they chirped in unison. 'With real eyes.'

They gave me some tech laced with sarcasm so heavily encrypted it never really thawed into effect. It was like being flogged with a double helix. I finally extracted the fact that Siri had sent them an c-mail just before her crescendo, but the feed had been jacked to their forge at the time and the message funnelled into a blank skeleton gun which had lain ready for impression.

'What was the message?'

'A command trail,' they said. 'Two million keystrokes.'

'All this theory's like eating hair,' I whined, impatient. Then the truth sunflared over my brainlobes—the only way to achieve the offence density Siri craved was to hack it, initiating a thousand thefts, frauds and intrusions in a split second. The programme she created to do it now informed the design of the gun cooling in the Twins' forge. They opened the panel and retrieved a firearm resembling a tin ammonite with a chicaned barrel and pupstock Steyr grip. Spiral cylinders were real fashionable then. All part of life's kitsch tapestry.

'Etheric sampler in the butt,' said the Twins. 'This gat's her legacy and culmination, shadowboy, her tub of warm ashes. She'd want to be home.'

'You mean I should take it back and scatter the ammo? No, not me. The cops are right about a gun eventually getting used whether or not there's a reason.'

'True of them, shadowboy. Be careful.'

My car had been replaced with an inflatable replica which burst when I put the key in the door. So I was on a clunker train to Beerlight. Carriage to myself until this big guy in gut braces bellies in. Looks at the empty seats, then lumbers right over to me, dropping down opposite. Regards me with a head like a throw cushion as the light and dark pass over us both.

'Staring is its own reward.'

'It certainly is.' In the pocket of my full-length void coat, the ammo-guzzler zinged against my palm.

'Shave the fuzz from the face of a moth, and what do you get?'

'Fatty Arbuckle?'

'Think again.'

'You?'

'On the nose. Tubs Fontanel's the name. Fontanel by name, fontanel by nature. Retired cop but I keep my eyes open. Know why I consider myself always on cop duty?'

'Any impediment to imitation'd throw you back on your labouring character?'

'Nah. Watch this.' He hauled himself up, stood in the aisle, and started throwing flat, startled shapes with his arms and legs. This galoot danced like a cartoon robot. Then he sat down, panting and chuffed. 'Know where I learnt to dance that way?'

'The laughing academy?'

'Nah.' He took out what looked like a cell phone. 'Know what this is?'

'Scrambler hotline to the circus?'

'Nah. Two-end scanner. I hear about a ventilation job I go round and scan the floor pattern. All began two years ago. I was flippin' through crime scene photos—you know, chalk body outlines on the floor? Got this flicker-book effect, like the outline man was dancin'. And I thought—get a choreographer in here, we're sittin' on a goldmine. Got dance numbers from every month last year. Multiple homicides I string together for, like, big production numbers. That thing I just did? Combination o' fifty crime scenes, January, central DC. I'm based in DC but I just hear about the fashionable events in Beerlight, yeah? Vortex, goofy crime scene, chalkline's a doozy, wanna record it. You from Beerlight? How's the local colour?'

'Red.'

'I get it. You got the chair there? We got gas in Washington. Folk say the killin' jar's just as cold-blooded as some homicides, but I think it's a crime of passion. Yeah rare's the day I forget to bless those who gave us a blank cheque on enforcement. Them and the bicthought media. Support us you're objective, criticise us you're biased. I could point to a dozen trite precedents. But the respect ain't there. What happened to faith in a higher authority?'

'Burned in a wicker man?'

'Nah. Average Beerlighter's got a morality like a ferris wheel. What Is it with you people? You hear me, boy? It'll be shuffleboard and orange walls before you realise you're runnin' naked through an alligator ranch ...'

His words had galvanised me into sleep—boredom was always the heaviest rock in the law's armoury. And I dreamt I was a clown driving a dyna-mite truck. Cliff edges blurred like sawteeth. Siri was sat next to me in red-fleck dungarees. 'What did the Twins say?' she asked calmly. 'Was it more art than science or was it based on exacting principles?'

'C-c-can't you see I don't give a damn about that?' I shrieked, wrenching the wheel, and the tyres blew out, waking me.

Tubs Fontanel was dressed the same as Siri from the dream, and looking as astonished as an inevitably snipered senator. Arterial blood misted and swirled between us, settling in a soft rain. I'd blown a hole in my thigh. The retired cop's bewilderment was perfectly apparent.

'What the f...'

I bowed to his judgement so fast his nose broke. The train was grinding into the station. He was snuffling something about paraffin and death as I leapt to the platform and made for the barrier with a few dozen others. I included a bullet now, and a thin gore trail. Yelling behind me—I turned to see Tubs bent over, gasping, light falling into him and being extinguished. He was a vacuum. Through the barrier, feeling squirly.

As I crossed the concourse everything was incredibly high res. I could see infringement thresholds overlapping as people jumped queues, threw punches, glared, every head a poisoned chalice. Kirlian stormfronts collid-ed around the rushing crowds. Mindmade law lines crisscrossed the air, weak and tangled as gossamer. As I passed through they shrivelled and vanished like burning hair. I stashed the gat in a locker, and blew.

Back at my barnacle-encrusted office I told the whole thing to my girl-friend and technical adviser, and she said it couldn't have been more Freud-ian if the gun had gone off as I went into a tunnel. I told her Freud was projecting, she kicked me in the balls and I blacked out for sixteen hours, waking only when the cops arrived.

'And that's how I ended up in a yelling cell with you guys,' I told the two interrogators affably.

'So you wouldn't know why the President was found with his head in the mouth of an embalmed Kodiak bear. Utterly naked and quite dead. Five yards of Chinese firecrackers up his ass.' They showed me photos of the crime scene.

'Can I keep these?'

'Atom, your story ain't even halfway good. And void without material proof. But we can bust open every last safe locker in Beerlight grand and if we find a gun, we'll do you as an accessory to the Siri job. We got you either way.'

The cops soon decided my death was unnecessary—something I'd been thinking for years. I could have said anything and breezed the polygraph, the Siri bullet handling the conscience response. But it wasn't a heroic dose—the gunshot was accidental, motiveless, self-inflicted. No intent. The Twins were scornful.

Worst of all, the cops had the gun, though they didn't know it. There were a thousand lockers in Beerlight station, and a gun in every one.

Steve Aylett is author of The Crime Studio *(Serif) and* Slaughtermatic *(published by Orion in October).*

So, the second story in this issue that proves that hard-boiled is not necessarily hard hearted. When I started to read 'The Ghosts of Ponce de Leon Park' I thought I knew what I was in for. I was wrong, and the ending (especially) blew me away. One of the best short stories I've read...

The Ghosts of Ponce de Leon Park
Fred Willard

"**WE CAN THUMB SOME MORE** or just walk down the railroad tracks to Ponce," Bob said.

"My legs don't feel so good," Del said. "The doctors at the clinic said my circulation is bad."

"I know, man. You already told me. Maybe walking will get your circulation going."

"Maybe so. I don't know about that. I just know my legs don't feel good."

Del looked down the rail bed. A tree line on either side hid it from the apartments and the shopping center and as the line curved gently in the distance to the left they also hid the destination.

"How far is it?" he asked.

"Maybe a mile."

"I guess we might as well walk it. We might stand around that long waiting for a ride."

They walked between the rails matching strides to the wooden ties.

"I don't know if I can keep this up," Del said.

"We can slow down."

"It ain't the speed it's the reach."

"The gravel's harder."

"I'm going to walk over to the side on the dirt," Del said. He stepped over to the worn path on the edge of the right of way.

"It's softer here," he said.

"That's your problem," Bob said. "You're too damn soft. It's like you never worked."

"I worked plenty."

"Down there is where the snakes are," Bob said.

"I don't see any damn snakes."

Del was slowly falling behind Bob's strides on the railroad ties.

"Hold on. What's the damn hurry?"

"You're in bad shape."

"It's the circulation. The doctors said I might get gangrene. Then they'd have to cut my legs off."

"That's the other thing, your circulation. I can tell you hadn't been working not without any circulation. So where did you get that stash of money?"

"I ain't got that much."

"But where did you get it? You been sucking dicks?"

"Why did you go and say something like that?"

"Well have you?"

"Hell, no."

"Where did you get the money, then?"

"Sold blood."

"No wonder you can't walk."

"You never sold blood?"

"I never been in bad shape like you are. "

"So if I'm in bad shape, why don't you just slow down? It ain't polite running off like that."

"I'll slow down, but this cut–through scares the hell out of me sometimes."

"Why's that?"

"All sorts of bad shit happens back here. The skinheads catch you and they kick your ass. They killed a couple homeless along these tracks. Stomped this one guy till his heart exploded."

"Now you're frightening me. What do they do—hide in the trees till you come by?"

"No. They just use it as a cut-through. They walk over from Little Five Points go up to Piedmont Park to beat queers. Keep your eyes open. We see anybody, we can get off the tracks and hide. I just don't like thinking about it."

"You wouldn't run off and leave me, if you saw the skinheads coming, would you?"

"I don't know, man. There wouldn't be much point in my sticking around for an ass whipping if I couldn't do nothing, would there?"

"I'll try to walk faster, but my legs are killing me. If we see some skinheads, help me hide in the trees before you run off."

"I'll do that, Del."

The track had been following a gentle curve, but as it straightened they could see Ponce de Leon Avenue ahead.

"It isn't that much further," Bob said.

They didn't talk as they tried to make time. Del's legs felt raw. They were swelling and he walked with them stiff in a fast shuffle so he could keep up. He counted steps to help the time pass. When they were almost to Ponce he said, "My legs are no good, I got to lay down."

"We farted around so long we can't get nothing at the Open Door or St. Luke's," Bob said. "I guess we might as well spend the night in this kudzu field. You want to buy us both a dinner since we missed it because of your damn circulation?"

"You can get us dinner and a couple pints of sherry," Del said.

They walked to the kudzu covered field to the right of the tracks, and found a little depression where they wouldn't be as visible and unrolled their bedrolls. Del pulled some money out of his stash and handed it to Bob.

"Why don't you take a water bottle?"

"Okay, I got to go to Green's then up to the Zesto, so it's going to take me some time, so just hang on."

"I ain't going nowhere," Del said.

When it came down to it, Del didn't know jack-shit about Bob. He thought Bob could just as easy take off with the money and not come back, buy himself a decent dinner and keep all the wine for himself. He had the look of someone who knew how to take care of himself, all right. His jeans, work shirt and heavy shoes were a lot newer than Del's, whose clothes looked like they were about to rot off. Not that Del cared anymore, but he thought they smelled like it too.

At the shelter in Nashville, Bob had got hung with the name Normal Bob. He wasn't so normal, but he had the good luck to show up after Crazy Bob who got his instructions from a dog named Tick that nobody else could see. Mostly the dog told him to howl. So Bob became Normal Bob to tell him apart from Crazy Bob.

Normal Bob was going back to Atlanta so Del planned to tag along. Del had a little stash of money and Normal knew the city so it seemed like a good partnership.

Del laid out in his bedroll and put his head on his little bag of clothes and watched the puffy white clouds drift across the early evening sky. In a little while, the night would unzip its bag of tricks and spill the predators into the hundreds of pockets of darkness along this street of appetites, and by then Del hoped to be fed, drunk and sleeping unnoticed among the weeds.

Now that he'd got the weight of his legs, he noticed he was getting the shakes in his hands, but there wasn't nothing he could do about it till Bob got back with the wine. He lay like this about an hour, till twilight, when he heard a man approaching, looked up and saw Bob carrying a couple of sacks.

"I got us both a Chubby Decker Plate."

He handed Del a pint bottle. Del broke the seal, and took three or four gulps, and fought to keep them down. He didn't want to waste any of it.

"You going to eat anything with that?" Bob asked.

"First things first," Del said.

"You shouldn't have made this trip. It was too much for you," Bob said.

"Had to leave Nashville."

"It must have been big trouble," Bob said.

"No, I just wore out my welcome too many places. Life was getting too hard."

"Well, a lot of little trouble can be just as bad as big trouble, " Bob said. "Tomorrow morning we can head up to St. Luke's for breakfast. Talk to the guys there. See what's going on."

"I don't know if I can make it," Del said. "I don't think I'm going to be able to walk at all."

"I can call the Grady wagon then, they can take you to the hospital."

"I'm afraid they might have to cut my legs off."

Bob tried to change the subject.

"This place we're sitting is historic, It's the back end of the old Ponce de Leon Baseball Park. That magnolia tree would have been at dead center field. The Atlanta Crackers used to play here. I came to the games with my old man. They tore the place down when they built the new stadium for the Braves. Turned it into this parking lot."

"I never liked this place none," Del said.

"You been here then?"

"I lived in Atlanta a couple months when I was a kid. I came here with my father once," Del said. "What do they call that building across the street?"

"That would be the old Sears and Roebuck. It's got city offices now, so they call it City Hall East."

"I remember the Sears and Roebuck, you got off the trolley and walked across the street to the park."

"That's right, man, they still had the old electric trolleys when the Cracker's played here."

"I never had no luck here. We shouldn't have stopped here."

"Hell, You were the one who wanted to stop, Del. You said your legs were bad. You never should have left Nashville with your legs like that."

"I know that, now," Del said. The memory of the old ball park pinned him to the ground like a stack of cement blocks on his chest.

2

Del woke up in the middle of the night breaking a fever. There was a bright full moon.

"I got to pee bad, man and I can't move my legs," he said. "I need help getting up.

Bob didn't answer so he pushed himself up a little bit on an elbow and saw the ground where Bob had been sleeping and had crushed the kudzu, but Bob and his bedroll were gone. Del felt for his money stash and it was gone, too. At least he left one of the pints.

There wasn't nothing he could do but lie there until somebody came along to help. He held the pee as long as he could then wet the bed. It felt uncomfortable as it soaked his pants and ran up his back. He didn't think he could go back to sleep, but that wasn't the worst part. Something much more frightening was happening because time was messing up somehow and he was also back in his parents little shack they had rented in West Atlanta when he was nine years old.

"I was thinking about taking the boy to a ball game," his father said.

Del pretended he wasn't paying attention but he hoped his mother would say yes. She was the one who had a job, and she always watched every penny she made. That's what his parents always fought about.

"I guess we ought to do something for him," his mother said. She walked back to her bedroom, where she kept her money, and closed the door so nobody could hear her hiding place. When she came out she handed a couple folded dollar bills to his father, and some change, too.

"Why don't y'all get yourself a hot dog. That way I don't have to cook nothing for you, tonight."

She went back to her room and laid down. She worked so much she was always tired. Some days she went to bed as soon as she got home from work.

After a while his father said, "Okay, boy, it's time to go to that ball game."

He followed his father up to the trolley stop, trying to keep up with his funny bobbing walk. They sat on a hard bench for a few minutes till the trolley came.

"Mr. Driver, I need a transfer for me and my boy." He said it like they always did things together.

The driver tore off two scraps of paper, and handed them to him, and then his father made a big to do about handing one to Del.

"Now you hold onto this, Son. It's what makes you able to ride the second trolley."

They both sat down.

"I like this sideways seat the best," his father explained.

"Me too, " Del agreed.

After a few minutes his father pulled the cord that rang the bell and said, "Time to get off."

They were at another bus stop and Del sat on a bench like the other one.

"Now you sit here, till I get back. No matter what happens, just stay there."

He crossed the street and went in a liquor store and when he came out Del could see a bottle stuck in his front pants pocket. When he sat next to Del he took it out, and held it to his lips and swallowed three or four times.

"Here. You want some."

He handed it to Del who took a sip but thought it tasted sour, like puke. He pretended to like it, though.

"Here comes the bus." His father put the bottle back in his pants.

"They don't like you to drink this stuff on the bus," he father explained.

Once they got on it seemed like they were at a party.

"Anybody going to see the Crackers?" his father asked.

A bunch of people laughed like his father had told a joke.

"Seems like most of us are," a woman said.

"Have a seat, son."

He sat Del down in the sideways seat, then walked back four or five rows to where there was a bunch of men sitting. He said something, they laughed, and a couple of them looked up toward the driver, then the bottle came out and they were passing it around.

Del looked out the window and watched the people on the street until they stopped next to this big brick building with a tower on top like a castle.

"That's the Sears and Roebuck."

A woman sitting next to him said this when she saw him looking at the building.

"Everybody off the bus," his father said. The men with him laughed like this was pretty funny.

People were already starting to line up to buy tickets, so his father ran ahead and bought two seats in the white bleachers. They went up this ramp into the park and he followed his father and the other men under the wooden seats to a refreshment stand where a man was cooking hot dogs on a grill.

Dell asked, "You going to get us some hot dogs, daddy?"

"Don't have no money left," he said. "But wait a minute here. I got something in my pocket."

He reached in his pocket and pulled out his white handkerchief. He bent down on one knee, and laid it out like a neat square, then stepped back and started doing a little dance like a buck and wing and giving out yelps.

He was pretty good at it, but Del didn't like to watch.

Pretty soon a crowd had gathered and people were dropping nickels and dimes, even a few quarters on the handkerchief.

"Thank you very much, folks." his father said. He scooped up the money and handed Del a quarter.

"You keep this in case you need it. Don't spend it on food or nothing. Just hold onto it. Now go on up and get us our seats and I'll be along in a little while."

The men from the bus had gathered around his father again and Del knew he wanted to drink with them, so he went to get their seats in the bleachers. A boy his own age tried to sit down next to him, but he held his hand out over the seat and said, "My daddy's going to be sitting there," so the boy moved over a space.

Pretty soon the teams took to the field and everybody cheered. Del didn't know much that was going on but he acted like he did, so nobody would think he was stupid. He didn't know how to play ball. His parents moved around so he never really got to have many friends and the few boys he knew didn't have the equipment. Still, it was real beautiful to watch. The lights made the field seem bright green and the uniforms stuck out like a cartoon in the newspaper. Out in the distance there was this dirt bank covered with kudzu and a big magnolia tree and over to the right, a railroad track. It didn't look like how he'd imagined a ball park, but he liked it.

He actually started figuring out the game, at least part of it, and he'd get excited with every pitch, and cheer with the crowd when the players from Birmingham would swing at a pitch and miss.

He was having fun until he figured out that his father wasn't coming to his seat, and then he only watched the game because he knew he ought to be having fun since he probably wasn't going to get to come back.

The Crackers won. As the crowd left, he didn't see his father and he knew he wasn't here. In his pocket, he felt the quarter and wondered if this was the time he was supposed to save the money for, or if there would be another one. Finally he decided this must be the time, because spending it was the only way he was going to get home.

"I'd like a transfer, Mr. Driver." he said

The man gave him a funny look, but handed him the transfer.

Del was pretty sure he could spot the street where he lived, but he wasn't too sure about the stop by the liquor store, so he sat in the sideways seat twisted around with his face pressed against the window. It turned out to be easy to see because of the lights, so he rang the bell and got off the trolley.

He was quiet going in the house. He was starving and got a piece of bread. He hoped his mother wouldn't notice and get mad.

"That you boy?" she called from the bedroom.

"Yes ma'am."

"Is your father with you?"

"No ma'am, he ain't."

"I should have known," she said. "He don't care nothing about you. He just wanted the money so he could get a drink."

"He won't be coming back neither," she said. "I told him the next time he took to drinking he couldn't come back, but sometimes that man needs a drink so bad he'd trade his whole life for it."

<h3 style="text-align:center">3</h3>

Del woke up, or he thought he woke up. It seemed like he was back in the kudzu field and there were men standing around him, but something reminded him of the mission back at Nashville.

It was the picture the reverend had taken him aside to see. Some old drunk had painted it from the Book of Revelations showing skeletons on winged horses, the four horsemen of the apocalypse riding above the battle field at Armageddon. He hadn't understood then what the preacher had meant, showing it to him like that, but now he knew that he had been shown his death.

He might as well have put his hands on Del's head in benediction and said, "Go forth my son, and die by skinhead," because Del knew the four men looking down at him were going to kill him. They didn't have any hair and their skin was stretched tight and showed their skulls. The moonlight made it seem they had bleached bone instead of flesh and their eyes had retreated in their sockets. They leaned over Del lying in his bedroll and his own piss.

"He smells rank," one of the men said.

"Let's put him out of his misery."

"It's my legs," Del said. "They ain't no good."

"Don't worry old man, God's going to give you a new body."

Del saw the heel of the boot coming down on his face, felt bone crunching, and heard a sound like loud ringing in his ears. He let go of everything and didn't know nothing they did after that.

Del was unconscious and then he saw the kudzu in front of his face again. There was a man standing next to him. The man knelt down and put his hand on Del's shoulder.

"Hello, son. I've been wanting to talk to you for a long time."

Del knew he was dead because it was his father's voice. He stood up quickly, held his arm in front of him and marveled at it. It was milky white under the full moon and had perfect skin like a baby's, like he had never worked in the sun or fallen down.

The dark green kudzu was silver where it was kissed by the light and his father's face was beautiful like a blessing Del had never seen in this world.

"I've been wanting to tell you that I always loved you. I didn't leave you that night, and that's the truth. Some bad men took me away from the ball park in their automobile. They took me out of town and killed me. They cut my gut open so my body wouldn't float, and they wrapped me in burlap, and tied cement blocks to me, and they threw me in the Chattahoochee River. I swear, son, that I never meant to leave you that night. I always loved you. And now I've been sent down here to take you up to heaven," he said.

Del picked up the bottle, took a little sip and saw the hunger on his father's face as he looked at the sherry. He wouldn't offer him any. He'd wait for him to ask… or maybe even beg.

"If you just come from heaven, how come you want a drink so bad," Del asked.

"They sent me down to get you, son. You don't go with me, you got to stay by yourself."

"You always were a liar. How do I know it's heaven you're taking me to?"

"Could you give me a taste of that wine? Then we could go up there. Don't you want to be with the other people? Your mother's up there."

Del turned around, kicked his dirty bed roll and started walking fast to the railroad, then running down the tracks leaving his father far behind. Now that God had given him his new body, he didn't need nobody or their stinking lies. From now on he would travel alone.

Fred describes his story as " …hopeless, violent, pessimistic, narcissistic, all the stuff that makes me proud to be an American." *He is the author of* Down on Ponce, *just published by No Exit Press, and well worth you investing your pocket money in.*

A Story by I
Paul Duncan

I HAVE OFTEN BEEN FRIGHTENED by the thought that, no matter how long I know someone, no matter how intimately, there is always a part of them I will never know, and can never second guess. I have always tried to look inside people, to find out what made them what they were, how their mind worked, so that I could predict their next action or thought. I considered myself quite adept at this and have, over the years, been quite successful at it.

This skill has proved helpful in both my life and my profession.

(My profession is not your concern, and I do not wish to disclose it. I will not give you any clues in that area. There are no hints in this text. You will, no doubt, read this text looking for clues. Because of the publication this appears in, you will be suspicious. At this stage, you may even go so far as to speculate whether I am a criminal, a policeman, a writer, or a combination thereof. You will never know—it is irrelevant. I need my anonymity.)

This story starts with a friend. I have known this friend, on and off, for many years. I met this person, whom I shall call A, whilst I was at B University. We were an odd couple, and people commented that we had nothing in common. This was true, but I have found that most friends are different from each other—the differences allow us to see each other in a different light, and hence grow as people. The worse kind of friend is one similar to ones self—people hate to be constantly reminded of their own faults.

After University, we worked together at C Ltd for a while, and then lost contact. I moved to D City, married E, moved to F Street before settling in G Road. It was a good time for me. Everything was simple and life was sweet. Then, after ten years, I accidentally bumped into A again and my life fell apart.

How do two people bond? There is no quick application of superglue, and instant symbiosis—it is a long, invisible process where millions of emotional gifts and favours are exchanged. Before you know it, you have reached a compromise, an equilibrium, an understanding. You can spend hours in the company of the one with whom you have bonded, and it feels like seconds.

This was my feeling towards A when we met. However, as I was later to understand, A had obviously changed. We had been meeting regularly for a little time when, over a drink, A said:

"I'd like to ask a favour."

"Go ahead."

"Do you know the people across the road from you?"

"Not really. You know, just a nodding acquaintance."

"Could you keep an eye on them for me? You know, make a list of people coming and going from the house, times, that sort of thing."

"…err…"

"I know it's a bit of a weird thing to ask, but it'd be a great help to me. I'm… I can't really tell you what's going on, but it'll make sense at the death."

Although I was more than a little confused by the request, I agreed. A was always a bit more eccentric than I, and I was always too 'square' for most people's tastes. Besides, it was kind of exciting to be spying on someone else.

At first, E was somewhat sceptical about the whole thing and wouldn't have anything to do with it. Our road was in a respectable neighbourhood—nothing much happened and, if it did, it was behind closed doors. Nevertheless, over the first four weeks, I established that my neighbours, H and J, had a kind of routine: a) first thing in the morning the children (K, M and N) would be sent off to school; b) during the day packages would arrive via delivery vans; c) throughout the evening people would arrive with ring binders, knock on the door, enter, spend a few minutes inside, leave, and drive off.

I did not find any of this suspicious. Obviously, my neighbours worked at home, they ordered their clothes and other items from catalogues, and they had friends or relations around in the evening. They even had grocers and video libraries coming to the door. The window cleaners were around every couple of weeks. The other day I even had a guy offering to clean out my guttering for £12.

You would think that watching people would be boring, that there would be long periods of nothing happening, that your interest would waiver. I didn't find that to be the case. It became a habit to watch them. I would watch television, do some cooking, gardening, clear out the garage, and always one eye would be kept on my neighbours. Inside the house, my clipboard was always by my side, ready for the next scrap of information.

When outside, I would surreptitiously look at my watch and memorise what to write down. (I able to develop my own set of standard phrases and short-hand initials because H and J had a very rigorous routine.)

E would come home from work and ask me what news I had, what was going on, having caught the bug too. Ritually, E would look through my notes before coming into the kitchen and kissing me. When I told A about this, A laughed knowingly.

"It always happens," A said. "Curiosity always gets the better of them."

One day, when I went for a walk down to the newspaper shop, I forgot my money, went back, and realised my neighbours had gone out. It was instinctive. I didn't know how I knew—there must have been some subtle change that only my senses realised—but when I looked over to their house it was empty. I was shocked.

I thought for a moment. What should I do? I have to know, for certain, if they are there or not. Otherwise, there'd be a gap in my notes, something unknown.

Although, I had never visited the neighbours, I decided to knock on their door. Knock, knock. Wait, wait, wait. No answer. No sound of movement from within the house. Where have they gone? What are they doing?

I didn't like standing there. I felt exposed. I looked up and down the street, saw nothing but neat rows of grass and tarmac. (Except for the O house—they had an old caravan decomposing on their drive, and the carcass of a car in their garden.) There was no-one around.

Quickly, I walked up to the window and looked in, shading my eyes.

It was messy. Cups and saucers all over the place. Cigarette butts, ash trays. Newspapers, plastic bags, junk mail. All strewn across the furniture and floor. It looked like they spent their lives slumped in front of the box. What a waste, I thought.

Fearing detection, I retreated back to my house and wrote down everything I could remember. There was a certain thrill, a sense of thwarting danger, in the whole exercise. E got the whole story that evening and listened intently over dinner. I remember that we made love that night.

The experience of missing the neighbours, of not knowing where they were, had the effect of making me more vigilant, more determined to chart their every move. My neighbours had done something wrong—they were to blame for something, all I had to do was find that something.

I was now rooted to the sofa in the front room. I had phone, fax, laptop, TV, video, camcorder and binoculars to hand. If I didn't own it before, I got it delivered pronto.

I phoned libraries to get births, deaths and marriages in their family. I talked to people in the local council offices and found out about the property and the history of the land they were on. The last census gave me more information. I was hooked up to the Internet and so did some background checks on them, see if they owned any companies. I checked newspapers to see if they were mentioned in any articles. No stone went unturned, no fact unchecked.

Looking across the road at them, I knew the neighbours by the shape and movements of their silhouettes. I could predict the sequence of events in their lives. I played little games with myself, timing how long it took them to wash, dress and breakfast, when the post and deliveries would turn up, when the visitors would arrive and depart. I plotted average times of visits by visitor, trying to work out what could be said in that time. I took down the registration numbers of the visitors' cars, traced them through P (a friend from way back), got names, addresses, and repeated the whole process for every one of them. Q, R and S were retired, lived an hour away, were in different professions, educated in different places, moved in different circles, didn't know one another. They were completely anonymous. When I checked T, I was sure I'd hit the jackpot (even told A as much), because T's name kept popping up, but it all led nowhere—T owned a business, was known in the community, was completely harmless.

There were no clues.

They were not suspicious in any way.

They had done nothing wrong.

I had reached the stage where I no longer went out. I had everything delivered to me. Even A started coming to the house. I was spending all my time looking, searching, excavating, digging, hewing data but finding no nuggets of information worth having.

Work around the house was forgotten. E would come home and get shirty with me. It was not a good time.

Frustrated, I tried to think in a different way. Perhaps I was looking for the wrong things? Instead of looking at what was there, what I knew, maybe I should be looking for holes in the data, for things that I did not know. I rifled through the material I had collected, looked at video footage of the visitors, their dress, their expressions, and found nothing. Wherever I went, I always returned none the wiser.

I decided to go back to the beginning. Given time to think, there were certain questions in my mind. First, what had the neighbours done to warrant me keeping tabs on them? Secondly, what had A to do with it? Thirdly, why was I keeping tabs on them?

When A came round for the daily report, I came straight out with it.

"I've been checking on the comings and goings of H and J for months now, keeping you up-to-date. Sure, it's been interesting in a weird kind of way, but I'm fed up with there being no answers. I want to know why I'm doing this? Why did you ask me to do this A? What have they done?"

A looked at me. I could tell that facts were being weighed up, a decision being made.

"It's for your own protection," A said.

I was a little taken aback. "But, I haven't done anything wrong."

"No. But you might."

A left me time to think about that. "But what has that got to do with my neighbours?"

"They are watching you. They are waiting for you to do something wrong."

All I could come up with was a weak, "Eh?"

"When I found out they were watching you, I thought it best to tell you to watch them. I figured that if you watched them long enough, you'd find something on them, you'd have someone to blame."

"But why me?"

"Why not? Someone has to take the blame. Why not you?"

A got up and left. I felt like a blank page.

"But I can't blame them for anything." I muttered. "I've looked and looked. They haven't done anything wrong."

The following morning, I saw U. U looked suspicious. I decided to find out as much about U as I could. I followed U, and photographed U. U did not disappoint me. If I do anything wrong, then I know who's going to take the blame.

Paul Duncan is a founding editor of Crime Time, and is currently working on a biography of writer Gerald Kersh.

Eddie Duggan, a long time contributor as a critic, with a story of low-lifery in London

One for the Road
Eddie Duggan

IT WAS ONE OF THE LAST pubs along the Edgware Road, way up beyond Staples Corner, where North London thins out before giving way to the expanse of Hertfordshire. Pubs and other landmarks flick past the windscreen: Welsh Harp; boat shop; Red Lion; Volkswagen garage; Kings Arms; bingo hall; next set of lights. Left at the lights and then an immediate right across the path of oncoming traffic to park in the service road parallel to the main road.

Across the traffic of the Edgware Road, the detached sandstone and red-brick building looms up, one of those large 1930s pubs, all roof and tall chimneys, standing between a small, 1970s, plate-glass-fronted supermarket to one side and a wooden greengrocer's stall, shuttered sides closed and large wooden wheels chained to a lamp-post, to the other. A broken wooden lettuce-box and traces of vegetable matter lay strewn beside the entrance to the Public Bar.

The Public Bar, with its bare wooden floor, chipped paintwork, and broken window, contains three kids, barely seventeen, sitting close to pints of fizzy piss masquerading as lager while a fourth chases three red balls around the heavily-stained baize of the small pool table. From the jukebox, Chrissie Hynde's nasal whine implores the listener to cease sobbing. A connecting door leads from Public to Saloon Bar; the contrast in atmosphere as cruel as a witty metaphor to a dull intellect.

A little too brightly lit, the L-shaped Saloon Bar packs in too much beige plush to be comfortable. Heavy beige drapes hang at the windows. Upholstered benches run along the left wall; a row of little wooden tables with iron legs, each surrounded by four padded stools, runs down the centre. The heavy door closes itself gently, cutting off Chrissie Hynde in mid-sob while the Saloon Bar jukebox stands alone, silent and garish as an elderly whore.

Two figures sit talking quietly in the angle of the L while a scrawny, furrow-faced little man, clearly not the landlord, stands lost behind the large bar. The newcomer moves quietly across the carpet to the bar.

"Half a pint of your best bitter please."

Needlessly, the till declares the barman's name, Joey, by way of a small screen at the back of the bar. After paying for his drink, then sipping twice from the small glass by way of preparation for the next stage of his journey, silent foot-steps carry the newcomer uneasily across the carpeted expanse toward the seated figures.

The two heads break away from a whispered conversation, turn accusingly toward the stranger as he begins lowering himself to a sitting position at the table next to them. The stares are met with an appeasing eyebrow-flash and a nod as bottom of the awkwardly-held half-pint glass taps loudly to announce its sudden contact with the wooden table.

'Alright…?'

A glance quickly takes in the detail of the two as the stranger's sitting motion concludes. One, a near hippy-type, with greasy, shoulder-length black hair draped around a pointy-featured face with beard and moustache, wears a green army-surplus style jacket with numerous pockets. The other, with short, dark wavy hair, is clean shaven. Marks etched on both cheeks remain as a vivid reminder of an adolescence severely blighted by acne. An oxblood leather jacket—not the ubiquitous bomber, but a half-length job with patch pockets, epaulettes, buttons and belt—completes the trousseau. Two almost-full pint-glasses, one yellow, one brown, face each other across the dirty Embassy ashtray; four empty glasses stand off to one side.

The stares continue; the leather jacket starts, 'What…?'

'Do you know Bill? Wild Bill?' asks the newcomer, alternating a conciliatory glance between each face. 'Someone down Paddington told me I could find him in here.'

'Wossit to you 'oo we know?' Leather Jacket continues aggressively.

'I thought you might know when he'd be in, that's all.'

'That might depend on what you want,' offers Green Jacket sharply.

'It's business. I heard he's got something to sell. I want to talk to him about it.'

'Well, he might not be in till late. But if it's business, I reckon I might be able to help you out … depends what you're after.'

'It's personal.'

'There's no skag around if that's what you're after, but there might be some jellies later if you need something.'

'What? … No … Someone I know who knows Bill told me he's got something he wants to get rid of … that I ought to see him in here to talk about it.'

'You're looking for a tool then?'

Sipping at the half pint glass, the stranger nods.

'Yeah, well I reckon we can sort you out with Billy. Have you got any transport?'

An affirmative reply prompts the emptying of glasses and the three file out into the early evening light. Across the Edgware Road, Green Jacket stands by the front passenger door of an elderly rust-coloured Nissan Bluebird, Leather Jacket at the back as the doors click open. Pulling out of the service road, the Nissan turns right across the Edgware Road's early evening traffic.

'Do a left at the lights ... right at the bottom of the hill.'

The houses disappear, leaving a strip of road running through a bleak urban landscape of concrete slabs and dry mud. A mini roundabout leads onto long, curving outer ring road that circumscribes a vast housing estate. Dull, dark, greyish-brown boxes are fitted together in a child-like, nameless, architectural style, much discussed by social psychologists and radio pundits in the wake of the eighties riots. Interconnected cuboid shapes, low-stacked boxes above narrow gaps, form a warren of roads, walkways and underpasses for teenage joy riders to rampage through between appointments with magistrates and social workers. The contractors' JCBs have buried the ghosts of old Hendon aerodrome too deeply for them to be much troubled by the rumblings of a new generation of young heroes.

'Pull in there,' instructs Green Jacket, nodding toward the parking bay adjacent to an entry-way in the estate's dark outer wall. Nearby a steel bus-shelter that might once have had windows provides a place of refuge for a fluttering collage of litter. Nobody waits for a bus.

'Have you got the money then?' asks Green Jacket.

'I'll talk to Bill first.'

'You can't. He won't wannus just taking anyone up. He wants four for it. Givvus the money and I'll go and get it, bring it out for yer.'

A long, slow inhalation preceding a reply that doesn't come stirs Green Jacket to exclaim: 'Look, don't fuck about, we're doin' you a favour. Just givvus the money and I'll go and get it.'

A thin wad of twenty pound notes passes quickly between hands. Green Jacket quickly thumbs the notes, 'Twenty-forty-sixty-eighty-one, twenty-forty-sixty-eighty-two, twenty-forty-sixty-eighty-three,' fanning out the last five notes, 'and one's four. And what about something for sorting you out? A drink—call it commission?'

'Yeah ... forty on top' suggests Leather Jacket from the back seat.

'When I see it.'

Green Jacket folds the notes back into a wad and they disappear into a pocket. 'Wait here.'

The absurdity of the situation begins to dawn on the purchaser: sitting in car with a stranger with whom he has exchanged fewer than half a dozen words, while a second stranger has just calmly walked away with four hundred beer tokens. What if he doesn't come back? How long will he have to wait? How long should he wait? Will this one in the leather try to get away? The chain of thought is broken as Leather Jacket opens the car door. All these thoughts, together with a new one: 'Fuck—he's doing a runner' are expressed simultaneously in a single, embarrassed-sounding 'Hey!—'

'I'm 'avin a piss, alright?!'

Leaving the back door open wide, Leather Jacket turns to face the car and relieves himself against the side of the vehicle.

Fear of being suckered into handing over four hundred pounds briefly gives way to distaste as Leather Jacket appears to spend a little too long shaking the drips of piss from his prick. Leather Jacket eventually gives a little bob as he tucks himself away, dropping the flaps of his jacket to cover the dozens of small dark spots that pepper the front of his light-coloured trousers, so many piss splashes that have ricocheted back from the wheel arch.

Closing the door as he lowers himself back into the car, Leather Jacket produces a tobacco tin, opens it, and begins building a small joint. The thick, sweet, smell of hashish fills the car as a maroon Ronson Comet hisses a jet of burning gas. Thick, grubby-pissy fingers twist a roll of cardboard into place and quickly light the joint before slipping the tin into a safari-style patch pocket. Smoking two thirds of the spliff in silence, Leather Jacket thrusts it between the front seats in a gesture of profferance.

'Hhmm! … ? No, no thanks.' The silence broken, he continues, 'What's taking him so long?'

'Just wait. 'E'll come back.'

The door of the flat clicks shut as Green Jacket, his right hand pocket sagging under newly added weight, performs a task of mental arithmetic while pondering how the details of the story might be shaped so as to maximise his personal profit. He muses on how he will present to his associate Bill's bargaining acumen as such that he would not be moved from the newly-upped asking price of three-fifty, leaving a profit margin of a mere fifty quid. Obviously, as he himself has done the majority of the work, he is entitled to most of the profit. A thirty-twenty split seems more than generous. Forty-ten wouldn't be unreasonable. Setting off along the walkway, Green Jacket smiles inwardly in acknowledgment of his own skill in a neatly managed scam, the pleasure heightened by a coca-flavoured dripping sensation in the sinuses, induced by a hard sniff.

A little over a fortnight previously, Bill had let it be known to a select group of saloon bar associates that a certain piece of hardware had come into his possession and he would be prepared to pass it on to a new owner for the considered sum of three ton. He had let on to no-one, however, how he had acquired the matt-black 9mm Glock automatic pistol.

Bill's standing among his peers would be enhanced if it were thought that he were well-enough connected with the criminal fraternity to be able to come into possession of a shooter. The appropriate kudos would not be gained, Bill was sure, were it widely known that he had come across the weapon by merely lifting a floorboard in order to gain access to a blocked air-brick in the kitchen of an empty house in which he had been labouring for fifty pounds a day to supplement his dole money.

Green Jacket had reasoned to Bill, albeit expressed differently, that, as he had found a punter, he was morally entitled to some commission. While Bill accepted the premise he was less than chuffed with the figure proposed. Green Jacket produced a small, round mirror on which he set up two generous lines of reasonable coke—not pharmaceutical, but not cut with too much crap—to help sweeten Bill to the deal. This was followed by twenty minutes of reasonable and good-natured haggling over a spliff and a can of lager, which were provided by the host, bringing the deal to a conclusion.

Bill couldn't admit that he was scared—shit scared—at having had a gun under his bath for the past two weeks. If Bill's missus found out, she'd be off again—and probably for good this time. While he would be relieved to see the back of the pistol, he attempted to manage the deal with as much brava-do as he could muster, so as to not appear too keen to get rid of the weapon at the first opportunity. The agreed sum of two-fifty would finance the purchase of a widescreen Nicam telly, a widescreen video or, hopefully, even both.

Green Jacket emerged from the gap between two walls he had disappeared into half an hour earlier. Walking quickly, his head moved from right to left, scanning the approach from each direction as he approached the orange Nissan. He was breathing quickly as he ducked into the front passenger seat. 'Right. I've got it. Now givvus the forty quid.'

'I want to have a good look, decide if I want it.'

'Look, don't fuck about, this isn't fucking Tesco's. I'm not the fucking nigger with the video in *Jackie* fucking-*Brown*. You've got what you wanted, it's not fucking sale-or-return and I ain't a fucking charity. Now givvus the forty fucking quid and we can all fuck off. '

The green-sleeved arm held its right palm open, in a Christ-like gesture, while the left lay folded over the bulging pocket. The palm closed around the two purple notes, folding them and slipping them into a top pocket in one easy movement, concluded with three short jabs, tamping the notes securely down. Then the right hand joined the left hand in a concerted movement to slip the bulging jiffy bag out of the pocket.

'Right, here you go,'said Green Jacket, amiable now, passing the jiffy bag. 'Be very fucking discreet with this, OK?'

The business-end of the weapon stares out of the padded envelope, returning its owner's gaze like the dull, single eye of the urethral opening of a black steel prick.

'Look, put it away, put it under your seat or something. Drop us back at the pub, OK?'

Its passengers seated in a suspicious silence, the car follows the arc of the outer ring toward Mill Hill and the M1. The apartheid of residential planning, owner-occupiers on the left facing council tenants on the right, gives way to the shared amenities of a tube station and a parade of shops. Green Jacket breaks the silence: 'Drop us at the lights, OK?'

As the car slows to a halt, the two kerbside doors open simultaneously to allow the passengers out. Leather Jacket slams the rear door closed with a force much harder than necessary. Green Jacket turns, leaning into the car before closing the door to remark : 'Listen, you've not been here, you don't know me—be very fucking discreet, OK? Be cool with that thing.'

Driving south along the Edgware Road, a thought breaks simultaneously in the head and the stomach pit of the driver of the orange Nissan: he didn't ask if it was loaded.

This is Eddie Duggan's first attempt at fiction. The names, characters and locations in this story are ficticious. Any resemblance to any real nutters or real places is entirely coincidental.

Last issue we promised you the runner-up entry in our Ellis Peters memorial anthology competition. Well here's the winner, and the runner up will be next issue. Oops, sorry...

The Great Brogonye
David Howard

ABOVE THE VINEYARDS the grey walls of the castle rose to announce that the Brogonye family had risen to prominence in the town.

I was Wilhelm Brogonye. No longer a prominent member of the family, and tomorrow I would be even less prominent.

I would be hung by the neck. Dead.

Marietzburg is a small Bavarian town of little importance. The nearby Marietzburg Falls were spectacular, it is true. But they were not enough to persuade most people to remain in the town. So in 1904 my brother and I left.

Ralf was destined for America. A part mythological country which was pronounced with a breathless awe by the inhabitants of Marietzburg.

A magic land where everything was possible they said.

'And what of you Wilhelm,' they asked, 'where are you bound for?'

'India,' I replied. Silence. 'They have need of doctors out there', I added by means of further explanation, but I could see that I had already lost their attention.

'America,' they muttered. 'No one had ever gone to America before.'

America was like Marietzburg, but much much better.

It wasn't long before news about Ralf began to reach Marietzburg. He'd joined a Circus troop travelling the southern States. Found himself a wife in a town called Cincinnati. And ended every circus performance by mesmerising audiences with what he called 'a death-defying high-wire act'.

'And what news of Wilhelm?' they asked my father in the market square of Marietzburg.

'Oh, he's still in Calcutta,' my father replied. 'Helping the sick. He's a good boy.'

Yes, they agreed, Wilhelm was a good boy.

But America, what a place.

Ralf's letters home now had a Manhattan postmark. He'd left the circus, and his wife. Hadn't there been children too?

Me? I hardly wrote at all. After all, what interest were malaria, typhus, and leprosy compared to the temptations of America?

Soon Ralf's letters began to be accompanied by clippings from the New York newspapers.

'That can't be my son,' my father exclaimed, pulling the front page of the *New York Times* from the latest envelope. 'It's not true, Mimi, tell me this is impossible.' He pushed the newspaper across to my mother's side of the table.

She took one look at it and muttered something incomprehensible in Russian, her native tongue.

'Heaven help us,' she declared moments later, 'he's even calling himself The Great Brogonye.'

It wasn't often the people of Marietzburg were lost for words, but when the newspaper photograph was passed among them...

Well. A circus act they could understand, but this! A high-wire walk between two New York skyscrapers. It was madness. Whatever next, they said.

Next was an even higher walk between two different buildings; followed by a walk across some famous falls; and an escape from a sealed metal coffin thrown into the Hudson River.

When The Great Brogonye was presented before President Theodore Roosevelt, the photograph even reached the front page of Bavaria's own newspaper. Now the people of Marietzburg could read for themselves about the latest exploits of The Great Brogonye.

But their eyes would always alight on the same word.

That word was 'millionaire'.

'And what news of Wilhelm?' The question was asked less and less in the narrow cobbled streets of Marietzburg.

And not often in the castle above the town either.

Here, I must partly share the blame.

I see that now.

My journeys home—and they were few, were not without motive.

The Mission in Calcutta was not thriving.

At first my father was generous. But as my requests grew larger his excuses grew ever more fanciful.

He had to buy more vineyards to expand the business; the castle needed expensive repairs; the river barges were old and must be replaced.

'Why don't you ask The Great Brogonye,' he suggested dismissively one night on the eve of my return to India.

It was only then that I realised that to my father Ralf no longer existed.

He was now The Great Brogonye.

At first my letters to Ralf received no reply. The situation at the Mission was now becoming critical. We had run out of quinine and were short of many other essential drugs.

On top of that the Mission building itself was in disrepair. I now spent several hours a day engaged in repairs when I should have been inside caring for the sick.

In despair, I wrote again to my father. It was nothing less than a begging letter and didn't deserve the generous response it received. A small cheque. Enough to keep the mission going for a month at least.

But from Ralf there was nothing.

Then one day a letter arrived via my bank in Calcutta. Noting the New York postmark, I ripped the pages from the envelope and hastily read the contents.

Dear Wilhelm,

Please do not send any more of your unpleasant letters. I receive many requests for money every week and cannot possibly choose between one so-called charitable institution and another.

In such circumstances I have refused all such requests, and must also decline yours. Ralf. The Great Brogonye.

I could scarcely believe what I had just read and can remember very little of the events of the next week.

My anger was only broken by an unexpected letter from my father.

Ralf had been injured in an accident. He knew few details, except that one of Ralf's performances had gone badly wrong and he was now in hospital with extensive burns to his face and arms.

Although I was shocked by the news, my lack of compassion for Ralf was only slightly less surprising than the knowledge that my parents were going to visit him in New York—it was the first time I had ever known them leave Germany.

The plans were already set. They would travel to France where they would board a new ship of the British White Star Line.

That ship was the S.S. *Titanic*.

The news of the *Titanic* took several weeks to reach Calcutta. By that time Ralf, not as critically injured as it first appeared—although his facial injuries were such that he now wore his performing mask in public, had already returned to the family castle at Marietzburg.

In my absence, Ralf had quickly assumed control of the family wine business. A situation which soon become official in the eyes of the state of Bavaria.

I was in bed with malaria when a copy of my parents' will arrived from the family lawyer.

For a man fighting for his life, the news of his disinheritance is laughably unimportant. It was only when the fever broke that the depths of betrayal began to darken my already weakened thoughts.

I cannot now blame the malaria for the plan that began to congeal in my mind.

I've heard it said that we all have a darker side. It was then that I discovered mine.

The next day I was up early. I felt curiously elated as I greeted my staff at the Mission, who were as surprised to see me as they were curious about my renewed vigour.

Hope is as infectious as any disease, and hope is what I now had for the survival of the Mission. But first I had to put several events in motion.

That night I wrote a letter home to Bavaria. The following morning I asked Gitsa, one of my nurses, to write out two copies of the letter and address them to my brother in Marietzburg and our family lawyer in the nearby town of Umsdorf. Gitsa, who speaks no German, diligently reproduced the letters in her own hand and gave them to me without question.

Not many of us have the chance to announce our own deaths, but that's what I did when I posted those two envelopes. Although I hated leaving the Mission in the care of my staff, I could see no other alternative.

I now worked my passage by ship to Venice, and then made my way north through the Swiss valleys until I reached Bavaria. I avoided all towns where I had acquaintances, although with my hair now drooping over my shoulders, and a beard which wouldn't shame a pirate, I hardly even recognised myself.

I took lodgings in Umsdorf, a town half a mile downstream from the Marietzburg Falls. Although Umsdorf was the last navigable town on the river, some barges travelled further upstream to a small private quay my father had built for his business just below the falls.

It was here that I now passed on my way into Marietzburg.

Darkness had fallen some hours before but as I entered the market square I still kept my face to the cobbled ground. I had many friends in the town but I quickly grew confident that my disguise together with my absence from the town for most of the previous eight years would protect my identity.

For my purposes, it was the ideal time to return to Marietzburg. The grape harvest had brought the usual ragbag of workers into the town, and soon I was sitting between a pair of them in an ill-lit tavern.

I was seeking confirmation of what I had first heard in Calcutta and I quickly guided the conversation in the direction of the castle and its new occupant.

'The Great Brogonye is not so great now, my friend,' one of them declared, lifting the beer I had just bought him to his rugged, sunburnt face. 'Even Rudi here would have more luck with women if he wore a mask all the time like The Great Brogonye.' He laughed, waved his hand in the general direction of his companion, and spilled beer down his beard. Noting the surprise on my face he now turned fully to me.

'Where have you been not to hear all about the Great Brogonye?' he muttered disdainfully. 'Maybe he's worried if he takes his mask off he'll crack a mirror, eh … and now this, more foolishness.' He pointed towards a large placard barely visible through the grimy widow of the tavern.

Finally outside in the cool air, I found it difficult at first to believe the information the placard conveyed. To celebrate the wine harvest and the fiftieth anniversary of the Brogonye Wine Company 'The Great Brogonye would perform a feat so unusual and so dangerous that he had attempted it only once before—at the famous falls at Niagara—The Great Brogonye was going to go over the Marietzburg Falls in a wine barrel.'

The stark outline of the castle's turrets stood like sentinels guarding the town below. It was a week later and my plans were almost complete. I'd waited in the woods all day watching the final preparations for The Great Brogonye's jump the following morning.

Night had now fallen and the castle workshop pressed into service to make the specially strengthened barrel for the jump was now deserted.

Waiting for cloud to conceal the moonlight, I left the shadow of the woodland and silently crossed the cobbled courtyard. The large barn doors of the workshop were closed, but as I knew from my childhood at the castle, entry was easy. I pulled both ill-fitting doors towards me and eased myself through the gap created by decades of wear in the mechanism.

Once inside, the wooden barrel loaded on to the cart for its journey to the falls was immediately visible. I pushed grain sacks into the gaps between the barn doors and the frame, and satisfied that no light would be visible from outside, lit the oil lamp. I now jumped on the cart and inspected the wooden barrel. I needed to work quickly. Taking a hand-drill from one of the workbenches, I drilled quarter-inch holes through all the knots in the wood—well over fifty in all. I then re-filled the holes with a mixture I had made earlier in the day and disguised my handiwork inside and out with a mixture of Indian Ink and water.

Removing the sacking from the bottom of the barrel, where it had been placed to protect The Great Brogonye from the impact of the fall, I now tipped a mortar mixture bought in Umsdorf into the base of the barrel to a depth of four or five inches.

I then sawed a piece of wood to exact dimensions and secured it firmly into position to form a false base to the barrel just above the mortar mix.

With the sacking now returned to the base of the barrel, I inspected my work, moving the oil lamp around the barrel inside and out before I was satisfied that all was well.

Outside again, I made my way across the courtyard to the Coopers workshop. From several dozen I chose a barrel as near as possible to the one I had just been working on—for my purposes it would not have to be so strong. And using sacking to smother the noise of the cobbled courtyard, rolled the barrel to the woodland I had emerged from three hours before.

From there it was all downhill—literally. Until I eventually emerged from the woods at the bottom of the grass track and set off in the direction of the Marietzburg Falls. It was past midnight before I was able to conceal the barrel beneath bracken and branches at the bottom of the falls.

I now had one more task to perform. Slowly I took the phial of hydrochloric acid from my tunic pocket.

Taking care to remove all traces of my stay, I left my lodgings early next morning and vanished into the charcoal-grey of first light. My reappearance at the Marietzburg Falls a while later coincided with the first shafts of sunlight broaching the trees on the far bank.

Feeling vulnerable in the open, I quickly changed into the passable replica of The Great Brogonye's costume I had stitched together during the past week. Necessity had taught me to sew in Calcutta, and with a rudimentary knowledge of chemical dyes learnt from medical school, I was able to reproduce the bright red and yellow colours of The Great Brogonye's costume.

Retaining nothing except a six-foot length of rope and the black leather face-mask which completed the Brogonye's costume, I bundled my discarded clothes into my leather hold-all, piled it full of rocks and flung it into the river. In seconds the treacherous waters beneath the falls had consumed it within their twenty-foot depths. Retrieving the barrel from beneath its camouflage, I rolled it down the grass slope until it slid into the water. At first the power of the torrent tried to rip the barrel from my grasp. I clung hold, forcing the barrel several yards upstream to where the flow ebbed.

I was now within touching distance of the fifty-foot high wall of thunderous water that was the Marietzburg Falls. Already soaked, I now had no choice but to plunge into the alpine meltwater myself. It was breathtakingly cold, but to my relief I was still able to touch the riverbed.

Hanging on to the rock outcrops on the riverbank with one hand and the barrel with the other, I hauled myself through the barrage of cascading water and up on to one of the boulders that littered the base of the hollowed-out rockface beyond. Exhausted, I sat for several minutes, my eyes closed to the new world I had just entered.

From my position inside the falls it was impossible to see anything beyond the impenetrable wall of water before me.

I waited patiently for several hours and it was only the approaching sound of a brass band that made me aware that a large crowd was gathering on either side of the falls. Taking my timepiece from its waterproof pouch, I saw that it was only minutes before The Great Brogonye was to make his jump.

My pulse pumping in my temples, I quickly tied one end of the rope to the rockface, pulled on my face-mask and lifted the barrel into the swirling water.

With some difficulty I hunkered myself down into the barrel, my grasp of the rope keeping me from leaving the rockface too early.

Above the roar of the waterfall, it was still surprisingly easy to discern what was happening in the bright sunlight outside. The crowd cheered when The Great Brogonye first entered his barrel; they applauded as he rolled into the swirling water; and now, as The Great Brogonye raced towards the fifty-foot drop, the cheering and clapping diminished to nothing.

Wiping the water continuously from my eyes, I scanned the cascading torrent, searching for the Brogonye's barrel as it fell.

Then suddenly it was there, the weight of the barrel spinning and cutting through the wall of water as it came fully into view right above me. If I hadn't moved quickly the barrel would have smashed on top of me. Instead it plummeted into the swirling water beyond and disappeared from view.

It all happened too quickly for me to see properly. But the knot holes in the barrel that I'd filled with clay would have dissolved by now, sucking the water into the Brogonye's barrel where it would be absorbed by the mortar, dragging them both to the riverbed twenty feet below.

I now let go off the rope, fixed the lid of the barrel into place and braced myself as the weight of the failing water took us under and into the white water beyond.

I had padded the inside of the barrel but nothing could prepare me for the pummelling I now received. In the space of seconds, I was rolled a dozen times and tipped upside-down so that my head was smashed continuously against the top of the barrel. I lost consciousness for a few seconds. Not long enough. The barrel now smashed against a rock, splitting the wood, allowing water to seep inside. Still the barrel kept tumbling, the inflowing water choking the breath from my lungs.

Then suddenly all was still. The power had been drained from the river and I was just floating along.

I pushed against the lid, and suddenly the vacuum of the barrel was filled not only with sunlight but a swelling applause.

A barge which was delivering wine for the festival was diverted to pluck me from the barrel and convey me safely to the shore. From there I was hauled on to a cart draped with the yellow and red of The Great Brogonye and conveyed into town. I used my elevated position to search the river for the other barrel. Nothing.

The Great Brogonye was dead.

I was paraded in the market square, lauded over by all, and slapped on the back so many times my shoulders ached. Despite my protestations, I was persuaded to say a few words.

I spoke falteringly about my parents; my father who had asked me to 'perform something memorable for the wine festival'; and my mother who had 'always tried to put a stop to such foolishness'. That met with a peal of laughter from the crowd because my words echoed their own memories of my parents.

My confidence grew.

'I would also like to pay tribute to the dedication of my brother, Ralf. Who gave his life for the sick of Calcutta.' I was tempted to continue, but I was surprised how easy it was to speak about myself like this. It was as if now I'd slipped into The Great Brogonye's costume, Dr Wilhelm Brogonye had ceased to exist.

Wisely perhaps, I resisted the temptation to ask for donations to the Mission. Best not to push my luck. After all, now I had become The Great Brogonye, heir to the Brogonye Wine Company, the Mission would never be short of money again.

'And now ladies and gentlemen, I have one final announcement to make.' I paused for effect before continuing. 'What you have witnessed here today was the last ever performance by The Great Brogonye.' And with a flourish I frankly enjoyed, I removed my black leather face-mask.

At that there was silence as they absorbed the blood-red burns melted into the side of my face. In truth, the dilute hydrochloric acid burns I had inflicted the previous night were more impressive than they would be long-lasting. And besides, sympathy would be the perfect cover for any doubts that I really was The Great Brogonye.

'And now friends,' I continued, 'although I cannot recommend dropping over a waterfall to give you much of an appetite, let the feast begin.' I now raised my goblet to the air expecting it to be full of wine. It was empty.

'It seems we're the only wine festival in Bavaria with no wine,' I declared.

It was then that I was told about the accident at the jetty. The crew of the barge delivering the wine—I now damn them to hell!—had been distracted from their duties by the jump of The Great Brogonye. The six barrels of wine had fallen from the barge into the river.

I was just about to announce the delay when the cart carrying the wine rattled into the market square. The crowd, already excitable, cheered ever more loudly.

Except for me.

I'd just realised there were seven barrels on the cart and one of them wasn't silent.

John Harvey's Slow Dancer Press is a welcome addition to the independent crime fiction publishers in this country. The first books published by them are reviewed, and indeed advertised, elsewhere in this issue, but here is a selection to whet your appetite, courtesty John and company, and their curious quest to publish books by people with 'Smith' for a last name...

Gumshoe
Neville Smith

A CHANCE MEETING early in their careers between director Stephen Frears, famous now for such films as *The Grifters, My Beautiful Launderette and Dangerous Liaisons*, and award-winning writer Neville Smith, led to their collaboration in what is still one of the finest—and funniest—*noir* pastiches being made.

As Frears describes in his introduction to the Slow Dancer Press re-issue of Smith's novel, Neville would labour away at the script. bringing in new material every day, each page more entertaining and surprising than the last. The film's excellent cast—Albert Finney, Billie Whitelaw, Frank Finlay, Janice Rule—brought Smith's characters brilliantly to life on the screen. With the novel, written m the wake of the original screenplay, we have time to savour not only the wisecracks and but also, alongside the witty and knowing parody of Chandleresque private eye style, a vivid evocation of the social and political life of sixties Britain.

Here are the opening chapters Neville Smith's *Gumshoe*, which is now available again for the first time in many years.

CHAPTER ONE

He looked like the kind of guy your mother would like to marry your sister. If you had a mother. If you had a sister.

He wore a three-button Italian suit, a Billy Eckstine-style flex-roll, buttondown collar, a slim-jim tie. Neat, flat-cut hair topped the lot off. The perfect brother-in-law, circa 1957. He leaned back with his feet on the desk, bored out of his mind, looking at me sitting opposite in my vintage Grenfell trench coat (Hawkes of Savile Row, W1 By Appointment); I wasn't bored.

I'd been making a pilgrimage to this guy's office every week for a year, only missing those occasions the dole people changed my days for signing on. The guy didn't mind. I should say 'man' really, not 'guy', because he's always chiding me for the way I speak, when he isn't trying to copy it. You know what psychiatrists are, always trying to find a level on which to approach you. Always trying to show how like them you are. It's supposed to reassure you. It never works.

I ought to explain what I was doing there. My girl had married my brother and I'd gone hypochondriac badly. That isn't funny. My quack had recommended the shrink. It's all on the National Health, everyone can get it and a lot more should. If you feel you need it, apply now, because the way things are going, Heath and his gang might make it illegal. They're making it pretty hard now even if you're not a nutter, so jump in, it's not so bad. The theory is still 'care, from the cradle to the grave,' but the Cosa Nostra (Smith Square branch) are just hurrying the process along and making you pay a bomb for it. My name is Eddie Ginley.

"What are you thinking about?" he said.

"Nothing." I twiddled the *Echo*. "I'm thirty-one today."

"Happy birthday," he said.

"Thanks doc."

"How's the club?" He stretched and yawned.

"You really want to know?"

"Yeah. Sure."

"Great. I'm just doing the bingo calling at the moment, slip in a few gags here and there, I get to wear a tux. Tommy says he'll let me do a spot soon. He's weaning me in. That's what he says."

"Tommy's the boss?"

"Yeah."

He lapsed into silence again. I looked around the office I knew so well: his desk, his Grundig—it's funny how psychiatrists like to have something

German around them, even if, like mine, they're not analysts—his note-pad, the paintings on the wall done by children, the packed mantelpiece with his blood pressure machine, his dusty old stethoscope.

"Your turn."

"I can't think of anything to say," he said.

"What am I here for then?"

"I like you Eddie. It gets to this time in the week and I think, 'Great. Eddie's coming. We can have a laugh. Crack a few gags.' That's all really."

"Great. Meanwhile, head man, what about my cure?"

"What cure, Eddie?" He smiled and felt for his fags and as usual he wasn't carrying any, so I lobbed him my Luckies and Zippo.

"What cure?" came his voice again as he scrambled under his desk for the lighter. His face, red from exertion, peered over the edge of his blotter. "I told you when you started that you can't cure hypochondriasis. I just help you to live with it. Some great people were hypos—Darwin... er..." He struggled to think.

"Hitler?" I offered.

"Well, yes," he conceded, "but I was trying to offer encouragement."

"Elvis Presley."

"Is he?" The psych leaned across his desk with real interest, eyes widened as though I was giving him some real hot showbiz gossip.

"No, But it would really encourage me if he was."

"Oh!" He was really disappointed. He fell back in his chair and at last lit the Lucky. I had to prise the Zippo out of his grip as he gazed at the ceiling. I've lost three lighters to him that way, it must be part of the therapy.

He perked up again and leaned across his desk, eyes narrowing, fag drooping at the lip, "Listen, kid. You want some stuff? I can get you some real high grade scratch. No bum gear. For real. Shoot you up pretty good. You like, gringo?"

I started to laugh, he looked hurt.

"What was wrong with that?" he pleaded.

I stopped laughing, "Nothing. What's the film?"

He thought hard. "Well, no single film really. I mean, I can't remember any one particular character saying it, it's just the *genre*. You know."

I laughed again.

"Come on. What was wrong?"

"Nothing. Except scratch is—money, not dope. And as for gringo..." I shook my head. "Really, doc, you ought to pay more attention."

He got up and walked round the desk and sat on the edge of it looking down at me, "I try, Eddie, I really try. I watch old films on the telly and even write down bits to tell you. I can never remember them."

"You can always go back to medicine, doc."

He grinned down at me, "Okay, Eddie, I'll see you again next week."

"Right, doc." I stood, shrugged my trench coat back into place and made for the door.

"Actually," he began and I turned and looked at him, "what I was attempting to say there was, do you need any pills?"

"Valium? Librium?"

He rolled back his top lip in what he thought was his best Bogart manner, leapt from his desk and adopted his Cagney stance. The voice was a mixture of the two. Or near enough.

"You… You just name your poison. Just name it kid. You dirty rat you!"

"Nah. I don't want anything. Even when I'm really low I only take them for a couple of days, then I forget and I always end up throwing them down the bog."

"Doesn't it help you?" he asked.

"Not me, doc, but it makes the chain easier to pull." He didn't laugh and I'd rehearsed that gag all week to tell him. That's show business.

"Here," I called as he turned to look at his appointment book. I threw him the rolled *Echo*. He opened it. He couldn't miss the advert I'd placed because I'd ringed it in black. Actually, someone else must have ringed it too because that evening someone else rang about it.

I didn't rehearse that. Honest.

The advert read.

SAM SPADE
GINLEY'S THE NAME
GUMSHOE'S THE GAME
Private Investigations
No Divorce Work
051-246-4379

It was a gag. A birthday present from me, to me. I got the idea from a detective novel. I read a lot of detective novels. American ones all the time, except for Ambler, Greene and Lyall.

So. The psychiatrist was reading the advert and I was on my way home to catch up on a little ironing. I was at home when I got rung.

CHAPTER TWO

I live on the top floor of a house in Gambier Terrace and my front window faces the Anglican Cathedral. My room is sort of L-shaped, with one door leading off to my own bathroom, a hardboard partition separating it from the kitchen area. The door leading downstairs to the street faces my bed, which is below the aforementioned window. In the corner, by the door, there's a curtained cubbyhole, which is a wardrobe, and contains my wardrobe. I hang my trench in there, next to my three-buttoned suit like the shrink, I'm vintage 1957. Well, I look at it this way, I'm thirty-one, right? I can't go with what everyone's wearing these days. Now the late fifties, that's my time., that's where I'm sticking. That's where I'm stuck, too, with almost everything, clothes, records—movies I'm stuck with in the forties. The mountain of trivia that is enclosed by my skull hails from way back. Anyway, next to my suit is my new tux,. I'm still paying for it so it must be new, but I'd give you odds you'd never think so when I've got it on. I've got some good things in my modest little stash, a wall 'phone in the kitchen for instance, and my bookshelves are. crammed with several interesting titles—nearly all the Penguin green backs; lots of different books really, a pretty catholic taste that remained when my ugly Catholic religion got the boot. Next to the bookshelves is my record collection and my hi-fi set-up; Thorens 150 deck, Nicco amp, and Celestion 15 speakers for the buffs out there. On the little mantelpiece I have, there is a ten-by-eight of Lauren Bacall, a ten-by-eight of me in my tux—a Jerome's special photograph ("Look showbiz," the photographer said)—a framed colour photograph of the 1970 League Champions, my cufflink collection and a birthday card: "Now you are 31!" A joke one. Ellen sent me that.

I was sitting on the bed ironing (I've got this board that you can adjust to any height—I'm pretty hip to modern methods of cutting the housewife's workload) with the headphones on giving Buddy Holly and the Crickets a play, when I got the ring. Actually a track had finished and I'd taken the headphones off between songs because your ears can sweat something wicked under the old earpieces, when I heard the 'phone. I whipped the 'phones off and crossed to the 'phone, as I will in such instances, and picked it up.

"The Ginley Residence... just a minute, I'll see if he's in." I crossed to the amplifier and pulled the headphone jack out. "That'll Be the Day" blasted into the room. I went back and picked up the receiver.

"He's in the music room at the moment, running through a number with the band."

I held the receiver towards one of the speakers.

"Can you hear? I'm sorry, you'll have to give me the message, he can't possibly be disturbed." And then this incredibly distant, seemingly sexless voice gave me the message, which I only just got at first go because of the sound of the record. I repeated it. "Exchange Hotel, Room 105, 7.30." The voice said, "Okay?" and rang off. Well, it was my birthday, someone knew I was a pretty lonely fellow, so they were throwing a surprise party. it was no party, but it was a surprise all right.

CHAPTER THREE

The Exchange Hotel backs onto the station of the same name and fronts onto Tithebarn Street. It's big and white and those in the know reckon it to be the best in the city, although I wouldn't know, never having stayed at the joint— only been through it, so to speak. There's an old-fashioned portal and steps leading up to revolving doors, and inside, the reception hall, or foyer, or whatever, is like a green-carpeted, cream-painted, Victorian basketball court without the nets. There's a long desk to the right, and the night I presented myself there was a pretty girl receptionist and an old Welsh one behind it. The latter had a face like a chewed pink caramel, with those blue, rimless, fly-away specs women like her like to sport, and I could tell she was Welsh because she was yacking into the 'phone in that language. The pretty receptionist approached with a smile but Taffy looked up, saw me, and whipping the 'phone down asked me what I wanted sir, gnashing the false choppers. I didn't like her. Some of my best friends are Welsh, and have faces like chewed caramels, and most everyone I know over forty has false choppers and if she's behind a desk earning a wage she's one of us and not THEM, but she came on so obsequious, like it was going out of style, So I gave the pretty one my M.G.M. smile (I'm saving up for caps and a nose job) and asked and was told, prettily, that room 105 was on the first floor, left past the lounge, and that I couldn't miss it. Taffy gave her a look that would have freeze-dried her and I made for the stairs. As I walked up I made a mental note to be nice to Taffy when I came down, being instantly remorseful as I nearly always am when I play hard with anyone. Some people get me like that though; really fix me. It's just that you've got to be on the side of the person who works for a living, the person who hustles a wage. That's a tough enough life. But there are those people for whom service means servility and they seem to love it. Waiters, hotel receptionists, the guys who work the restaurant cars on trains. Not all of them, but why do those who serve have to be creeping bastards? Beats me. On the first floor a tray-carrying waiter who was in no way servile marked me down straight away.

"The bandroom's in the basement for tonight," he sneered.

"Why for tonight?"

"We don't run to a proper one so we've put you in the luggage-room. In the basement. We moved the luggage first, of course."

"Of course."

"We know you bastards. Booze. Groupies."

"Yeah."

He peered at me suspiciously.

"Where's your instruments

There was no answer to that, so I flashed my buzzer and he went puce and even showed me past the lounge to the corridor where I could find Room 105. I always carry my buzzer—the clubs I've not been a member of that it's got me into! My friend Arthur showed me how to make a buzzer. It helps if you're unemployed. You see you take your dole card and fold it in half across, and flash the half with the crown on it that says "Official", and people think you are a copper. Arthur had a mate once who used to do it with a ration book (remember them?). But he must have been pretty fast because you have to keep your buzzer in your inside breast pocket for best effect (unless you wear a trench like I do where you can whip it out just below waist level and they've hardly had time to register but still think you're a copper) and one of those old ration books would get stuck if you weren't quick, and by the time you'd got it out you'd have lost your cool. Arthur's mate used to do this to get into clubs, until he got caught. He was very silly really, because he went to this club, whipped out his ration book, got in, and no sooner did he have a bevvy and a bird lined up, than the boss of the place stuck a wad of notes in his hand and gave him the high sign. So it's drinks for all hands and the manager's muttering about how unusual this is and Arthur's mate is throwing money around and dancing with all the birds like he's got first divi on Littlewoods, when the real fuzz arrive and wonder where their kickback is. The manager points out their 'colleague' on the dance floor, with pound notes bulging out of his pockets, buying drinks all round and pulling the birds. The real coppers give him the tap on the shoulder and Arthur's mate, thinking they're muscling in on his talent, tells them to push off or he'll do them for obstruction. They ask which division he's with, and where's his identification, so he smirks and waves his ration book and shouts, "Z Victor One to B.D.!" He got done for imper-sonating a police officer and asked for two hundred similar offences to be taken into consideration. He got five years. I never forgot that and always stick to dole cards. Anyway you have to cut the ration book into a quarter of its size and stick a photo in it. It's too much trouble.

I knocked on 105 and went in. The room was in pitch darkness, except for a television switched on showing an old movie, and I waited for the lights to come on and everyone to shout "Surprise!" and shower me with presents. Nothing happened, except that from somewhere a voice spoke. A flat, expressionless, business-like man's voice. The voice of a man who, when he told you, you stayed told. The lads had really tried, I thought, they're really making my birthday something to remember.

"Shut the door," the voice said. I shut it and leant against it.

"Do they charge you extra for the light?" I quipped.

I figured I'd play along until the punch line. Don't spoil a good gag. If your mates have tried, it's only fair you should try too.

"Cut the cracks."

"Just trying to make small talk, mister."

"It's not needed."

"Make your play."

"To the right. There's a dresser," he said. "A package on it. Got it?"

I could make out a chair with a high back now, facing the television, and I could see smoke curling up and smell cigar. I had to give it to the lads, they spared no expense. Or Tommy. This had to be Tommy's doing.

"This the package?" I held it up although he couldn't see it.

"There's no other."

"Okay. What's the pitch?"

"Pitch?" He seemed surprised.

"The job."

"It's all in the package."

"The folding green?"

"What?"

"Money. Twenty dollars a day plus expenses."

I tell you I can pinch material from anywhere. With the best of them.

"Twenty dollars? It's in sterling. That's what was agreed." He seemed really surprised now.

"Don't flip your wig buster," I cautioned him, "I can live with it."

There was a silence for a moment so I looked at the movie on television. Judy Holliday was telling Broderick Crawford that he could use a little education himself if you asked her. One of my favourites. I was just beginning to enjoy it for the fifth time of seeing when the voice cut in sharply. "What are you waiting for?"

"I was just going."

I opened the door. The lights have just got to come on now, I thought.

"Happy Birthday to you, Happy Birthday dear Eddie..." But no.

"I was just going," I said.

"We want results."

I laid it on the line: "Broad at the shoulder and narrow at the hip and everybody knows you don't give no lip, to Big Ed."

No answering laughs, no chuckles, not even a titter. I reached for the light switch; there wasn't one.

"I hope you're as tough is you sound," the voice said.

"Dig this. Nobody steps into this baby's sunshine," I said. Quick as a flash. And stepping into the corridor, I closed the door. I could hear the movie carrying on inside as I waited listening for a few moments. Well, I wasn't going to open the present till I got to the club. I'd let Tommy and his lads see my pleasure as I opened it. I walked down the corridor and as I turned the corner a small neat man wearing a small-brimmed hat passed me.

"Nutters," I laughed and nodded my head towards 105. He looked blankly at me and walked on, but then he didn't know the lads.

I had to leg it for the fourteen bus because I was way overdue at the club and having settled into one of those long seats near the exit for a quick jump off for the club, I looked at the package. Brown paper covered, about ten by six, heavily sellotaped. I tore off the tape and lifted a corner of the paper. Inside was a stiff cardboard box. No card. A book. A book for my birthday. They'd never asked me what I read, so, knowing Tommy, it was probably the life of Judy Garland or something. By Mel Tormé. Have you read that thing? I'm waiting for the double album to hit the shops. Woolworths of course. On Embassy. Natch. And I like Mel Tormé *singing*. The box had a flap, also sellotaped. So I'd sneak a peek and re-wrap and come on at the club as though I'd never looked. Whatever book was inside was stuck, so I turned the parcel upside down and shook it. Out came a photo of a dame and a wad of rubber-banded Bank of Funland notes in tenners, and something else fell out that crashed heavily to the floor, and when I picked it up it was a toy gun. Except when I looked at the notes to see 'pay the bearer ten laughs' I saw the good lady herself's head and ten pounds. And the gun I was holding like Joe Friday was giving the lady opposite a double hernia with fright. And the next thing was that I needed that quick exit from the bus, and I was leaning on a wall miles from the club shaking from fear and anger and wondering what the hell kind of birthday present was this to give a fellow?

Julie Smith

New Orleans Mourning
Julie Smith

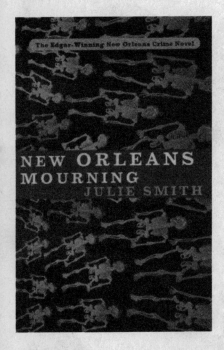

Strange things happen in the world of crime publishing; sometimes stranger than events in the books themselves. Take the case of Julie Smith, for instance. In the United States she is a major figure, an author whose name is mentioned in the same breath as Sue Grafton, Sarah Paretsky, Linda Barnes. And not just because her principal character is a woman: like the others mentioned, she writes well, sells well. The strange thing is, until now, she has never been published in Britain.

New Orleans Mourning is the first of Julie's series featuring police detective Skip Langdon, and, with the others, shares the same racy style, the same knowledgeable evocation of life in the Crescent City. On its original publication it was awarded the Edgar for Best Novel from the Mystery Writers of America; since then it has sold over 200,000 copies in the USA. Here are two early chapters from the novel.

THE MONARCH OF MIRTH

THE QUIET WAS DEAFENING. Skip had forgotten that part, though she'd been here before on Mardi Gras—as Tricia Latimore's guest, when they were both at McGehee's and nobody their age had invited them anywhere. She was at the Boston Club today for no other reason than that she knew these people, she was at home here—or so her brother officers imagined. True, her father had elbowed his way into Rex, but certainly not into this bastion of blue blood. And that didn't begin to tell the story. There was Skip's own peculiar identity crisis to reckon with. But Sergeant Pitre wouldn't know about that, and wouldn't care. She was handy, that was all. She'd been on the scene and no one else who had had been brave enough to beard the Brahmins in their lair.

Skip had been working parade routes, along with a third of the cops in the city, and she was scheduled for a twelve-hour shift like everyone else. The system really wasn't too bad. During Carnival a third of the department did their regular jobs from 6 A.M. to 6 P.M., a third took over from 6 P.M. to 6 A.M., and that freed everyone else for parade routes.

Skip's day had started with Zulu and a fight among three men and a woman. The woman's escort was obviously 'from away,' as New Orleanians put it. "Forget doubloons," Skip heard her tell him, "But if you catch a coconut, guard it with your life."

For once, Skip was standing with her back to the parade, watching the crowd, as regulations required. The speaker was a blonde woman wearing a UNO sweatshirt. Her friend had on a denim jacket. Skip's eye strayed over the crowd and a coconut thrown by a Zulu warrior whizzed over her shoulder. The man in the denim jacket, apparently impressed by his date's assessment of its value, jumped up, caught it, and cradled it in the crook of his arm like a football player catching a pass. "All r-i-i-ght!" Skip yelled. A few people clapped and hollered.

"Hey! Hey!" yelled the man with the coconut, and suddenly he was down. The crowd parted. Two well-dressed men were trying to wrestle away the coconut. Skip started toward them. "Okay, okay! Knock it off!"

The blonde glanced at her briefly, hesitating only a moment, and jumped on the pile, closing her teeth around the polo-shirted bicep of the topmost man. Skip paused, giving the three a chance to work out their differences. She stepped back to give the two ruffians room to run. Caught up in the spirit, she shouted: "A round of applause, ladies and gentlemen!" The crowd cheered, the blonde bowed, and her gentleman friend presented her with the well-earned coconut.

A satisfying morning. Unlike most of her peers, Skip liked working parade routes. It was a relief from having to make small talk with the likes of Marcelle St. Amant Gaudet, who had ice-blue chiffon behind the eyes.

It was a relief from a lot of things. She could remember the party at the Pontalba, where the host lowered a bucket from the balcony and shouted, "Alms for the rich." Unamused, his girlfriend tried to stop him, and he dragged her into the bathroom. There were some thumps and screams, then silence. Finally the host emerged carrying handfuls of frosted, permed, freshly cut hair, which he scattered among the guests.

The shorn girlfriend, apparently undaunted, spent the afternoon methodically seducing each male member of the host's family, racking up, by Skip's count, older brother, younger brother, and two cousins. She later told friends his father had been perfectly willing as well, but too drunk to get it up.

Even as a prepubescent hellion, Skip had liked the street at Carnival. Not Canal Street particularly, where the crowds were so thick people stood in the streets about an inch from the floats literally smack up against them, so that if there was trouble the entire U.S. Army, much less the New Orleans Police Department, would be helpless. And where you couldn't even get your hands above your head to reach out for throws and where, if you were claustrophobic, you'd faint and be trampled to death because no way could you get your head between your knees.

What she liked was St. Charles Avenue, like Canal closed to traffic for the Rex Parade. But even here, famous as the site of 'the family Mardi Gras,' it could get rough. She'd forgotten how rough, how violent it could be, and she was relearning that morning. Yet in past years she'd given the cops as much trouble as certain drunk, foul-mouthed sorority types were giving her today.

The huddled masses stood several hundred deep on both sides of the avenue, some with ladders for their kids or themselves, some with toddlers on their shoulders, risking the kids' lives, in her opinion—one bump and baby hit the pavement. As a cop (instead of the dedicated troublemaker of old) she was truly shocked at the way they pushed and shoved and hollered for throws. They really did holler and beg—just like the guidebooks said they did. It seemed to be proper Carnival etiquette for the hoi polloi. The aristocrats (the male ones anyway), grandly conveyed on floats, were supposed to demonstrate their largesse by casting trinkets into the crowds. Little strings of beads, mostly, and Carnival doubloons.

She wondered how the knights and dukes of Rex decided on whom to bestow the coveted gewgaws. Did they search out the prettiest girls? The most flamboyant drag queens? The least aggressive little kids? The recyclers, of course, those who caught throws and rethrew them, bargained for nudity. In the last few years it had become a fad in the Quarter for women to take off their blouses for beads.

If Skip were on a float she would have insisted, she thought, on rewarding those in the most amusing costumes. Like that man across the street who'd apparently got himself up as an Italian restaurant. He had a round, table-like arrangement around his middle covered with a red-checked tablecloth and topped with a plate of papier-mâché spaghetti and an old wine bottle complete with colorful wax drippings. She also liked the grasshopper with a little grasshopper kid just about knee-high to him. If you were going to behave like an idiot, which was the whole point of Carnival, you could at least go all the Way.

There were a lot of popes this year, as His Holiness had earlier favored the city with a visit. Here and there was a two-legged Dixie beer can, and the random screwball who had sprayed himself gold or silver. Inevitably, there was a film crew trying vainly to make some sort of visual sense of it all. Skip wondered if the filmmakers would bother to record the prodigious number of kids in fraternity sweatshirts carrying Hurricanes or beers—or every legal go-cups—and barfing all over one another. The drinking age had recently been raised to twenty-one, but the unofficial tall-enough-to-reach-the-bar rule was still very much in effect. And you could drink on the street as long as you didn't do it out of a bottle or glass, but on Mardi Gras who could enforce the go-cup law?

Skip was absolutely convinced that most of the damage done by Carnival drunks was perpetrated by the football and beer-bust crowd. She ought to know, having done quite a bit of it herself in her day. She was well aware of the legendary kinship between cops and criminals. It was only recently that she'd come over to the side of law and order.

A roar was gathering up the avenue. The sovereign float, the one bearing Rex himself, was approaching. The closer it came, the pushier people got. Skip knew this was the wrong time to let her attention stray—and all too well, she knew she wasn't supposed to turn her back to the crowd—but one of Rex's pages was calling her.

"Hey, Skip, whereyat, dawalin'?" Probably Tricia Lattimore's little brother, who was at the age where kids thought aping the yats was funny. She was dying to say hi. And that wasn't all—she had to get a look at one of her oldest acquaintances in his moment of glory. She turned around.

There he was—the King of Carnival, Rex himself, the Monarch of Mirth, all in gold and positively exuding noblesse oblige. Despite all the fancy sobriquets, he was known to his intimates as plain Chauncey St. Amant. He was a well-padded gentleman, like most New Orleanians of a certain age, and he was in his element playing Old King Cole the merry old soul. Skip hoped his arm wouldn't fall off from too much waving. She'd known him since her rubber pants days.

He looked up and waved at someone on one of the balconies. Automatically, Skip's gaze followed his. The float was just parallel to the balcony, one she knew well. Today it was draped with Mardi Gras bunting—purple, green, and gold. The single occupant standing on it was dressed as Dolly Parton in cowgirl finery.

Dolly had on her trademark curly wig, a red satin sequined blouse, blue satin skirt, fawn gloves, balloons in her bodice, and two-gun holster. She had on a white mask with eye shadow in three colors and sequined rouge spots. As Chauncey waved, she drew one of her six-shooters. She twirled the gun, clowning, and pointed it, leaning on the balcony. Not very amusing to a cop, but Chauncey was appreciative enough to throw her a doubloon. And then he fell off his throne.

The band in front of the float was playing "When the Saints Go Marching In," so Skip never heard the shot. All she knew was that one moment Chauncey was admiring Dolly and the next minute he was down on the floor of the float. Knowing instantly what had happened, Skip started to draw her own gun, but there wasn't a chance. She was pushed from all sides, had to fight to remain standing. One of the filmmakers, determined to miss nothing, hit her on the side of the face with his camera. "Oh, God! Sorry. Are you hurt?"

"Shove it!"

"But did you see? Dolly…"

Her partner yelled, "Goddamnit, Langdon, quit acting like a broad!" She had time for one last look. Dolly was gone.

"It was Dolly!" she yelled back. "Dolly Parton!" But none of the other cops seemed to hear. Could she make a run for it? Get to the apartment house, intercept Dolly as she came out? Not a chance. You couldn't run two steps in that mess, couldn't walk, couldn't do anything but fight for your life. By now some of the other cops had their nightsticks drawn' and Skip knew she had to use hers too.

For a moment fear shivered through her body. This was a mob. Somebody was going to get hurt. And then anger replaced the fear. Goddamnit, these people were assholes. They were trying to kill her. Especially the self-important bastard with the camera. He was going to take her out, and ten little kids as well. Nightstick horizontal, she gave him a good shove and he had the gall to look surprised.

"Get back, dammit!"

He stared at her as if he hadn't heard. "But Dolly..

"Back!"

The crowd closed in and he nearly lost his balance. Skip lost valuable seconds trying to keep him from going down. And then it was her against the mob. All she remembered afterward was pushing with all her strength, pushing till her arms hurt, for about a week and a half.

She later realized it had probably been no more than ten minutes. And then she was summoned to the float, where the Monarch of Mirth was laid out as if on a bier, his bloody mask beside him, a round hole in the royal temple.

Sergeant Pitre started to speak, but Skip interrupted. "Dolly Parton!" she blurted, causing her fellow cops to stare as if she were delirious.

She pulled herself together. "A woman dressed like Dolly Parton shot him. From that balcony."

As she pointed to the balcony, a second-storey one on the river side of the avenue, she thought about the implications of its ownership—it was Tolliver Albert's. Albert was 'Uncle Tolliver' to the St. Amant family and practically a member of it—Chauncey and Bitty's best friend. He was an antique dealer, a charming bachelor in his fifties much favored as an extra man at Uptown dinner parties. A social fixture. And yet someone dressed as Dolly Parton had stood on his balcony and shot Chauncey. "I saw it happen," she said.

"You saw the shooting?" Pitre's voice was belligerent, as if he weren't willing to bestow the exalted status of star witness on a rookie female.

Quickly, Skip sketched out what she'd seen. Pitre barked orders, dispatching other officers to the Dolly chase. "It's Tolliver Albert's place," said Skip. "He'll be at the Boston Club."

"Unless he's Dolly."

"The St. Amants'll be there too," Eventually the parade would have gone down Canal Street and stopped at the club, where the whole family would have been in the reviewing -stand, and where Rex would have toasted his queen—if Chauncey hadn't been murdered. As it was, Mardi Gras was stopped in its tracks.

"I know where they'll be, Officer Post-deb. You're a friend of the family, right?"

Skip nodded, though she wasn't, really. She was just an old acquaintance, the daughter of their doctor, someone they probably thought of as often as they thought about their coat-rack. True, she'd gone through McGehee's and Newcomb with Marcelle, had even been a bridesmaid at her brief marriage to Lionel Gaudet, but that was only because Lionel was her cousin. They weren't friends Marcelle lived on her trust fund, lunching a lot and playing tennis; she interested Skip about as much as a stale beignet.

By now emergency vehicles were starting to arrive. Pitre held up a finger, commandeered one of the squad cars, and beckoned Skip to get in with him. "Come on. We're going to inform the next of kin."

Normally homicide would do that—they must have thought Pitre could get there faster than they could. Pitre was obviously too intimidated to go alone to a place where half the swells in New Orleans would be gathered. Skip was sure he meant her to do all the work, and she relished the idea. She had never fit in with the Uptown crowd—at least not in her own mind— but Pitre didn't have to know that. After that post-deb remark, she was going to enjoy humiliating him by doing this job and doing it right. Even as she vowed revenge on Pitre, it came to her exactly what the job would entail; that Chauncey St. Amant was actually dead. She'd seen the murder, but she couldn't quite take in the dead part. This must be what shock is like, she thought—a kind of numbness that pushes tragedy out of your head.

The crowds on the parade route were thicker than Southern flattery, but Prytania, a block from St. Charles, was a ghost street. They turned onto it and flew. Skip was glad they were flying—she didn't want someone to phone the Boston Club and break the news ungently.

THE KING IS DEAD

PITRE ROUNDED UP the others while Skip went to the ladies' room to get Bitty. Bitty fled from her and stood still, once outside, staring wildly around as if disoriented. "I'll take you to the others," Skip said, and led her to the small third-floor room they'd been assigned. She tried to be fast, unobtrusive, but a hush fell as -,he walked through the crowd with Bitty St. Amant, elegant, fragile Bitty, Skip towering above her, the two of them looking like beauty and the beast.

Pitre, who'd taken off his hat, nodded at her. Skip called Bitty by her last name, as she had been taught—a girl whose daddy was from Mississippi wasn't on a first-name basis with parents of peers. "Mrs. St. Amant," she said, "I'm so sorry. Mr. St. Amant's been killed."

Skip could see that they were prepared for the worst. When two cops turn up looking somber in the middle of a Carnival party, the best news one could expect would be a nonfatal accident. But being prepared didn't help.

Bitty and Marcelle wailed together in one high, desperate voice. Bitty fell, automatically it seemed, into Tolliver's arms. Skip saw his face twitch in pain and then she looked at Henry. She couldn't tell what she saw on his face, but if it was grief, it was mixed with something else—something a little like triumph, Skip thought. But Henry was a mean brat she'd never liked. Perhaps she was making it up.

Before she had time to ponder further, she was holding Marcelle, who was sobbing against her uniform. She seemed to have fallen as automatically on Skip as Bitty had fallen on Tolliver. Skip thought it odd that neither had chosen Henry. But then Bitty changed partners. She held Henry as if she were the daughter and he the father, shaking and holding tight to him. She seemed very small and thin in her plum-colored suit. Tears welled in Henry's eyes and escaped. Skip thought she might have been wrong about him.

Pitre withdrew. Skip didn't know how long she held Marcelle, who kept saying, "Daddy, Daddy," over and over, loud at first and then more softly, crying till she was cried out. When she stopped crying, Bitty did too, as if brought up short, and for a moment they all stared at one another. Then Pitre came in again with a couple of homicide detectives who'd just arrived. They were two of the department stars, Frank O'Rourke and Joe Tarantino.

Skip told the story of what she'd seen, in a small room the club lent them, and then Tarantino said, "Stay while we interview these people. You know them, don't you?"

"Yes." Everyone in the department seemed to know her life history.

"Maybe they'll feel more at ease. with you here."

They called Tolliver in. He wasn't his handsome, dashing self. His skin was oatmeal, his posture a memory.

"Mr. Albert, did you leave the party at any time?"

"Of course not."

"Would you check and make sure you have the key to your apartment?"

Looking vague, as if the request hadn't registered, he pulled out a leather key case and showed his apartment key.

"Does anyone else have a key to your apartment?"

"My cleaning lady."

"Anyone else?"

Tolliver hesitated. "Why? What's this about?"

"Could you just answer the question please?"

"Mrs. St. Amant does."

"Did you see Mrs. St. Amant leave the party?"

"What is this about?"

"Did you, sir?"

"No!"

"Do you know anyone who was planning to dress as a cowgirl today? Or Dolly Parton?"

"No."

"Anyone who owns such a costume?"

"No."

"Do you own such a costume?"

"No. Why are you asking me these things?"

"Because, Mr. Albert, someone dressed as Dolly Parton shot Chauncey St, Amant from your balcony."

He already looked like a man who'd just lost his best friend. Now he turned from oatmeal to cream of wheat. He sagged against the chair back. "No. You're mistaken."

Tarantino raised an eyebrow at Skip.

She said, "I saw it. I know your house, Tolliver. It was your balcony."

"I live in an apartment. It couldn't have been mine."

"It was your apartment."

"Did anyone," he finally asked, "see Dolly coming out?"

Instead of answering, O'Rourke said, "Is there a back door?"

"Yes."

O'Rourke sighed in resignation. Dolly had probably slipped out the back.

After Tolliver, they invited Bitty in.

"You have a key to Mr. Albert's apartment?"

"I water the plants when Tolliver goes away," she said. "He takes buying trips. I've had a key for years."

She was so calm Skip thought she must be in shock.

"Mrs. St. Amant, do you have the key with you now?"

"Why are you asking these questions?"

"Did you leave the party at any time?"

She shook her head, Her lips pursed slightly, then straightened out, and Skip saw a muscle start to work in her jaw. "What's going on? Why do you want to know?"

"We'll tell you in a minute. Can you hang on for just a couple of questions more?" Tarantino's voice was soothing. Skip knew he was afraid she might go out of control before they found out where the key was.

Bitty nodded, her lip., getting tighter,

"Where is the key now?"

"In my purse. I put it on a chair somewhere."

"Would you mind making sure it's still there?"

Bitty sent Skip to find the purse and rummaged through it for her key ring. "Here it is."

"How long has your purse been unattended?"

"A couple of hours, I guess."

"Who knew you had a key?"

"Why, everyone. I'm always having to water Tolliver's plants after lunch or something, and I usually say where 1'm going."

They asked her the Dolly questions and then gave her the bad news about the balcony. The tight line of her lips broke, She screamed as she hadn't when they told her Chauncey was dead—a delayed reaction, Skip thought. The screams kept on, one after another, until they called Tolliver to hold her.

Marcelle's and Henry's interviews added little. Marcelle had not left the party; Henry had gone out for some air—for about thirty minutes, maybe forty-five.

"I think," said O'Rourke, "that we ought to go to Mr. Albert's apartment and have a look."

They brought it up with Tolliver, who gulped and looked at Bitty. "I don't want to leave Mrs. St. Amant. Could someone else go with you?"

"Marcelle, you go," said Bitty. "Please." She took one of Henry's hands and held it. Apparently she wanted to be surrounded by the remaining men in her life.

Marcelle looked trapped. She said, "Skip, will you come?"

Skip looked at O'Rourke and Tarantino, They nodded.

"Sure."

In the backseat of the dicks' car Marcelle turned to Skip and let tears once again come into her eyes, which seemed the size of small plates. Marcelle was a famous beauty. She had gotten the best genes from both parents—Chauncey's dark coloring and Bitty's Phidian profile, She'd married young and divorced early. She might not be Skip's favorite conversationalist, but for all her pampered existence, she was a gentle enough soul.

"Skippy, it's political, don't you think? My daddy had enemies. Mother used to warn him all the time- 'Chauncey, you shouldn't be so outspoken. There's a lot of nuts in the world.'she was right, I guess. It's got to be political, don't you think, Skippy?"

Skip didn't know whether Marcelle spoke for the benefit of the dicks or whether she just didn't mind talking in front of them. She said, "I just don't know," and wondered if it could be political.

For the first time she started to think of the difference Chauncey St. Amant's death would make in the political and cultural life of the. city. It would be a huge loss. He had been a member of the Boston Club, which did not admit Jews, blacks or women, but he had publicly spoken out against the club's policy. That might seem a small thing to outsiders, but in the circles in which Chauncey moved, it was radical. It would probably have been his undoing if he hadn't been the son-in-law of Haygood Mayhew. And that was just a tiny facet of his genuine commitment to civil rights.

He was president of the Carrollton Bank, which had one of the best affirmative action policies of any large corporation in the city. It had black and female vice presidents, and minorities in plenty of other executive spots. And he was a prominent liberal Democrat who had helped elect the current black mayor, Furman Soniat. Lately, though, there had been talk that he might run for office, possibly for the state senate, though Soniat was thinking of moving up himself.

He was also a jazz buff and one of the founders of the New Orleans jazz and Heritage Festival. In addition, he had taken on several young musicians as his personal protégés, helping them find gigs and giving them what he called 'artistic subsidies' when they needed them. Invariably his protégés had been black, and some of them had taken advantage of his generosity, spending the money on drugs and ending up in jail, which gave the racists in Chauncey's crowd ammunition against his liberal civic ideas ammunition of the sort that is whispered rather than aired in the press. But a couple of unfortunate incidents hadn't stopped Chauncey on either front. He believed in civil rights and he believed in music, and he supported them. Not that he didn't also support the symphony (in the years when there had been one) and the museum—he believed in the arts, period—but because New Orleans jazz was largely performed by black people, his love of it had been lumped with what, even in the high-toned Boston Club, was still called 'niggerlovin' (by its cruder members, anyway).

So Marcelle was right. He had lots of enemies. Racists and ultraconservatives who simply wanted to maintain the white male status quo. He'd had those for a long time. However, lately, as his political ambitions had come to the fore, he'd made enemies in his own political camp as well. Black politicians and ultraliberal whites who wanted to see Mayor Soniat in Baton Rouge had turned on him for attempting to split the liberal vote. He had political enemies, all right. But Skip wondered how any of them could get a key to Uncle Tolliver's apartment.

It was a famous apartment by New Orleans standards, having once been featured in Architectural Digest. It was slightly ornate for Skip's taste, but given her current spartan living conditions, she gasped with pleasure on seeing it again. It had the twelve-foot windows that opened from the floor, fourteen-foot ceilings, and anachronistic fireplaces of almost every building in New Orleans; perfect surroundings for the antiques Tolliver collected so lovingly.

He had painted the walls terra-cotta, a rich backdrop for the blue-and-white Chinese porcelains flanking an ormolu clock on the mantel. An American primitive hung over the collection. The rug was one of the quieter

Chinese ones, the fabric on sofa and chairs, on the other hand, an assertive print that screamed Brunschwig & Fils.

Skip thought she would have killed for a mahogany desk she was sure must be Sheraton. But a very dark, simple coffee table was obviously meant to be the center of attraction—the stage for Tolliver's most spectacular orchid performances. Smaller (though equally priceless-looking) tables were crowned with blooming orchids as well, but this one held a massive display of the plants Bitty watered, grown in a room in back that Tolliver had converted into a tiny greenhouse. The gun that must have killed Chauncey, an odd-looking old revolver, was lying beside a plain clay flowerpot.

In the middle of the elegant carpet was a tumble of clothes—a blonde curly wig, red satin shirt, blue satin skirt, gloves, mask, and D-cup bra with wadded-up rags that had given the balloon effect. A two-gun holster with one gun still in it had been flung onto a needlepoint footstool that jutted out at a funny angle in front of its chair. Dolly must have kicked it askew in her rush to undress.

The three of them had checked the place out, then called Marcelle inside to see if anything was missing. Looking at the pile, she made a little sound, as if she'd been jabbed in the solar plexus. "The clothes," she said. "You can trace the clothes, can't you? Surely whoever sold that outfit would remember."

They all moved closer and looked at the items, not touching. The wig could have come from Woolworth's. The other things looked cheap and sleazy. Probably the murderer had bought each item separately, and from someplace that sold a lot of similar merchandise.

O'Rourke sighed. "We might have better luck with the guns."

They might indeed, Skip thought. She didn't know much about firearms, but these looked odd.

Skip moved out to the balcony. There were plants there—a Norfolk pine, jasmine, some smaller things. There was even a Christmas cactus in a clay wall sconce between the windows. Two old-fashioned wrought-iron chairs were grouped on either side of a damp, dirty circle on the floor. On one of the chairs sat a gardenia plant in a pot the size of the circle. Skip's stomach flip-flopped as she realized Dolly must have removed the pot so she could stand where she needed to to get the best shot.

The men left Skip with Marcelle while they looked around, came back to report that nothing had been disturbed. "Mrs. Caudet, where can we drop you?"

"I'd like to go home to change, please. Before I go to my mother's."

They took Skip back to police headquarters, questioned her for an hour, and left her exhausted. Exhausted and feeling cheated. She would have given anything to be O'Rourke or Tarantino today.

Lieutenant Duby called her in. "I've had a request from the chief."

Chief McDermott. Her dad was his doctor. Some said that was how she had gotten her job.

"He wants to use you as a sort of special investigator on this. You've been detailed to homicide for the rest of the week."

Skip clasped her hands in her lap, as her mother had taught her to do more than twenty years ago. She couldn't have heard what she thought she had. She said nothing.

"The chief wants you to go and do what Uptown girls do—do you understand?"

Skip did. They wanted her to spy.

"Cooperate with O'Rourke and Tarantino, okay? And report to me. Any questions?"

"Starting now?"

"Tomorrow."

She was still on parade routes. "I'd better get back to work."

"Langdon, what time did you report this morning?"

"Five o'clock."

"You're a casualty, officer. Go home."

Feeling only slightly guilty, she left his office, pondering the mysterious ways of Comus, Momus, and Proteus, the gods of Carnival. She'd become a cop to escape the Uptown crowd and now the very thing she'd hated most all her life her tenuous place in it—was going to help her in her new life. She was going to do work hardly any rookie ever did, and all because she was an Uptown girl. Yet it wasn't for once because of her family's influence. Oddly, it was because of Skip herself; because she had expertise no other rookie had. The irony of it made her head spin.

Duby called her back. "You've got a phone call."

"Here?"

"Obviously here, officer. You're detailed here. Take it in homicide."

The detective bureau was divided into crimes against property and crimes against persons. You had to go through property crimes to get to the room homicide shared with robbery. It was roughly the size of an amphitheater and decorated with a single picture—a poster of a snake crawling on a naked woman. Homicide's desks were clustered neatly at one end of the room, robbery's at the other. There was no one at either end.

Shrugging, Skip chose a desk at random and asked for her call.

"Officer Langdon? About time. This is Dolly."

It was a man's voice. Skip wondered how in hell she could get a trace when she was the only one in the whole place. No way that she knew of.

"I saw you," she said. "Did you see me?"

"You didn't see me, honey. I was shit-faced over at Maidie Blane's."

Skip sighed and stopped worrying about the trace. "Cookie Lamoreaux. Très amusant."

"Awful about Chauncey. I heard you saw it."

"Word travels fast."

"Actually, I had the inside track. I've got a houseguest saw it too. Old buddy from California here to do a film on Mardi Gras."

"Oh, that asshole."

"Hey, he speaks well of you. Says you saved his ass."

"He nearly cost me mine."

"He's got something for you."

"I've got something for him too."

"I'm putting him on, okay? I said I'd make the introductions."

"Hi," said a new voice, quite a pleasant one—a little businesslike, but a little friendly too. "This is Steve Steinman. I saw your name tag and Cookie said he knew you. Weird, huh? I didn't know it was such a small town."

"In some ways it's a village." (Some ways that she hated like tarantulas.)

"Thanks for helping me today."

"No problem. It's my job."

"Listen, I think I got film of the thing. I thought maybe you could tell me who to show it to. The names of the investigating officers."

Skip's ears started to ring. "You've got it on film? The murder?"

"I'm not sure yet. It's being developed. I won't get it till ten o'clock or so."

"Tonight?"

"Uh-huh. Should I just drop it by the cop shop?"

"It'll be a madhouse around here. Why don't you bring it by my house? I'll take it in first thing in the morning."

Sure. After she'd watched it six or eight times.

"Why not? Cookie says you're okay. Says you're the only cop in town he'd trust."

"He was drunk when he said that, right?"

"Guess so, come to think of it."

"That's Cookie."

She gave him her address.

DOWN ON PONCE
by Fred Willard

Sam Fuller is a retired marijuana smuggler who has never figured out if it was a bomb or just a leaking gas line that blew up his boat, nearly drowned him and killed his closest friends. He did know that the Colombians were ruthlessly rolling over independent gangs, making it a good time for him to leave town — especially since he was still alive, but…officially dead.

When a man offers him $30,000 to kill his wife, a fatal series of events leads Fuller to go into hiding on Atlanta's Ponce de Leon Avenue. Called Ponce by locals, it is a haven for the homeless, the lawless and the restless.

Fuller accidentally gets involved in the disintegrating operation of a Dixie mob boss, Billy *"Dong"* Chandler, and a struggle for control between Chandler and the respectable businessmen who have been laundering his money. He knows that Chandler must have an enormous cache of money hidden somewhere, and he wants to do the right thing — steal it.

"A dazzling debut novel, a rollercoaster ride through an underworld filled with wonderfully skewed characters, as dangerous as they are perverse, whiplash dialogue that will have you laughing out loud, and more twists than a hangman's noose. Willard's hard-boiled, hilarious and harrowing page turner deserves a standing ovation."— William Diehl author of SHOW OF EVIL and PRIMAL FEAR

NO EXIT PRESS

ISBN: 1 901982 31 9   PRICE: £6.99pb
A NO EXIT ORIGINAL PAPERBACK

The Verdict

Everything under the sun reviewed by people with time for crime...

Yes, it's time for the annual Lawrence Blockathon. On this page a review of Tanner on Ice, , and then, the great man speaks, somewhat laconically, to Brian Ritterspak about the new book(s). Let the games begin!

It's that man again...

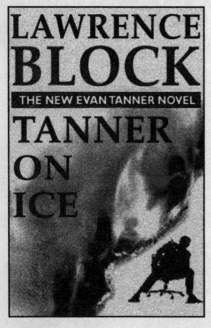

Tanner On Ice by Lawrence Block, No Exit Press, £10

It's always difficult to review Block's books. Principally this is due to the thing that makes them such a joy to read—the man's sheer facility with words. Block (dear, dear, Larry...) leaves you in danger of having little to say, except for the superlatives heaped on him by other reviewers.

Tanner, aficionados will already know, is the eponymous hero of a series of books written over twenty-five years ago by Block and representative of the (then) enthusiasm for spy stories. Block's spin on this is that Tanner doesn't sleep—a blow to the head in the Korean war has rendered sleep uneccesary to him.

Block's problem with *Tanner On Ice* was how to revive a character he last wrote about 25 years ago, without him being of pensionable age *or* being stuck in a time warp. Block solves this one in a manner (no, I'm not telling you how) suitably amusing, if a little too familiar to us comic book fans.

Unlike *Hitman*, *Tanner On Ice* is a laugh riot, from Tanner's Internet immersion course to the plot, which involves the destabilisation of a country. There are women, there are guns, there are cliffhangers. Block pulls off what is essentially a parody, without you noticing it. Another hit, I'm afraid.

Robert 'Bob' Galbraith

A quick chat with
Lawrence Block

CAN WE START BY TALKING a little about your latest book?

There are three new ones in '98. *Hit Man* (Morrow and Orion) is an episodic novel about Keller, a sort of Urban Lonely Guy of assassins. It's just out in the UK so I don't know how it's going there, but it was partticularly well received in the States, where reviews were very generous and sales exceeded the publisher's fondest hopes. I hope I'll do another novel about Keller, but don't know when. Then there's *Tanner on Ice*, just out in the States from Dutton and coming soon (though I don't know exactly when) from No Exit in the UK. It's the first appearance of freelance secret agent and all-around eccentric Evan Tanner since 1970; I I wrote the book Spring of 97 in the west of Ireland, though it takes place largely in Burma. I had great fun with it, and it seems to be going well over here. And in October Morrow and Orion will both be releasing *Everybody Dies*, the 14th Matthew Scudder novel, and one everybody seems keen on, including (he said, blushing) myself. It's dark and violent and I love it.

You've assimilated any influences that you may have had, but who were they? Who were the writers who inspired you in your fledgling efforts... one guesses Rex Stout?

I don't really know. A lot of mainstream realists—John O'Hara, Thomas Wolfe, James T Farrell, etc. And Somerset Maugham. Fredric Brown, Evan Hunter, Hammett and Chandler and Ross MacDonald. I don't think a lot in terms of influences. Musicians do, but writers are less usefully approached this way.

Can you look back on your early unpublished work with affection? Is any of it publishable—or will it remain in a bottom drawer?

Hell, it's all published.

How do you regrad your erotic pieces?

With wonder.

Okay... How do you regard your writing peers? Is there anyone whose work you never miss—and how many writers not within your field do you try to keep up with?

I make it a point never to say anything about living writers, but it's no secret I'm a big fan of my longtime friend Don Westlake.

Can you talk about the Chip Harrison/Leo Haig Books?

I can talk about almost anything, so why not? The first two are emphatically not mysteries—in fact the first, *No Score*, was almost entitled *The Lecher in the Rye*. I liked the character and wanted to do more, so I figured he had to go to work for a private detective—that way he could stay the same age forever. And I had enormous fun with the two mysteries. I don't think I'll do more, but if there's one thing I've learned, it's that one never knows.

The vexed issue of violence: how do you feel a writer should approach this in the 90s?

Write what you want. Period. If they don't like it, fuck 'em.

And sexuality? Should a contemporary writer opt for frankness or discretion?

Same answer.

Do you feel it's possible for a writer (genre or otherwise) these days to be apolitical? Or does the state of Western society create a political stance, indirect or otherwise?

Well, I'm apolitical.

Tell me a little about your working methods.

They vary from book to book. Handwriting, typewriter, computer. At home, away. I don't have one way of doing things, and I keep reinventing the wheel with every book.

What do you feel is the principal appeal of the kind of fiction you write?

Beats me.

The other arts... Is it important for a writer to be au fait with films? And is music a factor in your inspiration?

Au fait! Ooh la la, how Continental! I like to go to the movies and I like to listen to music, but I don't think either one makes much of a difference in my work.

Many people are lucky enough to be able to remember a teacher or mentor who was influential on them. Do you have such a figure?

Not really. There was an 11th grade English teacher who encouraged me, and I remember her gratefully, but I didn't have a mentor, and I've never had the urge to be one to anyone else, either.

Which comes first with you: plot or characters? Is the former always important, or can a novel of strongly drawn characters sideline narrative to any degree?

I dunno.

Is there a city that gets your creative juices flowing more than any other—apart from New York?

Well, I set most of my books in New York, and it's where I choose to live. I'm sure I draw energy from the city. But we travel as much as we possibly can, and I think that energises me, too.

How would you describe your relationship with your publisher and editor? Have you had any grisly experiences in this area earlier in your career?

I've mostly had good relationships. I don't get a lot of editing.

Do you bear your potential reader in mind when writing, or do you write principally for yourself?

I write with the intention that the books be read, certainly. But I try to write precisely what I would want to read. I think I would be doing my readers a signal disservice if I made an effort to give them what I think they want.

How do you feel about the fact that a writer is often a commodity, to be packaged and sold by a publisher?

When was it ever otherwise?

And after your next book?

The one after the book I discussed earlier will be a Burglar book, out in the States in July of 1999—but only if I get to work and stop spending far too much of my time answering questions...

The Judgement of Strangers by Andrew Taylor, Harper Collins, £15.99 ISBN 0002325586

Hard to know what to make of Andrew Taylor. I suspect that if this is the kind of thing you like then you'll go for it in a big way. This is an oddly compelling book even if it is written to something of a formula (I hate a book that starts with a mutilated cat and I hate a cat called Lord Peter—but there you go). At times the writing is obvious and strangely flat, but it is also wonderfully evocative of its time and recreates 1970s suburbia with a bit of an edge. Somehow you keep turning the pages to see what happens next.

This is the second in an 'interlocking yet separate' trilogy and I confess to not having read the first nor being particularly inspired to keep an eye out for the third. Whilst this is probably a draw back in trying to give a fair review, one thing I will say is that the publisher's claim to this being a major literary work which 'transcends the genre' (a silly phrase in itself which was recently debunked by Nicholas Blincoe in The Observer) just doesn't hold much water. It's a clever and accomplished book, but is lacking the quality of genuine surprise that a writer of, say, Gwen Butler's ability, manages to deliver on a regular basis.

Taylor's own description of the trilogy is that they are "psychological thrillers concerning time and angles, love and murder with their roots deep in the middle ages". If he hadn't told me this I wouldn't have thought it possible. But, in fairness, if you want to pursue the matter yourself then e-mail Mr Taylor at taylor@lydmouth.demon.co.uk

Peter Walker

Tooth and Nail by Ian Rankin, Orion Paperbacks, £5.99, ISBN 0752809407

Before Ian Rankin fans rush off to buy Tooth and Nail—THIS IS NOT A NEW BOOK. This is the third Inspector Rebus novel, Wolfman, re-titled, re-packaged and re-released. Originally published in 1992, Tooth and Nail sees Inspector Rebus off his usual Edinburgh patch and down South aiding the Metropolitan Police in their hunt for London's latest serial killer of women, one who both murders and mutilates.

Rebus, not keen to go in the first place, finds himself in that familiar 'fish out of water' plot with London coppers eager to see this so-called serial killer expert 'Jock' fail. We have the usual jokes about his Scottish accent not being understood, hostility from some police and some very telling descriptions of London life seen from a visitor's point of view.

Frequently, when a detective is off his (or her) home patch the novel deteriorates—see the endless TV Christmas specials—but this doesn't. Rebus is his usual self, but seeing him in a different milieu adds to his character rather than detracts. Seeing his style of detecting at odds with those around him, makes him seem even more unique and intuitive than usual. As a visitor he is requested not to step out of line, but when push comes to shove there's no senior officer breathing down his neck and he can detect in his own way, secure in the knowledge that he could always jump on the plane and be back home within a couple of hours.

The serial killings are rather grisly; women's corpses are turning up all over London and there seems to be no pattern to the killings or victims, and no forensic evidence to make a link. The sub-plots involving Rebus's ex-wife and daughter and a glamorous Canadian psychologist add vulnerability to his rather passive character.

A great stand alone novel that doesn't require a comprehensive knowledge of Rebus to fully appreciate it.

Ellen Cheshire

The Little Death by Michael Nava, Alyson Publications, £6.99, ISBN: 1555833888

When two worlds collide you expect casualties—but this is all out war.

Henry is a burnt out young lawyer, farmed out to work the dead end shifts by his company after loosing his last case. Hugh is an unknown quantity...in the can after being picked up outside a 'fag bar' in down town San Francisco. After getting the charges dropped on some minor technicalities, Henry is sure that he will never see Hugh again.

They meet under strange circumstances—and, ultimately, Hugh dies under strange circumstances… but not before voicing his conviction that his paternal grandfather wants him dead.

Henry is convinced that this apparent suicide of a strung out, gay, heroin junkie is murder… and, fuelled by love, is determined to prove this to be the case. His route is fraught with danger; the death of a junkie is not a strange enough occurrence to warrant too much of SFPD's attention, the death of a gay junkie, with an extremely powerful family looming in the background, warrants even less attention than the death of a small cat.

Whilst pursuing the truth and justice for his lover he is thrown into a seedy world where unpleasant tasks are dealt with by paid staff, the guilty have clean hands, and gets involved with a family with more skeletons in their closet than can be found at the local cemetery.

This book is not what it seems, the characters are strong, and the story line one of the most powerful that I have read in a long time. I found myself angered by the apparent indifference of the professionals surrounding Henry and the case, caught up in the frustration of endless brick walls and joining Henry on his journey around the maze that is 'establishment' like the proverbial laboratory rat. And who killed Hugh? It was simple to understand who pulled the trigger, the strangest twist of all was who paid the reaper.

Helen Bryant

The Mysterious Bookshop

For the old and the new in crime fiction.
Rare and second-hand a speciality.
We have hundreds of books for £3.
Sample our special offer of
4 x £3 books for £10!
We also have Signed US First Editions, Sherlockiana,
Thrillers, Audio, True Crime, Reference, plus all the new
UK paperbacks and hardbacks – often also signed!
Find us at:

82 Marylebone High Street, London W1M 3DE

and get on to our mailing list
for mail-order and our essential newsletters.

Telephone: 0171 486 8975, or
Fax: 0171 486 8953, or
e-mail : MysteriousLON@compuserve.com
You can also visit our US website at
www.MYSTERIOUSBOOKSHOP.com

Like A Hole In The Head by Jen Banbury, Gollancz, £9.99 , ISBN 0575065931

Like A Hole In The Head... yeah, and you need one to follow the plot (if there is one) in this book.

Jill, who is completely *mad*, and needs to be slapped, is sold a rare book (a signed copy of Jack London's *Cruise of the Snark*) by a dwarf (oh and by the way, Jill 'works' at a bookstore run by another mad person). This book is not his, he is, in fact, an actor (and a *bad* one at that). He is accompanied back to the store by a giant (look I *told* you this book was weird) who, when Jill says she's sold the book on, sets fire to the dwarf's hair.

In fact Jill has sold the book to a guy she wants to sleep with – who turns out to be a child actor who never made it as a grown up one. *He* does sleep with her, then switches the book, and takes the original to a book fair – where he is sure to get plenty of money for this extremely rare novel.

What takes place after that is anyone's guess. Jill steals her male friend's motorbike (no, not the book stealer, *another* male friend) and zooms off to Las Vegas to this book fair to retrieve the book before the giant torches more pertinent parts of the dwarf. Sleeps with someone else because she needs a shower, and finally, after *pages and pages and pages*, finds the book.

Please let me out now, I promise to be good and read the rest of the books...

Helen Bryant

Fall Girl by Elizabeth Botsford, Blaze Publishing

When the novel's first line (also printed on the back cover) is *"Most girls learn about sex from riding horses, but Zoe had learned from dancing the samba..."* you know you're in trouble.

When the blurb on the back cover continues with *"Explore the world's most intriguing city"* and the city turns out to be Hong Kong and we are asked to *"experience the power struggles"*, *"Laugh your way through a jolly good read"* and instructed not to miss *"the zany political thriller"* you begin to wonder what crime you might have committed, to make reading this novel a fit punishment.

Sold as *"an ideal gift for the adventurers (armchair or otherwise) in your life"* I began to have serious doubts about what I'd find on the 279 pages between the pale blue covers.

Zoe, the novel's heroine, is a beautiful (of course) vivacious 25 year old English financial trader based in Hong Kong. The 1987 stock market crash is the catalyst from which the novel's adventures (I use the word generously here) spiral. On the eve of Zoe's roof-top 25th birthday party the crash happens, the party breaks up, her flat-mate throws up and her boss mysteriously dies. In the days following the crash the power struggles in Hong Kong's political, religious and financial worlds change and Zoe finds herself on the run from the police after her "creative accounting" (fraud) is uncovered.

Zoe surrounds herself with a circle of eccentric characters to rival Dorothy's journey to Oz. Her journey to freedom is littered with members of sinister cults, a flamboyant samba dancing banker, an eccentric elder stateswoman with dogs whose eyes pop out, undercover detectives, an intrusive photographer and an alcoholic flat-mate. What she fails to find is an intriguing plot or even a coherent one, a lead character to care about, or indeed any character to engage with.

I'm trying hard to find at least one redeeming feature, as this is Elizabeth Botsford's first novel after having spent a *"wasted youth qualifying as an attorney in the UK and California"*. She followed this by working in the Hong Kong Headquarters of the largest law firm in the world, the European Commission in Brussels and the law firm which represented the late Princess Diana. An impressive legal CV by the look of things and she should have stuck to it.

My sincere commiseration to the allocated reviewer of her promised second novel.

Not to be recommended to anyone.

Ellen Cheshire

Mangrove Squeeze by Laurence Shames, Orion, Hbk, £16.99 (£9.99 Trade Pkb), ISBN: 0-7528-1002-2 (TPB: 0-7528-1433-8).

Shames dedicated his last book, *Virgin Heat*, to Key West *"for being so humid and so strange, such a congenital place to write about"*. It certainly shows in his books. Maybe there is a thesis in here for someone who can link location to writing style, but there does seem to be a case for a Florida sub-genre which specialises in a style of writing which is darkly humorous, rich and compelling.

Shames often gets mentioned in the same breath as Elmore Leonard, whose early Florida based novels also use the same kind of quirky, offbeat characters for a serio-comic effect. Or, more commonly, Shames is midway between Leonard and the more obvious comparison with Carl Hiaasen. But Shames has reached the point where he can be his own man. If anyone is to be held up as a bench mark my money would be on Charles Willeford. Shames, like Willeford, has the authenticity of his locations and the ability to create believable characters who do and say funny things. He also has that sureness of touch in the way he builds up toward a climax which makes his books hard to put down.

This one involves the intertwining of the various elements which make up Key West. The developing relationship between a new arrival and a local journalist clashes with the usual local corruption and the latest big ecological threat—this time its the Russian Mafia who have a lot of plutonium to sell. Full of on the nail dialogue, funny and believable.

He has steadily built up a cult following and should break out into a wider audience if he consistently writes books that are this good.

Peter Walker.

Scapegoat by Daniel Pennac, Harvill, £9.99, ISBN 1860464432
The Fairy Gunmother by Daniel Pennac, Harvill, £6.99, ISBN 1860464459

Here's something a bit different. The central character is Benjamin Malleussène, a professional martyr—when customers at the department store where he works complain, Ben is called in to take the blame. He cries, they relent, the store is saved.

Ben is a bit of a martyr in his private life as well—the oldest of a clan of brothers and sisters, each with different fathers, and with a mother who has run off with yet another man. Ben has to fill their stomachs, hearts and souls. He also has a smelly and epileptic dog, Julius, complete with lolling tongue.

If this isn't enough, in the first book *The Scapegoat*, a series of bombings are killing the store's customers—and Ben is present at each death. Suffering from periodic deafness, taking blame for the bombings and surrounded by a bewildering array of characters, things don't look good for Ben. And if you think *that's* complicated, hah! I've left out bizarre characters like Theo, constantly dressing up to photograph himself in the store's photo booth, and who has also taken charge of a group of geriatric druggies, using the store as a kind of crêche for them.

The second book, *The Fairy Gun-mother*, begins with a racist cop being shot dead while on stake-out duty, protecting the elderly of Belleville from indiscriminate attacks. He's shot by an old lady when he tries to help her across the road (which is covered by an ice patch in the shape of Africa). The recoil gives her a good head start over the ice as she makes her getaway. This novel divides its time between Ben and a cop called Pastor (he's very good at getting confessions out of people) who, working separately, have to find out who's killing old people, who's supplying *drugs* to old people, who put the love of Ben's life, Julie, in a coma, and, oh yes, who killed the racist cop. As usual, Ben is to blame for all of these things and more.

Pennac used to be a schoolteacher, and the looking after and protecting of children comes to the fore in these novels. Often the children know more than the adults, but don't have an adult's capacity to deal with information. Another predominant theme is the reading and enjoying of books. One character, Risson, runs the book department of the store, whilst in *Scapegoat* Ben tells the children a story every night about tough cops Harry Hyena and Sid Burns, *"meaner than Phil Coffin and more bent than the Bouncing Czech,"* using the bombings as the story's basis. In fact, the French title of *Scapegoat* is *Au Bonheur Des Ogres* (*The Happiness Of Ogres*)—ogres being mythical creatures that ate children—a pun on

Emile Zola's novel *Au Bonheur Des Dames* (*The Happiness Of Women*), which is also about a department store. There are many delightful touches throughout the books—like French pastry they're tasty, rich but light.

Originally published in 1985 and 1987 respectively (but released in reverse order in the UK for some unknown reason), these are the first two novels of the Belleville Quartet which, when I recently looked in a French bookshop, seemed to have expanded to five or six novels. Perhaps someone has mis-translated along the way and the books are just about the Belleville Quarter (District) of Paris. And talking of translation (both by Ian Monk), some of the translation of *The Fairy Gunmother* is annoying due to Monk using specific English words and phrases instead of French ones. For example, all the ex-druggie oldsters visit a Derby And Joan Club, an institution which does not exist in France. It grates, and I had to go away and mutter for five minutes before returning to the book. Thankfully, there's none of this in *The Scapegoat*.

So, if you want to read something that's witty, inventive, shocking and great fun, p,p,pick up a Pennac.

Paul Duncan

Nothing But Trouble by James Maw, Sceptre, £12.00, ISBN 0340674989

This is a peculiar book. It's a rather smug buddy-novel that is peculiarly irritating because, while it has the ingredients of a good novel, it never really works as a whole. It kicks off with the assassination of a South American bishop and then cuts abruptly to a very silly scene in which Mills Clearwater, an American student at some vague and unspecific Oxford college, 'gowns up' for breakfast, calls a porter 'Sir' and causes a fire with an electric toaster. The plot plumbs even greater depths as Mills (*"as in Dark Satanic…"*) falls in with Jude, *"…a comprehensive school boy from South London"* whose working-class credentials are established by uncertain parentage, comprehensive education and, to cap it all, *"…until a week before he'd been working as a welder's mate at a paper mill."*

We learn that Jude is so named because he was conceived when his mother shagged a parkie after seeing Paul MacCartney and *Hey Jude* was her favourite song. Shame it was a Lennon song. Jude apparently knows how to make *"…a pheasant casserole"* and plucks, guts and cooks the roadkill he encounters on an unlit cycle ride through Oxfordshire. It's a pity Jude—or is it James?—doesn't know enough about preparing pheasant to hang it for a few days.

Mills Clearwater is the son of the Governor of Texas, who is in the running for the American Presidency. Poorly brought-up and misunderstood Mills cannot of course be allowed to screw up his father's campaign, so he scarpers for South America where he gets involved in all sorts of unlikely shenannigans as he is pursued by variety of even less likely characters. Jude, meanwhile, is left kicking his heels with Mills's granny in the Governor's mansion in Texas until he decides to go and save buddy Mills. Whether Jude is successful or not in his bid to save Mills, I'll not let on; nor will I reveal the outcome of Governor Clearwater's shot at the White House: these discoveries can be pleasures for the reader. I will let on, however, that I found the ending (not to mention the middle) as unlikely as the rest of the book.

The book doesn't really come off terribly well. The dialogue is poor in places too. It's a shame because there are some nice bits—mainly the travel writing: the vivid descriptions of the landscape show Maw drawing on his experience of back-packing in South America. However, this book was sent out to be reviewed for a crime-fiction magazine, not a travel mag. And that's a shame too. *Nothing But Trouble* is aptly titled—but perhaps, like the pheasant, it would have developed a better flavour if it had been hung longer.

Eddie Duggan

Mama Stalks the Past by Nora DeLoach, Bantam (US) $21.95, 0553106627

An engrossing tale of deception and skulduggery in South Carolina, wittily told, with occasional bursts of harsh reality to leaven the mix.

Hannah Mixon is possibly the most obnoxious neighbour that you could have (and I know whereof I speak), and makes no secret of her dislike for Simone Covington's Mama—her next door neighbour. So when she dies and leaves Mama the bulk of her fortune the small town of Otis, South Carolina is agog, and Mama fears that tongues will start to wag... When it's found that Hannah was murdered Mama *knows* that tongues will wag.

Simone is a paralegal, but Mama, well, Mama, as well as being the best cook in Otis, is a detective of sorts (previously appearing in *Mama Solves a Murder* and *Mama Traps a Killer*). Mama doesn't want the Mixon land, but the only way she can see to rescue her reputation is to find out who killed Hannah, and perhaps that's just what Hannah wanted.

Although this all sounds a bit too cosy in a 'grits and sweet potatoes', downhome sort of way, in fact the contrast between occasionally acerbic narrator Simone (the novel's first words are *"I was pissed."*) and her more traditional mother constantly keeps the book the right side of real. The contrast between old and new South is well delineated—Otis is nearly a character in itself. The neatly underplayed treatment of her father's possible alcoholism and the overwhelming concern for keeping land in the family are mixed with more traditional mystery elements to provide a first class entertainment that still articulates black concerns in a human and informing manner. I hope someone in the UK picks up this series. It's nice to see black people in an American crime novel who are neither victims or victimisers.

Wendy Lawrence

Small Towns Can Be Murder by Connie Shelton, Intrigue Press, $22.95, 1-890768-05-7

It would sound harsh to call this a desert cosy, but almost, that's what it is. Female sleuth Charlie Parker (!) and her assistant Sally Bertrand visit Laura Armijo, a friend of Sally's in her home town in New Mexico. During the visit Laura learns that a friend has died of a miscarriage, an event she feels is tied in to her friend's abusive husband, Richard. Charlie agrees to try and find out what happened.

Charlie is partners with her brother Ron in a private investigation agency in Albuquerque, and is embroiled in an ongoing argument with him about guns – she is opposed to them, but as she and Ron were trapped by a killer in a previous case (*Partnerships can Kill*) he wants her to be able to protect herself. To add to the confusion Charlie's helicopter pilot boyfriend is in town and wants her to move to Hawaii with him.

The three plot strands are capably and grippingly entwined, and Shelton doesn't shirk from confronting big issues – spousal abuse, gun control – while keeping us deftly entertained with an enjoyable and resourceful character. Soft, but with a hard centre. Or vice versa.

Wendy Lawrence

The Sleeper by Gillian White, Corgi Books, £5.99

What is a psychological thriller? It is a term used frequently by publishers and reviewers (I'm sure I've been guilty in the past) as quick and easy phrase to describe a thriller that does not fit neatly into any obvious category—and *The Sleeper* is one such example. These psychological thrillers often tread that fine line between good and bad, one where the story slowly unfolds around the protagonists' actions and where, usually, deeds buried deep in the past (both emotionally and psychologically) catch up with them in the present.

The Sleeper is no different, and as the novel's title itself conjures up, its focus is on this idea of hidden secrets being reawakened and destroying events currently taking place. The events, in the present, from which the past returns are set over the magical days around Christmas, as the reader flits between celebrations in two homes. Christmas at the Happy Haven Hotel, which is anything but a happy haven, has been disrupted by the disappearance of one of its elderly residents, their Christmas celebration is contrasted with that of the Moons, where their remote farmhouse has been snowed-in with the electricity and phone cut-off by the unusually bad weather.

When a body is discovered in the basement of the Moons' farmhouse, this triggers a train of events that escalates, leading to tragedy and misfortune for the entire family. Inter-cut with the internal reminiscences of one of those trapped in the farm-house, a taut and tightly written nov-el emerges. One that both thrills and disturbs—the thrills are woven with intricate details surrounding fami-lies, family gatherings, growing up and growing old, which are both funny and tragic.

The combination of domesticity and murder, passion and jealousy, mysticism and insanity merge into this deeply dark and chilly thriller, or should that psychological thrill-er?

Ellen Cheshire

Child's Play by Reginald Hill, HarperCollins, £6.99

The television success of a cele-brated novelist's detective can be a double-edged sword: the author's bank balance may swell satisfyingly, but readers can end up with a cast-in-stone view of the protagonists that owes more to actors than the origi-nal author. The success of Reginald Hill's irresistible Dalziel and Pascoe books after the TV series was assured, and one hopes that Hill won't start subsequently changing his charac-ters as Colin Dexter has done. This novel demonstrates how thorough-ly Hill merits his pre-eminent posi-tion among crime writers in a trench-ant tale of murderous intrigue that stretches back to Italy in World War Two, even if this is hardly vintage Hill. Andy Dalziel is coping with internal police politics when the

death of an Italian in the police car park soon has both Dalziel and his heavyweight superior investigating the complex mystery that began when a soldier went missing during the war. As usual, characterisation is vigorous, and Hill marshals his nar-rative with inexorable precision to a nicely-judged climax.

Barry Forshaw

Unruly Passions by Kate Charles, Little, Brown £16.99, ISBN 0316645494

Since Trollope, the ordered, sanc-timonious world of the clergy has been a fertile ground for dramas of self-interest and character assassina-tion as bloody as anything in the sec-ular world. And while Charles' styl-ishly written early novels have veered towards the cosy at times, she is at pains with this one to move things fairly swiftly into dangerous territory. Which is a good thing: a thriller about a woman who is one of the first of her sex to achieve the office of Archdeacon (together with acknowledgements to various cleri-cal figures and superscriptions from the Alternative Service Book) is in desperate danger of being sedate home counties fare (not a pitfall Charles is always able to avoid). Charles keeps things edgy by intro-ducing sex in the form of a man: Hal, the husband of Margaret Phillips (the Archdeacon). His involvement with a best-selling authoress who becomes obsessed with him, and a vicar's wife with a disabled child, leads to theft and finally violence. If Charles, who invokes *Hello!* magazine during the course of her narrative, steers at times towards that magazine's choice of adjectives, there is still a steely core to her narrative that makes this a compelling (if not too disturbing) read.

Barry Forshaw

Tiger Sky by Rachel Billington, Macmillan, £16.99, ISBN 03336262

Billington's use of crime novel techniques is cleverly dovetailed with her non-genre skills, and this is a stylish exercise in the same arena as PD James' most successfully realised novel, *Innocent Blood*: the release from prison of a murderer, and the attempts by those around the criminal to come to terms with the past. (Although, it has to be said, James' book is a much more striking work.) Here, Joe Feather is a killer who murdered his lover when he found her in bed with her ex-husband. After eight years, Joe is released from prison and returns to his village community, most of whom are outraged at his release. As locals try to force him out of his childhood home (Billington shows a topicality here that gives an edge to the narrative), a group of women work to help him and win him acceptance in the community. And it's this group that Billington is adept at depicting, giving each woman's personal agenda a satisfying solidity. In particular, Julie, Joe's probation officer, is a powerfully drawn character, using Joe as a conduit to

work through her own problems. Her eating disorder is given the weight of the more serious issues in the book (no mean task for Billington, given that the narrative inevitably has to cope with a fresh crime). Joe's steady realisation that his own house has become as claustrophobic prison as any jail is another powerfully rendered aspect of a book that shows an author using existing conventions for her own accomplished ends.

Barry Forshaw

Eleven Hours by Paulina Simons, Flamingo £12.99, ISBN 0006551114

Simons gleaned much praise for her earlier *Tully* and *Red Leaves*, and this new suspense outing certainly exerts a grip from page one. If the writing is penny-plain rather than elegant, that could be argued as the right approach for the tale Simmons has chosen to tell. In a hot Texas shopping mall, heavily pregnant Didi Wood is bundled into a car in the parking lot by an obsessed young man. We are soon into familiar pursuit territory, as Didi's husband Rich tracks her down by car and helicopter, aided by a laconic FBI man. A nice tension is set up by the latter's insouciant confidence (we are allowed to doubt, along with Rich, whether or not the agent can really deliver when the chips are down), and Didi is characterised with a degree of freshness that allows one to forgive the odd conventionality of plotting. Dialogue rings true and there's a nicely judged acceleration of pace as the final confrontation approaches. While Simons doesn't go in much for subtleties, that's no problem within the terms of the approach she's set herself: the eleven hours of the narrative pass very swiftly for the reader.

Barry Forshaw

Upon a Dark Night Peter Lovesey, Warner Books, £5.99. ISBN 075152025X

A young woman is dumped unconscious in a hospital car park, and awakes to find that she has lost her memory. The amnesiac is taken to a hostel until her memory returns. The opening of Lovesy's astringently written thriller is conventional enough, but his very individual manner kicks in with the introduction of Ada, the huge and overwhelming shoplifter who takes the girl (called Rose by the social workers) under her wing. The relationship between the two women is very adroitly drawn, with Ada a marvellously realised character. When Lovesey's sleuth Peter Diamond becomes involved (while investigating a suspicious death), events conspire to suggest that Rose is the key to another gruesome murder. Lovesey creates the ambience of Bath with all his customary skill (has anyone plunged to their death from a house in the Royal Crescent in a novel before?), and the plotting has the satisfyingly complex structure that the author has taken out a patent on. Perhaps, at times, the sheer energy of Lovesey's

earlier writing is conspicuous by its absence, but aficionados will be satisfied.

Barry Forshaw

Arm & a Leg by David Ralph Martin, Heinemann, £16.99, ISBN 0434004391

Martin's first book marked him out as a charter member of the streetwise school of tough and gritty UK crime writers, and this second assured outing largely consolidates his position, even if it exudes the usual second novel 'marking time' feel. Those who like their thrillers undisturbing should steer well clear, but aficionados of the kind of book in which no holds are barred will relish this one. In terse and punchy prose, Martin details a world in which few of the old verities hold sway: DS Hallam moves in a Bristol of dangerous drug deals and psychopathic cop-haters. With the imminent huge raid by Bristol CID on major drug dealers, Hallam finds that the complication of the vicious Baz and an exploding riot ensure that his recovery from a chisel wound will not be happening in tranquillity. Biting, dynamic stuff, handled with a careful eye for pungent detail, and only the occasional misstep.

Barry Forshaw

Moon Music by Faye Kellerman, Headline, £16.99, ISBN: 0747276579

Kellerman has a legion of devoted fans for her Decker series, and she pulls off the difficult task here of inaugurating a new protagonist. It may be a tad foolhardy for a crime wrier to call her hero Poe, but the father of the detective novel would not object to some of the grisly material on offer here. And Detective Sergeant Romulus Poe is a sharply drawn figure, with some novel touches. Another important character in the book is the town of Las Vegas, presented here with a kind of debased gothic splendour. If, at times, the invention falters, Kellerman is soon back on track.

Poe is assigned to a case in which the horribly mutilated body of a showgirl has been found (giving pause to even the jaundiced residents of Vegas). Matters are complicated when Poe finds that the dead girl had a relationship with his partner, Steve Jensen.

The plotting is skilful, recalling Kellernan's best work in *Day of Atonement* and *Milk and Honey*. She's also good on Poe's ambiguous relationship with the anorexic wife of his partner.

Vegas is a promising setting, and Kellerman's Romulus Poe looks set for a healthy run. But why do the parents of detectives always have the prescience to give their children outrageous names?

Barry Forshaw

At All Costs by John Gilstrap, Michael Joseph, £10, ISBN 0718143396

There's a novel concept at the heart of Gilstrap's successor to the lively *Nathan's Run*: the two protagonists, Jack and Carolyn Donovan, have been on the run for thirteen years. Their supposed crime (of which they are innocent) is the massacre of sixteen people and the sparking of one of the USA's most devastating environmental disasters. As the FBI pursue his desperate protagonists, Gilstrap is adroit at handling the uncertain relationship between the Donvans and their son, Travis, who has not been told why his family never settles in one place for long, and is finding the unspecified fear is having a grim effect. The narrative acquires a powerful momentum when a freak false arrest pins the Donovans down, and they are obliged to try to prove their innocence. And anyone who knows their conspiracy theory thrillers will not be amazed to hear that the ramifications of the case reach all the way to the Director of the FBI. The usual film deals have been made, but the key question for the reader is: does Gilstrap deliver? And, despite the odd pedestrian moment, the answer's a conclusive yes.

Barry Forshaw

The Wire in the Blood by Val McDermid, HarperCollins £5.99, ISBN 000649983X

While many crime writers share a common style, there are those who have a voice quite unlike anyone else. McDermid is such a writer, and this latest page-turner has all the panache McDermid displayed in the Gold Dagger Award-winning *The Mer-*

maids Singing. The villain here is as memorable as any the author has created: a charming, urbane manner is the public face of a truly disturbed and horrifying psyche. Dr. Tony Hill, expert at profiling the dark worlds of serial killers, is heading up a national force to discover if there's a link between several missing teenagers. One officer, Shaz Bowman, has an outrageous theory, and soon Hill and his colleague Carol Jordan are part of a terrifying hunt in which the rôles of hunter and hunted are alarmingly reversed. Some may doubt that such a taut narrative needed to spread to nearly five hundred pages, but McDermid has the reader blissfully unaware of the book's considerable length.

Barry Forshaw

Gumshoe by Neville Smith, Slow Dancer Press, £6.99, 1871033446

Ginley's The Name, Gumshoe's the Game (No Divorce Work)

When Eddie Ginley (a Liverpool bingo caller and would-be stand-up comic) celebrates his birthday by putting a notice in the paper, his dream comes true. Unfortunately, his carefully constructed fantasy world of damsels, gunsels and private eyes becomes all too real when someone calls his bluff and offers him a job. The mysterious fat man gives him a photo of a girl, a thousand pounds and a brand spanking new Smith & Wesson. And you know what you do with a Smith & Wesson, don't you? You just put your finger on the trigger and pull.

This is Neville Smith's novelisation of his own original screenplay for the 1971 film, directed by Stephen Frears *(The Grifters)*, and starring Albert Finney. A pastiche, it still works as a novel because of the unrelenting normality and realism of the characters. Although Ginley may spend his time quoting films and private eye clichés, his basic humanity, stubbornness, loyalty and honesty still shine through. There's also a nice supporting cast of characters: the sentimental club boss who spends his money getting fake photos of himself with celebrities; the Scots hardman killer who makes tea for Eddie; the old friend who, posing as a repairman, used to nick tellies, and is now working for the council, guarding empty houses. Everywhere Eddie goes, he gets what he wants, not by force but by being nice to people.

A downright enjoyable read—the dialogue is sparkling—you should go out and buy this now. You know how to buy, don't you? You just walk to the bookshop and pay.

Paul Duncan

Do Not Exceed the Stated Dose by Peter Lovesey, Little, Brown, £16.99, ISBN 0316644439

A collection of short stories is always a tricky thing to bring off, but Lovesey's customary professionalism ensures that this is a real treat. If there are moments when Lovesey is on auto-pilot (and one or two of the stories are unexceptional), he's adroit enough to make us forget that distracting feeling. Marshalling all the expertise he brings to his excellent crime novels, Lovesey creates a collection with a startling range, dealing with both the sordid and the genteel. Along with the ordinary-man-in-danger scenario, Lovesey provides welcome outings for his standard detective protagonists, Peter Diamond and Bertie, Prince of Wales (the latter featuring a strange narrative involving the Henley Regatta). Those who lament Lovesey's pensioning off of the much-loved Sergeant Cribb will be given pause by the vigour and inventiveness of this book.

Barry Forshaw

Dead Even by Brad Meltzer, Hodder & Stoughton, £10, ISBN 0340658169

Meltzer cleverly mixes a hip and witty grasp of character with the mechanics of a cracking legal thriller to produce another winner along the lines of his best-selling first novel *The Tenth Justice*. Sara Tate has just begun her new job as prosecutor in the Manhattan District Attorney's Office. She is married to Jared Lynch, who is about to become a partner at a top Wall Street law firm. When they find themselves taking opposing sides in the same case, the result is not just a threat to their lively marriage, but to their lives as well. The couple find themselves in danger from parties to the case on both sides, with a terminal prospect: no matter who loses, the other dies. It takes some skill these days to make a novel work in the over-crowded Grisham-style thriller stakes, and Meltzer wisely avoids sounding like any of his rivals. In this excellent book, he shows a richness of characterisation that is more skilful than many a better known writer in the genre.

Barry Forshaw

Caught in the Light by Robert Goddard, Bantam Press, £16.99, ISBN 0593042662

Goddard's success as a novelist whose primary virtue is a compulsive (if middlebrow) readability will be consolidated with this powerful and complex thriller (and it's more unequivocally a thriller than his previous books—although, as a novel of character, it has depth and truthfulness). Photographer Ian Jarrett, on an assignment in Vienna, falls in love with a woman he encounters in a chance meeting. After separating from his wife in England, he finds that Marian, his new love, has vanished mysteriously from his life. His increasingly obsessive search for her leads him to a Dorset churchyard and a psychotherapist, Dorothy Sanger, who believes she is the reincarnation of a woman who lived in Regency times, and who may have invented photography before Talbot. The fascinating revelations that follow may owe a touch to the novels of deception of Boileau and Narcejac (who wrote *Vertigo*), but Goddard is very much his own man, and the word-of-mouth among readers that ensured his early acclaim will be as vocal as ever in support of this book. Goddard's success is perhaps a little surprising given his conventional attributes, but, God, do readers still flock to an old-fashioned storyteller.

Barry Forshaw

The Soldier in the Wheatfield by Philip Hook, Hodder & Stoughton, £14.99, ISBN 0340682167

Hook's publishers are selling him as the Dick Francis of the art world, and although this idea has been tried before, it's rarely been carried off with the aplomb we find here. Dirty deals in the world of German Romantic landscapes is actually more plausible than Francis' unrealistically crime-ridden racetracks. Hook's hero, Parnello Moran, finds himself in mortal danger when a painting he buys at a New York auction is almost immediately stolen. The history of the painting, linked to a German Wehrmacht officer and an appalling crime in 1942, leads Moran into a whirlwind chase across Europe to a final rendezvous with the strangest secret of all… the secret of the soldier in the wheatfield. The author works for Sotheby's, but keeps his expert knowledge as a persuasive backdrop to a propulsively written thriller.

Barry Forshaw

The Last Cut by Michael Pearce, HarperCollins, £14.99

In his Arabic series, Pearce has been responsible for one of the most unusual and entertaining sequences in crime fiction. The Mamur Zapt is the title given to the Welsh captain Gareth Owen serving in Edwardian Cairo; the sense of time and place is conjured with striking verve, and Owen's conflicts with his British and Egyptian masters lends a real bite to these cunningly plotted books. The latest leans towards the delightful vein of humour so often mined by Pearce: a dam which allows water to flow through Egypt is at the heart of a labyrinthine plot, with the mysterious Lizard Man bearing a grudge against Egypt's irrigation system. When a young woman's body is found at the site of the dam, Owen is reluctant to believe he is dealing with traditional ritual sacrifice. But is he? Pearce keeps us diverted and confused right up to the set piece ending.

Barry Forshaw

The Pistoleer by James Carlos Blake, Canongate, £8.99

The crime novel and the western are inextricably linked, and sometimes the links seem to jump out at you. Although Blake's sympatheic portrait of John Wesley Hardin might seem to owe more to various Billy the Kid stories than to contemporary films, the connection between our modern serial killer heroes and the gunman whom death seems to follow around should be obvious. We start with the abuse in childhood (the outlaw's usually comes at the hand of legal, rather than parental authority) and we take the structure of the road novel as a framework for the deaths.

In westerns, killing makes some men more attractive to women. Some of the best sequences in *The Pistoleer* are those narrated by women. Not only does Wes get some good booty, but the women have their own perspective on it, a perspective not usually a part of the genre. Serial killers, unfortunately, never seem to have that same attraction for women.

If at times Blake becomes overly romantic, the novel doesn't suffer for it. The kaleidoscope of narrators give him lots of scope for irony, and provides a panoramic view of the West which few novels have time or scope to attempt, much less deliver. This ranks with Geoff Aggeler's *Confessions Of Johnny Ringo* and Loren Estleman's *Bloody Season* as among the best 'bad man' novels in recent years.

Michael Carlson

New Orleans Mourning by Julie Smith, Slow Dancer, £7.99

New Orleans Mourning won an Edgar Award in 1991, and it's taken seven years for it come into print in Britain, courtesy of John Harvey and Slow Dancer. It's a novel rich in the lore of New Orleans, and for my taste, its gumbo has too much okra and not enough boudin, if you know what I mean, cher. There's a lot of sizzle and not a lot of steak, in the language of the more mundane parts of America.

Really this is a story of New Orleans society, a sort of Tennessee Williams homage wrapped up in a murder. Skip Langdon, Julie Smith's female cop, comes from the fringes of society, but has been an outsider all her life. Being a cop brings her satisfaction, but doesn't help her fit in to her parents' world any better. Think of Betty Thomas from *Hill Street Blues*, and stick her into an episode of *Dynasty* moved to Mardi Gras with liberal doses of booze, drugs, and blacks, and you've got this acorn in a nutshell, you.

Smith tells the story in a third-person narrative which takes first-person viewpoints. This is always difficult to pull off, and especially so when all the third and first persons sound alike (except for Yankees, who exist to have local colour explained to them, and blacks, who exist to keep the damn city alive). So the book weaves its way through 300 pages of minuets, before actually picking up pace and becoming gripping as the dark family secrets begin to be revealed. Then it ends, and so many loose ends are left hanging you know there's gotta be a sequel just to explain them. The blurbs say Smith writes like Jazz should sound, Lord help us if Jazz sounded like that. I keep hearing baroque music: intricate, repetitive, and interminable.

Michael Carlson

Black and White and Read All Over?

King Suckerman by George P Pelecanos, Serpent'0s Tail/Mask Noir, £8.99, ISBN 1-85242-610-1

FORMER ARMED-ROBBER and bad-ass black man Wilton Cooper teams up with terminal-wigger redneck, Bobby Roy 'B. R.' Clagget and two black country-boys, the Thomas brothers. The path of this dangerous band crosses with that of black record-shop owner, Marcus Clay and his dope-dealing Greek buddy, Dimitri Karras, with grave consequences.

As well as providing the title of this latest offering from George P Pelecanos, *King Suckerman* is also the title of a [fictional] nineteen-seventies 'blaxploitation' flick about a pimp—but *"not any old pimp. The baddest player there ever was"* (p. 14). The *King Suckerman* film is not so much blaxploitation as an Iceberg Slim-style tale of the grimmer aspects of black urban life, of which one of the novel's black characters remarks, *"I bet some white man wrote that movie; produced it, too"* (p. 15). This comment serves to raise the question of the status of Pelecanos's text, which is itself an example of a non-black writer representing black experience. Is Pelecanos's novel just another piece of blaxploitation, or is it something more than a wigger-text simply leeching on black style? Similar questions have been raised about the use of popular culture, black style and the representation of black characters in the films of Quentin Tarantino.

King Suckerman invites comparison with Tarantino's films not just because of the centrality of popular culture, black or otherwise—music, film, drugs, fashion, television—in the text and in the characters' lives; or because of the portrayal of violence and vernacular speech (particularly, perhaps, the emotive terms 'motherfucker' and 'nigger'), but also because of the narrative structure.

One of the more interesting aspects of this Pelecanos novel, and one of the more interesting aspects of Tarantiono's work, is the way in which the story is told. Both Pelecanos and Tarantino adopt the technique of cutting between apparently discrete, disparate, plot-lines which are brought together, carefully crafted into a complex weave of differing points of view. The disorienting shifts in time that characterise Tarantino's narrative style—re-running the same scene from a different point of view—are also employed by Pelecanos. A scene might take place which unfolds as if seen from one character's point-of-view. The reader completes the scene, only to be taken back over it, but from a different point-of-view. While it would be interesting to see how a film version of *King Suckerman* might be scripted by Tarantino, that is not to be; there is however a film of *King Suckerman* already in production, starring Sean "Puffy" Combs (aka Puff Daddy).

King Suckerman marks something of a turning-point for Pelecanos. It is not, however, a turning point of quite the same order of magnitude as, say, Walter Mosley's *Always Outnumbered Always Outgunned* (also published in the UK by Serpents Tail). Mosley's *Always Outnumbered Always Outgunned* marks a break with a familiar series character and shows Mosley, the writer of several Easy Rawlins novels, maturing and exploring different registers and different techniques. The same can be said—up to a point—of *King Suckerman*. It shows Pelecanos exploring different registers and different narrative techniques. In this sense Pelecanos is showing signs of maturing as a writer; but, entertaining and well-crafted as this novel is, the lavish praise that is routinely heaped upon him for the frankly rather vapid Stefanos series still seems a little premature.

One of the most grating aspects of Pelecanos's style is the way in which it is like what French sociologist Jean Baudrillard calls a *simulacra:* a perfect copy of an original that never existed. Hence, one suspects, the gushing reviews and the frequent comparisons to Dashiell Hammett, James M. Cain and, more recently, Jim Thompson, that are blurbed across the covers of Pelecanos's novels.

That said, Pelecanos does seem now to have gotten away from creating the sense, which permeates the earlier narratives, that he is trying too hard to establish both his own and Nick Stefanos's credentials. *King Suckerman* offers welcome relief from that feeling of writing-as-continual-performance, that gosh, look-at-me/isn't-it-great-to-be-looked-at-ness that encumbers the Stefanos novels. But while *King Suckerman* is a great improvement over Pelecanos's earlier novels, there is still some slack in the text. For example, the baggy prose that constitutes chapters six through to nine could be much crisper: the present forty-two pages could be pared down to fifteen or twenty pages, with the effect that the pacing becomes much tighter.

Nor has Pelecanos been bold enough to leave behind the certainty (not to say unit sales and easy praise?) of the Stefanos series this time out. *King Suckerman* is something of a half-way house between a bold new venture and a 'prequel' to the Stefanos novels. The young Nick Stefanos is shown in his early days as a dope-head domestic electrical goods salesman in Nutty Nathan's. In attempting to make *King Suckerman* serve as a prequel to the Stefanos novels, Pelecanos shows that the line between 'consistency' and 'repetition' is a thin one which, here at least, he appears to follow with some uncertainty.

In the first Nick Stefanos novel, *A Firing Offence*, for example, Stefanos walks *"…down the noisy wooden steps to the stock room. The musty odour of damp cardboard met me as I descended the stairs"* (p. 22) while in *King Suckerman*, *"Karras went down a shaky set of wooden stairs. The musty odour of damp cardboard hit him as he stepped onto a concrete floor littered with warranty cards and cigarette butts"* (p. 155).

In *A Firing Offence*, *"McGinnes pulled a film canister and a small brass pipe out of his pocket and shook some pot out of the vial"* (p. 22). In *King Suckerman*, *"McGinnes … took a film canister and a small brass pipe from his pocket and shook some pot into the bowl"* (p. 159).

Stefanos describes himself in *A Firing Offence* as *"…usually wearing some kind of rock-and-roll T-shirt, tight Levi's cuffed cigarette style, Sears workboots on my feet"* (p. 22) while in *King Suckerman* *"Stefanos [was] wearing Levi's cigarette style, one turn-up at the cuff [...] a pair of Sears work boots and a Led Zeppelin T-shirt."*(p. 156).

Even though these are the same characters in the same location, the similarity in the descriptive prose goes beyond the call of consistency and comes uncomfortably close to laziness or self-plagiarism.

The themes of fatherhood and male-relationships give *King Suckerman* an extra dimension. The main male characters lack the steadying influence of a father figure. Heroes Marcus Clay and Dimitri Karras are men without fathers as, of course, is Nick Stefanos. Their relationships with women are often obstacles to, or tests of, the depth of their 'real' relationships with other men.

While drug-dealer Eddie Marchetti is a 'bad father' to Vivian Lee, his symbolic daughter, his associate, Clarence Tate, is a caring, nurturing father to his own 'motherless' daughter. Bad-guy B. R. Clagget has a savage bully of a step-father in the place of a 'real' father which 'explains' his deviancy. Mega-baddie Wilton Cooper cuts across the lives of all these men like an awful father-figure, the Titan who must answer to his sons.

For all its right-on style, *King Suckerman* retains a sense of conservatism and there are some scenes of cloying moralism. Marcus Tate, for example, often speaks with the novel's moral voice, openly courting regeneration by continually demonstrating self-awareness and regretting his wrongdoing. Even pussy-hound Karras exercises some moral judgement with respect to his drug-dealing and his sexual inclinations. Episodes of male-bonding intersperse the action scenes of a novel that can also be seen as a tale of clichéd masculine loyalty.

Male sexuality is something of a cliché here too: the good-guys are shown as 'healthily' heterosexual and get to grapple with the more profound aspects of relationships with women. The baddies are homosexual or inept heterosexuals (suggesting an equivalence between social deviancy and 'sexual deviancy') while the naive young white-boys seem to spend a disproportionate amount of story-time polishing Onan's flag-pole.

As noted, the film *King Suckerman* plays like an Iceberg Slim story—the tale of an unrelenting black pimp, mean and hard on his hoes, fucked over by The Way Things Are. For record-shop employee Rasheed, the film tells it like it is. The film also prompts Wilton Cooper to buy a copy of Iceberg Slim's *Pimp* for B.R.—telling him, *"most of what you saw in that movie ... they took straight that shit straight from Ice, man. Read that and you'll know what's really going on"* (p. 77).

Is there really any point then in Pelecanos bringing his formula and polish to black experience when, thanks to Iceberg Slim (and the Payback Press), it's available in its raw state? Perhaps the difference is that Iceberg Slim offers an authentic version of black experience—for characters such as Wilton Cooper and Rasheed, who *know* how it is—while Pelecanos writes for the white boys: the Dewey Schmidts, the Jimmy Castles and the Jerry Baluzys.

Pelecanos is improving as a writer and a stylist—the reservations discussed above notwithstanding. There's still a lot of promise in Pelecanos. Let's hope he hasn't peaked yet.

Eddie Duggan

Eddie Duggan teaches on the Literary Studies course at University College, Suffolk. He is currently researching *The Maltese Falcon* for a PhD at the University of East Anglia. His website is <http://www.ejmd.mcmail.com>

The following Stefanos novels are available in the UK:

A Firing Offense, Serpents Tail/Mask Noir (1997), £8.99, ISBN 1-85242-563-6

Down by the River Where the Dead Men Go, Serpents Tail/Mask Noir (1997), £8.99, ISBN 1-85242-529-6

Nick's Trip, Serpents Tail/Mask Noir (forthcoming: Autumn 1998).

JENNIE MELVILLE
WINDSOR RED

CHARMIAN DANIELS, on a sabbatical from the police force takes rooms in Wellington Yard, Windsor near the pottery of Anny, a childhood friend. The rhythm of life in Wellington Yard is disturbed by the disappearance of Anny's daughter with her violent boyfriend. Dismembered limbs from an unidentified body are discovered in a rubbish sack. A child is snatched from its pram. Headless torsos are found outside Windsor.

Are these events connected? And what relationship do they have to the coterie of female criminals that Charmian is 'studying'...? All is resolved in a Grand Guignol climax that will leave the most hardened crime fiction fans gasping.

Price: £4.99 ISBN: 1-902002-01-6. Available from all good bookshops, or post free rom: CT Publishing, PO Box 5880, Birmingham B16 8JF

email ct@crimetime.demon.co.uk

From Hell: The Jack The Ripper Mystery by Bob Hinton, Old Bakehouse, £7. 50, ISBN 1874538964

With such a plethora of books on Jack the Ripper, with almost as many theories as writers, a new writer must have a special impact to succeed. Bob Hinton has and does.

Apart from this book reading as smoothly as a novel, he has researched with extra care. He has checked bayonets and surgical knives as weapons. He has compared the crimes with such cases as the Panther, The Sunset Strip slayers, and the killing of President Kennedy. He analyses several other East End 19th. century murders. He gives a new insight into the Jack the Ripper murders and stresses many matters glossed over by other theorists—and very tactfully indicates several errors in their illustrations.

His suspect is the mysterious George Hutchinson, and indeed there are some odd points hitherto ignored. Why would a well-dressed man be wearing *spats* at midnight—normally changed by lunchtime? Why was the watch-chain shewing on a cold night when the overcoat would be buttoned? How could he see the colour of the boot-buttons on such a dim night, when he contradicts himself over the facial descriptions? Hinton considers Hutchinson to be a typical stalker, and moreover one who fits the psychological profiling already applied.

In his analysis he includes prejudice—how even the most balanced individual must have some, even if unconcious. Then he turns to the whole range of motives, and the different types of killings, building up his case calmly, precisely and with obvious enthusiasm. He starts with earlier murders and attacks than usual, and considers one of the victims to have been an unsuccessful (and unlucky) novice blackmailer. He is the first I have read who considers the famous letter a hoax because of the educated tone and lack of passions which he shows in other Killers' missives. He shows the pattern of the murders of several killers, like Gacy and Bundy and JTR.

An excellent first book with plenty of thought, theory and fact.

John Kennedy Melling

Freedomland by Richard Price, Bloomsbury, Hbk, £16.99, ISBN 07475 39812

It's a sultry night in June. A young woman, Brenda Martin, walks as if in a trance through the city of Dempsy's notorious 'Darktown' district. This is the Armstrong projects, a crime-infested black neighbourhood and Brenda is a lone white woman. But she's not a junkie looking for a quick fix. Her hands are lacerated and bloody yet she appears oblivious not only to her surroundings but also her physical pain. She eventually reaches a local hospital where she reveals that she has been the victim of a carjacking. The wounds to her hands resulted from landing on the ground after being hurled out of her car by a black assailant. Later, she discloses to an interviewing police officer that her four-year-old son, Cody was asleep in the back of the car.

Thus begins the prologue of Richard Price's novel *Freedomland*, an intriguing book which sees the author returning to the claustrophobic urban jungle he depicted so memorably and convincingly in his acclaimed epic, *Clockers*, a few years back.

When Cody, the car and the assailant fail to materialise after an exhaustive police search, an accusatory finger begins to point in Brenda's direction. Did she fabricate the whole thing? Is she the one responsible for her son's disappearance?

Well, what on the surface may seem like a simple case of whodunnit turns out to be a complex and compelling book.

Those readers familiar with Price will know that his vivid descriptive prose needs no introduction. He can evoke the sights and sounds of urban America unlike any other writer I know. He has an expert feel for recreating the slang-ridden street idioms of cops and lowly ghetto dwellers. After a time, the most brutal profanities seem to possess an almost poetical cadence.

Whereas much contemporary crime fiction has the stylised self-conscious artifice of a Hollywood movie, *Freedomland* comes across with the stark authenticity of a documentary film.

One of the book's main protagonists is black middle-aged detective, Lorenzo 'Big Daddy' Council. He's overweight, asthmatic and has the distinction of being a former juicehead who saw the light just in time to save his career (though not his marriage!). Darktown is his turf. He's a respected figure there and has the community's acceptance but as a policeman he is aware that there will always be a tincture of mistrust and the notion that he sold out.

The other major player in *Freedomland* is reporter Jesse Haus, a hardened, predatory newsmaker living by her wits. In general, the police regard reporters like Jessie with contempt but as is evident in *Freedomland* it is often a symbiotic relationship involving give and take on both sides. After all, cops and reporters are both in the information business.

Although Jesse's job involves a cynical exploitation of crime victims, Price paints a sympathetic picture of her. Indeed, we see that all human beings, even the morally reprehensible, are complex, ambiguous creatures worthy of our understanding and compassion.

When the news of the child's disappearance becomes public, all hell breaks loose. Police from the neighbouring district charge into Darktown like stormtroopers, rounding up young black men and bullying them in an attempt to extort information. The potentially explosive situation is exacerbated by the rapid influx of a bizarre media circus which sets up camp near the site of the alleged crime.

This is a grittily realistic human drama. You sense the grim desperation of America's black urban underclass who are eking out a bleak existence in a hostile environment. This is not so much the American dream as the American nightmare.

The result is a morally complex, arresting picture. There's a brooding unease that permeates the whole book. Darktown is a powderkeg ready to go blow, a smouldering crucible of palpable racial and social tension. What Price manages to achieve through his characters is a sense of compassion and empathy in the reader without resorting to cheap clichés.

This is definitely the best book I've read this year. However, Price (despite his credentials as an Academy Award nominated screenwriter) is virtually unknown in this country. His work is not devoted exclusively to crime but he does very much focus his attention on America's impoverished underclass from which crime and its effects are rarely absent. Highly recommended!

Charles Waring.

A Sight for Sore Eyes by Ruth Rendell, Hutchinson, £16.99

Rendell is rarely off form, and this tense and involving tale definitely ranks among her best. The central character, Teddy Brex, is a neglected and damaged child, whose unloving parents have left him with a view of humanity as vile and unpleasant. Rendell plays Brex against Francine Hill, similarly damaged after being discovered by her father sitting by the body of her mother. Francine, her skirt red with blood, is mute, and only nine months after the murder does she manage to speak – but cannot identify the killer. With consummate skill, Rendell plays with the idea of beauty, and what lies beneath: as Teddy and Francine become attractive people, the horrors lurking beneath their exquisite surfaces create a page-turner that has all the psychological insight we have come to take for granted with Rendell.

Barry Forshaw

The Fu Manchu Omnibus Volume 3 by Sax Rohmer, Allison & Busby, £9.99

The rediscovery and rehabilitation of Sax Rohmer as one of the great thriller writers continues apace with this delicious collection of the evil deeds of the Oriental criminal mastermind (and his implacable opponent Commissioner Sir Denis Nayland Smith of the Yard). Those seeking politically correct yarns should look elsewhere, but readers interested in seeing what kept an earlier generation utterly enthralled will find much to captivate them here (and there are those on this very magazine who are happy to see Rohmer dusted off for the Nineties). The plotting in the three books collected here (*The Trail of Fu Manchu, President Fu Manchu* and *Re-enter Dr Fu Manchu*) moves like the proverbial express train, and it's not hard to see why Rohmer influenced writers from Ian Fleming (Dr No is a thinly disguised Fu Manchu) onwards. PC or not (and if you're a CT reader, you're probably not the easily offended sort), this is greatly enjoyable fare. *[And, dear reader, there will be a Sax Rohmer/Fu Manchu retrospective in the next Crime Time—Ed.]*

Barry Forshaw

Secret Prey by John Sandford, Headline, £16.99

In the latest of Sandford's stylishly written Prey series, Deputy Chief Lucas Davenport of the Minneapolis PD is up against a ruthless killer in a plot that pays homage to the classic British murder mystery: Davenport himself is bemused by the neat motives all the suspects have, and looks forward to the final scene where the detective gathers them all together. But there's nothing sedate (in the Christie manner) about Sandford's high-octane narrative, which unspools its powerful effects while broadening the initial death of a company chairman into a scenario involving far greater matters than the murder of a single man. The prose is lean and pared down, and the 300 odd pages will turn very quickly for most readers.

Barry Forshaw

I Should Have Stayed Home by Horace McCoy, Serpent's Tail Midnight Classics, £6.99

This is a very welcome reprinting of one of the least known of the great Hollywood novels, a book with many similarities to McCoy's well-known *They Shoot Horses Don't They*, and also seemingly the inspiration for Billy Wilder's screenplay of *Sunset Boulevard*.

Ralph Carson and Mona Matthews are movie extras, looking for the big break. Mona curses out a judge during a friend's trial, the resulting notoriety gains them entry into Hollywood society, and corruption follows as sure as the sun sets into the Pacific. Carson becomes toy boy to Mrs. Smithers, rich and influential. Not only does he despise himself (remember William Holden in *Sunset Boulevard*), but McCoy uses the situation to show us exactly why Carson, and a million other good looking kids with talent never will make it in the human jungle of Hollywood. The setting and tone is eerily familiar from Wilder's movie.

It all gains impact from McCoy's hardboiled prose; nearly sixty years later it catches the reader and won't let go. You're drawn along, much as the characters themselves are, like marathon dancers who can't keep going but can't afford to stop. A brilliant little book, much deserving of this reprinting, and more attention. Bravo, Serpent's Tail.

Michael Carlson

Sixty-Three Closure by Anthony Frewin No Exit Press, £6.99

Lee Harvey Oswald passed through Britain, one way or another, on his way to defect in Moscow. Just exactly where, when, how and why has never really been confirmed, but it provides the foundation for Anthony Frewin's latest conspiracy thriller. If *Sixty-Three* doesn't actually provide us with much closure, it's more because that British link is tenuous, and whatever questions it may raise about the Oswald the agent or Oswald the patsy, it doesn't go very far to providing the answers to the bigger questions.

London Blues, Frewin's previous novel, was set in the middle of the Profumo affair, and as such was able to provide a more convincing and compelling set of conspiracies. Because the characters were directly involved in the incidents at the core of the story, it was a more involving narrative.

Here, Christopher Cornwell, (homage to McCarry's Paul Christopher and LeCarre, perhaps?) who like Frewin, works as an assistant on movies, is drawn into a mystery which has already caused the death of his best friend. If, in the logic of conspiracy thrillers, it's never quite clear why certain people possessing knowledge are killed, while others who possess the same knowledge, and are aware of the killings, are allowed to live, that's a minor point. The story bogs down at time with details of meals and courtship in the boho world of Hertfordshire, but it picks up again for a frame-up climax that packs more punch than everything which has led up to it.

Though you wonder how helpless Cornwell's solicitor girlfriend would really be. You also wonder why he never saw *Defence Of The Realm* and realised what you have to do with sensitive and dangerous information when security services are after you.

London Blues was a tough act to follow. If *Sixty-Three Closure* isn't able to do that, it may be because the real mysteries of Oswald, in Dallas and in Britain, overshadow it too much.

Michael Carlson

Small Vices by Robert B Parker, John Murray, £16.99

My reaction to Spenser is like Homer Simpson's to doughnuts: is there anything he can't do? Although the world's toughest politically-correct sensitive man has become a parody of himself in recent decades, *Small Vices* has a hard edge that reminds us of just how well Robert Parker can do this stuff when he tries.

Spenser is hired by a former DA to look into the conviction of a ghetto black, Ellis Alves, for the rape-murder of a white college student. His public defender is convinced he was innocent and she blew the case, and the former DA is inclined to agree. So Spenser starts to investigate, and dredge up a dumpster full of ugliness: corruption, bigotry, class barriers, all in the leafy suburbs of Boston. What makes it interesting is that if Ellis Alves is innocent, the likely suspect is Clint Stapleton, adopted son of a wealthy white family. But Clint, although light-skinned, is also black.

It's the richest background Parker has provided in some time, full of contrasts and echoes. Spenser and Susan are debating whether to adopt a child, and of course children are at the core of this story. Then, as the mystery reaches saturation point, Parker switches the story 180 degrees, by bringing in a professional hit man. It allows for some padding, but it also works because it gets us back to the core of Spenser's character, the original hard boiled stuff that has got softer boiled as the years go by. Though the young girls still seem to go for the increasingly middle-aged ex-boxer!

Parker handles the finish with enough panache to make it almost believable, and that's good enough. This is the best Spenser novel in some years, and that is, after all, high praise.

Michael Carlson

Snap by John Burns, Macmillan, £16.99

Anyone ploughing their way through a Media Studies course should immediately torch their text books and read John Burns's *snap*. *Snap* is the second outing for Burns' anti-hero Max Chard, a typically hard-drinking tabloid hack who has learnt the art that many journalists take a lifetime to master—how to successfully fiddle your expenses. And Burns, an award-winning crime reporter with the Daily Express for many years, knows about such things.

He also knows how to re-create the atmosphere of a News Desk under siege from an over-wrought editor and a circulation in free-fall. Not that Max Chard spends much time at the *office*. When not cuddling a G&T or his long suffering girlfriend Rosie, he's out there on the concrete of London searching for that exclusive that will make his name.

In the sad absence of a Profumo or a Watergate, Max settles to investigate the murder of a Dutch au-pair involved in drug dealing. Although Chard's investigative techniques owe much to Police methods, he also employs schemes far removed from the Police rule book (is there really one?)

Burns also scatters just enough herrings to throw the reader off course but still gives you a sporting chance to solve the case. Although many crime writers can achieve this balance, there are not many who can write such fresh, sharp and witty dialogue along the way.

If you like comedy thrillers, this is the book for you.

Macmillan also tell me that *Hack*, the first Max Chard novel (originally published in a low volume paperback original by Masquerade Publications in 1996) is published simultaneously with *Snap* as a Pan paperback priced £5.99

David Howard

**The Reckoning by Keith Baker,
Headline, Hbk, £16.99,
ISBN 0747218447**

Consider this. Tom Gallagher is a man haunted by spectres from his past. He was an FBI agent whose carefully orchestrated plot to apprehend members of an organised crime syndicate went horribly awry, resulting in the deaths of two of his colleagues. Not only does Gallagher feel the onerous weight of guilt for what he perceives as his responsibility for these deaths, but he also has a failed marriage on his over-burdened conscience. He suffers a mental breakdown, finding solace and a dubious friend in the dreaded bottle. Eventually pensioned off by the FBI, he returns to his native Dublin to pick up the pieces of his fragmented personal life. But his daughter, Emma, the offspring from his marriage and now a high-profile minister in Irish government is estranged from the father she never knew. Gallagher's attempts at reconciliation with Emma come to naught. In fact, it seems that he is seeking to undermine her governmental authority when he writes a newspaper article that threatens to compromise her political position.

However, just when you think our beleagured hero will do the honourable thing and borrow a rope from his neighbour, one day, out of the blue, Gallagher is confronted by a face from the past. The face belongs to one of his old adversaries, Gilbert Leslie, a nefarious criminal mastermind who conceals his not only ruthlessness but a pychotic sexual neurosis behind a facade of corporate respectability. Although Gallagher recognises Gilbert as his personal nemesis, he is forced to galvanise himself and confront the past so that he can begin living in the present.

OK, so it's not the most original of ideas but Keith Baker's adroitly-written tale about an international organised crime syndicate choosing to infiltrate the Irish economy to launder drug money is a tense page-turner.

The Reckoning is a conventional thriller but Baker spins a cleverly-plotted, enjoyable yarn. The central character, Gallagher is in the mould of the once-classic, now somewhat clich,d flawed hero who's gone to hell and back, but, as you can probably guess, comes out a better person for it in the end. Baker utilises all his current affairs journalistic prowess to paint a convincing picture of the Machiavellian skullduggery and corruption that permeates democratic politics. Baker also provides an arresting set-piece of political Russian roulette in an tense exchange between government and opposition MPs in the Irish parliament.

This is a story that melds media-manipulation, political intrigue, organised crime, drug cartels and computer-hacking with its hero's own personal redemption. The fast-paced action is charged by nerve-jangling scenes of graphic violence and an impressive showdown in a shopping centre.

Ultimately, Baker's ambigious ending suggests that the fight against organised crime is a somewhat futile one as the real perpetrators have ways and means of eluding justice. But I guess that's life: not everything ends happily ever after.

Charles Waring

Head Injuries by Conrad Williams, Frontlines/The Do-Not Press £5

To use Morecambe as a setting for a violent and haunting thriller is a brave thing for an author to do. Morecambe?!? But Williams uses the very ordinariness of his setting in an extremely clever and evocative way, making every banal location of an English seaside town atmospheric and threatening. The hero, David, is summoned to Morecambe, despite his wish never to return to the place. Like the town in winter, he feels empty and dispirited by his life of drink, substance abuse and casual sex. A meeting with his old friends, Helen and Seamus, soon brings spectres of the past to destructive life. The friends attempt to pinpoint the source of the violence that has been menacing them, and Williams' graphic descriptions of the sex and mayhem that ensues defines the book as suitable for only the least shockable of readers – even if William occasionally gives the impression of striving rather too hard for effect. Lean, compelling prose marks this out as a thriller of real distinction.

Barry Forshaw

Dirty Laundry by Don Taylor, Serpent's Tail, £8.99

The anti-hero of Taylor's sharply written first novel, Errol Oldfield, is living under considerable pressure from his chequered past, sexual fantasies, and drink-fuelled paranoia. While working in a downmarket discount shop (and supplementing his income by dipping into the till and salmon poaching), he pursues the alluring divorcee Maxine. However, Maxine is fixated on the star striker of the football team in the north-eastern town in which Taylor sets his novel. Errol's actions become more extreme, with catastrophic consequences. There's a canny synthesis here between the gritty realism of American writers like James Elroy and the working class fantasies of Dennis Potter. The narrative is wild and surprising, with the protagonists behaving every bit as badly as in the American West Coast novels that inspired Taylor.

Barry Forshaw

Tooth & Nail by John B. Spencer, Bloodlines / The Do-Not Press, £7

Property speculation, with no holds barred, is the name of the game for Reggie Crystal and Terry Reece-Morgan. Between them they have half of west London in their pockets. However, their own personal problems are about to tear them from their positions of power. Crystal's bizarre sexual practices, and Reece-Morgan's desire to end the life of his invalid wife, create a recipe for disaster when the psychopathic Darren comes into their lives. John B. Spencer is a writer with a singularly distinctive voice, and brings to his very British milieu of Rackmanesque greed and violence a racy grasp of plotting and utterly authentic dialogue. The characters may be unlovely, but we watch them as fascinated as we might be by the squabbles of reptiles. Spencer has shown a steady growth through his last five gritty novels, and this is well up to par.

Barry Forshaw

Bad to the Bone by James Waddington, Dedalus, £7.99

Setting a blackly comic novel in the commercialised world of sports cycling already marks out Waddington's hilarious and surreal book as something different. But when we are also presented with sharp insights into drugs, health, exploitation and sanity, it's quickly apparent that this is a book in danger of biting off more than it can chew. Triumphantly, however, Waddington makes his breathless narrative (set against the backdrop of the Tour de France) a riveting read. Akil Saenz, the handsome and athletic cyclist – who well may be the greatest the world has ever known – is poised to win an unprecedented sixth Tour de France when the doctor of a rival team mysteriously ensures that he is beaten by inferior riders with bizarre mental deterioration accompanying their phenomenal riding skills. Grotesque murders are also taking place, and Saenz realises to his horror that he will have to work with the sinister Dr Fleishman to achieve his much hoped-for glory. You've never read anything quite like this, and Waddington is clearly a unique talent to watch.

Barry Forshaw

Filth by Irvine Welsh, Jonathan Cape, £9.99, H £16.99

Welsh has set himself a difficult task with the unprecedented success of *Trainspotting* and his other books. By striking off in a different direction, he may lose a few of the readers who wish him to stay in the comic drug milieu he has made his own. But those who recognise that a good writer has to freshen the brew will find the new book a fascinating, witty and innovative novel. Detective Sergeant Bruce Robertson begins his Christmas with a week of sex and drugs in Amsterdam. But he's in bad shape: an unshakeable cocaine habit and his messy string of extramarital affairs make it difficult for him to focus on the grisly murder he's obliged to solve. And as Robertson careers through the lower depths, he encounters an adversary very close to home that makes this tale of a corrupt, misanthropic cop as funny, disturbing and intelligent as anything being written today. The fainthearted are given fair warning by the title: Welsh makes the *Trainspotting* locales seem like the home counties with the vividly described sleaze of his new book.

Barry Forshaw

A Long Finish by Michael Dibdin, Faber and Faber, £16.99, ISBN: 0571193412

It's easier to admire some writers than actually be caught liking them. With his latest Aurelio Zen mystery, supposed crime heavyweight Michael Dibdin has tipped even that scale.

Consider: this, like the others, is published by Faber and Faber, which automatically bestows a certain prestige when the broadsheet reviewers comes a knocking. A publisher with a pedigree, and one willing to finance that authorial grail: the hardback printing. Dibdin, it says, is a *serious* writer.

And Dibdin can write. If you've ever read any of the Zens you can testify to that. On a basic level—words in front of other words, nicely milled sentences, elegant paragraphs—he'll turn in an entirely proficient job. But that's not at issue, not when he's authoring books as anaemic, as thoughtlessly bland as *A Long Finish*. It sets up a cast of exotically monikered Italians and some mildly diverting plot details about wine and murder and patriarchy and family, and resolves them neatly. It's superior mystery spinning of a kind that, even under her own name, Ruth Rendell can do in her sleep. It's writing that never gets its hands dirty.

Psychologically Dibdin can't hold a candle to Barbara Vine or even (on TV rather the page) Morse, and his characterisation is lamentable racked against, say, fellow countryman John Harvey. (For all the bumbling pretension, Aurelio Zen is a mere aperitif to Resnick's meaty desperation.) The humour is staid and middle-class, and for a book with such an exotic setting, a sense of place is woefully lacking.

This very polite, very *professional* book is at least better than his alleged 'thriller' *Dark Spectre*, but is as equally unsatisfying as either crime writing or contemporary fiction. On this evidence, Aurelio Zen, if not Dibdin himself, would do well to retire quietly from the game.

Gerald Houghton

Pretty Ballerina by John Wessel, Viking, £9.99, ISBN: 0670866083

Chicago. Some of Ritchie's videostore customers will pay handsomely for anything from the early *ouvre* of Cassie Ryan. Not *D-Cup Zombies* or *Biker Bitches From Hell* nor any of the fake-blood stuff. That has no frisson, no *jolt*. Not like *Pacific Rimmed* or *Personal Breast*. Not the films this baby doll made *before* she was legal.

But that's not why this former Lolita lovely hires ex-PI and sometime gaolie (sic) Harding. No, what Cassie Ryan wants is someone to find her kid brother Kim who vanished twenty-two years ago from off of a church bus—all that remains of a family slaughtered by her psychotic. And now she's receiving cryptic notes that stir old memories. Reopen old wounds.

Wessel's novel is unpretentious stuff. Taking its cue from the infamous Traci Lords debacle, it elects to play a tight game, swiftly establishing its stock cast—rich porn collectors, enigmatic Vietnamese detectives, veteran stone-killers—then moving about the board until only the guilty and the damaged remain.

Nothing so frighteningly original then, but at least a game played with a degree of wit and verve on Wessel's part. One in which he almost pulls off the difficult trick of rendering Harding both smart-arse *and* likeable. Almost. And at only 240 pages, it certainly doesn't out-stay its welcome.

What it can't do, however, is leap the hurdle anyone penning a book like this sets for themselves: the solution has to come from within characters we already know. As a consequence there will always be a degree of *ho-hum* about the resolution that no amount of clever, rain-soaked manoeuvring will overcome. Bearing that one minor caveat in mind, *Pretty Ballerina* comes cautiously recommended.

Gerald Houghton

The Silent Cry by Kenzaburo Oe, Serpent's Tail, Pbk, £6.99, ISBN: 1852426020

This is a disconcerting read for so many reasons. Not the least is the 68-year-old author's 1994 Nobel Prize for Literature; a sense of expectation settles in before you even part its pages. And all the more with *The Silent Cry*, published originally in 1967,

held up by the awarding Committee as the very pinnacle of Oe's achievement. There is an almost unique burden upon relatively slender shoulders.

Nor does it stop there. Our narrator is Mitsu, with his one-eye, dipsomaniac wife and institutionalised child who *"showed no more response than a vegetable."* His troubles though—his *real* troubles—are shaped more like philandering sibling Takashi, who returns from American misadventures with thoughts of the family home. Soon the brothers up sticks for rural Japan, intent on selling up the homestead and recovering a fondly recalled hut *"with its well-remembered scent of green thatch."*

What Mitsu and Taka find, however, is the force of tradition and history intent on interceding. There is a sitting tenant—literally—in the considerable shape of *"Japan's fattest woman"* Jin, tensions between the indigenous population and immigrant Koreans, memories of a sister's suicide, and thoughts of a celebrated 1860 rising.

All of which rather generates a false sense of security in this absorbing, occasionally crude comedy of manners. For the latter half is far stranger, far darker, finding as it does Taka as nominal leader of a new rising in the valley. One that no longer masks its hatred for the Koreans, one that loots the local supermarket, and one which culminates in tragedy and, just possibly, redemption.

Spirits haunt the pages of this

complex, challenging book, with their formidable questions of guilt and responsibility rendered with a clear head and in deceptively accessible prose. And, yes, there is a murder, the book does turn violent and confrontational (shades of JG Ballard) as order breaks down, but this is far from being easily labelled crime fiction. It is not a book to be approached that lightly nor forgotten so quickly.

Gerald Houghton

Dirty Laundry by Paul Thomas, Vista, £5.99, ISBN: 0575603933

Wallace Guttle, a PI who gets off on the sex-ploits of his targets, gets three bullets in the forehead for his troubles. Businessman Victor Appleyard took a final dive off of the Auckland harbour bridge, leaving a merry widow and a whole mess of trouble for disgraced reporter and failed gigolo Reggie Sparks. Maverick cop Tito Ihaka is just trying to make sense of it all.

It's hardly promising when a novelist comes billed as *"the down-under Carl Hiaasen"* by his publisher, but this second from New Zealand's Paul Thomas very nearly fits the bill. Like those of his Floridian cousin, the plot—which revolves around the 1970 suicide of a young woman at an exclusive public school—is ludicrous, needlessly convoluted and extremely diverting. But more pointedly, Thomas' deft characterisation and sense of violent absurdity save *Dirty Laundry* from simple pastiche.

This book is not just a comic American thriller transplanted to the Southern Hemisphere, finding in its mix of erstwhile SAS-loons, Oz Mafiosi and psychotic, blood-drinking Maori gangs an original voice with a real feel for location.

Vista are already promising two more Thomas books (including his award-winning debut, *Inside Dope*), but don't wait until everyone wants a piece: hitch a ride aboard this particular bandwagon now.

Gerald Houghton

Magic Hoffmann by Jakob Arjouni, No Exit Press, £6.99, ISBN 1874061718

After four years, Fred 'Magic' Hoffmann is finally out again—free at last and ready to live. Four years of biding his time, of waiting for the moment when he would finally leave the prison gates behind and meet Nickel and Annette again, his partners in crime, with whom he planned and executed a not unimpressive bank robbery that greatly surprised everyone in his small home town. Sure, his friends got away and Hoffmann got caught—but he knows they won't let him down, they're waiting for him with his share of the loot, and then off to Canada they'll all go, the inseparable trio, living a life free of bourgeois constraints. Making their dreams come true, doing everything they'd ever seen in the movies, and giving the finger to all the squares left behind in Germany.

TANNER ON ICE
by Lawrence Block

THE FIRST NEW EVAN TANNER NOVEL FOR 26 YEARS!

Evan Tanner, a globetrotting adventurer to put Indiana Jones in the shade, not only had his sleep centre destroyed in the Korean War but now he has been on extended vacation...in the deep freeze for over 25years! Thawed but not shaken, Tanner has a lot of catching up to do. No sooner than he's reacquainted himself with Minna, his "adopted daughter" and now a beautiful and desirable women and mastered a crash course in Internet learning than he is recruited for another covert assignment - to destablise the government of Burma (or should that be Myanmar?) and he finds himself in Rangoon (or is that Yangon?) Mix in exotic surroundings, an exiled Russian beauty, foreign intrigue, cross and double cross, a mysterious dead man and you have an edgy and entertaining puzzle that only Lawrence Block could create.

Praise for Burglar in the Library:
"Extremely funny and laid back"—Literary Review
"A genuine treat"—The List
"The pace is brisk, the dialogue snappy..and the hook of the Chandler first edition is lovely"—TLS
"..a homage to the golden age of murder mysteries"—Donna Leon, The Sunday Times

Lawrence Block is one of the most respected and best-selling names in mystery fiction and has won three Edgar and four Shamus awards. He is the author of eight Bernie Rhodenbarr, "Burglar" mysteries and this is his eighth Evan Tanner novel, all published by No Exit Press

ISBN: 1 901982 33 5 PRICE: £10hb
A NO EXIT ORIGINAL

It all does go horribly wrong, of course. A lot has changed during those four years that Hoffmann has been locked away. Although he considers himself clever beyond measure, he is too thick to realise that he has become a relic from the past. His verbal mannerisms get on everyone's nerves and his jokes are considered offensive these days. What was a slick rebel in the Eighties is a convicted criminal now, an embarrassment to all, a man the outside world would rather have forgotten about.

Unperturbed by all this, Fred sets out to track down his friends. To his surprise (and confirming the reader's suspicions), this proves to be harder than anticipated. Also, Fred discovers that not only the times have changed—the people he thought he knew are quite different, too. When he finally meets up with Annette in Berlin, he is shocked to find out that the shared dream of starting a new life in Canada was never more than a fanciful flight of the imagination to her. It appears she's quite happy now, managing a film studio in what after the Berlin wall came down has become Germany's hottest city. Never mind, thinks Magic Hoffmann, finding Nickel is more important anyway, since he is the one who has Hoffmann's share of the money. Canada is only a few phone calls away...

This is about as much as I dare reveal of the plot without fear of spoiling the book for the reader. Whether *Magic Hoffmann* is about *"one man's refusal to be brought down by his country and 'his friends'"* (as the publisher claims) or simply the fascinating and sympathetically told story of an incredibly stupid git, readers will have to decide for themselves. Thanks to the talents of author Arjouni, the story of hapless underdog Fred Hoffmann is funny and occasionally quite poignant, but never predictable. This is not so much a crime novel but rather an exploration of friendship and the uneasiness we feel when confronted with a friend from the past who doesn't seem to have changed at all. If this was a British novel, it would soon become an acclaimed Channel 4 film, starring Robert Carlyle and directed by Mike Leigh in one of his jollier moods. A highly recommended read.

Frank Thielmann

Cold Writer

Nothing Personal by Jason Starr, £6.99, ISBN: 1 901982 05 X

If you were one of the lucky people who discovered Jason Starr with last year's *Cold Caller*, you'll be so pleased he's got another book out that you probably won't stop to ask if it's any good. So I'll save you the trouble—it is *very* good. If you expected him to repeat the first person hell of *Cold Caller* you'll be disappointed however. *Nothing Personal* is a third person narrative detailing the problems of a sort of groteque extended family: Joey 'The Jinx' DePino is a compulsive gambler, his wife Maureen overeats, Leslie is anorexic and her husband David has panic attacks. When Joey concocts a perfect, but sick, plan to pay off his gambling debts and David confronts his Chinese mistress who has been stalking his family, four problematic lives are about to collide. It's the general lack of concern for anyone but themselves which makes Starr's characters so perversely appealing. You find yourself agreeing with their twisted logic and having to pull back, saying *"hey...just a minute."*

It's impossible to find a matrix from which Starr's flexible and commanding prose style evolved. He reads unlike anyone else, with a totally surprising use of language (both idiomatic and precisely detailed) that never ceases to exhilarate. Some, it has to be said, have found it too heady a mix – but those prepared to enter his world know that they're in an exhilarating *terra incognito* with few sign posts to help them. Sometimes, with Starr's characters, we think we've identified someone cut from familiar cloth, but we are soon disabused of such notions. Protagonists behave with a totally convincing logic in terms of their motives, even when their motives are off-the-wall.

But it's Starr's plotting which puts him in the upper echelons of current crime writers. If, at times, plausibility may be stretched, this is at the service of the kind of narrative that has an almost operatic gusto and vigour. Of course, his name is only gradually becoming known to the majority of crime readers – but that makes those of us who've discovered him able to retain a satisfying smugness about our own perceptiveness. For a little time longer at least.

Brian Ritterspak

So, what's it like documenting the lives of all-American psychopaths anyway? Over to you, Jason...

MY NEW NOVEL is *Nothing Personal*. Like my first novel, *Cold Caller*, it is set in New York, but *Nothing Personal* is a bigger, more complex book. There are two major characters—a compulsive gambler and an ad executive; two main plots, several subplots, and the story is told from multiple points of view. After *Cold Caller*, which has a more traditional noir first-person style, I wanted to try a different approach.

Hemingway was the first writer I was inspired by because his style is so seemingly simple to imitate. For this same reason I went through my "Raymond Carver phase." But after a while I realised that Carver and Hemingway are much more complex than they first appear and the

trick is to find your own voice. Of course, from this time, I have some work that will always stay in my bottom drawer: except for a few characters and plot ideas I'd like to rekindle someday, most of my early writing sucks. When I was moving a couple of years I threw out most of it and eventually I'll probably throw the rest of it. And believe me I'm not the type of writer who has no objectivity about his own work—I have no hidden treasures.

I've read almost every Elmore Leonard novel. I also like Russell Banks, Patricia Highsmith, James M. Cain and James Michener—to name a few writers whose novels are stacked on my night table right now. I probably don't read as many new crime novels as I should.

I don't think there is any set rule with regard to the more extreme elements of crime fiction. Some writers, like Eddie Bunker, use a lot of violence in their work and it works—others have a lot of violence and it seems gratuitous. Personally, I like well-written violent crime novels because, let's face it, crime, by definition, is violent.

With regard to sexuality, I think this depends on a writer's style and preferences. I try to only put scenes in my novels that push the action forward, and I try never to include a sex scene just for the sake of having a sex scene. But if I thought the sex scene was important to the plot or funny or served some purpose, would definitely include it. I probably wouldn't hold back either—in fact, I'd probably go over the top with it. In *Nothing Personal*, there is a sex scene early on in the book, but it's only there because I thought it was necessary.

I try to write for at least a few hours every day. Some days I just revise—other days I write 5-10 pages. I try not to put too much pressure on myself. I know if I write a few pages a day every six months or so I'll finish a book. When I finish my rough drafts, my wife edits and suggests all sorts of changes. I stubbornly refuse and then a few hours later I realise she's right and I give in.

Why do people read crime fiction? Entertainment. Escape. Fun. In all likelihood, the winner of the next Booker Prize won't be a crime novel. But that doesn't mean that a crime novels can't make statements—I just think the statement should be within the context of entertaining, plot-driven novels that people enjoy reading. Perhaps that way the statements can be even more powerful.

My writing is heavily influenced by movies—maybe even more so than books. Sometimes I try to envision my books as films as I'm writing them. It helps me visualise the scenes—make sure there's enough action. I sometimes use lyrics from songs, but I wouldn't say that music is an influence. And speaking of movies, *Cold Caller*, was recently optioned by the producer of the forthcoming movie *Fight Club*, starring Brad Pitt, Helena Bonham Carter, and Ed Norton. Kevin Allen, who directed the movie *Twin Town*, is attached as director, and a screenplay is currently being written.

I had a professor in college, John Vernon (not the actor who played the villain in *Point Blank*), who encouraged me a great deal. The fact that he was a successfully published novelist was also an inspiration. We talked about plot and character, I recollect. With me, the precise order of importance in this area varies. Sometimes I come up with the plot idea first, sometimes I think of the characters. But I don't think character can ever be too strong.

New York—since I've lived here my whole life and because most of my novels and stories take place here, this is my city in every sense of the word. I think it's important to write about places you know well. But I have ideas for stories and novels that take place in other cities that I hope to write someday—but for the time being I'm sticking with New York.

I've only had great experiences with publishers so far. My first two novels have been first published in England by No Exit, which I guess is kind of unusual for an American writer, but it has worked out great. *Cold Caller* was sold back to Norton in the States and there will also be publications in Germany and France. Maybe grisly experiences await me, but so far, so good.

I try only to think about the mechanics of the plot and the characters while I'm writing, rather than any hypothetical reader. Hopefully, if it works for me it'll work for readers. I'm also very secretive and superstitious about unfinished works. I fear that if I discuss an unfinished work it will remain that way forever.

I think more people are reading than ever. Just look at the success of Amazon.com. If you use the Internet you have to know how to read so the future. And the Net is a way of travelling. As for actual travel: I suppose it depends on what the writer's travelling budget is. But I'd like to see myself as a writer of the world.

My next book is a darkly comic crime novel set, once again, in New York. Stylistically, it is another departure for me. There is a major character who is a professional criminal, which is also a slight departure for me because the characters in *Cold Caller* and *Nothing Personal* are strictly amateurs.

Gumshoes, blues and the latest news: Slow Dancer Press

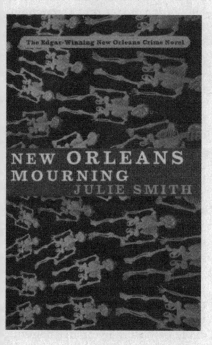

by Ian Bell

WITH A TRIPLE WHAMMY of something old, something new, something borrowed and something blue, John Harvey's Slow Dancer Press, previously associated with poetry, launches its crime list this autumn.

The first of the three handsomely presented initial titles is something old, a reissue of Neville Smith's 1971 Liverpool PI novel, *Gumshoe*. Originally published as a 'novelisation' of Smith's own original screenplay, the book is inevitably a bit thin in characterisation and atmosphere, but it is occasionally very funny in expression, and it rips along engagingly. The central character, winningly played on screen by Albert Finney, is Liverpool bingo caller and would-be comic Eddie Ginley, who through a series of accidents finds himself acting as a private eye, caught up in a complex sanctions-busting scam. Voiced as a pastiche of Chandler (again!) the story has its echoes of Billy Liar, as well as of the jokier side of crime fiction. A bit like Mike Ripley, only funny. The early 70s period setting now lends charm, with references to Edward Heath and his gang, the Rhodesia crisis, Everton as league champions, 16mm film and the newly-arrived 'colour' TVs. Less charming was the references to black characters as 'spades', but you can't rewrite history I guess. This reissue contains a brief foreword by the film's director, Stephen Frears, but he has disappointingly little to say. So a good enough start, and remember to look out for the movie popping up late at night on your colour TV.

The second title is both something borrowed, and something new, in the UK at least. Julie Smith's *New Orleans Mourning* was published in the States in 1991, but this is its first appearance over here. Winner of Edgar Allan Poe Award for Best Novel, it is very welcome indeed. Set in a beautifully realised New Orleans, it is worked around the attempts by Skip Langdon, a rather ungainly female police officer, to solve the murder of a prominent citizen very publicly carried out at the Mardi Gras parade. But although the plot is complex and intriguing, and the central character both idiosyncratic and plausible, the book uses these generic features to give a meticulous account of life in Louisiana. The nuances of social class and prejudice along racial and sexual lines are fascinatingly developed. Sometimes reading like a cross between *Fargo*, and *Midnight in the Garden of Good and Evil* the novel gives a terrific portrait of place, class and race. If Smith's other seven Skip Langdon novels are

anything like as good as this then they would be very welcome. Any more, Slow Dancer?

And finally, something blue. John Harvey himself has edited a collection of eighteen original short stories, *Blue Lightning*, all of which have some musical element. And as readers of the Charlie Resnick series must know, Harvey's own extensive knowledge of jazz runs throughout his writing. Not all the stories have a lot to do with crime, but there are good pieces from well-known writers including Liza Cody, Michael Z Lewin, Walter Mosley, Ian Rankin and James Sallis. Harvey himself offers a Resnick short story, but without the supportive context of the novels, it looks light-weight. In fact, this anthology is really for dipping in rather than for tearing through. The best stories are very good, and even the weaker ones are professional. Of the three books published, this seemed the weakest, but it still had its moments.

So Slow Dancer make a pretty good beginning, enterprising in the choice of issues, professional in presentation. Future publications include new work by Brian Thomson and Bill Moody, indicating ambition and thoughtfulness. Independent publishers are always welcome, and in the crime field they can be influential too. John Harvey says that the next Resnick novel—his tenth—will be the last, alas. Let us hope that through Slow Dancer he continues to help animate crime writing.

Books in Brief:
Short Sentences

Legacy by Murray Smith, Michael Joseph, £16.99, 0718143353

Big Jack Fitzrowan, baronet and electronics millionaire dies sailing his yacht off Nantucket sound, precipitating a bit of a kerfuffle dynasty-wise. For Big Jack's firstborn is illegitimate and missing. If found, said missing sprog will inherit most of BJ's fortune.

This does not of course leave the rest of the family in the best of moods—down in the mouth would be a fair description of their general mien. All sorts of folk get involved—mistresses, cops, you name it... and then ('fess up, you were waiting for this) it turns out that Jack's demise might not have been the accident it seemed. Great fun, by the man who bought you *Strangers* and *Bulman* on the telly. Just for elevating Don Henderson to icon standard he deserves a cheer or two. Check this out if you like big, bold, plot-driven adventure.

Wendy Lawrence

One of us by Michael Marshall Smith, Harpercollins, £14.99, 0002256002

Here's something different for techno-thriller fans. Hap Thompson, an ex-

everything (con, husband, barman) is working as a REMtemp—having other peoples dreams for them—when he's offered work caretaking memories (those of you who've seen *Johnny Mnemonic* will be having the impression that *you're* caretaking someone's memories by now I dare say...). This is squarely illegal, but very profitable.

One night hap takes on a bigger memory than usual and his client disappears. Unless he can find her he's off to chokey for what he holds in his head, and worse, something *really nasty* lies at the end of the memory...

It's little surprise that Smith's previous book is in development with Spielberg. He delivers high-concept ideas with a warmth and humour that's unusual in this field. One to watch out for.

Wendy Lawrence

Sejanus by David Wishart, Sceptre, £16.99, 0340684461

From beyond the grave amateur detective Marcus Corvinus (...errr, did I mention we're in ancient Rome? No? We are.) receives a commission from the Empress Livia. She would like to have Emperor Tiberius's deputy and likely successer, Sejanus, killed.

Approached by two senators who want him to dig up some dirt on Sejanus, Corvinus accepts. The book, like its predecessors *I, Virgil, Ovid, Nero* and *Germanicus* is witty and entertaining with a ribald nature that gives you a genuine feel for the age that Wishart is recreating.

Wendy Lawrence

High Crimes by Joseph Finder, William Morrow, $24.95, 0688149626

An efficient courtroom drama from the author of *The Zero Hour*. This one's already been made into a film due to the seemingly endless appetite people have for this sort of book. I blame the cancellation of *Perry Mason* and *Crown Court* myself.

Claire Heller Chapman's world falls apart when her husband Tom is arrested by a team of government agents and accused of a brutal crime. Which of course, he says he didn't commit (men!).

Claire, a high-profile criminal defence attorney and a Harvard law professor, must put her reputation on the line to defend Tom in a top-secret court-martial. As she searches for evidence that will clear Tom she finds a high-level conspiracy that threatens the lives and careers of herself and her loved ones.

Wendy Lawrence

Death of a Good Woman by Max Marquis, Macmillan, £16.99, 0333654072

In Max Marquis's fourth novel about Detective Inspector Harry Timberlake an investigation into the murder of a quiet, church-going woman leads him into the criminal underworld seeking a murderer.

Mary Docker is found stabbed forty-three times with a kitchen knife, but despite his best efforts Timberlake can't discover a motive, never mind a murderer. Only odd events in his own love life prompt him to consider a connection between the murder of Mary Docker and those of several high-class call girls. *Death of A Good Woman* is a distinctly different variant on the traditional British Police Procedural.

Wendy Lawrence

The Contractor by George Brown, Piatkus, £17.99, 0749904399

You either like this kind of book or you don't. It's CIA conspiracy time again, and we go back to 1974 as the San Franciso Police Department stumble onto a deeply incriminating CIA secret. Somewhere in South-East Asia is an agent who penetrated the enemy and supplied the highest quality information. But the price has been high—too high. And the agent known as Contractor must die to cover the CIA's tracks. Good of its kind, George Brown can certainly detail a conspiracy and the writing has a nicely sardonic edge to it.

Bob Galbraith

The Bone Yard by Paul Johnston, Hodder, £16.99, 0340694920

This book has a hero (no, don't stop me now) called—wait for it—Quintilian Dalrymple. I'll type that again - Quintilian Dalrymple. It doesn't get any better, does it? Anyway Johnston's first novel won the John Creasey Best First Novel award, in one of the years they remembered to give it, not that *that* means anything.

In fact *The Bone Yard* is a treat — 'darkly satirical' as they say (although the author seems more than a bit aware that that's what they say). Funny as well.

It's the future, 2021 to be exact and it's Edinburgh, and Edinburgh's a 'crime-free independent state' — so Blair's plans worked out then — and it's all very totalitarian. The 'subversive blues-haunted' (have dust-jacket blurb writers no shame? I can imagine Johnston crying over that one) Dalrymple is trying to solve a case in which—get this!—music tapes are being planted inside murder victims. The most amazing thing about this (to me, anyway) is that cassettes still exist twenty-odd years hence. I'd have taken a bet that recordable CDs and MiniDiscs would have been objects of scorn by then, let alone the humble cassette. The cassettes are of banned music, although as the first one is by Eric Clapton perhaps that's just wishful thinking.

Try Jack O'Connell if you want *real* dystopian gloom, but this is still an entertainment of quality. The symbolism is a bit cack handed in places, but it's nice to see someone trying something different.

Wendy Lawrence

ABC Murders by Agatha Christie, HarperCollins, £15.99, 0002310147

What can I say about the blessed Agatha that everyone else hasn't said already. Carp, wail and moan, but most crime writers would be jobless without her. The reissues continue apace, with this, one of the best of the Poirot series. If you don't know the plot, you're probably a teeeenager, but here goes; a serial killer (yes, they did exist prior to *Silence of The Lambs*) is killing people at random, in alphabetical order, leaving an ABC railway guide at the scene of the crime. Poirot receives letters from the killer, taunting him to catch the murderer. Does he? Of course he does, but not before two hundred or so enjoyable pages are devoured.

Wendy Lawrence

Gypsy Hearts by R. M. Eversz, Pan, £6.99, ISBN 0330350579

Set in Prague after the collapse of Communism, Eversz's witty and involving thriller pits a ruthless but sympathetic con-man hero (an ex-pat from LA) against a duplicitous woman who is every inch his equal. Using all the apparatus of the crime genre (wildly twisting plot, calculating characters, sudden death) Eversz creates a fascinating hybrid between the literary novel and the thriller, with the occasional straining for effect being a minor blemish. The sense of place is probably this compelling tale's strongest card, and Eversz's anti-hero might just end up as a latter-day rival of Patricia Highsmith's Tom Ripley.

Barry Forshaw

Capsule Comments
by Barry Forshaw

The most cursory glance at the new lists demonstrates the amazing range of writing in the crime and thriller genres today. Those who loathe the more sedate forms can luxuriate in the most blood-bolted of narratives, while the classic British detective story is alive and well (even if it's relocated at times to ancient Rome or nineteenth-century Egypt). Of course, it has to be said that the range of writing is perfectly matched by the range of accomplishment: the most powerful and finely-honed prose rubs shoulders with writing so execrable that it wouldn't pass muster in *The Sun*. So – what are the goodies and baddies?

John Burns' *Hack* (Pan, £5.99) has an ambivalent attitude to its tabloid crime reporter. At times Burns' own Fleet Street experience is worn rather too much on the sleeve, but the narrative moves convincingly. Reggie Nadelson's *Hot Poppies* (Faber, £14.99) is another entry in the Artie Cohen series, with a convoluted plot that owes not a little to *Gorky Park*. But the flat, spare prose is the thing here, and Nadelson has a cutting New York sensibility that informs these bitter Hammet-style chicaneries.

With *A Crime in the Neighbourhood* (Viking, £12.99), we are in debut novel territory. But Suzanne Berne quickly allays the usual fears when reading a tyro effort. Utilising her own childhood in 1970s Virginia, there's a skilful use of metaphor in the fashion in which Berne counterpoints the Watergate conspiracies with the dark family secrets of her narrative. Using a boy narrator (reminiscent of Richard Ford), Berne spins a solid tale with a grisly and satisfying dénouement.

If Robin Cook's *Toxin* (Macmillan, £16.99) seems a bit of a journeyman effort, that might be because we've become too familiar with the tropes of the medical thriller. Hard-core Cook fans will like it, but it won't win any converts. Ironically, Elmore Leonard's **Cuba** (Viking, £16.99) may disappoint his crime readers, but this Robert Stone-style non-crime novel has all the wisecracking acerbity and pithy characterisation that his aficionados know and love.

The division between the "cosies" and more sanguinary fare is blurred in several new books. With Natasha Cooper's *Creeping Ivy* (Simon & Schuster, £15.99) a mother's reaction to the disappearance of her daughter from the local playground, we may be in danger of a warmed-over narrative – particularly when barrister Trish Maguire is presented as the plucky heroine familiar from a hundred similar books. But Cooper is good on betrayal and guilt, and the final result has a nicely mordant tone.

Frederick Forsyth's encomium on a book jacket means as little as Stephen King's these days, but his plug for Murray Smith's *Legacy* (Michael Joseph, £16.99) is largely justified. More a novel of appalling behaviour than the kind of action adventure that Smith has dealt with before, this is unexceptional but gripping fare.

A couple of reliable names deliver the goods in Raymond Flynn's *Busybody* (New English Library, £5.99) and David Wishart's *Sejanus* (Sceptre, £16.99). Flynn's newest DCI Graham is no more or less than a par-for-the-course entry in a reliable series, but Wishart's latest in the increasingly overcrowded field of the ancient Roman thriller has the kind of meticulous detail that we've come to enjoy in the doyen of this genre, Steven Saylor.

How does a writer internalise the ubiquitous Chandler influence? It's possible to hack out diverting facsimiles, but Robert Wilson's *Blood is Dirt* (HarperCollins, £6.99) uses that wonderful narrative voice in a perfectly individual fashion. The great Nelson Algren is also invoked in this throbbing, sweaty tale.

Another debut and the heart sinks again. But not for long: Denise Mina's *Garnethill* (Bantam, £15.99) is an authoritative and trenchant piece, dripping with black humour and casual brutality. Mina is, as they say, a name to watch.

No reader of this magazine needs a commendation for anything by James Ellroy; suffice it to say that *L. A. Noir: the Lloyd Hopkins Trilogy* is available from Arrow at a give-away £9.99. Ditto Kinky Friedman, and a similar marking-of-the-card is necessary for *Roadkill* (Faber, £5.95). Alan Spence's *Way to Go* (Phoenix House, £12.99) won the Scottish Writer of the Year award, and although we're getting a tad over-familiar with Glaswegian crime, the

undertaking industry is a fresh (if that's the word) subject. The dialogue is a scabrous delight. More acutely observed dialogue is on display in Donald Harstad's *Eleven Days* (Fourth Estate, £9.99), with a truly exhilarating blood-shedding version of the police procedural.

But to end on a more restrained note: Ruth Dudley Edwards' *Publish and Be Murdered* (HarperCollins, £15.99) may not do anything for readers of Mark Timlin, but puts the boot into political correctness with satisfying force.

Out In Paperback - Previously Reviewed

Death Minus Zero by John Baker, Vista, £5.99, ISBN 0575602023

"The supporting cast work splendidly, and York itself is evoked in an effective series of settings. Dark and seedy, leavened with ample wit, I enjoyed this book and can imagine it making an entertaining television series"

Martin Hughes

The Reluctant Investigator by Frank Lean, Arrow, £5.99, 0749321806

"Lean writes pacy, readable fiction. If this book is to be judged by the highest standards, then I must confess to a number of reservations about it, but importantly the author does not lose sight of the need to entertain his readers; in return, I suspect that most of them will be willing to forgive the implausibilities of some elements of the plot. I must also say that I did not fully understand the significance of the title—

Cunane strikes me as being, by and large, a far-from-reluctant detective and none the worse for that … in some respects a rather more ambitious book than the average private eye/serial killer novel."

Martin Edwards

The Hanging Garden by Ian Rankin, Orion, £9.99, ISBN 0752821261

"…Rankin freshens the brew with some adroit plotting—and if the Bolshie DI hero is desperately over-familiar these days, Rankin is able to distract us with a hundred tiny details that keep thing percolating nicely. What a nice touch, for instance, to describe the contents of a cramped office while Rebus is waiting for an important phone call—it's this kind of cliché avoidance that keeps us turning the pages. And when the Yakuza make a mid-book appearance, we're well into the kind of mix that made earlier Rankins such fun. If the truth be told, something radical is needed for the next Rebus tome, but this is more than enough to justify that poll position he's now holding."

Barry Forshaw

Act Of Violence by Margaret Yorke, Warner , £5.99, ISBN 0751520241

"Set firmly in the English village world of cul-de-sacs and cow shed conversions, the reader is drawn into the tale by the conversational tone of the text which induces the feeling that one is somehow present amongst these people with their little lives and petty concerns, yet their individual natures remain opaque, adding to the overall effect of a distant familiarity…

"… I've not encountered a book like this before nor felt so unsettled by a work of fiction in a long time. This is an effective thriller, very English, very believable and all the better for it. "

Martin Hughes

Out in UK Hardcover

Hitman by Lawrence Block, Orion, £16.99

"Keller is a killer, a character who's appeared in a number of short stories previously published by Lawrence Block, now brought together as a novel, and they fit together so seamlessly that you'd hardly know it unless you'd come across them in their original form.

"Keller is a whimsical sort of cove most of the time, but occasionally he gets a little down like we all do. Not about his job, but about things like stray dogs and the state of the rain forest, which is fair enough I suppose. In fact he dispatches his victims with equilibrium and elan, and shows no sign of regret or conscience which I suppose helps if your job description is: Hired Killer. Not that Keller regards himself as such. More a sort of helping hand to a better place.

"Lawrence Block is one of the finest crime writers operating right now and I liked Keller a lot. As a matter of fact I liked him even better after held got rid of his dog and his girlfriend, but then I'm a hard hearted sort of bloke and I don't care who knows it. I hope this character runs and runs."

Mark Timlin

Historical Crime
Gwendoline Butler

Here are four historical detectives stories, all well researched, from different countries and different times. Each story has its own character.

The Riddle of St Leonard's by Candice Robb, Arrow, £5.99, ISBN 0 7493 2365 5.

To anyone with a feeling for the history of medieval England this book is a delight, as much for the ample and necessary glossary—did you know that the Anglo Saxon for the plague was manqualm?—as for the plain elegant way it is written. The dialogue is sensitively handled so you feel, yes, people *did* speak like this in fourteenth century York.

The City of York, with the Archbishop second only to Canterbury, under the threat of the plague is the scene for the series of puzzling deaths at St Leonard's Hospital. The deaths are of pensioners, which will bring money to the indebted hospital. But are they murders

A sense of place is very strong in Robb's writing; York, well mapped with the St Leonard's Hospital and the Archbishop's Palace, together with the roads, and all the country points of plot interest marked, as was the 1930's custom. Like the glossary, this map is a pleasure to have. Westminster and Windsor Castle, joined by the river Thames, appear in the sultry heat, in this lethal, plague ridden summer.

People are important too—the canny, intriguing clerics, the Keeper of the Hanaver, Richard de Ravenser and Thoresby, Archbishop of York, jockeying for position, with an eye on their own advancement, are the very essence of the politics of medieval England. I was glad to meet the character Erkenwald, clearly of Viking descent, testifying to the continuing Viking influence on York centuries after their arrival. Owen Archer, war hero, detective and his wife, who has her own career as an apothecary, are attractive, but it was the figure of the child Alisoun, a sturdy, aggressive girl orphaned by the plague, loving her horse that is all she has left in the world, who won my heart. Fourteenth century York knew real poverty and we see in this book the thin line between surviving and dying of hunger. The child Alisoun does survive, partly due to her own qualities, but many did not. It was a tough, brutal world.

Within this network of people and places, the plot moves briskly on, making an enjoyable read; you want to go on reading which is the ultimate test.

It is the author's fifth book and a sixth to come, which I shall welcome.

The Devil in Music by Kate Ross, New English Library, £5.99. ISBN 0340649267.

This adventure, set in Lombardy in the 1820s, of Kate Ross's detective Julian Kestrel, with his servant Dipper, is an exceedingly rich canvas of character, scene and plot. It is a broad and well painted canvas too, rather like a battle scene of the Napoleonic wars. In it, there is savagery, and humour and sacrifice.

But it is almost too crowded, too full of painted scenes. The hero, if indeed he is that, Julian Kestrel, is too lightly painted in and does not dominate the scene as he should, since it is he who must solve the mystery of several murders. He is crowded out by the characters who walk beside him. Lovely ladies, brave soldiers.

This is Lombardy at a time of insurrection when the yoke of Austrian oppression is resented. It is also a story of music, singers and opera.

We are treated to a panoramic view of Northern Italy in the years after the defeat of Napoleon when the struggle to throw out the Austrian rulers began. It is a beautiful country of lakes, mountains, castles and opera houses with handsome cities like Milan and Turin. Against this background the secret, underground opposition the Carbonari is fighting against the Austrians. In addition there are two murders, the mystery of which Julian Kestrel is brought in to solve.

Not everyone in this complicated scenario is exactly what they seem. Several characters are given a kind of dualism— pretending to be someone else. Crucial to the plot, indeed it *is* the plot, but hard to believe, so you have to suspend disbelief. But do this, just as you would with a Verdi opera with which, in the catalogue of family hatreds and revenges, it bears some resemblance. Ride with it though, and enjoy a galloping good tale. But you have to be feeling in a mood for romance.

The Valley of the Shadow by Peter Tremayne, Headline, £5.99. ISBN 074725780

There were times when reading this novel that I felt the author was more interested in showing us how much cleaner and more civilised was Celtic Ireland in the seventh century than the Anglo-Saxon kingdoms across the channel.

In the small clan territory of Gleann Geis under the Chieftain Laisre who serves wine (even if it is poor stuff) at dinner to its guests who stay in a hostel where they have hot baths at their command and a privy on the stairs. All sweetly scented.

I found myself wondering how this was managed and what economy supported it. Barter, we are told—they have no coinage. Although as one reads on, we learn they are not above accepting the odd coin as a sort of tip. So what about the drainage system and the hot water? The water is heated by wood fires, yes, but water is very heavy, who carries it so that two hot baths a day are on offer?

But still, there is murder and plenty of deceit in this sweet smelling fiefdom which the heroine detective Sister Fidelma must solve. She is a royal lady, a Christian and a high ranking lawyer. Fidelma is calm and always in control, she rises above all threats because she has been raised to the Niadh Nasc, the Order of the Golden Chain.

The Celtic names like Cruinn and Dinach and Artagal are hard at first for the Anglo-Saxon tongue to manage, place names like the Cruacha Dhubha even harder, this slows the reader down, but once having mastered the art of gliding over them, the reader can enjoy the smooth unravelling of the plot by Sister Fidelma. She is one of those detectives who knows all by a kind of instinct, in which she is a little like Miss Marple.

Fully to appreciate *The Valley of the Shadow* you have to enjoy reading about the court life of small Celtic kingdom; this reviewer did. If you are in the mood for detection in the seventh century this is one for you. It has charm .

Murder on the Appian Way by Steven Saylor, Robinson, £6.99, ISBN 1854878913

Any historical crime book that can tell you that Pompey had a double chin, that Mark Anthony drank ten year old red wine and let you see Cicero plain is worth reading. And there is more fascinating detail like this in Steven Saylor's book, all well-researched and accurate. Here is a rich Roman house, that of Pompey: his bathing rooms were lit by sky lights from above and with tiny windows at eye level in the wall through which could be seen glimpses of the sea, the three rooms with the water kept at just the right temperature of cold, warm and hot plunges. After this a massage from a slave and then the bather was wrapped in warm, soft towels. This was luxury but it depended, as Saylor shows, on slave labour. Slaves who were sometimes treated well, but who could be executed, or sent to the mines, or the galleys. The dialogue is straightforward, often witty, more Shavian than Shakespeare, and none the worse for that.

The mystery which Gordianus the Finder, detective, Roman citizen, must clear up is the death of Publius Clodius whom his enemy Titus Milo is suspected of killing, this at the time of consular elections. His adventures illustrate clearly the turmoil of Roman society when the Republic was in its death throes and Imperial Rome was about to be created under the Caesars.

As well as giving the reader a mystery to solve in the death of Publius Claudius, Saylor presents us with the picture of a rich, bureaucratic. violent society with a respect for the laws but which is based, in the end, on soldiers. Roman civilisation had behind it Babylonian, Egyptian and Greek societies from which it drew much. They were rich civilisations which knew both luxury and brutality; Saylor lets us know that as they were, so was Rome. You feel that the clever Finder was lucky to survive. You needed a clear head and some luck to come through in that society—also a powerful patron, of which Gordianus is wily enough to have more than one.

Fiction but it reads like the story of a real man. It was much enjoyed by this reader.

Shakespearean Whodunits
edited by Mike Ashley, Robinson,
£5.99, ISBN 1854879456
Reviewed by John Hall

The front cover tells us that the short stories in this volume are 'murders and mysteries based on Shakespeare's plays,' and this is amplified in the short introduction, which explains that some of the stories look at incidents in the plays in a search for alternative readings, and some consider the consequences of the events mentioned by Shakespeare.

By definition, all the stories are 'historical' to some extent. Any writer of historical fiction has a big gap to bridge. The main problems are background and dialogue; our American colleagues perhaps show up worst here, but the British writers are not all entirely happy with the details. Take money: one does not expect a non-specialist to know what the 'English' was, or how its value altered with geography, but the everyday currency is another matter, and when a servant is promised a sovereign for services rendered, and is given two crowns; or when an informant stays silent after being given a noble but is expected to spill the beans for an extra payment of a groat, one does just wonder if there was any primary research. This sort of thing smacks of secondary knowledge, and the Hollywood version at that—Errol Flynn producing a bulging pouch from his codpiece and telling his sidekick, 'Here are a hundred gold marks.' If he had said, 'Here are A HUNDRED MARKS IN GOLD,' that would have been fine; although the two sentences look similar, they are quite different, and that difference makes a difference. Does this matter? Yes, because if you know the right usage then it interrupts the flow. (If you don't, you'll probably be hopelessly lost in the first place.)

Dialogue is even more important—'spill the beans' and 'sidekick' are acceptable in a review written in the closing years of the twentieth century, but not in a medieval romance, and many of the writers in this collection lean too far towards modern idiom—fine, in a parody, but it sits uneasily with what is intended as a serious historical setting. It matters because the reader can get the impression that the general outlook on life was identical in 1198 or 1598 to what it is in 1998, and that isn't so; fair enough, hopes, fears and ambitions may be broadly similar, but they are phrased and pursued differently. When Shakespeare's lines are quoted in a modern matrix the results can be particularly bizarre, almost as if the writer is making fun of the original. However, some of the writers get it almost perfect, Steve Lockley ('A Sea of Troubles') and Peter Tremayne ('An Ensuing Evil') manage to be intelligible to a modern reader whilst preserving the flavour of the original texts.

As with the recent Robinson collection of Sherlock Holmes stories, a high proportion of the writers here have a background in SF and fantasy, and some of the stories are best regarded as fantasy with a light sprinkling of detection. This is particularly noticeable in some of the stories based on legend rather than history, and whether you like this approach or not is a matter of taste. Some of these stories do presuppose a good knowledge of the Shakespeare plays to which they refer, and drag in a multitude of characters, not all of whose names are immediately familiar, and consequently some of them rather lost me.

Personally I was happier with the first half-dozen tales, based on King John ('When the Dead Rise Up,' by John T Aquino), two Richards ('The Death of Kings,' by Margaret Frazer, and 'A Shadow that Dies' by Mary Reed and Eric Mayer), and three Henrys ('A Villainous Company' by Susanna Gregory, 'The Death of Falstaff' by Darrell Schweitzer, and 'A Serious Matter' by Derek Wilson), where the writers had a solid factual background to rely on. But for me the gem of the collection is 'Toil and Trouble' by Edward D Hoch, a look at the events in Macbeth from the point of view of the three witches.

The book must be regarded as a bargain, at less than six pounds for over four hundred pages. If you like Shakespeare and a blend of fantasy and detection, you'll like this. And—despite the minor gripes earlier—it would be a very critical reader who could not find anything here to intrigue or delight. Recommended.

Audio World
Ellen Cheshire

A Sight For Sore Eyes by Ruth Rendell, read by Tim Piggott-Smith, Random House Audiobooks, £8.99

Ruth Rendell's *A Sight For Sore Eyes* is a strange mix of stories concerning unhappy and indeed, in the most part, abnormal people whose lives are linked by the impossibly handsome, but lonely, Teddy Brex.

The personal stories cross class and cultural barriers as an intricately woven but nonetheless dull tale is spun. Teddy Brex is a lonely and beautiful young man who was neglected by his parents as he grew up. When he falls in love with Francine (the 'sight for sore eyes') he finds it had to believe her story of a claustrophobic and suffocating upbringing.

Their stories, told in third person, are cut together with biographical information on those who touch their lives. Some of the stories are set before they were born, and others happen concurrently with the events in the present. Perhaps, not surprisingly, since this is *Crime Time*, both Teddy's and Francine's lives have been touched by death. Francine in the dim and distant past and Teddy's more recently and far more 'hands-on'.

Perhaps it was the third person narrative style, compounded by Tim Piggott-Smith's cool and emotionally detached reading that failed to ignite any passion or life into this psychological thriller. Or maybe like many other Ruth Rendell thrillers there is just some essential missing element, which no actor can bring to life.

Ruth Rendell novels are complex, with the smallest detail being an essential piece to the larger jigsaw puzzle she creates. Through abridgement much of this is lost and as such I've found her work one of the least effective when translated to this medium.

Trial Run by Dick Francis, read by Martin Jarvis, Penguin Audiobooks, £8.99
Reflex by Dick Francis, read by Martin Jarvis, Penguin Audiobooks, £8.99

Trial Run, published in 1978, and *Reflex*, from 1980, are the latest two additions to Penguin Audiobook's growing Dick Francis audio book collection, making the current total of cassettes seventeen out of a possible thirty-six. At this rate, I'm sure it won't be too long before Penguin have caught up on the back catalogue, thus reducing their output to one a year in line with Dick Francis's annual novel.

Trial Run, written prior to the collapse of the Iron Curtain and the break up of the USSR, is set in Moscow in the months leading up to the Olympic games. A minor member of the Royal Family is keen to participate in the games (in the horse riding events—what else?) and has received threats and warnings urging him not to participate. Randall Drew, once a great rider himself but forced to retire, is chosen to go to Moscow to uncover the truth behind the threats and the recent inexplicable death of another rider.

Reflex is set back on home ground in the race courses of English steeplechasing. Philip Nore, a full-time jockey and part-time photographer is drawn into intriguing mystery which relies, unusually, not on brawn but on a knowledge of photography. The father of one of Nore's colleagues, George Millace (a professional photographer), dies in a car crash under strange circumstances, this is followed by their house being broken into on the day of the funeral, followed by a fire that brings the house to the ground. Nore takes on an active role in uncovering the mysteries of Millace's box of photographic rejects.

The two novels were abridged by Andrew Simpson, who has managed to retain the sparkle and pace of Francis's novels, which combined with Martin Jarvis's marvellously warm but yet edgy reading, makes for a further two excellent additions to the collection. I look forward to more.

Zero Option by Chris Ryan, read by Christian Rodska, Random House Audiobooks, £8.99

Although described as a thriller, I don't think *Zero Option* will find many fans amongst *Crime Time* readers. It is not bad, it's just not my thing, but if thrillers set in and around the IRA and anti-terrorism are your thing then this is a very good yarn.

Zero Option is a pacey thriller where the hero Geordie Sharp, a sergeant in the SAS, has to take on a personal battle with the IRA after they kidnap his girlfriend and his young son. When Geordie Sharp takes on a top secret assignment to rescue them if it goes wrong the Government will deny his existence and all involvement. These are the risks Geordie is prepared to take when fighting for the lives of his family.

The plot is gripping and the consequences of his and the terrorists' actions are not glamourised, they are fully worked through and examined, leaving the listener in no doubt of the risks that men like Geordie Sharp take on our behalf. Chris Ryan knows only too well what these risks entail as he was himself in the SAS for many years before retiring in 1994 to write. This

ED GORMAN
NIGHT KILLS

The odd thing was how comfortably she seemed to fit inside there, as if this were a coffin and not a freezer at all. She was completely nude and only now beginning to show signs of the freezing process, ice forming on her arms and face.

But he could tell she hadn't been in here very long because of the smells...

Frank Brolan, successful adman, unwitting fall-guy. Someone has murdered a call girl and planted her in his freezer. Frank has to find the killer before the cops find him.

As the body count rises, with the killer leaving Frank's mark at every crime, Frank flees into the night and the city. He finds help in an unlikely duo—a teenage whore and a wheelchair-bound dwarf with a mind like a steel trap...

"A painfully powerful and personal novel about three out-siders—an alcoholic advertising executive, a man twisted and disfigured by spina bifida, and a runaway teenage girl—brought together in a noir unlike any you've ever read. Violent, melancholy, bitterly humorous, Night Kills is a 'relationship' novel of the classic mould. As disturbing and sad a crime novel as I've ever read."

—CEMETERY DANCE

Price: £4.99 ISBN: 1-902002-03-2
**Available from all good bookshops, or post free
from: CT Publishing, PO Box 5880,
Birmingham B16 8JF**
Email ct@crimetime.demon.co.uk

is his third novel, and the second Geordie Shape thriller, the first being *Stand By, Stand By* also available on Random House Audiobooks read by Christian Rodska.

The novel is set in many countries with a wide cast of international SAS operatives and terrorists; Christian Rodska makes an excellent attempt to differentiate between all the characters through a variety of accents and vocal mannerisms, which ease the listener through this rather complicated and indeed convoluted thriller.

In The Red by Mark Tavener, BBC Radio Collection, £8.99

In The Red, BBC2's recent three hour TV comedy/drama/parody/crime series had previously seen life as a seven part radio series. Originally broadcast on Radio 4 in 1995, *In The Red* starred Michael Williams as George Cragge (Warren Clarke on TV) and Stephen Moore as Geoffrey Crichton-Potter (Richard Griffiths on TV), and is one of three Mark Tavener crime novels to have been broadcast on Radio 4 with Cragge as the hapless reporter caught up in shady deals and grisly murders, but the only one available on the BBC Radio Collection label.

I doubt whether the television series will ever be considered a cracking drama—there was just something missing. Great cast, fun plot, but nevertheless a disappointment—though seeing a car crashing through the doors at Broadcasting House was quite a sight. However the radio series is of a different calibre, it is far wittier and far less over the top than the TV series and therefore a real gem.

In The Red is a light-hearted and fun drama which sees George Cragge, a Radio 4 crime reporter of the old school, solving a series of bizarre murders: bank managers across London are being ingeniously killed using one pound coins as the fatal weapon. The financial world has been shaken up and the beleaguered Reform Party are making a political success on the back of the murders—but who is the murderer? And what do they have to gain by the deaths?

The sub-plot concerning Cragge's disciplinary proceedings and the machinations of the two Radio Controllers are very funny. The Controllers' plans to bring about the Director General's downfall is beautifully underplayed by Stephen Fry as the Controller of Radio 2 and John Bird as the Controller of Radio 4; they were the only two actors to survive the transition from radio to TV and hence it is their faces that made it onto the cassette's cover.

Great fun with far more subtle digs at the Beeb than the overblown TV series. Let's hope that *In The Red* sells well and then maybe the BBC will bring out Mark Tavener's other two Cragge detective dramas, *In the Balance* and *In the Chair*.

The Wood Beyond by Reginald Hill, read by Graham Roberts, Isis Audio Books, £19.99

I have always been a great lover of Dalziel and Pascoe; both the TV series and HarperCollins' six audio-book abridgements read by Warren Clarke and Colin Buchanan have always hooked me. What I've enjoyed most in these adaptations has been the double act of the university educated policeman vs the school of life copper, the old school vs the new school, the young vs the old, the by-the-book vs the break-a-few-rules which is played out so well on TV and read on the audio cassettes. The novel abridgements released by HarperCollins seem to alternate between favouring one or other of the double-act, which is why HarperCollins has Warren Clarke reading those Dalziel at its core and Colin Buchanan, Pascoe. But the humour and comradeship was always present and dominant.

Therefore it was with great excitement that I settled down with Isis Audio Book's complete and unabridged The Wood Beyond, a Dalziel and Pascoe novel. The running time of 14 hours conjured up many happy hours in the company of Dalziel and Pascoe. How disappointed I was. The action seemed slow and it wasn't until side 8 (out of 24) that Dalziel and Pascoe were united. Usually an advocate of the author's original text being maintained, I wished on this occasion that much of the detail had bee cut to quicken the pace.

The Wood Beyond, published in 1996, has Pascoe at its core where he has to come to terms with family bereavement, followed by a revelation from the past that Pascoe in the present has to investigate much to Dalziel's impatience and annoyance. Dalziel himself is having to investigate the discovery of human remains in the grounds of a laboratory which had been broken into by Animal Rights protestors.

Graham Roberts, a regular on The Archers (he plays George Barford for any Archers' fans other there), reads well enough, but inevitably I have become biased towards the familiar voices of Warren Clarke and Colin Buchanan.

All Isis Audio Books can be purchased directly, for more details call 01865 250 333.

The Wire in The Blood by Val McDermid, read by Michael Tudor Barnes, Isis Audio Books, £19.99

Anyone who read or heard Val McDermid's first Dr Tony Hill novel, The Mermaid's Singing, will have eagerly anticipated its follow-up. Well here it is. The Wire In The Blood sees Dr Tony Hill in a more formal role within the police force, having been asked to set up a national task force of psychological profilers.

The opening chapters of this complete and unabridged audio book deal with the setting up and training of a group of police offices seconded to this new task force. However, one of the training exercises soon turns deadly when Shaz Bowman suspects that a serial killer is at work kidnapping and murdering teenage girls.

This opening sequence is intercut with the life story of a phenomenally successful showbiz couple (think Richard and Judy). Although it seems fairly obvious early on 'whodunit' this, by no means, makes the investigation simple and over the next fifteen hours and fifteen minutes the tension increases as the two stories become entwined.

Carol Jordan, the Inspector who became both professionally and emotionally involved with Tony Hill in *The Mermaids Singing*, is also on hand here to lend her cool and calm presence to this emotional and personal investigation for the profilers when one of his team is brutally mutilated and murdered.

Michael Tudor Barnes whose work includes roles in *The Bill*, *Softly Softly* and *Eastenders* as well as stage work reads this disturbing and in some parts sickening psychological thriller with charm and dignity as well as maniacal megalomania as required. The complete text reading retains pace, excitement, passion and terror throughout—not one word wasted and tension maintained throughout.

All Isis Audio Books can be purchased directly, for more details call 01865 250 333.

SIXTY-THREE CLOSURE

Anthony Frewin

THE NEW NOVEL FROM THE AUTHOR OF LONDON BLUES

After a close friend's apparent suicide, Christopher Cornwell receives several photos the friend mailed prior to his death. Cornwell subsequently discovers by chance the presence in one of the photos of Lee Harvey Oswald, the alleged assassin of President Kennedy. But how could Oswald be photographed in a small Hertfordshire market town when he was supposed to be living in Russia as a defector at the same time? As Cornwell investigates the story behind the photos he unknowingly becomes the target of an investigation himself, by a shadowy agency as determined to maintain its secrets now as in 1963.

"The great JFK conspiracy novel…the assassination in Dealey Plaza will never seem the same again. Darkly imaginative and believable…a totally original "secret history" of our our time"— Larry Celona, Chief Crime Correspondent of the New York Post.

Praise for London Blues "A dazzling existential thriller….a tour-de-force of English sleaze."—Martin Short

"A love letter to a sexual age that was both abundant and naïve"— Esquire

"A forceful, striking thriller"—Time Out

"A fascinating and compulsive portrait of London before it began swinging…a risk taking, formula defying book"—Melody Maker

"The quintessential Soho book"—Loaded

"Fifties atmosphere, powerfully evoked…"—Literary Review

ISBN: 1 901982 04 1 PRICE: £6.99pb
NO EXIT PRESS

Film

M (PG; July 6)
Dir. Fritz Lang. St. Peter Lorre, Ellen Widmann, Inge Landgut, Otto Wernicke.

I can't help reading something subversive into the BFI's decision to release the restored version of Lang's 1931 film in 1998. At a time when the release of child abusers back into society invokes the spectre of community paranoia, and Adrian Lyne's take on *Lolita* has re-awakened censorious Old England, the prospect of this examination of pitiful psychosis in the face of pitiless hypocrisy seems little short of polemical. Far from dwelling upon the grisly acts of child murderer Hans Beckert (Lorre), Lang and Thea von Harbou's screenplay focused upon the pathology of his accusers. The result is a powerful study of consensus in crisis, and one of the most accomplished thrillers of the early sound period.

We come upon a city galvanised by fear, only cuckoo clocks and church bells still on the move. *"Just you wait, it won't take long"* Beckert tells Elsie Beckmann (Landgut) as he buys her a balloon and takes her somewhere quiet so as to kill her. Meanwhile, Frau Beckmann (Widmann) anxiously watches the clock. With supreme economy, *Lang* charts Elsie's final hours; Beckert casting a deep shadow across a placard proclaiming his crimes as she bounces her ball against it, the ball later rolling fitfully into the grass as Frau Beckmann resignedly clears the table. When he sees another little girl reflected in a store window, the light from a set of knives framing his cherubic face, he whistles the *Hall of the Mountain King* theme from Grieg's *Peer Gynt*. We can only guess how Beckert destroys these little girls. All we know is the process in which he lures them away, they are missed, and the city duly goes into shock. As with the title—M—what is powerful is the suggestion that the sign conceals and the way in which the bars of a flatly rendered tune chart the chaos of Beckert's. strange love.

The memory of Beckert's bourgeois homunculus staring bug-eyed at the city is hard to forget. But this is as much because he embodies the city's corruption as that he is its scourge. Notice how Lang's camera, like a disinterested tourist, prowls through sausage-and-beer halls, stands by in smoke-filled rooms while businessmen accuse each other of touching little girls; each stage in its odyssey linked by voices telling of the investigative process. While the prolice re-read Beckert's handwriting and study their maps, the underworld guffaws at the notion that the state should take care of Beckert. For Lang, there is more at stake than what happened on that patch of grass. Clearly, the crisis is not Beckert, it's something in the air, call it history. Contrary to received opinion, Beckert was not based upon any particular case history. Indeed, it's not difficult to imagine how the serial killer phenomenon could flourish in a society racked by mad investment, massive unemployment, and aborted revolutions. Fittingly perhaps, we seldom see Beckert, making Lorre's final coup-de-théatre all the more stunning.

"Again and again I have to walk the streets. And I always feel that somebody is following me… It is I myself… Following…. Me…" Even Lorre's melodramatic gestures add to rather than dispel the complexity of his position, as well as the enigma of his psychosis. Cutting back and forth between this shrieking soul and his jury, a Brueghelesque rabble of self-righteous pickpockets and frenzied mothers, Lang analyses the two sides of a familiar equation. Remember; Lorre was a Hungarian Jew, an outsider on two counts in a Germany in which Nazi street squads itched to take power. It is one of those happy casting decisions which was not merely technically appropriate, but upon which history has conferred terrible resonance. *M* is a subversive film not simply because it trades in the molestation of underage girls, but because it dared suggest that something uglier stalked the streets. Thanks to the BFI, now it'll be tucked away in our video collections.

Richard Armstrong

Ghost Camera/The Last Journey (U)
Dir. Bernard Vorhaus, St. Henry Kendall, Ida Lupino, Hugh Williams, Godfrey Tearle.

Seeing its role as protector of the British film industry, rather than, as elsewhere, protector of a revealing aspect of the nation's culture, in 1927 the government introduced the Cinematograph Films Act. This provided a quota requiring cinema owners to increase the percentage of domestic product shown from 5% to 20% by 1935. The result was the infamous 'quota quickie', cheaply made films to meet the requirement, but churned out in the knowledge that audiences still preferred American movies. American screenwriter Bernard Vorhaus was only passing through when the Act was passed, but stayed for seven years. The bulk of the films he directed were produced by Julius Hagen at tiny operation Twickenham Studios. BFI Video has performed a real service by releasing *Ghost Camera* and *The Last Journey* for they demonstrate that the skid row aesthetic of the 'quickie' could be turned to genuine account. They also feature a native sensibility seen all too rarely in contemporary British output.

Neither of these thrillers are particularly well written or well acted, but both were shot and edited with breathtaking invention. Notice *Ghost Camera*'s courtroom scene in which editor David Lean cuts from the theatrical gestures of the young John Mills to ever tighter close-ups of the judge delineating his guilt. Notice the shifting locations signalled by zooms into close-ups or a London map in *The Lost Journey* as Vorhous pulls all his protagonists' stories together. Vorhaus also inserted an organically motivated subjective camera sequence long before the device entered the history books. In the absence of prestige writers and actors, the legacy of the best 'quickies' remains largely stylistic and truly vernacular.

Just as there is a delirious insouci-

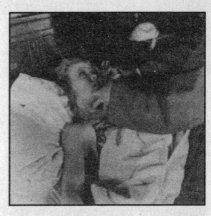

ance about their style, so there is an innocence about the world which they depict. It is an innocence which they, perhaps more so than the full-length features they supported, have no time or excuse to explain. When it is revealed that Ernest Elton (Mills) is guilty of murder, the awful word is spell out letter by letter in myriad cuts from telephonist to telegrapher to shocked neighbour. When bookish, bespectacled John Gray (Kendall) and May Elton (Lupino) go to the country to investigate, they respond to working-class rustics as though they are wild animals. The whole device of having metropolitan idlers getting mixed up in dirty dealings smacks of an Enid Blyton mystery. In England in 1933 a chap and a gal still knew their place, and the difference between what's done and what isn't. And maps of the world were still covered in blotches of red. Aside from their cinematic value, these little films are historical documents from a time when victims were poisoned in Mayfair drawing rooms and the democratic automatic had yet to leave pools of red in Hungerford and Dunblane. Remember: the Cinematograph Films Act was designed specifically to keep the pernicious influence of America out of British cinemas.

Envisaging Jean Renoir's 1938 *La Bête Humaine*, in which a *crime passionel* is played out against dank Parisian marshalling yards, *The Last Journey* (1935) tells of a train driver disgruntled by impending retirement and driven to destroy his train and everyone in it because he suspects his wife of infidelity. But his jealousy is remedied in a peculiarly British trice when Sir Wilfred Rhodes (Tearle), a Harley Street psychiatrist, is enlisted to unravel the poor chap's confusion as the train hurtles westwards. It is significant that the key characters in both films are middle-class. Whilst such as John's assistant and the innkeeper in *Ghost Camera*, and the train driver here, are at best local colour in tales revolving around the educated and efficient bourgeois protagonists. Loathe to plumb the ebb and flow of desire in the train driver's heart and mind, the decision to circumvent his passion with patrician cool strikes as terribly British. Determinedly unsexy, and containing the merest suggestion of appalling violence, these thrillers now seem stoically uninterested in the squalid compulsions which in many a French and American film drive lovers and killers. Yet they speak volumes about a society

which could mythologise a butcher of prostitutes, yet sever Derek Bentley's spinal cord for being in the wrong place at the wrong time. Suggesting the possibility, yet epitomising a Fourth Form take on sex which, until the 80s, dogged British humour, a prole in *The Last Journey* makes, a joke: "*I always regard marriage as a cafeteria. You grab what you want and pay for it later.*" Since the demise or the Cinematograph Films Act, we have hungrily consumed American movies, whatever the cost.

Richard Armstrong,

Palmetto (USA 1998)
Directed by Volker Schlondorff, screenplay by E Max Frye (based on James Hadley Chase's Just Another Sucker)
Wild Things (USA 1998)
Directed by John McNaughton, written by Stephen Peters
On its bright and shiny surface, the Sunshine State is not the most natural setting for noir, but there is a surprisingly large sub-genre which is set in the steamy heat and dangerous swamps of America's vacation land. Although surfaces are important to the look of noir, things are seldom what they seem.

Cape Fear might be the most obvious example of this, and many of John D MacDonald's bring the conventions of noir into a Florida setting. You can find elements of this in the novels of Harry Crews, and in Tom McGuane's *92 In The Shade*.

Lawrence Kasdan's pseudo-noir

Body Heat is the most obvious source for the feel of the first of the two movies under discussion here, with the Gulf Coast settings producing a shiny patina of sweat on everything that happens. But *Body Heat*, like most Kasdan, was second-hand, and it's hard to escape that feeling in *Palmetto*, not least in Elizabeth Shue's performance as a femme fatale which seems to be lifted from Kathleen Turner, who didn't do it so well in the first place. In this case, the Shue doesn't fit.

Except in the sense that, as an unconvincing Siren, Shue's seduction of Woody Harrelson emphasises one of the crucial factors of noir, the helpless, often dumbo, male protagonist, led about by his libido. Harrelson makes a fine lead, as hopeless as Fred MacMurray in the face of raw sex. Gina Gershon, of the funny lips and hard body, has become a fixture in neo-noir, and here she has her work cut out for her as the loyal woman Harrelson betrays.

Perhaps the reason so little of this works is because Harrelson is such a naturally comic actor, and sometimes seems to be undercutting the tension of the story. But that is more likely the effect of having a German director filming a noir story by a British writer who himself was regurgitating what he'd read and seen in classic books and movies.

You get the feeling Schlondorff, like Wim Wenders in *The End Of Violence*, is more concerned with showing some of the grotesqueries of America, and doesn't really care if the story itself pulls away from your interest.

The one actor who seems to be taking the whole thing seriously is Chloe Sevigny, on first thought an unlikely choice as a jeune fatale, but excellent in her role, bringing both energy and uncertainty to it. That doesn't necessarily fit in. It's hard to tell if *Palmetto* is actually trying to play with you, or if it's just giving you a knowing nudge and wink, but either way, it isn't very involving.

Wild Things eschews the steam for the south Florida glitzville made famous by *Miami Vice* and Carl Hiaasen. It even has an excellent score by George Clinton which pays homage to Jan Hammer's MiVi synthesisers, and shots of swamps and alligators just to remind us what we're doing here. But if Scholndorff seemed to be doing *Palmetto* for the fun of it, here John McNaughton appears to be on holiday from such serious stuff as *Henry Portrait Of A Serial Killer*.

Where Woody Harrelson's character is dumb and doomed from the start, in *Wild Things* Matt Dillon's high school guidance counsellor goes through a whole gamut of roles. This is true of the entire cast: no one is what they seem, and if this business of actors playing characters who are playing at acting becomes boring, it is another of the facets of noir. Thus Denise Richards, humanity's closest equivalent to Jessica Rabbit, starts out as fatale and winds up a victim. You can take the rest from there, but there are excellent turns from Kevin Bacon, Carrie Snodgrass, and, with a knowing wink to *Black Widow*, Theresa Russell, who would've been so much more happy being Ida Lupino in the 40s.

Neve Campbell, of *Scream* fame, is a B movie superstar who shows the real talent to move up the Hollywood food chain. She can act rings around of any number of RADA grads in Merchant Ivory costume: and how many Kate Winslets would you see doing a shallow end of the pool love scene with Richards? *[Er... It was Amanda Donohoe that LA Law imported for the 'steamy lesbian' scenes I believe? And of course Ken Russell never had any sex in his films, eh Mike—oh no, no sex in British films!—Ed]* There is this sense that McNaughton wants to hover just on the edge of exploitation, but he always pulls back, just like Matt Dillon pulls back while sitting on a motel bed with the female detective who's been shadowing him. It helps avoid diluting the atmosphere, since watching Campbell and Richards could cause you to forget what else is going on.

Bill Murray's presence almost does a Woody on *Wild Things*, but if you remember that almost no one here is what they seem to be, it almost works. McNaughton has added one interesting gimmick, a closing credits run of explanation, in scenes that make clear the ways the entire scam was thought out and the way it worked. This works better than one might expect, especially since McNaughton has signalled most of these twists in the films, so he can't be accused of playing unfairly.

Neither of these films will move into the pantheon, but *Wild Things* in particular is an enjoyable little tributary trickling away from the shadowy mainstream.

Michael Carlson

Zero Effect

Written & directed by Jake Kasdan, St. Bill Pullman, Ben Stiller, Kim Dickens, Ryan O'Neill

Like father, like son. Jake Kasdan is a Hollywood legacy. His father Lawrence's first movie was a pastiche of film noir, *Body Heat*. He did a similar pastiche of western clichés, *Silverado*, and a redoing of John Sayles' little charmer *Return of The Secaucus Seven*, as the big budget *Big Chill*. Kasdan *père* is fine with the mechanics, but there's precious little originality in his finished product, and there's no sense of chances being taken.

Twenty-two-year-old Jake has learned his lessons well. *Zero Effect* is, in effect, a remake of the Sherlock Holmes story *A Scandal In Bohemia*, with Bill Pullman's Darryl Zero as Holmes, with more than a touch of Nero Wolfe thrown is, especially in his relationship with his Archie Goodwin/Dr Watson, Arlo (Ben Stiller). The story involves blackmail, and Kasdan throws in just enough invention to keep it relatively fresh.

He's also a talented enough filmmaker to realise the value of good set pieces, and to allow the characters, particularly Stiller, the freedom to perform solo for the camera. Pullman gets to ham, which he enjoys; it must be a break after playing Presidents. He does a nice job of letting Kim Dickens develop into the Irene Adler figure, and gets a brilliant little performance from Ryan O'Neal, whose spoiled Harvard rich-kid persona was first set down in *Love Story*, before Kasdan *fils* was born.

It's amazing that a talent for derivative, inconsequential, forgettable entertainment should be genetic. Or perhaps it isn't. Maybe there are dozens of kids out there who could do the same sort of business, if only they would hold back from trying to push the envelope, if only they got the chance.

Michael Carlson

Books on Film
Michael Carlson

Hong Kong Cinema: The Extra Dimensions by Stephen Teo, BFI, £15.99
The Genius of The System: Hollywood Film-making in the Studio System by Thomas Schatz, Faber & Faber, £14.99
Once Upon A Time In America by Adrian Martin, BFI, £6.99

It is more than coincidental that Sergio Leone broke new ground with his spaghetti westerns just after the Hollywood studio system collapsed. There is a knee-jerk reaction in Britain which undervalues Hollywood product (and over-values domestic films) *[Presumably this is* not *that bit of the press who've moaned on about us producing costume dramas instead of action features for the last twenty years then?-Ed]*, yet Schatz's study shows clearly how the studio system, for all its faults, provided the platform upon which so much great art was produced.

We may have known that already, but Schatz's most interesting thesis, and the one which provided the basis of the recent TV series based on this book, is that the Hollywood moguls, immigrant Jews from Eastern Europe, used the studios to create an image of the America into which they imagined they were assimilating, and this image is the one America grew to believe was the true picture of itself.

Nowhere is this more true, nor perplexing, than in the gangster movies. Most of the moguls worked their way out of the slums, often in businesses run on the edge of the criminal world. The early studios were set up to dodge Edison and the patent companies, and the finances for films often involved people with connections to crime, like Joe Kennedy. Dan Moldea has chronicled the role of organised crime, and Ronald Reagan, in using the film unions in the 1950s. Yet through all this time gangsters were presented as Robin Hood figures, making their own way to the American Dream, only to discover in the end they'd gone about it in the wrong way.

Schatz's book overlaps a great deal with Neal Gabler's *An Empire Of Their Own*, which tells the story of the moguls themselves with more flair. But Schatz's thesis is one that bears more examining, and will surely lead that way.

Hong Kong movies, on the other hand, may seem an unlikely area for academic study, and certainly lots of fans of Tsui Hark and John Woo are going to be disappointed as they wade through Stephen Teo's comprehensive account of the glory years of cinema in the former British colony. *Hong Kong Cinema* makes an interesting complement to Faber's *Hong Kong Babylon* (see *Crime Time*, Sept 1997) which was less interested in reading the films and more interested in a portrayal of the business itself.

There is probably a middle ground, one that would feature more stills of Sally Yeh, Maggie Cheung, or Chow Yun-Fat. Teo's book has no pictures at all, a real loss when he's discussing films that are not generally available in the West. But as a thorough study and a sympathetic reading of Hong Kong's movie history, you'll have to go far to beat it.

Adrian Martin makes a specific link between Sergio Leone's films and the work of Hong Kong directors like Hark and Woo, and if you're looking for a link between traditional Hollywood themes and the stylised paring down of genre conventions to their raw essence that defined Hong Kong, you need look no farther than Leone.

Martin's approach to Leone's final film is a micro-analysis, and a very effective one. His understanding of Leone's visual sense, and his ability to fit that into the elegiac quality of this film speak well of his sensitivity to a filmmaker whose artistry is still grossly undervalued. If Martin at time struggles to make connections with other films, especially those usually regarded as 'art', the +overall point is valid, especially in America. Leone was able to take the basic elements of American films, especially genre films, and remake them into a new visual mythology which helped show the way for the next generations of filmmakers to construct a new sort of genre story- telling.

It would be useful to have more of that analysis in this book on the macro side, and more structural analysis on the micro side. Martin's study is arranged thematically, yet it's really at its most effective when it's dealing with specifics of the shooting, changes in the various scripts, and the deletion of many shot scenes. Here Martin illuminates Leone's working methods as well as his aims. *Once Upon A Time In America* requires a certain amount of suspension of disbelief, but it remains one of the great gangster movies, and more than that, the fitting end to the career of one of the most important directors of his time.

Comics
Steven Steinbock

The Spirit: The New Adventures. Created by Will Eisner. Kitchen Sink Press. $3.50

The Spirit, whose popularity is as ethereal as his name, is among the earliest and most unconventional of comic book heroes. In 1940, Will Eisner began editing a 16-page comic supplement syndicated by the Chicago Tribune which featured Eisner's tongue-in-cheek masked vigilante. Kitchen Sink Comix, the underground comic mainstay which has been reprinting The Spirit since the late 1970s, has pulled together an assortment of notables from the comic world to pay homage to Eisner and his masked criminologist.

Under his mask, The Spirit was cocky young criminologist Denny Colt. Believed dead by the underworld, he fights against an assortment of off-beat crooks with his young sidekick, Ebony White. Spirit lives in a secret hideaway beneath Wildwood Cemetery, is friendly with Police Commissioner Dolan, and is smitten with Dolan's daughter, Ellen. His young pal Ebony is so blatantly clichéd an African American that he makes Amos and Andy look like a pair of Black Panthers.

Eisner, whose protégés have included Wally Wood and Jules Feifer, is known for his use of shadow, perspective, page layout, and the unparalleled talent for telling stories with humor, twist endings, and sad moral realism in seven or eight pages. According to Alan Moore, *"Will Eisner is the single person most responsible for giving comics its brains."* Eisner has gone on to write numerous graphic novels such as *A*

Contract With God and *The Heart of the Storm* which deal with such serious themes as loneliness, aging, and anti-semitism. His latest book, *Family Matter* (to be published this summer by Kitchen Sink) involves a family's dark secrets being revealed at a birthday party.

In issue #1 of *The Spirit: The New Adventures*, Alan Moore and Dave Gibbons, the talents that brought us DC's *Watchmen*, reunite to give us three interpretations and elaborations on The Spirit's origins.

Issue #2 gives us a diverse array of artisans who interpret very different facets of Eisner's storytelling style. *Spinx the Jinx in The Game of Life* written by John Wagner (*Judge Dredd*) with art by Carlos Ezquerra is a sad, slice-of-life about a long-time loser who can't seem to go straight. The lightest story in this batch, and the one that best captures the zanier side of Eisner's Spirit is *Sunday in the Park with St. George* by Jim Vance and Dan Burr (whose *Kings in Disguise* (1990) is the story of hoboes wandering the Depression-era Midwest).

The Return of Mink Stole is by Neil Gaiman and Eddie Campbell. Scotland native Campbell is one of the few who have surpassed Eisner in the ability to tell a deep story in a few sketchy panels. In this tale, a mediocre crime writer is holed up in a beach resort hotel trying to write a *Reservoir Dogs*-like screenplay. Overcome by writers' block, he unwittingly comes to the aid of The Spirit and foils femme fatale jewel-thief Mink Stole.

I enjoyed each of these homages to Will Eisner's The Spirit, as I'm sure will anyone who is familiar with The Spirit. I wanted to see more of Ebony. Perhaps, in these Politically Correct times a monkey-faced black man speaking silly patois is verbotten, but I've never known Kitchen Sink to shy from incorrectness, political or otherwise. Perhaps the highest praise for Eisner's work is that these stories all pale in comparison with the original stories in their glorious black and white. Nevertheless, they are entertaining and worthwhile, and loving tributes to Eisner's Spirit.

Gangland. Edited by Axel Alonso. DC Comics Vertigo. $2.95

I have long grown cynical of the Vertigo imprint of dark horror titles from DC Comics. The success of off-beat and intelligent horror comics such as *Swamp Thing* and *Sandman* (written by Alan Moore and Neil Gaiman) gave rise to other titles which gave a mind-bending reinterpretation to super-hero stuff. Grant Morrison took *Animal Man* and *Doom Patrol* and turned the one into a psychedelic animal rights saga and the other into a distinctly dada-esque story that might have existed if MC Escher had written comics.

In the beginning of 1993, the entire line of dark 'mature readers' titles broke off, under the direction of DC editor Karen Berger, into the DC Vertigo line. By then most of its half dozen regular titles had already decayed into cheap imitations of themselves. Alan Moore had gone on to other projects.

While Gaiman's *Sandman* held a niche for itself with its gentle storytelling, the rest of the line began clambering over itself to see which one could surpass the others in weirdness, grotesquerie, and per-page four-letter-word count. The center had fallen out of the line, and its storytelling had lost its point. Dada isn't dada if the artist is trying to make dada. One can only read so many stories about cross-dressing immortals vivisecting children's minds before one puts the whole lot down.

Having made my diatribe, DC Vertigo has come up with an interesting crime anthology miniseries that is worth the attention of crime comic aficionados. Reminiscent of EC's *Crime SuspenStories* from the 50s, each of the four issues of *Gangland* will contain three or four stories by various writers and artists. Stories will cover the gamut of syndicated crime themes, be it in Chinatown or Moscow, prehistoric gangs as well as futuristic ones, gang-bangers and crooked cops, and extra-terrestrial enforcers.

Talents include those of Dave Gibbons, Joe R. Lansdale, David Lloyd, Jamie Delano, and others. Issue #1 is a mixed bag of interesting, often amusing, but ultimately forgettable stories. Of the four stories included, the best were *Clean House* by Brian Azzarello and Tim Bradstreet about a mob informer in the FBI Witness Relocation Program who comes home to find his family gunned down, and *The Bear* by Dave Gibbons, set in a Russia of the near future in which old scores stain the snow red.

While the purpose of the entire Vertigo line seems to be to shock it's readers, *Gangland* manages that goal without pretending to be intellectual. And it pulls the job off with wry flourish.

Batman: Other Realms, Titan, £8.99
Superman: Exile, Titan, £10.99

When graphic novels look reasonably priced it's a sign of the times. These two collections reprint (respectively) two Batman tales from Legends of the Dark Knight and a Superman complete saga from the late 80s.

The Batman offering is particularly tasty, offering Bo Hampton's *Destiny*, teaming the Batman with a descendant of Joe Kubert's Viking Prince and telling a parallel tale of the original Prince at the same time. *The Sleeping* by Scott Hampton finds the soul of an injured Bruce Wayne sharing a mysterious netherworld with two others marooned there. The nature of both heroism and evil are debated intelligently and convincingly. One for the library.

Superman: Exile deals with the Man of Steel's reaction to him having had to execute three interstellar mass (hey, we're talking billions here) murders. Having become slightly unhinged by his guilt he is worried that he may become out of control, so exiles himself to the stars. In the way of all things (comics, anyway) he learns to heal himself.

Both of these collections are reassuringly competent in their handling of long established characters—recommended.

'What are we lacking?' we asked. 'Opinionated writers' came the answer...

A Personal View
Mark Timlin

Photo: Caroline Rees

AT LAST, under the editorship of Barry Forshaw I've been asked to write a regular column for *Crime Time*. He's a very wise man I'm sure you'll agree. And it is a personal view, and all opinions are mine and mine alone, so don't blame him, or the proprietors, blame me. And of course, if you disagree, you can always write to me here. But remember, I'll be opening any envelopes wearing heavy gloves, so don't bother putting in the double-edged razor blades.

So, what was the most important event in the crime calendar so far this year? No. Not the annual CWA dinner, dance and drag party where those whose turn it was this year to get an award queued up, said nice things about each other, drank some cheap champagne and went home after handing out the Cartier daggers. Maybe I've not got one because I wear a Rolex. Ho-hum.

No. I'm talking about *Murder They Write*, the supplement that turned up in the Times newspaper on Saturday April 18th 1998. What a to-do. Oh to be in England, now that April's here (and to be a master of crime into the bargain.) But honestly, some of the names that were included. Oo-er missus, you had to laugh.

Talk about the old pals act. Why do I get this strange feeling that in the weeks running up to its publication, telephone lines were running hot with: 'If you include me, I'll include you.' No names here, but some of these people weren't as much Masters of Crime as Masters of a nice read for a maiden aunt in Cheltenham. And others—well, I'd never heard of them, and I thought I knew a bit…

Mind you, I'd've been well pissed off if I hadn't been included. In fact, my publicist friend Lucy Ramsey, who knew about the supplement, neglected to inform me it was coming out in case I'd been ignored. As if.

Of course I can imagine there was some gnashing of teeth and tearing of hair that Saturday over the toast and marmalade as the great and the good of crime writing hastily fumbled though with shaking hands to see if they were included. If you weren't—too bad. After the rubbish that was included imagine how bad a writer you have to be to be left out.

And I thought it was a bit daft to have the late greats on the list. Apart from anything else, they don't need the publicity. But if you were going to include the deceased, how about Ross Macdonald and John D. MacDonald. Real masters of crime. And Derek Raymond, the forgotten man of British crime who merely got an honourable mention in one of the accompanying articles, as did Ted Lewis (who having written probably the best Brit crime novel ever, *Jack's Return Home* aka *Get Carter*, should have been included for that book alone.) Terrific picture of Michael Caine, though.

And I read somewhere (but I really can't remember where) that it's hoped to make the supplement an annual event. Just one thing. If you're a master of crime this year, what precludes you from being one the next? It's not like the Billboard Hot 100 where you can come roaring in with a bullet (how apt) one week and drop out the next. Or is it? I'm trying hard, you see. Maybe this article will do the trick. And if it doesn't, how about asking me to give some input? I'd put you right, no danger.

And just one tiny point to whoever wrote the piece about me. Just to set the record straight, I did not have *"a spat with Headline"* as you put it. I left in order to get into hardback. Headline kept me alive for a number of years publishing two paperback originals a year, and I'm constantly grateful. Unlike other past and present Headline authors I've never gone around badmouthing them. *And* they put out TV tie-in covers of some of the back catalogue, which is more than you can say for Gollancz. But more about *them* another time.

As a postscript to the above, I've just read the latest *Shots* magazine and in the editorial it's suggested that next year the Times supplement should *"feature those who were mysteriously left out the first time around."* No way. Working on that premise, by the time it was ten years old every blue rinsed harpie who ever had a short story about the rock cakes being stolen at the vicar's tea party published in *Knitting Monthly* would be a crime master. Talk about cheapening the currency.

I also note that a novel by a certain lady crime novelist was given away with the June *Good Housekeeping*. Now I know where I went wrong. I didn't aim my books at the readership of *Good*-fucking-*Housekeeping*.

And another thing. I see that *Red Herrings*, the confidential organ of the CWA has gone public. Now anyone with £2.96 or £4 to the usual address can read it. So what's that all about? Anyway, with trembling fingers I opened the copy that was slipped to me by my spy at court and started looking for the confidential bits. The secrets of how to write a successful crime novel. The controversies that would start arguments raging in the broadsheet newspapers of this fair land. And what did I find? Nothing mate. Not a sausage. Just how nobody who wins those daggers ever expects to. How modest. How middle class. How sodding irritating. If you don't think your latest novel is the best of the year, tear it up and start again.

See you next edition. Or maybe not of course.

Timlin's Top Tips... (Oo-err missus)

The Defence by DW Buffa, No Exit Press, £10.00

Everyone's looking for the new John Grisham. The British John Grisham. The French John Grisham. The Martian John Grisham for all I know. And why? Because when they find him they'll sell a shitload of books, just like John Grisham does, that's why. And D.W. Buffa is the latest. But John Grisham he ain't. And thank God for that. Much as I admire Mr Grisham's work, one is enough. In fact Buffa is everything that John Grisham isn't: tense, taut, exciting, and absolutely believable. And don't look for the good, little guy taking on the big, bad guys. Buffa's hero, a lawyer of course, works for the defence and doesn't care if the accused is guilty or not. In fact, better that he is. Then it's just a game. Fair do's if you lose. And if you win, the accused can go on to commit other crimes whilst the lawyer gets fat on the proceeds. And this lawyer never loses. That's why he's so rich. But then something happens. A crime committed a long time ago reverberates through the years and the lawyer pays in a way he never expected to. Yeah. This'll do. But leave out the Grisham comparisons No Exit. You don't need 'em!

Tapping the Source by Kem Nunn, No Exit Press, £6.99

Any book that's flashed *"in the same league as the best of Chandler and James Crumley"* just has to go to the top of my reading list on curiosity value alone, especially when I've never heard of the writer. In this case I've never even heard of anyone with the Christian name Kem, but that's beside the point. So is it in the same league? I hear you ask with bated breath. Not quite, but close, and for a first novel it's really something. A little woolly in the middle perhaps, with the opportunity for a great shoot-out wasted and a question mark over the fate of one of the leading characters, all of which could've been sorted with some judicious editing. But who's complaining. On the whole *Tapping The Source* cuts it

And the story is simple. A sexually abused young girl runs from the California desert town where she was dumped with her brother by their delinquent mother. Two years later the boy is told that she has disappeared again. This time in more suspicious circumstances. Gone to Mexico with a trio of surfers and only they returned.

So he goes looking in the coastal town where she ended up. To blend in he learns to surf and discovers that he is a natural. And then? Well get the book and find out.

Kem Nunn can really write. The novel is taut, sensitive and atmospheric, and he has the surf scene with its hedonistic lifestyle down pat. It made me want to go out and buy a surf punk CD and get gnarly in my woody.

Mangrove Squeeze by Laurence Shames, Orion, £9.99

For as long as I can remember there's been a battle for the title of 'King Of The Florida Crime Writers.' For years it belonged to John D. MacDonald with his Travis McGee series. Then, sadly, he died, and the crown was contested by Elmore Leonard, Carl Hiaasen and James Hall. But now, as Leonard has fallen foul of the 'Crime writer for people who know nothing about crime fiction' accolade, and is frankly too popular, so that he can write almost anything to critical acclaim, and Hiaasen and Hall have got too eco-freako for their own good, another runner comes up on the inside straight—Laurence Shames.

So what have we here that merits such fulsome praise? Russian Mafia exchanging plutonium for rare artefacts under the guise of running T-shirt shops; an old Italian Mafioso who died on the operating table and thus was allowed to retire in peace rather than have his head blown off, who owns a Chihuahua so ancient as to be almost mummified; a beautiful woman left for dead in the boot of a 1959 Cadillac; a lovesick man who runs a crushingly unsuccessful hotel with the help of his father who suffers from Alzheimer's; two engaging drop-outs who live in a hot dog next to the airport (Believe me, it's true—you'll have to read the book.) And a whole load more, making up a cast of wonderful characters who inhabit a story beautifully told which works out just perfectly against all the odds. That's what we got

Laurence Shames right now is a hot as the Miami sun and if he continues writing books of this calibre can eclipse his rivals and snatch that elusive Florida Crime Writers crown. And I for one hope that he does.

TAPPING THE SOURCE

SOURCE

Kem Nunn

NOMINATED FOR THE AMERICAN BOOK AWARD—
Best First Novel

People came to Huntington Beach in search of the endless party, the ultimate high and the perfect wave. Ike Tucker came to look for his sister and for the three men who may have murdered her. In that place of gilded surfers and sun-bleached blondes, Ike looked into the shadows and found parties that drifted towards pointless violence, joyless violations and highs you might never come down from….and a sea of old hatreds and dreams gone bad.

"Kem Nunn is one of a rare breed, a novelist who knows how to plot and tell a story. There is amazing energy here"
—Elmore Leonard

"Forceful and gripping..in the same league as the best of Chandler and James Crumley. The all-time great surfing novel"
—Robert Stone

"Tense and driven with a sense of the apocalypse around the corner."
—Washington Post

"What Hemingway's Nick Adams did for fishing, Kem Nunn does for surfing. Through the sensibility of its hero and the sensitivity of its author, *Tapping the Source* puts you there and makes you understand."
—Saturday Review

ISBN: 1 901982 32 7 PRICE: £6.99

NO EXIT PRESS

And Finally...
Breese Books
John Kennedy Melling

AS SOON AS I SAW *Sherlock Holmes and the Greyfriar School Mystery* I promptly bought a copy as I was brought up on St Jim's and Greyfriars and often write about them in Mary Cadogan's *Story Paper Collectors Digest*. Reviewing it for CT secured the agreement of our amiable editor to interview Martin Breese, head of Martin Breese Publishing and Books, and to survey the whole dozen or more pastiches. We met for lunch at BAFTA, of which I have been a member for over thirty years and I found Martin to be an elegant, bearded man, erudite, well-spoken (and as voluble as myself). Luncheon lasted from 12.30pm till after 4pm, so many subjects did we need to cover in his remarkable career as a 'Renaissance Man.'

His first thirty years were spent as an advertising executive in South Africa, Switzerland and Britain, latterly with the famous Crawford Agency. When he spent the next ten years as a photographer with one of the quality Sundays, his subjects ranged from the great Billy Wilder when shooting *The Private Life of Sherlock Holmes*, to Bill Brandt whose photograph by Martin can be seen in the V&A.

The next change, or perhaps right-about-turn is more apt, was starting publishing conjuring books, more than eighty all told. Knowing all the great names—here we realised we knew each other's contacts, starting with John Fisher, TV producer and magician, and Paul Daniels, magician and entrepreneur. Martin demonstrated one neat close-up trick across the table.

Right-turn-again. He published *The Good Spy Guide*, novels, non-fiction— then a great success *Breese's Guide to Modern First Editions and their Values*. He sold a thousand copies at £37.50 and is now working on a new edition.

He has also directed for ten years a photographic Library of Ephemera, Retrograph Archive, specialising in the history of graphic design from 1860 to 1960.

So, where did Sherlock Holmes make his appearance? From my research for *Murder Done To Death* I know there are over one thousand parodies and pastiches of the Great Detective. Martin had known Val Andrews, author of *The Greyfriars Mystery,* for twenty years and he started producing audio cassettes, which he did not release, two of which were recorded by Val, who had already written some pastiches for another publisher, but wanted to make a change.

Martin does not claim to be one of those experts who know every comma and full-stop in the Canon like members of the Sherlock Holmes Societies, but this is no handicap. His policy is to buy the copyright outright from the authors as a more straightforward ploy than advances and royalties, which has worked out well.

A dozen already published and plenty more in the pipeline—several from Andrews, a couple from John Hall the Holmesian devotee, and others from JM Gregson whose earlier books were published by Harper-ollins. Sales in the United States are increasing, appropriately enough, with William Seil's *Sherlock Holmes and the Titanic Tradegy.* The technique is for Holmes to meet real-life characters and situations or prominent fictional personae, as had been done, for example with Sexton Blake and Raffles. The philosopher said if you make a better mousetrap the world will beat a path to your door, and the world is beating the pavements of Kensington Park Road.

The Breese Books Sherlock Holmes line
Sherlock Holmes and the Greyfriars School Mystery
by Val Andrews, £5.99. ISBN 0947533559
Sherlock Holmes and the Egyptian Hall Mystery
by Val Andrews, £4.95. ISBN 0947533435
Sherlock Holmes and the Yule-Tide Mystery
by Val Andrews, £5.99. ISBN 0947533117
Sherlock Holmes and the Titanic Tragedy
by William Seil, £6.99. ISBN 0947533354
Sherlock Holmes and the Baker St Dozen
by Val Andrews, £6.25. ISBN 0947533419
Sherlock Holmes and the Sandringham House Mystery
by Val Andrews, £6.99. ISBN 0947533532
Sherlock Holmes and the Chinese Junk Affairs
by Roy Templeman, £6.99. ISBN 0947533737
Sherlock Holmes and the Telephone Murder Mystery
by John Hall, £6.99. ISBN 0947533478

My interview with Martin Breese emphasised the current stages of his literary career of publishing; Sherlockiana and these eight books are a representative section of his present output. These are all pastiches, well bound and printed, striking covers selected from his *alter ego* the Retrograph Archive.

Some pastiches are purely and affectionately in the ambience of Holmes and Watson's fictional world, but the later trend has been for them. to meet either fictional detectives and personae, or to mingle with real-life characters and actual cases, crimes and tragedies, and this is the policy here as the titles shew.

Fictional—obviously Billy Bunter and the boys and masters of Greyfriars School in Kent, although the legendary Richards himself may be glimpsed in his publisher's famous office. Real characters—a selection—Maskelyne and Devant, the conjurors in the Egyptian Hall (now appropriately the offices of BAFTA where we met for lunch); the Captain and director of the Titanic with Jacques Futrelle, crime writer who perished in the sinking; King Edward VII and Horace Coldin the outstanding magician, and a venue rather than a man, the famous Mount Pleasant literary retreat at Reigate, translated into Belmont, rightly. Remember in the Doyle story, a commentator indicated that Colonel Takely must be Colonel Prendergast, as the French for 'take' is 'prendre'.

If I take the book that occasioned my interest in this series in the first place, *Sherlock Holmes and the Greyfriar School Mystery,* as an example. In the world of parody and pastiche, fashion occasionally partners fictional with real personae, and fictional with fictional. Ferrers Locke, Dr Locke's relative, has been studied exhaustively, perhaps more than the remaining nine-hundred-and-ninety-nine. Now we have Sherlock himself and Dr. Watson back at Greyfriars, the good Doctor's alma mater in 1912, he tells us in the 1928 introduction.

The theft of Mr Quelch's history of Greyfriars causes Watson to persuade Holmes to visit the School where Watson rose to Head Boy, or Captain of the School. They stay at the Cross Keys. Whilst there they manage to solve two other mysteries. Why was Wibley sneaking out of bounds each evening to visit the Theatre Royal in Courtfield? And who murdered jeweller H Silverman, whose shop adjoins Uncle Clegg's? With Sir Hilton Popper's aid, the killer is duly taken away. Joe Banks, the bookie, to whom Skinner owes £15, is flattened by Holmes' version of the Three Card Trick. Who leaves the note that Quelch's MSS will be returned if £15 ransom is paid? Vernon-Smith is regarded as the culprit. The detectives follow Quelch on a mysterious visit to Amalgamated Press, only to find his name unknown there. The MSS is found by deduction and returned, not quite in time to prevent the

Bounder's first lash in a public flogging—that is duly donated to the culprit. Quelch's secret is elucidated, with no inkling being given to the Head, so the former's unexpected literary career flourishes—for years, presumably.

The sense of atmosphere and period is excellent, with Frank Richards' rhythm matched exquisitely, and this should be a set book for all Greyfriars students.

The thirteen short stories are all much shorter than in the Canon but they fit remarkably well, as they might in CT or EQMM. All these books, of varying length from 112 to 256 pages, are well-researched and with accurate setting of scenes, personalities and especially rhythms. The Titanic is now a current fad with films, musical plays, books, souvenirs and actual artefacts. From my reading of the recent New York Souvenir I know the cabins, restaurants and decks are absolutely right, but I did wonder at the cast donning evening dress for the famous "first night out" (remember the HM Bateman-like scene when the leads in *Dodsworth* commit this solecism?).

Strangely Doyle, like Sir Arthur Sullivan and Dorothy L Sayers, could not reconcile his fame from his best output compared with heavier or stodgier works, so if you regret he didn't write more Holmes books and short stories, I can thoroughly recommend these pastiches to increase the knowledge of even the most fanatical Sherlockian fan.

There are five more books in this Series with more in the pipeline. These are; *The Travels Of Sherlock Holmes* (John Hall); *Sherlock Holmes and the Circus of Fear; Sherlock Holmes and the Theatre of Death; Sherlock Holmes and the Man Who Lost Himself; Sherlock Holmes and the Houdini Birthright*, (all by Val Andrews).

The new Catalogue will be a Collector's item, whether of books or ephemera.